Praise for
ILL MET BY MOONLIGHT . . .

"An entertaining historical fantasy . . . an enjoyable story, full of great bits of historical and fairy lore, with a likable cast and inventive use of traditional motifs and folklore."
—Charles de Lint

"A literate first novel, with the promise of good things to come." —*Publishers Weekly*

"By turns clever and charming, this delightful tale of magical intrigue is a confection filled with plot twists and surprises, impossible to put down."
—Deborah Chester, author of *The Sword, the Ring, and the Chalice* trilogy

"[Hoyt] knows her stuff—and enjoys playing with it. A refreshingly odd take on the origins of the Bard."—*Locus*

"A fanciful and charming interpretation of the origins of Shakespeare's plays as well as a tale of love and betrayal." —*Library Journal*

"An appealing portrait of [Shakespeare] coming of age . . . a finely paced romantic adventure." —*Starlog*

"A delightful Elizabethan fantasy." —*BookBrowser*

ILL MET BY MOONLIGHT

SARAH A. HOYT

ACE BOOKS, NEW YORK

ILL MET BY MOONLIGHT

An Ace Book / published by arrangement with the author

PRINTING HISTORY
Ace hardcover edition / October 2001
Ace mass-market edition / October 2002

Visit our website at
www.penguinputnam.com
Check out the ACE Science Fiction & Fantasy newsletter!

ISBN: 0-441-00983-2

ACE®
Ace Books are published
by The Berkley Publishing Group,
a division of Penguin Putnam Inc.,
375 Hudson Street, New York, New York 10014.
ACE and the "A" design
are trademarks belonging to Penguin Putnam Inc.

PRINTED IN THE UNITED STATES OF AMERICA

10 9 8 7 6 5 4 3 2 1

TO MY HUSBAND, DAN HOYT

"One half of me is yours, the other half yours—
Mine own, I would say; but if mine, then yours,
And so all yours."

The Merchant of Venice, 3.2.16–18

Prologue

❧

SCENE: *A vague place, the stage fogged over with thick white clouds that veil the backdrop, turning it into mere shadows and shapes, half perceived as though in a dream.*

ENTER: *An elegant young man, flawlessly attired according to Elizabethan fashion, in black velvet breeches, hose and doublet. The disarray of his auburn hair, his hand covering his left eye, the blood that trickles from beneath his fingers to drip onto his broad, fine white lawn collar—all give witness to recent calamity.*

Yet he speaks in the composed tones of an impersonal narrator.

"Between what happened and what didn't happen, what could have happened exists like a dream, suspended halfway between the safe, dark night of illusion and the harsh dawn of wakening reality.

"To peaceful Stratford, where we lay our scene, let us then go, and, within Arden Forest's ancient confines watch the drama about to unfold, the drama of treason, and love, and star-crossed passion.

"There, two households exist, nay, two kingdoms, which side by side have endured these many centuries with no strife. Now, mutiny breaks out between them.

"Two households, alike in dignity. Two young men chafe, each under his destiny, and curse the stars that have brought each to his subservient position.

"Will their travails change either? Can ill will bring good? Does treason ever turn good to ill? Is there a price to pay for elven love? Does deceit leave its mark upon the mind? Or can power be won at no cost?

"Watch, kind ladies and fair gentlemen, the fearful clash of these two realms which is now the two hours' traffic of our stage, the which, if you with patient ears attend, what here shall miss, our toil shall strive to mend."

Scene 1

ᗛᏋ

An Elizabethan town of whitewashed wattle-and-daub buildings, nestled in the curve of the gentle-flowing Avon. Ducklings waddle in the current and pigs walk the streets. Tall elms grow amid the houses, giving the very streets the feel of woodland glens. In an alley at the edge of town a poorly dressed young man stoops to open a garden gate.

Will stopped at the entrance to the garden, his hand on the rickety wooden gate. A feeling of doom came over him, like a presage of some evil thing.

A young man of nineteen, with overlong dark locks that curled on the collar of his cheap russet wool suit, Will felt as if he were about to walk into a trap. He looked around anxiously for what the trap might be, but saw nothing amiss.

The green garden ahead of him lay undisturbed. A few bees, from the hives next door, buzzed amid the flowers. The reddish rays of the setting sun burnished the flowers and made the vegetables a deep green. A fat brown chicken walked along the garden path, pecking at the ground.

Will shook his head at his fear, yet his fear remained. With his feet, in their worn ankle-high boots, solidly planted on the mud of the alley behind his parents' property, he looked into the sprawling garden for a hint of the great unnamed calamity that he knew awaited him just around the corner.

Half of him wanted to run in through the garden; the other half wished to hide, with animal cunning, behind the wall and spy . . . spy, he knew not on whom nor for what.

His mother's stories must be getting to him, her dark muttering about the velvet-clad gentlemen who visited Nan in Will's absence.

Will shook his head again and half chuckled at himself, but his chuckle echoed back strangely, visiting his ears like the cackle of a gloating demon.

He raised his white-gloved hand to his face and stroked the nest of soft hairs that only a young man's pride could mistake for a beard.

Nonsense. Sick fancies born of tiredness. It was all because of his job in Wincot, wearing him low enough that fancies preyed on his mind. His work, supervising the smallest children at their learning of the letters and numerals, would be dreary and arduous enough, but the two-hour walk each way to Wincot and back made it crushing.

This very day, Will had left Stratford at the crack of rosy dawn, when the pink tints of morn were no more than a promise in the east. Now, he came back home with the sun turned to bleeding glory in the west and night closing in on all sides, like creditors surrounding a penniless debtor.

Little wonder, then, that Will's mind should be filled with presages and wonders, with fears and unexplained dread. Little wonder.

He needed to rest and he longed for his bench by the scrubbed pine table; for the soft bustle his wife, Nan, made by the kitchen fire—her skirt kilted up on the left, displaying the length of her straight limbs and allowing her to move freely. Even now, she'd be clacking clay pans and stirring enticing smells from the poor vegetables and meager eggs, those homely, cheap ingredients, the best Will could provide for her. He longed for his newborn daughter, Susannah, for her mewling cries, for her wriggling in his tired arms.

He opened the gate and trotted onto the beaten dirt of the garden path with new decision. "Nan," he called.

This sound, too, returned oddly to his ears, like a long forgotten name, nevermore pronounced among the living. But Nan wasn't dead, nor gone, nor forgotten. Will had left her sleeping in their marriage bed—the broad oak bed given to him by his Arden aunt—when he'd dressed in the half-dark before dawn.

Still, his trotting slowed to a reluctant walk and he dared not call her name again.

Around him, the garden bloomed in green abundance. The neatly arranged patches of flax and herbs that Nan had planted in February, when she was already big with child, thrived. The roses she had brought with her from Hewlands, the Hathaways' farm in Shottery, bloomed big and round, casting their perfumes into the summer air.

Their scent mingled with the heavy odor of boiled cabbage, wafting from the house of Will's parents, next door. The two houses, built side by side, and both owned by Will's family, shared a garden and, until recently, had been used by the one family. But, on Will's marriage, his parents had made the house to the west private for him and Nan.

Will and Nan could only use the back and the top floor, since the front hall housed John Shakespeare's glover shop. But at the back, Will and Nan had their own kitchen, and, above that, their own chamber, and Will was as relieved not to have to share sleeping quarters with his siblings as his mother was glad not to have to share her kitchen with the woman she disdainfully called *the Shottery girl.*

Will's relief at this separation increased as the unsavory smell of cabbage washed over him, mingled with high-pitched screams from his three-year-old brother, Edmund, and the voice of his fourteen-year-old sister, Joan, raised in childish anger.

His home would never be that way, he promised himself, as he walked the narrow cobbled path between the rosebushes. Rather it would be like the home he remembered from his own childhood: well-ordained, with a few serving girls, and his Nan kept calm and rested enough to look after the children, who would be well fed and better dressed.

He had no idea how to manage this on his petty-schoolmaster allowance, but he was determined to manage it, somehow.

He rounded the corner of the garden path, beside the roses, and came into full view of his side of the house.

If only he didn't have to use his earnings to prop his parents' failing fortunes. If only—He stopped, his feelings of doom stronger than ever. Everything about this side of the house looked wrong.

The shutter on the window was closed, as was the door. Will frowned.

Nan never closed the door or the window while the last remnants of light could be gotten from the day.

Will's heart sped up like an unruly horse, and his feet raced upon the cobbled path.

The feeling of wrongness, of foreboding, overpowered him. Once, when he was very small, he had seen a dog swept away by the raging Avon at the flood. He remembered the small brown-and-white animal paddling futilely against the current even as it dragged him on and on to his certain doom. So, now, did Will's reason paddle against the current of dread that overtook it and pulled it on and on, unrelenting.

His running feet sped him to the door. Swinging it open, he peered into the dark, cool kitchen.

"Nan," he called. His voice broke, as it hadn't for years. No sound answered his call.

Blinded by the transition from daylight to dark, Will could see only vague shapes and dark shadows. He listened. No sound came from the kitchen or from upstairs. Nothing stirred. The close air reeked of wood smoke and the old mutton grease used for making tapers. But no tapers burned, no fire blazed in the hearth.

No blazing fire meant no supper. The young man's stomach twisted in a hungry knot. For a heartbeat, he forgot his anxiety and thought disparagingly of his wife who didn't even know enough to have her husband's food ready when he came home from his wearying toil.

These thoughts so resounded of his mother's bitter voice that Will frowned at them, reproaching the bitterness into silence. Nan was nowhere in sight. Perhaps she had fallen ill in another room, perhaps she was hurt, and yet Will, her wretched husband, could think only of his stomach. "Nan?"

He wished to hear Nan call back and name him a fool for his alarm. He wished it so hard that he almost fancied he heard it, very far away and faint. But he knew this for an illusion.

No matter how many times Will told himself that his fears were nonsense, that Nan must be nearby, that she must be well, dread leaped and danced in him like an obscene, mottled clown at a country fair, mocking his self-assurance.

As his eyes became acquainted with the dark, he saw

that the coals in the hearth remained banked, the ashes raked around them to protect the embers in the middle and reduce the danger of fire in the night. He'd done that the night before, and left all thus in the morning, when he'd walked out eating a slice of cold mutton and a piece of day-old bread for his breakfast. But Nan would have needed to undo this and feed the fire to prepare her dinner, and bake bread. Had Nan not had a midday meal? Had she been gone or ill for that long?

The dread grew in Will, stronger than ever, and the hair rose at the back of his neck. "Nan?" Still half-blind in the darkness, he pulled his gloves off, threw them on the table, and hurried down the narrow, shadowy corridor that separated the kitchen from the front hall.

The front-hall shop was darker even than the kitchen, but Will saw, without remarking, the hanging pelts and the wide, scarred workbench of his father's glover trade. His nose filled with the acrid smells of tanning—old meat, spoiled eggs, and stale flour—familiar to him from childhood.

Though wooden shutters were fitted over both windows, and the door firmly closed, *this* was no cause for alarm. These days this was the normal condition of John Shakespeare's glover shop. No doubt, Will's father would be hiding in his room, muttering about those who wished to catch him and make him pay his debts, though—that anyone knew—despite his ruined business, his slackening enthusiasm for work, he had no outstanding debts and no one pursued him.

Will took a sharp turn left, to the almost vertical stairway at the corner of the room, and hurried up it, his feet accommodating themselves to the narrow steps by long habit.

The entrance to the top floor was a mere square hole in the planks at the top of the staircase and, through this hole,

Will pushed his upper body into the top floor. The word "Nan" started but died on his lips.

Unlike the upper floor of the house next door, which had been partitioned into rooms to hold a large family, this one lacked any dividing walls to obstruct the view. Will could see the entire space at a glance, bathed in hazy light coming in through cracks in the wooden shutters that covered the three windows. Once, those windows had been covered by shutters made of lead and tiny panels of glass, but such luxuries had long been absent from the Shakespeare household.

The cheap woolen covers had been pulled neat and tight over the mattress of the good oak bed against the wall. On the bed, the fat black-and-white tomcat that Nan had brought with her from Hewlands, woke and stretched his paws in front of him, digging his claws into the bed covers. He looked at Will with an inquisitive eye and gave a little questioning *murr*. Beside him lay something, and, for a moment, Will thought he saw Nan, reclining there. He started to smile, when he noticed it was not Nan, not even anything close to Nan's size, but a small twig, broken from a bush, with green leaves still on it. What it was doing on his bed, he couldn't understand.

Will took a deep breath. The dread he'd felt in the garden returned, like a horse to an accustomed stable.

Slower, he climbed the rest of the way into the upper floor. On a peg on the wall hung Nan's good shirt and bodice and her embroidered kirtle, the clothing she wore to church on Sunday. His own good, black breeches and doublet hung on the other peg. Everything looked reassuring and accustomed, and yet the air felt heavy, impregnated with an odd floral scent.

Will nodded to the cat as to a respected acquaintance, while he went around to look in Susannah's cradle, beside the bed.

No sound came from the ancient rocking cradle, which had belonged to Will and each of his siblings in turn. Not the soft mewling of Susannah's cry, not even the sound of her breathing.

For a moment, in the darkness, he thought that Susannah was indeed in the cradle, though so immobile that his heart skipped a beat while a noose of panic tightened around it.

But as he reached into the small bed, he touched not the soft velvet of his daughter's skin, but something rough and harsh. Throwing the blankets back, he pulled the object out: a piece of a tree branch of sizable girth on which some wit had carved a rounded top and painted eyes and a nose and a mouth, all of it so crude it might well have been executed by one of Will's five-year-old pupils. It did not look like Susannah at all and, even in the dim light, Will could not imagine how he'd ever come to mistake it for her.

Puzzled, he turned the wood over in his hands, blinking in wonder. Who had done this? And what was this thing? It wasn't even a doll. What was it doing in Susannah's cradle? If a joke, it was a poor one. Had Nan played it? Why would she do such a thing?

Sometimes, in their scant six months together, Nan had hid herself in a far corner of the house when he got home, and made him hunt for her like a madman, until he brought her to ground in her hideout, desire and laughter interlacing in their embrace. But she'd never done it since Susannah had been born. And she'd never taken her joke to the point of leaving the fire unlit and a mannequin in his daughter's bed.

Worry rounded on Will like a hunting mastiff, nipping at his heels, trying to make him take flight. But his sluggish brain lagged, turning round and round, like a blindfolded beggar within a circle of mocking villagers.

Hemmed in by worry, it spun over the puzzle of Nan's absence, and knew not what answer to fetch.

His hands, working of their own accord, laid the mannequin back in Susannah's cradle and adjusted the small blanket over it, tenderly, as though it were Susannah herself. Why was Nan gone? And for how long? Could she have left Will for good?

She couldn't. She wouldn't. Oh, true, he'd not offered her a prosperous abode, nor did his earnings—halved as they must be with his parents' household—support Nan as he would like to support her. But then, Nan had known of his penury when she married him, had even known of it almost a year ago, when, sweet and laughing, she'd lain in the riverside fields with him, awaiting no sanction of parents, or law, or church.

Yet Nan was gone and Susannah with her. How to explain it?

Had Will's mother been right, when she'd talked of Nan's receiving visitors? Of velvet-suited dandies skulking around the garden paths?

Will couldn't credit it.

He thought of Nan as she'd been just the night before: Nan by the fire, Nan cooking supper, Nan warm and gentle in his bed. She couldn't have left. Not Nan. Not unless those gentlemen had taken her with them by force, and who would do that? Who would kidnap a poor man's wife and his little daughter? The shadowy persecutors of his father's fancy?

Will grinned despite his misery. These fears of his, these fantasies of doom, were like a plot hatched from his father's nightmares, his mother's fancy.

No, no. The world was a reasonable place, not populated by old wives' fears, old men's fancies, nor by the dreams of poets or the nightmares of philosophers. In this rational place, there had to be some good reason for Nan's absence.

Will's feet sought out the steps by feel as he made his way downstairs. Perforce, Nan's absence must have a cause as solid as the wood under his feet.

Before he reached the bottom floor, his frantic, searching brain had found one. Nan's sister-in-law, her brother Bartholomew's wife, was due to deliver any day. How foolish of him not to have thought of this before. Nan's kin would have come from Shottery to request her help.

Someone, probably Bartholomew himself, would have come from Hewlands Farm to fetch Nan, and he'd have brought his children, Nan's older nieces, to get them out from underfoot in the house. This thing in Susanna's cradle would be one of the children's toys, probably made by the child's own hand, which explained its crude imitation of human features.

Will smiled in the dark, musty workshop and sighed in relief. His mystery was solved, to his mind's content. Now he must go to Shottery and fetch his Nan. At Shottery, his kin by marriage would give him food and ale, and he could stay the night with Nan, or walk Nan home.

True, his legs were tired, and this walk would take away from his well-merited rest. But he'd rather put himself to the trouble of walking to Shottery and there spend the night with Nan than spend the night here, alone, in his cold bed.

Will closed the front-hall door behind himself, and squared his shoulders. After all, though only nineteen, he was a married man and married men had responsibilities. His wife would depend on him to come to her.

When Will stepped outside his kitchen door, the sun had fully set, its panoply of color hidden beyond the edge of the Earth. The sky spread over Stratford like a blanket: a deep, cloudless, blue dome with pinpoints of stars. Will blinked up at it. It looked like the velvet gown the Queen had worn when she'd come for the pageant the Earl of Leicester had put on for her at Kenilworth, when Will was less than eleven years old. Will had gone to see the pageant with his parents.

In his mind, Will saw again the shows for the Queen: the dancers, the plays, and, best of all, the dolphin, surmounted by the merman, navigating slowly down the river. That dolphin and merman, had fallen on young Will's credulous eyes like supernatural manifestations, and remained in his mind as a promise of a magical world that had never come true. The true world meant debts and hard work and short-lived pleasure purchased by long-lasting toil. He would never see the like of such wonders again.

An owl hooted from the barns at the other end of the Shakespeare backyard and Will jumped, startled. His foreboding returned, called by the ill-omened bird.

Along the garden path, a dark shape approached, an ominous shape, like a man with two heads.

Will swallowed and his breath halted, suspended, before the shape moved closer and a soft giggle revealed the imagined monster for a woman carrying a child.

"Nan, thank God," he said, before he realized that the woman was too short to be Nan.

The shape giggled again, the childish giggle of Will's sister, Joan, and, as it approached, the shadow revealed Joan's still round features, obscured by her unkempt curly hair.

"Goose," she said. "Your Nan is gone. Neither hide nor hair of her have we seen all day."

"She's gone to Shottery," he said, speaking his wish as reality. "To help her sister at her labor."

Joan stopped on the path, a little to the side, allowing Will to walk by her. As he went past, his brother Edmund,

on Joan's hip, three years old and weighing down
fourteen-year-old Joan, stretched out his hand to Will's
arm. Will caressed Edmund's chubby face, glancingly, as
he walked past.

"Mother says Nan is gone with the gentlemen as call
on her while you're at work," Joan said.

Will turned back. "Mother is like a witch poring over
her cauldron, brewing lies and plots around Nan."

With it said, he wished it unsaid, and bit his tongue in
belated reproach. What manner of son called his mother
a liar and a witch? Truly, the Bible warned of ungrateful
children, their tongues sharper than serpent's teeth. But on
the subject of Nan, Will's mother didn't speak as a dutiful
wife and mother, but as a raving hag, a lunatic spouting
infamy. She claimed that Nan had entrapped Will into an
ill-thought marriage that was as ruinous to him as disgraceful to Nan herself, and more, that Nan cavorted with
others while Will was away.

"Mother says she saw Nan go early morning, before the
sun came up, amid a large company, with twinkling lights
all around," Joan said, behind him. "No Shottery people,
for certain."

"Mother knows not what she says," Will yelled over his
shoulder, and ran across the garden toward the gate, taking
a shortcut through the rosebushes. The bushes prickled his
skin and snagged his clothes, but he did not care.

At the gate, a last, fugitive look over his shoulder
showed Will his sister still in the middle of the garden.
Though the distance didn't allow it, he fancied he saw her
amazed expression, wide-open mouth, eyes round in
shock. She'd be wondering why he ran. As though hus-
bands should stand quietly and listen to slander heaped on
their wives' names.

And where had Joan come from, with Edmund, after
nightfall? At any other time, Will would have gone back

and scolded the little girl, but now his Nan waited him. The thought of her enveloping arms and warm body beckoned him on. The thought of her warm voice, calming his fears, called to him like water to a parched traveler.

Will found his way through the alley to the path that crossed the forest of Arden, the path he knew much too well from his courting days when he had taken it every evening for a year, as much to bask in Nan's sweet presence as to escape the closed-in, vile atmosphere of home: his father with his fears, his mother with her fancies.

If only Will's father had stayed the course he'd first set. When Will had been very young, and John Shakespeare's business had thrived, John himself had been an alderman, an important man in the community.

Will walked the narrow path that countless generations of feet had beaten amid towering elms and sprawling oaks, and thought of his life and his family and the obligations that bound him. At nineteen, he was a married man, with a daughter. He'd married a woman with no dowry to speak of, and he had wed himself to an arduous, ill-paying career. He reproached his father for his father's mistakes, yet how could he hope to give Susannah a better start in life?

From behind him he heard the distant sounds of Stratford: the occasional cry of a baby, a woman calling for her son. From her voice, the woman would be Mistress Whateley. And, knowing the Whateley brat, Will suspected the boy was as likely as not to be out of the reach of even that shrill a call.

From farther away came the voice of a man, worse for drink, singing a mournful church song of papist times. Will caught the words *Dies Irae*—in fulsome, rounded Latin. That would be the owner of the Bear, the tavern where Catholics gathered to mourn the past.

Stratford was the only town Will had ever known, and

he knew it well. Its embrace could be comforting and safe like a mother's arms, but, like Will's mother, perhaps it held on too tightly and crushed that which it would preserve.

Perhaps Will should take Nan and Susannah to London and there attempt to find a trade that would bring him a better chance of fortune. But what trade? He had a good, logical mind, but a meager education, and what could a mind alone do for a man of no fortune?

When John had been prosperous, there had been talk of Will's attending university or one of the Inns of Court. With his precise mind Will could have made short work of university learning. Had he but done that, he could have become a real schoolmaster, not a petty schoolmaster, teaching older children their Latin, not the little ones their letters. He could have made enough money, then, to support a large family. Or perhaps he would have become a honey-tongued barrister, swift at unraveling legal knots. He could have supported his Nan, his sweet Nan, in style.

And even his mother would have been unable to spin stories about Nan's consorting with mysterious gentlemen in velvet and jewels.

Little by little, the city sounds receded, as the forest surrounded Will. Human voices became fainter, replaced by the hoots and scrapings of things scurrying and flying amid the old oaks that remained of a forest that, in the distant times of Arthur, had covered all of Britain.

Every rough spot on the path, every stone, every twig, made itself felt through Will's worn-out soles. His legs ached with a dull fatigue. He should have had his supper and he should be going to bed. He should be lying beside his Nan. But Nan was gone.

What if she hadn't gone to the Hathaways? What if she'd run away? She used to escape from her father's strict household, he remembered. She'd dressed in her brother

Bartholomew's old clothes and gone tramping about the forest of Arden for whole afternoons. Will wondered if she missed that freedom.

After Susannah's birth Nan had turned so silent. She no longer laughed at his jests. Waking up in the night to tend the baby made her look perpetually tired. And there wasn't ever enough food, either, only the meager white meat of egg and cheese, with the occasional bit of mutton. With her feeding the babe besides, Nan had grown thin and wraithlike. She didn't seek Will's pleasure as before, nor did her sight inflame him as it once had.

The trees whispered ominously around him, disturbed by wind.

Will sighed.

Things scurried and chattered in the undergrowth on either side of the path.

Ahead, some creature cried like a wounded child.

Could a gentleman really have been courting Nan? One of the richer merchants who came for the Stratford market, perhaps?

Will thought that Nan—Nan who labored nonstop, cooking and washing, mending and weaving and tending the garden—might well have taken the promise of a better life, had a gentleman offered it to her. What fool wouldn't?

Yet Nan was a fool in love. Nan loved him. Will was sure of this. He remembered the soft look that veiled Nan's deep blue eyes when she gazed on him. Yes, she loved him, too much and too well.

In the distance, a dog, or perhaps a wolf, howled at the moon.

Moonlight scarcely penetrated the deep darkness of the timeless forest, where each tree cast a whispering shadow, each bush resembled a skittering, squirming monster.

Sweet music sounded out of nowhere, rising like a river current, surrounding and enveloping Will.

He stopped, startled, at the sounds that were soothing, cool and harmonious and rousing all at once, gripping him in the tide of their smooth, sweet emotion.

Ahead of him, on his right-hand side, a great flash of light surged, like a flame that suddenly catches.

Fire. He flinched in panic, and put up his hand to cover his face. Fire, now. Fire come out of nothing. The forest, dry with midsummer heat, would catch easily. Will was too close to run from it.

But, as his dazzled eyes adapted to the light, he realized the blaze shone too pale, too mild, to be a conflagration. He lowered the hand that had shielded his eyes.

The flash of light solidified into a tall, white castle. Because its walls had an uneven transparency like clotted milk, Will saw rooms within it and glittering servants and courtiers in velvet and jewels walking up and down white marble staircases. At the center of the castle, a vast salon sprawled, furnished only with a red carpet and a massive gilded throne.

Noblemen and fine ladies, wearing jewels that sparkled like rival stars, stood in groups on either side of the throne. Brightly garbed minstrels played sweet music on strange instruments.

In front of the throne, on the red carpet, stood Nan, her fair hair arranged in heavy coils braided through with pearls, her slim body garbed in fine cloth that gave off the sheen of silk.

Around her, lights sparkled and twinkled, like the blinking beacon of the firefly.

Scene 2

ॐ

A palace in the air, sparkling with white walls and spacious marble floors. Columns like those in ancient Greek buildings support the far-distant ceiling, but these columns rise lighter and thinner than ever the gravity-bound laws of human architecture could permit. The ceiling itself shimmers in deep tones of pure gold, as does the throne. On the throne sits a creature who looks like a bearded man in his middle years. But his dark hair is smoother, his features more perfect than man ever possessed. He wears a crown and looks complacently around at an assembly of extraordinarily handsome courtiers. Around the walls and up near the ceiling, little fairies fly, their human shapes aloft on dragonfly wings. In a corner, a gathering of young courtiers play instruments with talent beyond mortal reach.

"Why, now, my brother. I'm glad you've graced this assembly." King Sylvanus, Lord of Elven Realms Above the Air and Beneath the Hills of Avalon, leaned forward on his gilded throne to look at his younger brother, Quicksilver.

The king's oval-shaped face composed itself to show

eager interest. His dark blue eyes, his small pink lips, all
of his well-proportioned features, arranged themselves in
an expression of solicitude. Yet beneath all that good will,
lurked something very much like disapproval.

Quicksilver sighed. He'd been hoping to go unnoticed,
amid the group of youths, more or less his own age, who
huddled to the left side of the throne and traded gossip
and news about the birth of the king's new daughter, the
death of his mortal spouse, and the human who had been
kidnapped to nurse the royal baby.

What other gossip had they traded, and what news had
leaked from their easy prattle to the vigilant ears of the
elven king?

Fearful but determined not to show it, Quicksilver
stepped forward, onto the red carpet in front of the throne.

He should have known that he could not remain hidden
for very long. Quicksilver saw himself clearly, in his
mind's mirror, and knew himself for the most lovely elven
lord of his age. Besides, unlike the other courtiers, he recoiled from gaudy clothes, tinted in colors borrowed from
butterfly wings and grafted from summer gardens. His
grief at his humiliating submission drove him to wearing
dark clothes. His court slippers were black, as were the
gloves on his long-fingered hands and the hose and
breeches that molded his long, well-shaped legs. His velvet doublet, dark as the midwinter night sky, outlined his
broad shoulders and narrow waist in gloom.

Quicksilver even disdained the white collar fashionable
among mortals and aped by most of his elven companions.
He wore nothing contrasting, save a large diamond clasp
that closed his doublet at the throat, and his own long,
glimmering, moonlight-colored hair, combed over his left
shoulder to his waist.

The jewel had come from his mother, sweet Titania,
late queen of the Fairy Realms. It was all Quicksilver had

inherited from his parents. Quicksilver's heart ached within him, mingling resentment and mourning. He should have inherited the kingdom. By elven law, the youngest child should have inherited, and that was Quicksilver. The youngest child, aye, and cosseted and coddled as the heir by fair Titania and her husband, Oberon, before their deaths. But all that, all law, all justice, was as nothing to the tyrant, Sylvanus.

The anger that coursed through Quicksilver tinged red the deep dark river of grief that drowned his soul. Yet, anger and humiliation, a bitter brew, hid themselves well in his sweet features, lurked unnoticed in his round, dark green eyes, as he danced forward, with mincing steps, to pay his respects to the usurper on the throne.

What else could he do? The fairy hill had accepted Sylvanus, goaded by Sylvanus's smooth words, his depiction of Quicksilver as a lowly shapechanger. That done, Quicksilver had been defeated. He could no more live without the hill, and its power that supported his elven soul, than a mortal could live without air or food.

Quicksilver tightened his hands into fists, until his well-kept nails bit into the tender flesh of his palms.

At fifty, Quicksilver had scarcely shed his elven childhood. He was barely old enough to speak for himself.

Five years ago, at his parents' death, he'd been a child in mind and law, more interested in his play pleasures than in the throne. By the time he'd realized he'd been robbed, the game had been played and the victor had claimed his place for good and ill.

Rightful king or no, Sylvanus was now the lord of fairies and elves, possessor of their vows of submission and, through those, of their glamoury, their supernatural strength, their very souls.

The might of all those conjoined powers surged through and from Sylvanus, like the discharge of heavenly power erupting from the thundercloud to char the Earth.

Quicksilver breathed deeply and stood before his brother, bowing his fair head slightly to the dark-haired, bearded majesty on the throne. "My lord."

His brother smiled. "I am amazed, my brother, that you come to us thus and grace the court with your presence. I heard you wished to leave our realm, entire, for another kingdom and its fair monarch."

Quicksilver barely stopped himself from gasping. His breath froze in his chest. The king had found him out. He knew of Quicksilver's plans, those ideas carefully spun in the dark recesses of the night, in the confidence of Quicksilver's intimates.

Who could—who would—have revealed to the king Quicksilver's plans of escape? Lady Ariel? He looked at the slim blonde on the other side of the room. No, she loved him too well to want him thwarted. Pyrite? Quicksilver forbore to search out his childhood friend in the group of male courtiers. He couldn't be the traitor, anyway. Bright, fair, prattling Pyrite didn't wish to keep Quicksilver near. The comparison between their looks bode ill for Pyrite. He'd much rather be friends with Quicksilver at a distance.

Quicksilver heard his own voice shape well-formed, facile words. "I do not wish to leave the realm of my birth, my brother, the realm of my parents." He meant it, as far as that went. He had no wish to leave, but leave he must, to avoid the usurper, his long reach touching Quicksilver's own soul. He must, to avoid the corruption of having to draw force from the tyrant who had stolen Quicksilver's own inheritance.

Sylvanus smiled. He extended his right hand to the thin air beside him. One of the flying fairies landed on it, dropping a rounded pearl of dew onto the monarch's palm. "I have here, my brother, a copy of a message from you to the lady Amaris, Queen of the fairy realm of Tyr-Nan-Og—asking her for the sanctuary of her kingdom, maybe the grace of her hand." The king held the dew between thumb and forefinger and, in that magic globe Quicksilver's miniscule image pranced, begged for refuge, and preened to entice that stranger, the maiden Queen of Tyr-Nan-Og. "Will you explain, my brother, then, what you meant by this message and"—the king gestured toward a troop of little flying fairies each holding a pearl drop of dew—"by the ones that followed it, and the ones that you received in return, in which Queen Amaris does not spurn you and even makes arrangements for your travel—all without consulting me?"

Quicksilver felt color burn in his cheeks, then vanish as he went cold with fear at the possible consequences of his failed plans. To contract marriage, or even to seek it out, without his king's consent would be treason, of course. To leave the kingdom without consent would be treason, also, for a member of the royal family.

"I meant not to displease you. Nor did I wish to. In faith, I had no great design in mind. But you know, my brother, that since our parents' death these five years ago, my heart is yet full of mourning." On a wild, crazed chance, like a deer brought to bay by a pack of hounds that will yet try to spear them on his antlers, and fight even as he bleeds into death, Quicksilver added, "If you'd give me a chance to go to another kingdom, and there pursue my studies and heal my pain . . . I've scarce completed the training in magic use that a noble in my position must endure. And the Queen of Tyr-Nan-Og will, I'm sure, vouchsafe me a stay in her court. That's all I wished of her."

And this was true, though the lady no doubt also wanted Quicksilver in her bed. But Quicksilver would rather not. He had been born with the capacity to change shapes between male and female at will—an ability more befitting lowly forest shapechangers than a member of the royal family—and in his duality he'd never found true love or even lasting desire with either gender.

Oh, Quicksilver would have married the queen for the power and the safety such a marriage promised. If that was the price for peace, then he would pay it. If he couldn't avoid matrimony, then he would marry rather than die. But matrimony had never been his intent. He'd just resigned himself to its inevitability. "I wanted a respite in different surroundings. Nothing more."

The king's eyes opened, in startled surprise, as though he'd never expected to hear a defense. For a moment he frowned; then he pouted. His small pink lips, so much like Quicksilver's own, drew into an unsatisfied expression, a pinch of disappointment, like the mouth of a child denied a sweet.

"No," he said. "No, my brother. You're needed here, not in Tyr-Nan-Og. You'll stay where it can be seen that we two live in harmony and that there is no dissension between us. Abroad, who knows what fools might start intrigues or deceits around your fair head. Young, innocent and trusting as you are . . . and with your dual, changing, capricious nature, your uncontrollable mutability . . ."

His brother always spoke thus, in veiled terms, of Quicksilver's power of changing between the male and female form, that gift—that curse—come to Quicksilver from some unknown ancestor. At least that was how the king alluded to it in Quicksilver's presence. Quicksilver knew too well that behind his back Sylvanus referred to his younger brother as the spawn of some dark thing that had crept, unbeknownst, into their parents' bed. Quicksilver knew that this had been one of the arguments employed to steal the crown from his too-young head.

Quicksilver's anger spiked, sharpened, like the new pain received when an old wound reopens.

Just at the mention of his strange power, Quicksilver fancied he heard tittering here and there in the assembly. Even the small fairies, the servants and helpers of Elvenland, skittered about on golden wings, casting wild patterns of light. Their own version of laughter.

Heat flared and waned on Quicksilver's cheeks in waves. His shame coursed through him like pain.

From across the room, he saw the lady Ariel, Duchess of the Air Kingdoms, beautiful, blond, and soft-hearted, stare at him with a pitying look. Her pitying gaze was yet another insult heaped upon him. Even when the pity arose from love, Quicksilver would not suffer pity.

And yet, what else could he do, but suffer it in good stead? The power of the hill, his need for it, bound him hand and foot to both pity and scorn. He was a prince with neither honor nor power.

If he left here, he could only go to another elven kingdom. And that pathway had just been barred. His careful plans of escape to Tyr-Nan-Og, the nearest and friendliest of the elven lands, had been discovered, betrayed, destroyed with a flick of the royal hand. Betrayed by whom? Quicksilver returned to the question with burning interest. Did his brother, then, have spies everywhere?

Quicksilver bit his lower lip, trying to call forth salty blood from flesh, trying to give himself pain that would remind him of his vulnerable nature, his undeniable need for the hill.

"Stay." The king leaned forward and watched Quicksilver as though reading his thoughts. Condescension mingled with a sharp, cunning look on the royal features. "Turn your thoughts, my brother, to the bright new day, and your joy to me, your rightful sovereign."

Quicksilver's blood thundered in his ears, a noise like

a storm at sea. "I thought, milord," he said, "that we were supposed to be mourning for your own dear wife, that mortal lady of passing beauty, who died just this week, giving life to your daughter."

Silence fell over the palace. It seemed to Quicksilver that even the servants in the distant rooms had stopped moving, stopped speaking. He knew he'd made a fatal blunder. He knew well that his brother—with his cold nature—had forgotten his wife before she lay deep in the dark ground.

Quicksilver had heard rumors of the new royal nurse-maid, arrived this day, who was expected to replace the queen on the throne and the king's bed as well. But to know it was one thing, to speak it aloud another.

Sylvanus, knowing that Quicksilver had no love for the late, mortal-born queen, would guess that by speaking of mourning the dead queen, Quicksilver meant only to taunt Sylvanus himself.

Holding his breath, Quicksilver waited for the ax to fall, for the royal displeasure to cut him off from hill and power, and send him into the world as a wraith, a pow-erless, hollow being, neither elf nor mortal, neither ghost nor living. None in the hill would oppose that punishment, either, for such provocation. One does not taunt sover-eigns.

Quicksilver waited, knowing himself doomed. What could have called his brother's renewed attention to him now? What could have sparked this need to render Quick-silver harmless, defanged; this wish to torment Quicksilver until, like a pup attacked by an old wolf, he rolled on the floor and exposed that which made him vulnerable?

Quicksilver's heart thudded erratically within his chest, like a trapped bird flinging itself at the walls of its cage and getting no more for it than torn wings.

Sylvanus laughed, a singing metallic sound, like the

hiss of a blade sharpened on good stone. "Yes, my dear wife is dead." He composed his face to sadness for a moment, then laughed again. "But, dear brother, your rightful sovereign is blessed with a daughter to lighten his days, a daughter who will have a nursemaid most fair. . . ."

At the words *rightful sovereign*, Quicksilver's nails dug with renewed vigor into his palms, exacting blood to punish his meek acceptance of his brother's foul lie. He must leave the hill. Oh, he must leave. And yet, he couldn't. He couldn't leave. Like a chained bear, baited by merciless, raging mutts, he must stay, helplessly straining at his bonds, while pain tore and rent his living flesh, his quick brain.

Quicksilver had so long clenched his fists that the pain of his nails biting his skin had dulled, had become an old, accustomed torment, like the pain of his having been passed over, like the aching torture of being who he was and not able to fix his nature to one, proper thing.

"Ah." The king's watchful attention, which had been intent on Quicksilver like the gaze of a cat on the mouse he tortures, softened and wandered behind Quicksilver's left shoulder and up, toward the open door of the royal salon. "The nursemaid that the raiding party has found to nurse my daughter, the princess, has arrived. Tonight, she is introduced to the court. Is she not passing fair?"

Forgotten, Quicksilver edged away from the throne, and melted again into the crowd of colorfully attired noblemen. With them, he looked toward the door of the salon.

The mortal had been arrayed in elven finery, decked out as the most worthy of the elven ladies, in a pale green gown studded with pearls. Through the deep slashes in her sleeves, a silvery fabric shone. A tiara of crystal and pearls had been set on her hair, and she wore pearl earrings on her too-large, too-red earlobes.

She advanced in the small, hesitant steps of one bewildered. All around her danced the small, chattering sprite fairies, skittering and flying, looking now like small humans with wings, and now like no more than pale, glowing lights.

As humans, they grabbed at the woman's arms and her skirts, and pulled her from the front and pushed her from behind. As lights, they danced ahead of her, enticing her forth.

Out of the corner of his eye, Quicksilver could see bevies of the fairy ladies across the room gather together, hide their faces behind their jeweled, plumaged fans, and whisper.

Oh, how they would dissect the stranger's dress and her looks, talk of her too-bulbous nose, the altogether common shape of her round face. Her feet would be judged too large, her hair too coarse, her hands too broad and work-callused.

Quicksilver wished he had worn his female aspect today, because the males among whom he stood had nothing but slavish approbation and simpering, whispered admiration for the mortal their king had already pronounced fair.

"Beautiful, isn't she?" Pyrite said. The shimmering green suit he wore lent brilliance to the brassy yellow hair that fell in curtains on either side of his mobile face. "Beautiful to take your heart away."

"Her eyes, like twin moons, have enchanted my soul."

"Her hair looks like wheat ready to be gathered at harvest," another nobleman put in.

Quicksilver gazed down at his open hands and saw the half-moon shapes his nails had cut into his palms. Dipping the ladle of his need in the river of the hill's power, he gathered magic to heal the wounds he had given himself. Even in doing it, he was aware that his brother had allowed him the use of that power; aware of Sylvanus's amused disdain that came with this gift.

Another young lord, dressed in silk that owed pattern and coloring to the blooming rose in a summer afternoon, laughed musically. "May this woman soon become our king's wife, and bring our sovereign lord a bountiful harvest indeed."

Others giggled.

The mortal advanced past them, too dazzled or perhaps too scared to look in their direction. At the foot of the throne, she curtseyed.

This grace, Quicksilver thought, might well have taken her the livelong day to learn.

She didn't look like a court lady, but like a broad-hipped farm girl, a peasant accustomed to harsh work. And perhaps the king meant it thus, having required a sturdy maid this time, since his last, highborn bride had proven so frail.

Quicksilver's hands tingled with new-healed wounds. His mind still seethed at being humiliated in front of the court. He focused his many-sided discontent on the nurse-maid and thought that he couldn't imagine what possessed everyone to suddenly see this creature as fair. Except, of course, that Sylvanus had declared her so and Sylvanus did not brook dissent.

The mortal straightened and looked around like a sleeper wakening. It seemed to Quicksilver that she trembled slightly.

"Ah, my dear," Sylvanus said. "How are they treating you? Have you all you need?"

She opened her broad red-lipped mouth, closed it with a snapping sound. A red flush tinged her pale, round cheeks, giving them a passing resemblance to harvest apples, a simile that, all gods be praised, went unremarked by the fawning noblemen who surrounded Quicksilver.

"Milord," the woman said. The broad vowels and rolled *r*'s of the region tainted her pleasant, low voice. "I do not have all I require. Your servants have seen me well lodged and I lack for no comfort, yet I shouldn't be here at all. My husband will be coming home and needing me, and missing his daughter that I brought with me."

The king's eyebrows arched. A vertical crease formed on the bridge of his nose. His pout came back, a dissatisfied sulking.

Quicksilver truly wished he'd come to court as a woman. Though it might have reminded everyone, once more, of his unseemly power, it would also have provided him with a fan behind which to hide the smile that kept trying to curl his lips upwards. He'd not expected the little peasant to be outspoken.

The storm gathering in the king's features dispersed as suddenly as it had begun. He leaned back. His powerful body relaxed visibly. His laugh rang out loudly, echoing through the halls and setting the whole, splendid company to fits of sympathetic giggling. "Thus I and all my enchanted kingdom are to be disdained in favor of a farmer, a butcher's apprentice or perhaps a lowly clerk in some law firm." He laughed on. "I'm offering you, milady, all the riches of both elves and fairies, the tall inhabitants of the hills and the small magical lights of the evening, all their riches, all their magic and"—he smiled seductively— "since you're so fair, even my hand in marriage, and a throne by my side. Yet, you stand there and tell me you require a husband. Well, and I grant you I'd be husband enough for you."

The company tittered again. The winged fairies flashed around the room, flaring into pale lights.

The woman recoiled, taking two steps back. Her fair but abundant eyebrows descended over her eyes, and she licked her lips, her expression one of shrewish calculation,

like a goodwife at the market faced with a higher price
than she wishes to pay. Her hand went to the front of her
pearl-embroidered pale green gown, as though searching
for the pocket of her accustomed apron. "I do not disdain
anyone. My husband is alive and well. I should be with
him. I seek no other." She raised her head a little, defi-
antly, and one of the many tiny braids affixed beneath the
tiara on her head, fell and dangled beside her ear, making
her look yet more mortal and more common, and somehow, perhaps because of that, more alluring—like freshly
baked bread and homely meals, next to which the dainties
of kings paled.

A hushed silence fell over the assembly. In the five
years of Sylvanus's reign, since King Oberon and Queen
Titania had disappeared one winter night and their power
vanished from amid their people, there hadn't been such
frank talk heard in this court.

Quicksilver could swear that even the sounds of
breathing stopped in the salon and the wings of the serf
fairies were arrested midbeat, as though each fairy, each
highborn elf held his or her breath, waiting for the king's
fury to be unleashed.

Instead, the king laughed again, his merriment echoed
by a string of relieved titters, an echo of flashing lights
and dancing winged sprites.

"So." The king grinned at the mortal. "So. But you can't
leave and return to your husband. It's my decree that you
shall remain here and nurse my daughter and raise your
own daughter as her sister. Soon, soon, we'll see if you
do not perceive the advantages of my kingdom, the joy of
my near-immortal people. We'll see if you might not long
to join us." The king rose to his full height, taller than
any mortal man. His limber figure made him look like a
mortal of twenty though among his own people he neared

middle age at three thousand years. "And now, we shall dance."

The woman's eyes clouded with tears, and her hands clenched into fists, the twin of Quicksilver's own. But she was even more powerless than Quicksilver, against the might of the hill embodied in the king.

That she had resisted him so far was miracle enough. That she denied him in front of his courtiers was astonishing. Most humans bent and swayed in the power of the hill, like limber pines tilting in the wind's fury.

The musician elves in the farthest corner, who'd been playing soft, subtle music, rose and struck up their instruments louder and faster, in a dancing tune.

"You, my dear, will dance with me." The king extended his hand to the mortal.

For a moment it all hung in the balance, and it looked as if she'd refuse the proffered royal fingers.

But a farm girl couldn't resist the elven king's glamoury. Her work-roughened hand, reddened by a hundred wash days, rested in his.

Before other couples joined in, Quicksilver had time to wonder at her grace, the skipping step with which she led the dance by the king's side. Then he noticed a young lady in white cutting through the crowd, toward him.

Ariel.

Her blond hair shone like a halo of light around her small, intent face which was set in unbearable longing, and her graceful figure seemed to lean forward, striving to reach Quicksilver. Her pale clothing lent her white skin a creamy pallor, like that of the finest silk.

She would come to Quicksilver, she would ask him to dance and loudly repeat it, making it unseemly for him to refuse.

Prince Quicksilver had no time and scant patience for

lovesick kings, and even less for lovesick elven maids of high birth and little mind.

Turning abruptly, before Ariel could reach him, he made for the wide, arched opening to the outside world, beyond the palace, beyond the enchanted realms of fairyland. He escaped toward the world of mortals, that place of crude and simple beings, which seemed to him, suddenly, to beckon like a promised land.

He rushed outside—past the black-diamond armored guards who bowed their heads to him—down the broad marble steps, to the cool dark night beyond.

He ran through the night, heedless, until he got far enough away from the bubble of light cast by the fairy palace. In the semidark, he leaned against the bark of a rough tree and took greedy breaths of air perfumed with the deep, earthy scents of trees and grass.

The voices of the small, scurrying creatures of the night surrounded him. *Hurry, hurry, hurry*, cried the mind of the mouse skittering through the undergrowth, while above him the sharper mind of the owl screamed of hunger and blood.

Quicksilver's anger sang in harmony with the owl, and his fear of his brother and his brother's power screamed in unison with the mouse.

Peevishly, he pulled off his gloves and, holding them both in his right hand, smacked them on his left leg as he resumed walking. His movement was intended to disperse his impotent anger, rather than to carry him anywhere. While he strode, unminding, through the forest around the charmed palace, his errors, his many-splendored mistakes, taunted him like mocking demons.

He should have said something in his own defense. He should somehow have salvaged his plans to leave the kingdom. He should have answered his brother's derisive tones, Sylvanus's implication that Quicksilver wasn't a proper elf, his intimation that Quicksilver might conspire against the kingdom. And he should, he *should*, have answered the barbed arrows aimed at his youth, his inexperience, his mutable nature.

With such flimsy excuses, such vile murmuring, his brother had managed to snatch the throne away. And no one had protested the usurpation. No one. With such flimsy excuses had Quicksilver been robbed of his inheritance.

Flogging his thigh, as one would flog a sluggish horse, he welcomed the stings of his blows, the pain that came through the black velvet of his breeches to remind him always that he had no power. No power to rebel. No power to do anything.

Maybe he *was* a child, maybe he was ineffective and foolish. Why else would he have allowed his brother to thus dispossess him? Even there, in the salon, he had found no answer to his brother's public mocking, his veiled challenge.

How could Quicksilver hope to prevail over Sylvanus's perfidy if he couldn't even reply to the king's taunting?

"Quicksilver, my lord, wait," a woman's voice called from behind him.

This high, harmonious voice almost set Quicksilver to flight. Yet he checked his feet in their attempt at running, kept them immobile on the woodland ground.

Ariel had found him and pursued him here. Why? Even she was not usually that importune, no matter how besotted.

Besotted. Thinking of her devotion, Quicksilver felt something dark and deep uncoil within him, something serpentine and cunning, that wished to vent his anger on anything, anyone.

This elven girl, an orphan, Pyrite's sister, even more powerless and even younger than Quicksilver, would be vulnerable to his wrath, his pent-up fury. And even if she was one of his few allies—and spies—in the court, Quicksilver knew he could safely hurt her. She would forgive him. She always forgave him.

Quicksilver breathed deeply, more furious than ever at Ariel's folly, her soft, yielding nature. His own folly was such that he might have liked her better were she harsher.

He rounded on her, with a cat's swift movements. "Milady Ariel."

She'd been running, full tilt, after him, and stopped, ten steps away, suddenly wary, as though something in his movement or his voice had given away his mood.

"Milord," she said, and struggled to catch her breath, and most becomingly raised her pretty, dainty hand to her pretty, dainty chest. "All evening long I've been wishing to speak with you."

Quicksilver closed his lips tightly.

Dressed in creamy velvet and lace, Ariel looked fair in this light, her lack of proper womanly charms masked by the shadows, her face small and earnest and anxiously turned up to him.

Words pushed past his lips, his fury biting through them. "I do not wish for your company. Someone betrayed me to my brother and it might well have been you, Lady Ariel." This statement sounded so unlikely that Quicksilver himself almost laughed at the words. Ariel could no more betray than plot, no more scheme than rebel. But it served to startle her. "It might well have been you."

She took a step back. Her hand clasped the lace at her chest. Her other hand—still holding the closed, white, feathered fan she'd used inside the salon—came up. But she never opened the fan, just held it closed near her face.

Her pink lips shaped a round, afflicted "Oh." She cleared her throat. "I've . . ." She shook her head. "As you know, I have my modest gift, my seeress gift, and last night I dreamed of your parents, the great Oberon, our Queen Titania that was. And in my dream, they—" She stopped abruptly. Her lips went pale and her eyes opened wide, as if something in Quicksilver's face scared her.

Quicksilver's heart beat faster, the very blood in his veins racing in frenzy, though he remained still. Ariel might be a twit, but she had a gift of dreams. And if she'd dreamed of Oberon and Titania, what had she dreamed? Was there hope his parents would return and reestablish the proper order of the world?

He clasped her arm in his hand, crushing her creamy silk sleeve to a crumple beneath his merciless fingers. "What dreamed you, fool girl, answer me?"

She opened her mouth, then closed it. For a moment it looked as if she could not command her voice to her wishes. "They came," she finally said, "as those shades of mortals that depart this world not in peace. Our king looked wan and ragged, and our queen—" Here, Ariel, who had been one of the queen's own maids, managed to squeeze from her eyes two crystalline tears, and stopped long enough to wipe them to a kerchief pulled from her sleeve. "Milady was also pale and wan, and devoid of substance so that through her, as though through great rents in her being, I could glimpse another world. It was a desolate world, as pale and devoid of life as she was. Naked trees stood out against a merciless sky, and the earth, the soil beneath her feet, boiled like a cauldron of evil. She wore only a white sheet, like the shroud in which mortals are confined at their death. And she said that by foul means were they slain, she and her royal husband, by foul means turned from this world to the place of shadows and nothingness—a place where no other elf has ever gone—where they expiate their former joys, their enchanted days. There . . ." Ariel paused.

"There where? There what?" Quicksilver's fury had

been replaced with shock and impatience. His parents had been murdered? By whom? And how? It wasn't easy to kill an elf. It was even harder to kill those who held the power of the whole hill in themselves. Quicksilver thought of his own, impotent fury at his brother, his repeated, empty fantasies of killing Sylvanus.

"There, in the land of shadows, your parents will remain imprisoned, powerless, waning, until you"—Ariel blushed and looked away—"until you, who are the legitimate heir of their power, should release them. By your avenging them, they will be freed to be born again into this world and the kingdom of fairy."

"Avenging them! How did they meet their death, then?"

"They said that they were slain when they rode north across the bridge of air, to sup with the Queen of the Northern Lights. They were stabbed through with a charmed dagger, by a mortal they met at the crossroads."

"A mortal?" Unbelievable. Mortals could attack fairies and elves, even the sovereigns of fairies—assuming they could resist the glamoury of elven magic and the raw power of the hill that such monarchs embodied. But mortals could not hope to succeed in such attacks. Even their iron was powerless to kill magical beings. They could do no harm. Not in vain were elves considered immortals. "To murder a king, or a queen, it would take charms, powerful charms woven onto the weapon. Charms that only our kind—"

He stopped.

Ariel nodded, setting her baby-fine pale hair in motion, its waves shining like beacons in the dark night. "Yes. They said that the one who benefited the most from their death had thus prepared the weapon for the wretched mortal."

The one who benefited most. Sylvanus. Sylvanus, the treasonous cur. Quicksilver had never suspected that much evil. Greed, yes—it lived in Sylvanus's chest, and pride, and ambition, revenge and more offenses at Sylvanus's beck than he had thoughts to put them in, imagination to give them shape, or time to act them in. But treason, that was sin of a higher order, a hand raised against the gods above and the spirits below. Quicksilver had never suspected greatness in his brother, not even greatness in evil.

In this new understanding, he looked all around with painfully clear vision. His parents' disappearance was no longer a mystery, nor did he wonder at his brother's usurping the throne.

He wondered, instead, why the moon still shone, on hearing of such horrors. There should be thunder and rain. Clouds should crowd and do battle in the sky. An earthquake should tear asunder Earth's fragile crust, crushing trees and animals in its unfeeling hand.

How could everything look so calm?

Love, love, love, thought the calling frog down by the river.

Life, life, life, twinkled the firefly close at hand.

Quicksilver breathed air that felt by turns too cold and burning hot, that scalded and froze him, mind and heart.

For Quicksilver, neither love nor life mattered any longer. Nor could he expect them to matter, even in the distant future. Gone was his dream of escaping to Tyr-Nan-Og to live a quiet life in an unclouded court, as the prince consort of a powerful queen.

His parents had died, not just changed forms as elves would, but truly died, as no elf should die. They'd been cut off from the wheel of creation that compensated elves for their exclusion from the heaven of mortals.

Without that wheel, Oberon's and Titania's souls would hang outside the world, struggling against the currents of time, buffeted by the hopelessness of those who would never leave the land of shadows.

From this remote, improbable land, his parents had sent a plea for his help, through Ariel's dream. They had asked the help of Quicksilver, their son, their darling, spoiled younger son, who was powerless to even prevent his brother's humiliating him before the court.

If Quicksilver ignored their plea, if he didn't aid them, they would fade away to nothing; to less than nothing, to that nothingness that haunted those who had never existed.

From what Ariel had said, they were close to nothingness even now.

He must avenge them.

But the one who had profited most from their demise was Sylvanus, and Sylvanus could not be killed. Not while he held all the power of the hill, the force of all the magic of every lord who'd sworn fealty to him—even, perforce, Quicksilver's magic and power.

Sylvanus could not be killed by an elf, an inhabitant of the hill he ruled. And yet, an idea quickened in the outraged prince's brain and all his other thoughts stopped, crushed and astonished under the weight of it. The traitor could not be punished by elven hand. But . . . by a mortal? Could Sylvanus's own scheme be turned upon him?

Quicksilver looked at Ariel, her drawn features, her big questing eyes, and disciplined himself to a controlled nod of his head. "Milady, I thank you. You have done well to tell me this."

"You—" She cleared her throat. Her long white neck stretched gracefully as she looked up at him. "You won't do anything in haste, will you, milord? It would be madness for you to try to attack . . ." She stopped short of pronouncing the king's name and, instead, waved her closed fan around helplessly. "To touch him would mean death for you, sweet my Lord." Her white hand held his arm, pale fingers gleaming on black velvet.

Sweet, she called him. And inside him, all the while,

such vile things rustled and crawled, tainting the unsullied ice of his soul with their dark trails. Thirst for revenge joined his aggrieved pride, and through this all Ariel would walk, like the child leading both lion and lamb.

Quicksilver shook his head. "Don't fear for me." His voice came out raspy and harsh with tears he could never, would never, shed, or not until vengeance was done. "But now you must return to the palace, before my—before *he*—wonders what you've been telling me, before *he* sends his spies for you." Quicksilver's feelings seemed strangely muted, like drums muffled by cloth. He should be raging and screaming, begging the heavens to avenge foul murder, yet he could manage no more than the feeling that he should do so. No accompanying echo arose in his heart.

Ariel nodded. Bobbing him a graceful curtsey, she said, "Yes, sweet lord." She grabbed his arm, and raising herself on tiptoe, with desperate suddenness, she set burning lips to his cheek for a feverish kiss.

Then she was gone, running like a scared being of the night, up the marble steps of the enchanted palace.

Quicksilver stayed where he was, his gaze following her. His hand rose to touch his cheek, where her timid kiss had heated his skin.

He let his hand fall and looked down at his gloves, which he'd twisted into a knot between his hands. He smoothed them with slow, unwitting movements.

With his enchanted vision he watched as, inside the palace, the false king danced with the peasant girl, while the whole noble company followed, round and round, tireless, like painted figures marching along the sides of a battle drum.

There had been a time that Quicksilver, too, had danced thus, wearing his slippers away in the pleasure of his own movement, in the rapture of the music lifting him. In both his shapes, he'd danced, graceful and gleeful and unashamed. But the couple leading the dance had been his parents.

His parents.

He wandered around outside the palace, keeping well in the shadow of the forest, trampling branches and leaves beneath his fine black court slippers, and startling insects and mice to desperate flight.

Hurry, hurry, hurry. Run, run, run, screamed small, afflicted mind-voices from the brush.

Oh, if only his parents' shadows would send him a willing instrument for his vengeance. Someone outside the realm, someone base and crude and mortal. Someone like the mortal his brother had commanded for his foul deed. Someone who would strike at Sylvanus's rotted-through heart and kill him and not be banned from the power of the hill forever.

And never mind if mortals who did harm the inhabitants of fairyland bought themselves death in that one action. What did Quicksilver care for the life of mortals, when his heart remained cold at his parents' plight and he had no more than a sense of what he *ought* to feel to guide him through his awful duty?

He stopped. A man stood in front of him.

Man might not be the right word. This looked scarcely more than a raw boy, with overlong bones beneath supple skin, his angles and jagged ends showing only a hint of future manly power. The hair on his chin was no more than a dispirited feathery growth.

Yet his skin glowed as pale and even and smooth as Lady Ariel's, and his forehead rose noble and broad. His small pink lips held an unexpected hint of stubborn strength. His dark hair fell in soft curls to his shoulders. His yellow-brown eyes were the eyes of a falcon intent on the chase.

Not unpleasant to the eye, the young man might have been mistaken for one of the elven king's own guards, except for his clothes, which were all mortal, and cheap. Russet wool, such as the poorest peasants wore, made up his garb, though it had been cut into a respectable enough doublet and breeches.

The garments showed the boy for a mortal. A mortal aspiring to middle class and falling short.

Yet he looked at the enchanted palace and saw it, where mortal eyes should perceive nothing but darkness and rustling trees.

Quicksilver sighed. This must be another Sunday child, blessed with enchanted sight. He wished the creatures wouldn't whelp on Sundays. It only caused trouble, for elf and human alike.

And yet . . . if the boy could see Sylvanus, maybe he could kill him, too. Maybe Quicksilver had found his henchman. Addling the mortal's wits, persuading him to cooperate could not be hard.

Quicksilver reached for the boy's thoughts and heard the tumult of them: *Nan, my Nan.*

The youth's eyes, fixed in a mournful gaze, turned to where the peasant girl danced with the elven king.

Ah, so this would be the butcher's apprentice, or the law clerk, or whatever he was, who'd married the woman that the elven king coveted.

And he would be—Quicksilver smiled—the willing instrument of Quicksilver's vengeance.

Silently, Quicksilver thanked his parents' shades for sending him such a one.

Then, by an effort of his elven will, he bent his body to his pliant mind, and, taking advantage of the gift his brother so disdained, wished upon himself his female aspect and changed his clothes to match his form. Thus armed, he set out to begin his vengeance.

Scene 3

⚙

A forest, thick enough to obscure the light of the cloud-veiled moon. A shimmering, translucent palace stands amid the trees, overlaying the dark trunks. Within the palace, the fairy company dances. Outside, Will watches the dancers. Quicksilver, in female form, looks on him, unobserved.

Open-mouthed, Will watched the finely dressed dancers, and Nan, dressed like a fine lady too, cavorting with the dark-haired man who'd sat on the throne in the translucent palace amid the trees. Will felt as if his wits had been addled by wine or sleepiness, and he couldn't think clearly from one end of a thought to the next.

The man looked like a king. He felt like a king, too, to Will's damped spirits, his muffled, despairing jealousy.

But king of what?

England had a queen, and no king, and may Elizabeth live and reign many more years, if it would avoid the civil wars that tore a country apart when a sovereign died with no legitimate heir.

Will shook his head. No kings in England. He must be dreaming.

Yet he felt awake. His feet hurt from the rocky forest path, and his bare hands felt the cool night breeze that made the bushes rustle and the trees whisper overhead.

Still, he must be dreaming. He knew the path through the forest to Shottery much too well never to have noticed a palace—and an enormous palace such as this, made of gleaming white marble. There weren't even ruins of a palace on this site, that Will might be seeing a ghostly projection of past glory.

In human memory, this forest was as it had ever been. Only its confines had shrunk more with each passing generation, till it was no more than woods, rambling through a small part of the country it had once covered.

Vague legends of Druids, the writings of Romans who'd first arrived in Britain, bobbed up in Will's mind, sending a shiver down his spine, clouding his thoughts like stories heard on a dark night, while the wind howls outside the shuttered windows.

Perhaps he was watching the unhallowed ceremonies of the pre-Christian savages who had once lived here.

But, no, such things didn't happen in this well-ordered world of flesh and blood. And if these were savages, why would Nan be among them?

No, it had to be a dream, all a mad dream. Only illusion could make marble walls transparent, a feat quite common in dreams, and not startling at all to the sleeping mind, though impossible in the waking world.

But if he was dreaming, what should he do? Did it matter where he wandered? And where had his dream begun? Had this whole day been a dream, and did he still lie snug beside his Nan in their bed, in the predawn mists of this day that his fevered brain told him was ending? Or had the dream begun sometime when his weary body had reclined deep within the forest, and he'd fallen asleep on a rough bed of moss and leaves?

He willed himself to wake, opened his eyes so much he felt they'd split. Nothing changed.

Will closed his eyes, and wished, and hoped that he would wake up in his bed, next to Nan.

He opened his eyes again to see Nan, dressed all in silk, covered all in pearls, hopping and skipping beside a royal personage that could not exist, within a semitransparent palace where no palace could rise.

Thus had she danced with Will, when he had courted her, at the churchyard at Temple Grafton in May of the year past. A year ago, little more, and he'd already lost her.

"Um . . . oh, um . . . good sir," a soft voice called, from amid the trees.

Will turned to look and, for a moment, forgot the palace and Nan and the impossible, prancing king.

In that moment he knew for sure that he wandered lost in a dream spun from a fevered brain.

The person standing amid the trees couldn't be real. Such beauty as she possessed—beauty distilled, refined with purity and grace such as the papist sculptors had tried to infuse into their idolatrous statues—such beauty couldn't exist in reality.

Not that the woman standing at the edge of the trees looked conventionally beautiful. Rather than the golden tresses much admired by poets, she had ink-black hair, so dark it gave off no reflection, even when moonlight, piercing the treetops, chanced to shine fully on her. Moonlight shone upon her high cheekbones, her oval, well-drawn face, her small straight nose and her large, large eyes that shone the color of polished silver.

Her pink lips turned slightly upward at the corners, a smile of amusement at his scrutiny.

She was dressed as finely as Nan in that dream-vision that had enthralled Will, and she did not look like some-

one who should be tramping about in the middle of Arden
Forest. Her glistening garb suited itself ill to forest paths.
Her gown fell over a fine chemise, both of them covered
all with glistening scrolls of silver-colored thread that
formed designs that now looked this way, now that, just
like the branches of a wind-whipped tree will form one
shape and then another, all of them beautiful, all of them
meaningless.

Her pulled-back long hair fell to her waist. A net of
shining silvery thread and pearls enveloped it without re-
straining it.

The woman stepped forward slowly, like a vision, her
movement more graceful than anything, save maybe the
flight of a bird on a spring morn.

The palace and Nan forgotten, Will had to control an
impulse to fall on his knees and worship this vision.

Next, he would be like those papist visionaries of old,
and run into Stratford claiming he'd seen the Virgin Mary
in the woods. Wouldn't that be a fine way of ending up
accused of conspiring with the Jesuits, or of turning the
people against their excommunicated sovereign?

Will's hand went to the front of his neck, beneath his
chin.

He'd always wanted to be in high places, but he'd never
meant to have his head displayed on a pike over London's
gate. Not that he would get even that. Common as dirt,
with no name and no arms, he'd end by hanging from the
gibbet while crows plucked out his eyes.

Gossamer-like and ethereal, the lady floated toward him
as if on air. A waft of perfume came with her—lilacs at
full bloom, a floral scent like the one Will had smelled in
his deserted room in Stratford, but stronger, more intoxicating. Will inhaled and felt dizzy.

The vision stopped short of walking through Will, and

smiled intently at him. "My kind sir," it said. "I need your help."

"My . . . help?"

The vision smiled. Her too-solid-feeling hand grasped Will's arm just above his wrist, where the sleeve of his secondhand suit ended. Her hand felt velvety-soft and very warm. "Your help, if you will give it to me. You are, I assume, the husband and master of that fine lady." She waved a graceful hand toward the translucent palace, within which Nan still leaped and cavorted. The lady's gesture made the twin globes of her breasts rise and fall within her low-cut chemise.

"Ah. Yes. Nan." So Nan was still there, too? A coherent dream this was, for all its incoherence.

"Good." The woman smiled. "My name is . . . um . . . Silver. Lady Silver, and I need your help in righting a great wrong . . . and in . . . um . . . getting your wife back."

"Nan?" Getting Nan back? But Nan . . . Had Nan really disappeared? In the world of rational men, Nan could not have disappeared. And if this was all a dream, then Nan would still be home, with Susannah, or else in Shottery, with her kin. And if this was a dream, what did it matter what Will did or how he responded to this splendid lady with her rounded breasts, her tiny waist?

Will's mind spun, in confused wonder.

"Yes, your wife. I understand you love her very much." The woman's smile seemed to mock the very idea of love between man and wife.

Will gave her a shrewd look. She was dressed and behaved like a lady, but was she a bawd, sent to tempt him?

Right. He smiled at the thought. Oh, certainly this was a bawd. A bawd in white silk walking the forest at night, beside a transparent palace, to tempt Will, petty-schoolmaster of Wincot, son of a ruined Stratford merchant. Perhaps she was a courtier inside that dream palace. Will smiled to himself.

His smile seemed to startle the dark lady. She cocked her head sideways and examined him, as though he were a strange, wondrous object brought from overseas in the belly of a ship.

"What—What has happened to my wife, and how may I help Nan? How may I help you—and Nan?" His mouth felt too dry. He licked his lips and gestured expansively toward the palace. If he was dreaming, he might as well find the rules behind the dream, that would allow him to rescue Nan, or at least to change the dream into something more pleasant. He eyed the lady Silver, her tightly corseted waist making an indentation between her ample bosom and her flaring hips. If this were a mad dream, then he'd dream what he best pleased. He longed to lay his face on the two satiny globes at her chest, but something in her eyes warned him against it.

The lady smiled, as though reading his mind, or maybe just the hungry expression in his eyes. "Your lady wife and your daughter have both been taken by the people below the hill."

The people below the hill? Below what hill, in this flat ground of forest and fields? It took him a while to realize what the words meant, to equate this with the *good people* of which his grandmother had muttered and his mother had spoken, long ago, when Will was a small boy.

He remembered his aunts and his mother, gathered in a furtive group by the fireplace, discussing mysterious, supernatural beings that inhabited mounds and disused glens, and intercepted travelers on their way through Arden Forest.

The women had to speak of such things behind the backs of their newly converted men, because the new, Protestant religion lacked the old religion's accustomed patience toward the ancient beliefs of the people.

From what Will had gathered when—a child of small years and tender imagination—he had listened to stories obviously not meant for him, the people below the hill must be the same as the beings who'd consorted with the druids. Magical beings, of unhallowed magic. His adult mind told him it was all nonsense, but dreams often were, so he thought on.

Some of his aunts and their neighbors had said these supernatural beings were a few of the fallen angels, the less guilty ones, who'd never been cast all the way to the depths. Others believed that they were the ancient, dethroned gods of the mistaken faiths. Others, yet, that they were the souls of the dead.

Will looked at the palace, and his heart turned within him. Nan amid the dead? No, it couldn't be. When she'd given birth he'd feared for her and the baby but nothing had come of it, and Nan lived, and Susannah with her.

He frowned at the beautiful lady in front of him, at her silver eyes that gazed into his.

Will's mother held with the papist belief in which she'd been raised, and even kept—well-concealed in the attic— an image of the Virgin Mary amid the angels, a painted cloth given to her by her prosperous father. But Will had heard the preachers say often enough that those apparitions of the Virgin, hailed by mystics of the past had been no more than deceptions of the devil.

Were these devils, then? Had Nan been captured by their deceptions, and had Will, with her, unwittingly fallen into their trap? And where was Susannah?

The lady smiled quizzically at him, while Will, uneasy, looked at the translucent palace, the dancing company. He remembered stories of the fairy people dancing, cursed dances that could hold those who joined in them captive for years or centuries. When the dancer emerged, he would crumble into the dust of the centuries he'd ignored while dancing.

Nan.

Will muttered the words of the Our Father under his breath, fully expecting the lady, the palace, and all to dissolve and leave him and Nan alone in the forest.

The dark lady laughed at his whisper. "We're not afraid of the divine. I'm sorry. Those are only legends. We are, it is true, bound by certain rules, as all creation is. But because we're different from you, doesn't mean we're unhallowed. We've respected the religions of men, and their beliefs, through the centuries, but they have no more power over us than we over them." Her laugh damped down to a muffled giggle. "No, my dear. If you want your wife back, you'll have to try another way." She wrapped her hands around his arm. "My way."

Will fought free of Silver's grasp and, half-maddened, ran to the immense staircase that led to the translucent palace's arched doorway.

He would rush in and grab Nan and pull her back. He seemed to remember, from the legends he'd half-listened to, that this was the way to reclaim a loved one stolen by the hill people for their unholy merriment.

Only, instead of climbing the staircase, as he intended, he ran through it—through the stone, and the walls, and the people, and the high columns, and through a series of crowded halls beyond. Guards and maids—all of them too pretty to be mortals—gathered in groups, or went about inscrutable errands.

He tripped on twigs and stubbed his toes on stones obscured by translucent courtiers, and he cried out the holy name in vain as he ran headlong into a translucent kitchen where fire that didn't burn him flamed in the hearth, maids and women tended pots that swung right through him, and roasts that he could neither smell nor touch turned on crystal-bright spits.

Above him, in the throne room, couples danced on and on, in indefatigable merriment. Looking straight up, Will saw, through the translucent marble floor, the length of his Nan's legs, encased in white stockings, moving beneath her green silk dress.

He ran back to the first hall he'd crossed, and tried to climb a spiral staircase to the floor above.

Instead of making progress, he ran deep into the marble of the staircase, and felt not even a tingle as he did so.

Encased in stone, his lungs still drew breath from the cool vegetation-scented air of Arden Forest. Fine lords and ladies walked up the staircase, not noticing him.

He heard a fine titter, a musical giggle.

The dark lady stood next to the staircase, and bid him come, with a gentle wave of the hand.

If any of the other courtiers saw her, they gave no sign. They didn't see Will. That was quite plain.

Reluctantly, Will came to the wave of the lady's hand. He'd gone back to thinking it was all a mad dream. Only in dreams did people walk through walls. Only in dreams did people run unnoticed amid the high and mighty. Only in dreams.

Yet, if this was a dream, Will would control it. He would do what he'd set out to do.

"I'm going to Shottery," he said, loud and clear, as he came near the lady Silver.

She smiled and kicked up her skirt with the tip of her silvery, pointed shoes, as if mocking him with a martial step. "To Shottery, then," she said. "And I'll talk to you along the way and tell you how you might rescue your wife and daughter."

She slipped her arm in his, and led him quietly out of the hall, through the wall, which she, too, crossed, as though it didn't exist. "It is no use," she said. "You cannot reach your Nan this way. She is in the world of the elves, in Fairyland, and you're in the world of humans. The two do no more touch than two leaves in a pair of tables, wax to wax, right next to each other, but unable to mingle the figures that the merchant has scrawled upon each. Credit and debit remain thus separate." Silver smiled.

"She is of my world, Nan is," Will said. Even in dreams, there should be some rationality preserved. "And Susannah."

Silver sighed. "Yes, but they were taken to ours, as I am in yours. This is a magic possible only to elves, not to humans. Humans must do something particular to acquire magic and gain admittance to Elvenland."

She'd led him by the arm onto his accustomed path through the forest and walked him along it.

The palace, with its lights and glimmering dancers, vanished from view, leaving the forest all the darker in its absence.

"So, what must I do to get Nan back?" Will asked, defeated. Even if this were only a dream, if it turned out that Nan had truly vanished, perhaps it was a prophetic dream and perhaps by following its instructions, Will could recover Nan nonetheless. "And is Susannah with her?"

"Well, Susannah is with her mother, and, should you recover your wife, the babe will be given to you. But first you must tell me your name, sir. And who you are."

"William Shakespeare. Will, son of John Shakespeare, the glover of Henley Street, in Stratford." He hoped, incongruously, that this fair lady wouldn't know the state of his father's business, as if it mattered what a dream, a chimera, thought or knew.

"Ah. And you're . . . a butcher's apprentice?"

Will tugged away the arm the lady held. Did he look

like a butcher, and born to such low calling? An insulting dream, this was, that he dreamed. "No. I'm a schoolmaster. A petty-schoolmaster. I teach in the petty school in Wincot."

The lady smiled, and her hand retrieved Will's arm and grasped it tighter. "A worthy calling, and you must be a man of learning. So it will not surprise you to know that in the sphere of elves and fairies, as in that of men, there can be treachery and base deceit. Nor, knowing as no doubt you do that all spheres are linked, the stars arrayed around the sun just like all worthy men are arrayed around your most high sovereign, you cannot fail to know that injustice in the world of fairies will lead to injustice in the world of men. And my own tribulations have thus led to your losing your wife." She squeezed Will's arm while she spoke in her low, sweet voice, of how if something went wrong in one sphere, it would go wrong in another. Will wanted to tell Silver that perforce he knew that mechanism, had learned it at his master's knee when he himself was in petty school.

But he couldn't find the voice to interrupt her as she explained it. Her bosom pressed tight against his arm, and it felt warm and springy, like freshly kneaded dough. Her scent filled his nostrils, making his sportive blood rise.

She so patently took him for a clod of the basest origin, incapable of knowing the simplest things, that Will couldn't dispute it.

Her intoxicating perfume, the grip of her hand on his arm, the way she moved like a vision floating, her superhumanly beautiful features, all of it conspired to keep him in awe-stricken, weak-kneed silence, unable to do any more than admire her. They walked down to where the river murmured amid the trees of Arden, and turned, following the path, toward the small town of Shottery proper, and Hewlands Farm at the outskirts of it.

Will's heart beat fast, very fast. Nan had been the only woman he'd ever touched, and never—even in dreams— had he thought to have such a fair companion as this dark lady.

"So, you see," she said, "I've suffered a great injustice. I should have been the rightful sovereign of the elven people, but my wicked relative usurped the throne, and because of that a great many calamities have come to pass, among them your father's decline, and the loss of your wife. Only by killing the king so that I may regain the throne, will everyone get back their proper due and thus will the world be set right again."

Will couldn't remember telling Silver of his father's misfortune, but he must have, because she spoke of it knowingly, with such deep understanding.

Her voice flowed like honey over warm bread: easy, sweet, and persuasive, penetrating and drenching every pore.

Hewlands Farm—the bulky square stone building where the Hathaway family housed—came into view in the moonlight. The scent of roses and stabled beasts mingled with Silver's perfume. No light shone from the windows.

Will stared at the house, puzzled. If a woman was in labor within, wouldn't there be more activity? But maybe it was all past, and the new mother contented with her child, and Nan, too, asleep somewhere within.

He remembered Nan dancing in the forest and told himself it had to be a dream.

And then that other piece of the dream, soft-spoken Lady Silver, still beside him, asked, in a seductive whisper, "So, will you be man enough to kill the elven king and regain your wife and daughter? Or are you only a boy, playing at being married?"

Her question stung like a blow. He turned around to

look at Silver's perfect features, her smiling lips, her re-flective, shiny, silver-colored eyes. "I'll do what it takes," he said, "to get my Nan back." His voice echoed, seem-ingly much louder than hers and stronger.

From the farmyard, a dog barked.

"Whatever it takes," Will said.

That this lady made his blood boil and set desire throb-bing through his veins as he'd never felt it, made his claim of Nan all the louder, more defensive. They'd been mar-ried six months and she was his own true love. He would not compare her to mad, fevered visions that couldn't be real.

Silver smiled. "Good boy. Only, I know you don't half believe it." She shrugged prettily, raising her shoulders and letting them fall again in a graceful movement. "No matter, you will. Go, go and make sure her kin hasn't sequestered your dancing wife, and when you've not found her elsewhere, I'll come to you again."

The lady smiled again and, suddenly, took Will's head in her two hands and brought her mouth down on his.

In the next moment, it stopped mattering whether she was true or a dream, as her hot mouth radiated heat to his body, her probing tongue acquainted itself with the depth and breadth of his mouth, her searching, hungry lips seemed to wish to suck his very soul away.

Will's heart throbbed, in joyful, painful dance. A din of unholy music filled his head, reverberated from the walls of his cranium, set his bones afire. Convulsively, he embraced the lady, feeling her body taut against his, her body perfect and pliant in his arms, her breasts soft and warm against his chest.

As suddenly as it had begun, the kiss ended. The lady he'd held in his arms vanished.

Alone, on a patch of moonlight outside dark Hewlands

Farm, Will wiped his mouth which, inexplicably, tasted sweet and spicy like the best wine.

Heat coursed through Will's veins and made him want to sing and dance for joy. He forgot he was tired and hungry. He felt as he had on wakening when he'd been quite small and the whole day stretched in front of him full of unending possibilities.

He sauntered down the path to the farm. He must have dreamed while he walked, and whatever restless sleep his brain had snatched while his body strode through the forest path had left him wonderfully renewed. Sleepwalking, he must have been, and no wonder, as hard as he'd been working.

Now, he would knock on the door and they would admit him to the chamber where Nan bid the night, and the fantastic nightmare would be over.

His blood surged in him and protested the idea of the dark lady's being gone forever, but he shook his head at it. A dream. Or if not a dream, a succubus that tormented sleeping men in their loneliness.

He remembered Nan in silk and pearls dancing with the royalty. That's what came from listening to his mother's nonsense. Now, he'd dream of it, and his mother's fantasies would pursue him until he knew not truth from folly.

He walked across the still-warm threshing yard and to the house proper, and knocked at the door.

It took a while to rouse anyone. As it would be if there had been a birth in the house. Everyone would be asleep and exhausted, of course.

But when Bartholomew opened the door, Will saw Bartholomew's wife right behind him, standing and swollen as big with child as ever.

Bartholomew, a tall, fair man with eyes so pale they always reminded Will of much-boiled blackberries,

frowned down at Will, his bristly eyebrows meeting in
disapproval above his eyes. "Hello there, Brother Will,"
he said, with forced heartiness. The long white shirt he
wore looked creased and grey smeared. "How come you
disturb our peace in the night? Is Nan well?"

*Nan. Bartholomew asked if she was well. Wasn't she
here?*

"Nan? Have you not . . . ? Is Nan not here?" Will
looked from Bartholomew to the other members of his
household, arrayed behind him: young men and women,
and small children. "Nan wasn't home. House dark. I
thought . . . Gentlemen in velvet, my mother said. But I
thought perforce Nan would be here. Is she not?"

"Wine," one of Nan's other brothers said, from behind
Bartholomew. "I much fear you've been drinking, Brother
Will."

The Hathaways were good religious people and disapproved of alcohol, except for the smallest of small ale.

Will shook his head. "No." He tried to discipline his
tongue to a coherent telling of his woes. Of a sudden, all
the tiredness of the day returned, its weight falling on his
shoulders like an accustomed cloak. "No. When I returned
home from work, Nan was gone and I couldn't find her."
He told the whole tale, even mentioning the block of wood
in the cradle, but leaving his visions and dreams out of it.

The women of the house exchanged glances at his
words, but didn't raise their voices.

It wasn't until Will, buoyed by a mug of weak ale and
a hunk of mutton, was ready to walk home again, that
Margaret, Nan's sister, spoke to him.

At the door, away from the family's men, she leaned
toward Will and whispered, in a breath reeking of old
mutton grease, "It is the good people who leave a stock
in the bed of a baby they steal, my brother. The good
people from beneath the hill."

Scene 4

✦

A rich bedchamber, furnished with a tall bed covered and curtained in green-and-crimson silk, embroidered more delicately than ever human needle stitched, with scenes of fauns and woodland animals. Beside the bed sits a double cradle, draped in white silk and lace and surmounted by a crystal crown. At the foot of the bed is a skillfully painted trunk, and past that, against the wall, a wide, wide mirror, in front of which a dark wooden table stands arrayed with brushes and combs and scents and ear-picks and everything a fine lady might desire. At the table, Nan Shakespeare sits, while near the bed, Ariel works, laying out clothes.

"No," Nan said, and put the fine crystal-handled brush down. Clad in a long nightshirt worked all over with lace, she felt like a doll, arranged and put on display. Her No resounded in the spacious room with its pale-green walls, and echoed off the gilded ceiling.

Deep within the hill, in her room in Fairyland, Nan felt a rage come over her, a rage not unlike what she'd felt at her parents' house, when enjoined to be a dutiful daughter. "I do not wish to ride with the king on his hunt."

While she spoke, Nan looked in the mirror, to see her little fairy maid, Ariel, go pale and straighten up, holding a dress to herself as if for protection. Not that Ariel was ever anything but pale. All milk white and pale gold, the girl looked like nothing so much as a fine statue carved in creamy ivory. And yet, Nan thought, she'd hardly be a girl. From the little Nan had understood of the life spans and ways of these people who had kidnapped her, Ariel— a mere adolescent—would be older than Nan, an old woman in mortal years.

Ariel's lips trembled, and her eyes rimmed with tears. "But, milady. The king wishes . . ."

Nan thought of the king, imposing and manly, strong and powerful. A man. Not like her Will, who was still in many ways a child, and whom Nan had led, by the hand and on tiptoe, through the threshold of adulthood. The king and what the king wished perturbed Nan and disturbed her reasoning. Sylvanus, fine and noble, attired in silk and velvets, had courted her.

She smiled at the mirror, bringing forth a puzzled expression from Ariel's tidy countenance.

Nan ignored Ariel's confusion, and wondered what her friends and companions would think of this. A king had courted Nan Shakespeare, who had been Nan Hathaway and whom no one, no one, had ever braved to court save that foolhardy boy, Will Shakespeare, too young and brash to fear her shrewish fame.

"Milady," Ariel said. She took a deep breath and squared her frail shoulders. "The king said you should go hunting with him, today. And this dress is what you should wear for it." Her long slim hand smoothed a confection of pearls and green silk, which she held in front of her own white gown.

Nan frowned. "No," she repeated. "I will not go hunting with the king." It wasn't the hunting or the killing. Raised in Hewlands Farm Nan had often had to kill chickens. Dressed in Bartholomew's clothes, she'd escaped from her father's too-tight rule, and wandered the forest of Arden, laying snares for rabbits and winging birds with stones from her practiced slingshot, a skill she'd learned from her four brothers.

But she'd come to the end of her patience and her obedient meekness. When the guards of the elven king had stolen her, they'd taken her in early morning, still tired, and they'd draped their magic over her like a golden blanket, making her sleepy and compliant. All the livelong day, yesterday, she'd been too stunned and scared, everything around her new and grand, and supernatural.

But now, a day and a night had passed since Nan had first been stolen, and she'd slept—in a silken soft bed such as she'd never before lain in—and she had thought, and felt awake and quick. She would not let herself be ruled anymore. If her father had never managed to rule her, no, nor her stepmother either, no matter how many times the switch was deployed or pious sermons preached to her, she'd not be ruled by these creatures, either, who were neither living nor dead, natural nor magic. Nor would she remain forever a prisoner in their nowhere realm under the hill. She meant to show them they had not, as perhaps they thought, kidnapped a hapless peasant, a willing heifer to do their bidding.

Ariel still stared at her, and still held the green, pearl-speckled dress, her mouth open in wonderment.

Funny creature, Nan thought. Did it shock her so much, then, that Nan refused to obey Sylvanus's will? She studied the reflection of Ariel's face. Did Ariel think Sylvanus that wonderful? An elf, Ariel might be, inconstant and mutable as all her kind. But she appeared concerned for Nan, and her features, bruised and tired, looked a mirror of Nan's own grief, the face of a fellow sufferer.

But Ariel was the sort who would suffer with patience, and Nan had no intention of doing likewise.

"Tell the king," she said, "that I am too tired, from feeding the babes in the night. Surely he'll grant me leave, then."

Like that, Ariel's face unclouded, and a little smile twisted her pink mouth. "Oh, certainly. That he will."

Nan smiled at Ariel in turn. Well, well. The little maid didn't seem squeamish about telling lies. And Ariel had known it was a lie, as rested as Nan looked and—Nan spared a glance at herself in the mirror, proud of her ruddy cheeks and clear eyes—as healthy. How far would the maid's complaisance go? "Ariel, I miss my husband," Nan said. "I've been married to him but a short time. You seem my friend true. If you would hide me and . . . and help me make my way out of the hill, to my home . . . then could I be with my husband, and . . ."

Before she finished asking, Nan knew the answer. Ariel dropped the dress and cast a shocked look all about as if she expected the magnificent walls to sprout ears or perhaps the golden oak door, on the far side, to open and allow an armed guard into Nan's peaceful chamber. "Oh no, milady," she said quickly. "You must stay here. Stay here and nurse our princess."

So decisive an answer, Nan hadn't expected. The maid condoned lying to the king, but not escaping him. Why not? Absently, Nan lifted the crystal-handled brush and ran its soft bristles down her silken wheat-colored hair. Too late, she remembered the banquet food she'd eaten the night before, and the injunctions found in every fairy tale against eating in Fairyland. Was it possible she wouldn't be able to leave even if she were to try?

"The food I ate last night," Nan said, looking out of the corner of her eye at Ariel, without fully turning to face the elf maiden. "Will it make me one of you?"

The girl started. "Oh, no, milady." Ariel took in a deep, startled breath. "No, milady. Never. We cannot give our food to mortals and bind them to the hill without the mortal's consent. That food you ate was charmed, true, but only charmed with transport spells to bring it from the tables of rich men around the country, to serve to you at our banquet. It was transported by magic from their tables, from beneath their very gazes. Our king himself . . ." And here, for no reason that Nan could imagine, Ariel's voice dwindled and diminished, and lapsed into speechlessness, like a brook that flows into the Earth and disappears. "The food, human food, was brought here expressly for you, and only the choicest."

Not trusting the mirror, Nan dared a sideways look at Ariel's face. She marked how wan Ariel had gone, how colorless her lips had turned at the word that had escaped them. The king. Was this maiden somehow grieved at her king? Perhaps, just perhaps, Ariel loved her king and resented his advances to Nan. So, she would agree with Nan's lying and avoiding his company, but not with Nan's escaping him, since that transgression would likely give him too much pain.

Ariel had turned around, all in a rush, and opened the painted trunk at the foot of the bed. "If milady will stay indoors, then we'll put on this gown."

To Nan's eyes both gowns looked much the same, both green and embroidered with jewels, both too lavish, too ornate, and too fine, and she didn't much care which she wore. She nodded at Ariel, while reasoning that, yes, surely that was it. The girl was in love with her sovereign. It would explain the girl's damped look, her bruised eyes, her grief-bearing countenance.

Nan's mind quickened, like a heart that jumps at a chance half offered. She didn't want the king, and if this maid wanted him, then perhaps . . . perhaps Nan could use

Ariel's love to snag the love of the king to its proper place. And perhaps he would let Nan go then. Perhaps other milk could be procured for the elven princess, or perhaps—sad to say—the king would disdain his first get when there was the chance of fathering others.

"The king," Nan said, baiting her hook, even as she picked now at this, now at that bottle on the dressing table, and reclined on the green velvet upholstered chair in front of it, admiring their workmanship, smelling their contents. So many bottles, some of them looking as if they'd been carved entire from a single crystal. And how different each fragrance smelled. All were pleasant scents, but some were deep and spicy and strong, others floral and light and airy. "He's a fine man in all parts the king is, is he not?"

Ariel started.

Looking at the maiden in the mirror, without appearing to observe her at all, Nan marked the wide-open eyes, the lips that parted to let fast breath through. She watched the blush that crept up Ariel's cheeks, like a tide climbing the riverbank in spring. Color seeped through pale skin, till red stood in vivid patches on Ariel's cheeks, giving her the look of one afflicted with a raging fever.

While Ariel's lips parted for a response, the door to the room opened and Nan jumped, startled, as one suddenly awakened. In flew a troop of the little winged creatures who did all the real work around the palace. Humanlike and exquisitely beautiful, the tallest of them did not exceed a palm in height. On their backs they had wings like a dragonfly's, only larger. They swooped in, lights flashing around their bodies, and pulled the covers on the bed, straightening them taut over the mattresses and making it all quite as neat as Nan herself did at home.

A pang for her Henley Street home prickled Nan's heart. She'd felt like a prisoner there, and resentful that Mother Shakespeare and Father Shakespeare intruded in

her life, watched her every step and took fully half of
Will's pay for their own maintenance.

But now, truly imprisoned in a supernatural gaol, she
longed for Henley Street and felt as though her heart had
remained there with Will.

Who was making her bed now? And how did Will fare,
with neither wife nor cook? A young dreamer with schol-
arly notions, Will might know by heart the arguments of
long-dead Romans, but had no idea how the bread was
made that she set in front of him every night, or how the
ale was brewed that he drank daily.

His mother would call him over to her side, and feed
him *her* bread and ale, and talk to him of how he had
been wrong to marry Nan.

A week of that, and Nan might well not have anyone
to return to, even if she escaped this gilded prison. Will
was so young . . . Her heart skipped a beat at the thought
of how young Will was, how frightfully trusting, how eagerly willing to please.

"Would milady have her hair dressed?" Ariel had recovered from whatever feelings mention of the king had
awakened.

Stepping behind Nan and, smiling at Nan in the mirror,
a smile of near apology, she took the brush from Nan's
hand, and started brushing Nan's hair gently.

Ariel's own hair was as bright as rays of the sun worked
into an artless kerchief over her shoulders and down her
back.

She wore a silk dress, as white as Nan's night apparel,
but cut lower, though perhaps it shouldn't have been. The
elven maiden had prodigiously little to display to the eyes
of men.

She had been introduced to Nan the night before, as a
Duchess of the Air Kingdoms and handmaid to the two
dead queens of the fairy realms.

Now, she'd be Nan's servant and companion. Which told a lot about the king's intentions toward Nan. Nan thought of him with mingled pride at his courtship and annoyance at his daring. Beautiful he was of course, like all his kind, and noble. But he was not Will. And thinking of Will caused Nan too much pain.

How much did Ariel's service cost the little elven maid? How long had she been in love with her king?

Nan remembered the king's hand, hot and unmerciful, clenching hers, and silently apologized to Will for the heat that had coursed through her own veins. She had not lied. The king was a fine man in all parts. And yet he was not a man, was he?

No, not a man and, despite the beautiful countenances that peopled his court, not an angel either. Nan had seen raw lust in his eyes and something else. Something dark, like a shadow lurking beneath his bonhomie.

Nan looked at the lovely Ariel's reflection and hugged herself. No, these were not angels, save perhaps the darker kind, banished forever from the sight of God.

Nan had heard stories about the people under the hill, and what she remembered made her wonder what company she'd fallen in with and how grievously she must have sinned, to deserve such exile. She'd heard of women taken by these beings because they'd missed church, neglected their prayers. What had she done?

It couldn't be the small matter of giving herself to Will while not yet married, could it? So many did it, and so often. And yet, perhaps she had enjoyed it more than most. Perhaps her lack of repentance . . .

She shivered.

What would Will have thought of this, of her servitude? And how fared it with Will, her own sweet Will who'd made her a woman and a wife, though he was himself barely more than a boy? She held onto the image of Will, to combat the remembrance of Sylvanus that kept coming to her mind, all velvety and fine, and smiling at her with lust in his eyes.

"Is milady well?" Ariel asked.

Nan nodded, but felt guilty color flow into her cheeks. Looking at herself in the mirror, she thought that she didn't blush prettily like Ariel. Her own blush was a coarse thing, an orange-red peeking through her sun-hardened skin. Once she had been as pretty and young as Ariel, but those days were long gone, and she had spent them in her father's farmhouse, scaring away what he mistook for suitable suitors, or wandering the forest, playing at being an unruly boy.

Without realizing it, Nan tapped her foot against the floor beneath the dressing table, and regarded Ariel's hands as they moved the brush slowly through Nan's long hair.

Nan's father had told her that her problem was that she wouldn't be tamed, couldn't be tamed. He'd made the point often enough, with a switch and a belt, both expertly handled by a man who'd raised four sons before trying to subdue his first daughter.

Yet Nan took her punishment and went on doing exactly as she pleased, not so much an ungrateful daughter as a hardheaded one.

So, why was she tamed now? Why did she cower here, within the hill, held prisoner by creatures that weren't even human?

Yesterday she had been half-asleep, her wits damped, like a fly in treacle, caught and swimming but making no headway.

But today . . .

Today, she would find her way out with or without Ariel's help.

Only, Ariel was a hindrance. With Ariel there, Nan could not hope to escape.

Nan had never had servants before. Oh, her father's house had its serving wenches, of course, as all prosperous farmers' houses did. But it would never have occurred to the late Richard Hathaway to have a servant brush his daughters' hair, or help them at their dressing. A dour man, with Puritan leanings, he'd have been more likely to have them brush the cows' tails, or saddle the horses for riding.

The advantage of such a household, so tightly run, and of being regarded as little more than a servant herself, was that an enterprising girl might leave her father's house, while everyone was fully immersed in the round of daily chores, and go for a walk in the woods, or a swim in the Avon. Nan had done it often enough. Denied school instruction, as most girls were, Nan had learned solitude like a hornbook, and knew by heart the seasons of the Avon and the flow of its waters. She had taught Will the paths to walk through Arden Forest, and he'd admired her knowledge of bird and animal, of herb and flower. He'd pronounced her mind the equal of his, if not superior, and she fully believed that her wit had captivated him more than her looks, her knowledge had sped him to marriage more than her fast and clumsy caresses in the fields.

But now . . .

She looked in the mirror. Her gaze met Ariel's and in that instant, Nan saw the elf maid not as an elf at all, but a suffering girl. The prison she imposed on Nan was prison to her as well. And Ariel's love for the king—was it love?

"Tell me about the king's late wife," Nan said, and her sharp, shrewd eyes watched Ariel as she'd watched the merchants measuring wheat at the fair in Stratford.

The girl looked puzzled. Once more, her fair eyebrows

descended over her pale eyes and she frowned, just a little. "She was a good lady," she said. "A kind lady."

"Was she like me, human, as I've heard?"

Ariel shrugged, raising thin shoulders upwards and letting them fall, a movement as slow and graceful as a swan opening its wings in the moment before startled flight. "Human. To begin with, human. But she wasn't taken by charm and guile. The . . ." And here, once more, Ariel's lips trembled and her voice faltered. "Our lord Sylvanus found her, wooed her, with stories and songs from a manor house in the north where he courted her, amid the crags of Scotland, and there he won her heart and from there he brought her." Ariel brushed Nan's hair vigorously, warming to her work and to the topic at the same time. "A stock was left in her bed, as ancient law commands, a painted piece of a tree trunk, or an enchanted twig that, by charm, looked and seemed to breathe like her, only mortally ill, and from that illness she appeared to die in days." Ariel looked up, and her gaze again met Nan's in the mirror.

Ariel's eyes were grave, serious, seeming to say more than her mouth could. "Long before she ate the charmed food and became . . . Sylvanus's subject and his wife, her people thought her dead and buried in the frozen dirt of the north lands."

Nan shivered, at the words as much as at the thought.

Had a stock been left behind for her, if ancient elven law demanded it?

Was Will, even now, mourning the death of his wife and daughter, never dreaming that both of them were alive and well, held captive, away from his bed and his home, his love and his care?

The thought so startled Nan that she had as if a glimpse of herself in her bier, her body in the ground of the Stratford cemetery. She almost saw Mary Shakespeare, her unloving mother-in-law, hosting the funeral and talking about how God had punished Nan's wickedness in leading Will astray.

She closed her eyes. It took her three breaths to compose herself, three more to realize that Ariel's answer, though it said much, added only one thing, to Nan's purpose nothing—that Ariel did indeed shy away from calling the king's name, or called him by a more private, personal name. Did that mean love? Ariel's eyes had looked most unloving.

Staring up at the elf-maid's clouded eyes, Nan decided that she must find an excuse to dismiss fair Ariel. But would fair Ariel go when dismissed? She'd hoped the girl would confide in her and, in the first blush of nascent friendship, would accede to leaving Nan alone and unwatched. That having failed, Nan would have to try to send the girl away without such an aid, and hope it worked. Maybe it would.

Maybe Nan could just escape, without bothering with the intrigues of this shadowy court, or the love of an elf maiden for her king.

Then Nan remembered the sort of private water closet they had here, nothing like the privy in the garden of the Henley house. It stood next to the bedroom, attached to it, and yet odorless as nothing but magic could make it. And next to the privy seat stood a bathtub, and the maids had chattered while they bathed Nan the day before, and implied that these baths in perfumed water were their daily habit. Not a weekly obligation, such as Nan and Will fulfilled in the half barrel set in front of the fire on Saturday night.

If that were true . . . "Ariel," she said, and reached back, to grasp the elven maiden's wrist, letting go of it again, very fast, when the flesh she touched felt cold enough to be the flesh of the dead. "Ariel, I would bathe, before I

see the king . . . since I think he might call on me to verify
why I'm not going on the hunt. Could I bathe? Could that
be done?"

Ariel's eyes opened wide in surprise, but then she nodded, bobbed a curtsey, and turned to disappear through a
small door behind the canopy of the bed.

The winged fairies had left too, somehow unnoticed.
Nan was alone in the room.

She heard the sound of running water from the bathing
room. The day before she had seen this: water cascading
from midair, transported there by the magic of the elves,
and by them converted to warm, softly perfumed liquid.
Moments later, Ariel emerged and bowed again. "Milady."

Nan got up, paused. "Yesterday, I was under some magical compulsion," she said. "But today I'm not, and I
would rather be alone. Would you, Lady Ariel, leave me
alone in the room and in the bath, that I might wash in
peace? I am not used to servants standing by while I un-
dress."

Ariel opened her mouth and took in breath, as if to
speak, then shrugged, nodded, bowed. "I'll be outside
your bedroom door," she said and retreated.

As soon as the heavy oak door closed behind Ariel, Nan
hurried to one of the windows—an unbelievably broad,
thin panel of glass, encased in a very fine wooden frame
which latched at the bottom.

Unlatching the frame, Nan pushed the window open—
open to the forest of Arden, trees and rocks, and blessed
freedom. She saw neither fairies nor elves on that side of
the palace.

Hurrying back into the room, Nan reached into the double cradle and pulled Susannah out. She'd nursed both
babies in the night and then again on wakening, and they
both slept contentedly. The fairy princess looked perhaps

a little rosier, a trifle blonder than Susannah, but they were alike enough to be sisters.

A shiver climbed up Nan's back. No, it would not be. Susannah would not grow up thinking herself the sister of this elf. She clutched Susannah to her, hard. The baby, in her borrowed finery of silk and lace, didn't move, only smiled at her mother's touch. Sleeping thus, she looked like a doll, and her sleep a morbid unconsciousness.

But Nan told herself the baby would be well as soon as they left this cursed place.

She wished for breeches, like Bartholomew's old ones that she'd often worn when escaping from her father's house to the freedom of the forest.

But no matter. She would make do. Hastily, she threw on the green dress that lay on the bed, not bothering with the bolster meant to hold the skirts out. Instead, she kilted the skirt up on the side, and tied it up, as she did with her own skirts, in the privacy of her home.

She would hie back from Arden to the alley behind the Henley Street house, get into her own house, and dress before anyone could see her in this unseemly attire.

And then—she realized she was gnashing her teeth— and then she would dispel anyone's notion that she might be dead, and undo whatever grief or fear Will might have felt.

She hefted Susannah again, a soft weight drooping in her arms, and put her long, unencumbered leg over the sill.

On the other side, she stepped onto yielding ground cushioned with pine needles, and tree leaves. Trees, so many trees, surrounded her. The sun shone in a distant haze above her, much obscured by clouds, and no brighter than candlelight seen through cheesecloth. Nan frowned at it. She'd get no direction from the sun, as if it also conspired at her captivity. And it was odd, too, for the

sun to be poised at noon, though Nan had just awakened.
She never slept that long.

Well, no matter. In whatever direction she started, she
would find a path she knew, or else come upon the flowing
Avon. She knew the place well enough.

So intent upon her purpose was she, that she walked a
few yards before she was struck by the peculiar silence of
the forest and a sense of wrongness.

The scent she smelled was not the oak and pine of the
forest, but a deep, unnatural smell of lilac.

The trees had an odd transparency, the sky above
glowed with a greenish-blue haze, and the sun shone like
a pale thing that gave no heat. Nan extended her trembling
hand until she should have touched a tree trunk.

Instead of touching it, her hand went through it, as if
through unfettered air.

Nan stood unmoving, the sleeping Susannah held in her
left arm, against her breast. She felt her daughter's soft
breathing, heard the beating of the small heart. Her own
eyes filled with tears. This was not freedom, but one more
contrivance of her gaolers. A land with neither taste nor
smell, a forest cleaned, sanitized, purged of what it was
and turned into what it couldn't be.

Looking down, she saw that her bare feet were set atop
pine needles and leaves, yet felt as though they touched a
cushion.

Slowly, she spun around, turning back, to look at the
palace behind her.

She wasn't surprised, didn't even feel betrayed, to see
Ariel standing there, outside the palace, in front of the
large window Nan had used for her attempted escape.

The strange thing was Ariel's expression, not gloating,
as Nan would have expected, but full of grave sorrow and
thoughtful commiseration. She walked up to Nan slowly,
and slowly set her cold little hand on Nan's arm.

"Come. I thought you would be here. I should have told you. You cannot go to the world of mortals. There is no way for you to escape and there is nothing I can do to help." Ariel hesitated, her expression even graver. "You can't go on your own, not without help from mortals. In this world of fairy you're prisoner, until someone from your own world shall release you. As we all are prisoner, each in our own troubles."

With her hand on Nan's arm, she led her back to the window, where instead of climbing through it, she made a quick strange gesture, lifting her right hand and waving it back and forth.

The wall opened and the stunned Nan was led back into her room.

Back into the captivity she'd never left.

For a moment she felt as if she'd been dropped, without warning, into a hole. For a heartbeat, she felt as if the very floor under her feet was a poisonous, slippery illusion.

In the next moment, she steadied herself. Her circumstances had changed fast and without warning before: when her mother had died, when her father had remarried, when her father had died leaving her a paltry dowry, when Will had got her with child.

Every time, each time, she'd solved her problems and emerged from them well enough. This wouldn't be any different.

She walked back to the cradle, set Susannah down beside the fairy baby, covered both with their white lace blanket, the texture and softness of cobwebs.

Then she undressed, and went to her bath, thinking she might as well bathe.

Stepping into the perfumed water, she looked at Ariel, who watched her, intent and puzzled.

This elf girl was so unguarded as to tell Nan that she was unhappy with her own situation.

Nan lowered herself into the warm, soothing bath.

Was it King Sylvanus's dark handsomeness that made Ariel's heart sad and caused her eyes to sink within those bruised rings? Was it his misguided passion for Nan that made Ariel sigh? Or was there someone else, something else, that held the fairy maiden in thrall?

No matter. Nan would find out, and she would use the knowledge to escape this miserable, shadowy existence and return to her Will. Her quiet, young Will with his diffident ways; his vile, tentative poems, full of puns and little else; his slavish, yet real devotion. Her Will, who'd never try to restrain her, not even from walking alone the paths of Arden Forest.

She reached for a soft cloth to wash herself. Elven wiles, magical though they might be, were no match for Nan, the shrew of Shottery. "Ariel, come and sit beside me," Nan said, gesturing to the chair beside the bath. "And tell me all about the people in this court, for I know nothing."

Scene 5

❧

Quicksilver's apartment in the fairy palace—a spacious room with marble floors and intricate tapestries hanging on the walls. The tapestries show war and banquets, and nude nymphs dancing in green glades. On one wall, by the broad, gilded bed, hangs a portrait of Quicksilver himself, so painted, with such magic, that by walking a few steps this way and that the look of the portrait changes and displays Quicksilver now as a fair youth, now as a dark lady. The rest of the room has refined and masculine appointments: a broad, red-upholstered armchair with a few dozen fat books beside it; a collection of swords lining the lower part of the eastern wall; a suit of armor in the southwest corner. Quicksilver stands in front of a full-length mirror while an elven servant helps him with his doublet.

"No, the other one." Quicksilver shrugged out of the black velvet doublet he wore, and into another one, obediently proffered by his silent dark-haired servant, Malachite.

The prince had just come back from hunting with the king's company the whole day, and his pain, his humiliation, burned in him like live coals. His brother hadn't so much as addressed Quicksilver all day and Quicksilver knew not whether to congratulate himself on not having to make small talk with the traitor, or burn at being thus slighted. The king had killed three stags, and Quicksilver none, and Quicksilver had walked away from the festivities and come to his room to bathe and dress for this night's work. Fine work, indeed, it would be.

Shrugging into the new doublet, Quicksilver admired himself in the mirror. Black velvet, like his breeches, like the attire he invariably wore when he was in his male aspect, this doublet fit him well, molding the width of his shoulders, outlining his narrow waist.

He adjusted the large diamond brooch at his throat. A prince, he thought he looked, a wronged prince, the color of his attire the external expression of his inner tumult.

Yet, how should a prince look who knows his brother has murdered their parents and now sits, remorseless, on his stolen throne? How should such a prince look? Quicksilver's eyes went, unmeant, to the armor in the corner, his war attire bestowed upon him by his mother but never yet worn.

Someone knocked at the door, and Quicksilver nodded toward it, indicating that Malachite should open it. The valet obeyed, understanding the unspoken order with the habit of many years standing. A changeling, long ago kidnapped by the elves for their own, he'd been brought up in Quicksilver's service.

The golden oak door opened noiselessly without hinges by a device known of the fairy race, and displayed the broad hall outside and Lord Pyrite's golden splendor. He wore a suit as red as a harlot's lips, and his blond hair was caught up in a towering pinnacle of golden feathers and fur. "Good eve, Quicksilver, good eve," Pyrite said as he strode past Malachite, ignoring the servant. His face

was wreathed all in smiles for his good friend Quicksilver,
and his reflected image, in the mirror, made a shocking
contrast to his friend's somber appearance.

"Good for those who think it good," Quicksilver answered, turning around to face Pyrite. He wondered what
this visit was about. Though Pyrite had once been a regular visitor to Quicksilver's apartments, his companion in
childish play, later in weapons-training and more mature
reflection, he hadn't visited Quicksilver in—oh—these
many months. Not since Quicksilver's complaints and la-
ments about being passed over for succession had driven
Pyrite away, maddened and exasperated.

"Leave off, man," Pyrite said, and smiled to soften the
words. The golden feathers in his hair bobbed up and
down as he tilted his head to gaze up at Quicksilver.
"Leave off," he repeated. "Do you know what a fool you
make of yourself, going around dressed all in funereal
attire, and mourning as though your parents had died five
minutes, not five years, ago?" He fingered the velvet of
Quicksilver's sleeve with open disdain and much too
much familiarity, but grinned ingratiatingly, like the imp-
ish child he'd once been. "Come, smile at me, be my
friend again. I have missed you, Quicksilver. I miss your
wit and your sparkling company. You were ever the stead-
ying force to my mad gamboling, the anchor to my tilting
ship. You always analyzed everyone's words and pre-
sented their actions to me for consideration. I have not
your sharp wit that sees into the hearts of men. Without
you, I bob and sway in every current. Be my friend, I beg.
Be yourself again."

Quicksilver made no answer, only raised his eyebrows
in questing doubt.

Pyrite hesitated. The appearance of joy slipped a little,
like a mask ill fitted to the wearer's brow. Then it returned, with renewed vigor, as though Pyrite had decided

to fasten it on anew. Yet Pyrite's voice held a hint of embarrassment as he said, "Look, Ariel tells me that you suspected her of having told your brother of your . . ." He cast a sidelong glance at Malachite.

Quicksilver wondered at that glance, since Malachite, given to Quicksilver by Titania when he was little more than a babe, had shown himself unswervingly loyal to Quicksilver alone. And perhaps, Quicksilver thought, that was what Pyrite feared.

"Ariel thinks," Pyrite resumed, looking at Quicksilver again, his smile more forceful than ever, "that you believe she betrayed you to your brother. And I thought not, you could not believe so. But . . ." He sighed. "Perhaps you suspect me?" He raised his fair brows in golden arches of doubt. The faint pinkish color on his cheek betrayed his true discomfiture. "You wouldn't suspect me of that, would you, Quicksilver?"

Quicksilver sighed. No. He hadn't suspected Pyrite of that. But now he knew not what to suspect.

Pyrite's eyes rounded. "Come, Quicksilver, come. You know I approved of your going and seeking your fortune, nay, your good rest in Tyr-Nan-Og." Pyrite smiled at the prince, displaying neatly set teeth, a little large for one of his race. "Truth, I told you so. You knew it well, were told it often in true plain words by thy true-telling friend. Can't you see it, Quicksilver?" He grabbed his friend's arm, and squeezed it and looked anxiously into Quicksilver's eyes. "Come, you and I were friends always, from our cradle. We were almost brothers. Think you I'd betray you?"

And Quicksilver saw everything, suddenly, with clear, unblushing certainty and wondered why he'd not seen it before. Pyrite truly would not have betrayed him. It wasn't only that Pyrite wanted Quicksilver away so that the prince's beauty didn't impinge on Pyrite's lesser splendor,

but also because Quicksilver's mourning grieved Pyrite
and worried his friend. That Pyrite worried about Quicksilver was a shaming thought and a comforting one, both.
The prince shook his head. "No. No. I never thought it.
Or if I did it was a nightmare, and it is forgotten." And
quickly, to hide his shamefully high emotion, he added,
"Yet, you serve the usurper who has taken the throne from
me."

Pyrite looked incredulous. He let go of Quicksilver's
arm and cackled. "That again? And whom should I serve?
I am a Duke of the Air Kingdoms and as such, I owe
allegiance to the sovereign of our realm, which Sylvanus
is. So long as Sylvanus is the king and your constant
friend, and my true sovereign, whom must I obey? Nay,
let me obey him and love you." He smiled at Quicksilver
again. "And let me see you out of these funeral rags. You
were the mirror of fashion in which we all saw ourselves
and knew our hearts humbled." He looked away. "My
sister says you avoid her." He cast a quick, searching look
at the prince and looked away again. "In truth, I think she
may be a little importune. But she means well. And you
loved her well, once."

Quicksilver sighed and forced a pale smile onto his
face. "I am changed," he said. "So changed, sometimes I
know me not."

Pyrite's smile wavered. "Well . . . and well . . . and perhaps you will return yet to your true self. If you'd gone
to Tyr-Nan-Og . . . And well . . . That may come yet, or
your brother might yet grant you a marriage closer to
home, where your friends can have the pleasure of your
company." He patted the prince's arm. "But meanwhile,
doubt me not. Doubt me not, nor my friendship for you."
He stared at Quicksilver, his enamel-blue eyes intent and
honest.

Quicksilver nodded, feeling tears flow into his eyes, despite himself. When he'd been Titania's pampered brat, he'd needed no offers of friendship and service, and after Titania's death, he'd got none. The duke's words, ringing true, echoed within Quicksilver's loneliness like a bell tolling over a vast countryside emptied by the plague. He'd never known how much he missed Pyrite's friendship or true kindness until now. On impulse, he offered both hands to Pyrite, who took them in his own. "I have something to do," Quicksilver said. "A duty which I must discharge and which I can't explain. But when it's over, I'll have need of loyal friends, and I'll count you among them." He patted Pyrite's shoulder.

Pyrite nodded. He too looked moved. He pulled away from Quicksilver, turned on his heel and left the room rapidly, as though afraid of displaying more emotion than he wished to betray.

Malachite closed the door and Quicksilver turned back toward the mirror. He stared at his own reflection blurred by the tears in his eyes. Strange how comfort came when least expected and how even Pyrite's facile cheer could touch him.

Had he been that friendless, then? That lost?

But Quicksilver knew the answer to that. The pain within him, his feelings of injustice at being passed over, had caused him to lash out without meaning, and sting with words his closest friends, his most certain allies. Sometimes he wondered if even Malachite was fully faithful or if Quicksilver's unpredictable temper had turned his bonded servant from him.

Malachite had stepped behind him and with practiced touch collected Quicksilver's hair in his hand, pulling it into a crystal clasp.

There was another knock at the oak door and Quicksilver, with raised eyebrows, signaled Malachite to open it.

This time the yawning oak door displayed the wan loveliness of Lady Ariel, Duchess of the Air Kingdoms.

Quicksilver turned from the lady's reflection in the mirror, to the real thing, standing at the door, clad in a pale dress, perfect and cold within the intricately worked lace that might well have been a shroud.

She looked past his manservant and fixed her gaze on Quicksilver. Her bloodless lips opened. "Milord." She shaped the word as though it hurt her.

He bowed. Ariel here? Ariel coming to knock at the door to his apartments? What was she playing at? Never before had she shown such daring, nor such determination. Was this Pyrite's doing?

"I would speak with you," she said. Color came and went on her cheeks, like the waxing and waning of the moon, now bright-colored, now white and blank.

He waved an impatient hand. "Then speak."

She gave a fearful glance toward his valet, then shook her head.

"Malachite, you may go. You are dismissed," Quicksilver said.

But before the servant could bow his dark head and turn to go, Ariel stopped him. "No. I do not wish to speak here. Not . . . not here. Would you come with me, milord, for a walk in the forest . . . in the forest outside?"

"Outside" meant the world of men, and Quicksilver weighed the matter carefully. What did Ariel have to tell him that couldn't be said in the palace? And did she know that, were it the most innocent of love declarations and her whole intent to avoid the wagging tongues of courtiers, yet they would be suspected of treason and not left alone for long after this?

He pressed his lips tight, bringing the weight of his displeasure on her. "Milady, you cannot mean you have such a secret that it can't be freely spoken here, in the palace, within hearing of all well-meaning subjects of my good brother." Let her hear that and take heed. If Malachite had been driven to discontent by Quicksilver's temper, then this chit of a girl could condemn herself, and Quicksilver with her, by her incautious words.

But she only shook her head again, and a smile came and went on her lips that only served to make them look yet more colorless and sickly. "It is not treason I intend, milord, unless it were treason to myself and that modesty a maid ought to keep."

Oh, she was good, Quicksilver thought. She not only had understood his warning, but she spoke as if she meant it. Malachite, head averted from such an unmaidenly declaration, blushed.

Quicksilver sighed with false reluctance. "You know, my lady, that I am too young and have not my brother's license to commit myself to matrimony, and that—"

"Oh, I would just speak to you!" Ariel yelled. Her hands fretted at the lace of her skirt, grabbing it in twin handfuls, then letting it go, marked with wrinkles that her ineffective hands could not smooth. She stamped her foot, her small white slipper slapping the floor with force. "I want to speak to you, of your feelings and your intentions."

Malachite looked as if he'd like to hide. A human, kidnapped in infancy and brought up in the fairy world, he nevertheless seemed to have an odd idea of propriety and never fully to accept the freedom-loving ways of most elven ladies.

"Very well," Quicksilver said, seeming cold and distant, though he admired Ariel more than ever. What a performance the maiden could put on. What an amazing performance. It made her look more beautiful than ever in his eyes and he found himself wondering whether the dark rings around her eyes were his doing, or the marks of her job as seeress. "Very well. Malachite, see to my room. Alter the brocade doublet as I've told you and have my bath ready for when I return tonight. I might be late. I have an excursion planned."

"Milord," Malachite said, and bowed primly. Only his half closed, averted eyes, betrayed what he was thinking: that Quicksilver's "excursion" would be to Ariel's bed, and he disapproved.

Quicksilver gave his arm to Ariel and together they walked out of the palace and through a magic portal to the world of men outside.

Away from the palace, he turned to her. "Ariel. How well you dissembled in there. I must compliment you on your performance." He grinned at her.

She stepped back, eyes rounded in shock. "Milord?" she said. And, in the wake of that, she blinked and her eyes shone as if filled with tears.

Tears? Why tears? Hadn't it been a performance? What was the foolish girl doing now?

She put out a hand to grasp his shoulder, though she never dared touch it, and let her hand fall awkwardly to her side. "You're not attending tonight's revels?"

Oh, so that was it. The infatuated little elf maid would require his attendance. Silly, ridiculous, but there it was and it must be borne. Though . . . to come to his room for just that purpose . . .

His smile widened as he explained with a vague, airy gentleness: "No. I have . . . ah . . . plans. Things to do." For one, he must visit Will in his mortal—and no doubt smelly—abode, and instruct him in the finer points of elven regicide.

His smile seemed to disquiet Ariel. She frowned into the full flow of it and asked in a voice little more than a whisper, "You're going to him, are you not?"

"*Him?*" Quicksilver asked. Who was the little fool jealous of now? Had he so much as glanced at anyone last night in the salon? Been near anyone? *Him?* Why, he hadn't even looked at a male in . . . An image of Kit Marlowe, lovely and vulnerable and all too, too mortal, passed through Quicksilver's mind and was pushed away.

"The human," Ariel said. "The human boy. Nan's husband."

Nan's husband? So the peasant was Nan, now, was she? Friends with Ariel? He looked at the duchess, bewildered. You never knew what stray Ariel might bring home, what bird with a broken wing, what faun with an injured hoof. But a human? A human that Sylvanus lusted after? Her folly was greater than Quicksilver's understanding.

"What speak you of?" he asked. "Of what?"

She blinked at him and spoke in a flat, serious voice. "Of Will. Nan's husband. I saw you with him yesterday. In the forest. I followed you, milord. I followed you and wish I hadn't. Nightlong I spent awake, thinking. Milord, do you love him?"

Ariel had followed him? Ariel had seen it, then, his transformation, his conversation with the mortal? At another time, this realization might have dismayed Quicksilver. He rarely let anyone see him transform and, since his parents' death, had taken great pains not to be seen in his female aspect. He'd spent the greater part of his time controlling what would have been involuntary changing.

But his having so readily found a mortal to commit his vengeance, his conversation with Will, the look in the boy's eye, his pleasing comeliness, and that oh-so-willingly returned kiss, all of it combined to give Quicksilver a feeling like that of full-moon madness, when parties raged all night and too much mead was drunk.

He turned a full smile on Lady Ariel, and chuckled a little as he answered, "In love? With a mortal, milady? I? You forget yourself, milady. And you mistake me."

Ariel looked like something made of yellowish wax. The hue robbed her of her delicate beauty and made her features appear stark and harshly etched. Her hands hung on either side of her body, as though she'd forgotten they existed. Were it not for the rise and fall of her chest, the rasping of breath in and out through her parted lips, she might well have been a statue.

She opened her mouth, but only to draw breath, with a gasping sound. She nodded, once—a quick ducking of the head down and up again. "You kissed him."

"Well?" Quicksilver smiled, still, though he managed not to chuckle. Why was Lady Ariel this upset? So she had seen him kiss the mortal. Why did she care? His smile grew wider, remembering. "And what if I did, milady? What would it matter? He is a mortal, my lady, not our kind."

Hell, but the boy could kiss. Where had he learned that? From his broad-hipped country wife? Perhaps Sylvanus would indeed get more than he had bargained for from the goodwife turned royal nursemaid. The thought of Sylvanus brought with it memories of Quicksilver's parents and of the dark task that hung over his head like an ax balanced on a fool's hand. "Milady, I'm waiting. Talk or be gone."

Ariel drew breath once more. "The mortal. You . . . You . . . kissed the mortal. You let him see you in your other form." She paused and opened her hands, palm out, on her skirt, as though those hands would go on talking where she could not.

So, that was it. A simple kiss had upset her. His familiarity with the mortal had galled her. He stepped beside Ariel, and wound his arm through hers. Hers felt smaller, so much frailer than the muscular arm of the peasant boy. She held herself stiffly, away from Quicksilver, refusing to budge at his cajoling pull.

He sighed. "Milady Ariel, the boy is only an instrument for what I truly seek. And what I truly seek is vengeance, as vengeance I should seek, for the foul deed against my parents." His voice fell to grave accents, as he spoke. "And if the crime came through a mortal, then through a mortal can it be remedied." He tugged at her again, gently, and she started walking beside him.

"But you let him—You—"

"I must convince him to kill the murderer." Quicksilver pulled Ariel along amid the tall, rustling trees. She looked small and frail enough to wring his heart. He remembered what it was like to feel small; he knew very well what it was like to be powerless. Yet, this passion of Lady Ariel's for him must be discouraged, for his good and hers. Nevertheless he needed friends. He must proceed carefully. "I must convince that mortal to do my vengeance and must keep him confused enough that he won't look beyond the pretty scenery I am drawing for the harsh truth beyond."

Ariel opened and closed her mouth. Color came and went in waves on her face, now tingeing her high cheekbones pink, now leaving them harsh and waxy-dreary. "If he—milord—If you do try vengeance, you will both die. And Nan will be left without a husband . . . and I will be . . . Nan and I . . ."

She wailed too loudly.

Quicksilver looked toward the lighted palace behind them, and wondered if such a lament might not be heard by the guards, even through the veil between the realms. He fancied the rustling along the forest floor had changed, from the random slithering of forest creatures to the purposeful movements of Sylvanus's spies.

Forcing a laugh, he covered Ariel's mouth with his hand. "Hush, milady, hush. I have no intention of dying," he said. "The mortal, now . . . Who knows what mortals do and why? Their lives are cheap and they whelp three to a season, like blind kittens behind a barn, and they die the same way, blind and foolish, for no reason at all, in a war they don't understand, or in a tavern brawl, to a dagger wielded by one they thought a friend. If he dies, nothing much is lost." Quicksilver spoke in an urgent, eager tone, but barely loud enough to be called a whisper. He felt Ariel's warm lips move against his palm, and lowered his hand slightly.

"You do not care, then, if he dies?" Ariel asked. She whispered too, but in such a rush that it gave her words the feeling of a long-suppressed scream. "If the boy dies? The boy Will? Nan's boy? But you seemed—Oh, you seemed to care for him. I know it is rare, almost impossible, for one of us to truly love a mortal. Even when we do, our love is not enough to satisfy them. Their love, as ephemeral as they are, is the sturdier brew. And yet there are legends of elves who love mortals and, in thus stooping toward their inferiors, become like gods in their intensity. And you seemed, you seemed to care for him. But you don't? You truly don't? You're that cold, then, milord, that cold that you'd send him to his death?"

"It is all a play, my dear, nothing but a play. The play's the thing, but the thing we play at is not always that which we are." He grinned at her. Color had returned to her face, tinting her cheeks and lips a deep pink and making her look lovely and alive. As they were, chest to chest, face to face, he could feel her hot breath on his face. Her dress rustled against his doublet, as breath made her chest rise and fall.

"What would make you think, fool girl, that I cared for that mortal, or any other?"

"Once you cared for a mortal." Ariel's hands rose, to rest on his shoulders, but she held them in tight little fists as she spoke. "There was that other mortal, the one whose name I forget, the one who became an actor."

Kit. The name came into Quicksilver's mind like an arrow, carrying with it the memory of the exquisite auburn-haired divinity student, whose bed he had shared for a scant summer. He thought of Kit's large questing eyes, his searching lips. How long had it been? Three? No, two years. A fine one Kit had been, though he'd turned a little mad, as mortals always did, who tasted fairy love. "Kit Marlowe," he said gently.

Remembering both young men made Quicksilver feel that Ariel looked paler, less real in his arms. That was the thing about mortals. Dumb and ephemeral they might be, and yet life coursed through their veins so strongly; their hearts beat with such desperate force.

Ariel nodded, her gaze worried, as though she sensed that Quicksilver had gone beyond her, to memories she didn't share.

"We were so young," Quicksilver said quietly, as one who reads an ancient epitaph. "Both so young." Kit had accepted both of Quicksilver's forms and Quicksilver had been innocent and foolish enough to hope that it might last, that they might . . . He let the dream drop into the night of forgotten chimeras. "He went a little insane. He no longer believes in the religion he studies and instead he lives a mad, perilous life, a barbarous one full of intrigue and danger. He craves excitement and passion such as even I can't give."

Ariel nodded. "But that's what we do to mortals, don't you see? Loving us makes them mad, because even when we return their love, it is only with elf love, designed neither to endure death, nor to taste sickness. Even our love for each other is a cold flame that gives no heat, and our love for them is not even that. What they crave . . ." Her eyes spoke on, of craving and foolish hopes. "If one of us could truly love a mortal, forgetting what they are, truly love their weakness as well as their fleeting beauty . . ." She shook her head. "If love like that existed, then maybe the mortal would not go mad. Yet maybe he still would. Maybe the greatest elf love can't equal humans' loyal attachments. It is because of us and other creatures like us that they speak of the love of gods driving humans to madness." She spoke as if to herself, as though studying a difficult lesson in a forgotten primer.

Quicksilver nodded gently, and took her fists from his shoulders, first one, and then the other, smoothing them into open hands, and setting them back against his doublet. His own hands went around her waist, which was small enough that his hands nearly encompassed it. "I know, my dear, but there's no danger of it for this boy, because once he does what I—" He stopped short of naming the fatal task. "If he fulfills what I want him to do, then he'll be dead, dead for daring to touch the king of the hill. The power of the hill will kill him, like a hand squashing a mayfly. And mad or not, it will not matter."

"Then you don't care?" she asked again anxiously. "You truly don't care for him?" She looked odd, not so much eager as scared.

Scared of which answer? Quicksilver shook his head. He tracked a new rustling on the forest floor and pulled Ariel toward him as she stepped back. He had no time to wonder at her fright.

Chances were that anyone, even his brother's spies, seeing them like this, would suspect Quicksilver of no worse thing than intending to seduce Ariel. To make it more plausible, he lowered his head toward hers and kissed her lips, tentatively. Her lips felt soft, like the petals of a newly opened rose. There might be more sport here than just throwing off Sylvanus's spies.

"When you were with that other youth, Marlowe . . . When you spent time with him, I thought to die of jealousy. I thought you loved him truly."

"Impossible to love a human." Such attachment and so foolish. Yes, Lady Ariel would need to learn her lesson, would need to leave Quicksilver and his dark path, his twining, confused nature, alone. But not yet. Not yet. Ariel's loneliness called to his own, like the live, warm sun called to the buried seed. He pulled her to him. "There will never be any reason for you to be jealous over me, milady."

"Oh," she said.

He pressed her close to him, and lowered his lips to her trembling ones, and kissed her, sucking at her tongue, feeling her chest against his, tasting the mint flavor of her mouth, hearing her heartbeat speed up.

She started to pull back, then surrendered to his embracing arms, his searching hands.

The rustling he'd been hearing and tracking resolved into steps. Human steps. Or at least elven, since no human, ever, stepped that lightly. The sound came through the forest, toward them. Still pressed close to Ariel, still feeling her warmth and movement through the fabric of her dress and his doublet Quicksilver listened to the steps, giving close mind to their cadence.

Had they been the heavy, uncouth steps of mortals, he would have continued his amusement. Chances were that cutpurses or drunks making their way through the forest in the evening light wouldn't be able to see the elven realm. And even had they been Sunday children, able to see elves, they would never have been able to touch them, lest Ariel and Quicksilver willed it so. They could have done no more than—at most—spread tales of wild spirits mating in the forest glens.

But the steps, as they approached, confirmed the light springiness of elvenkind. In fact, if Quicksilver didn't have supernatural senses, he would never have heard them. He pulled his mouth away from Ariel's, and took a finger to his lips, commanding silence, while he tracked the sound of the steps through the forest.

Three, no four elves, walking in near silence. Would these be Sylvanus's guards? Had word of Ariel's dream and Quicksilver's response to it spread already? His arm around Ariel's waist, Quicksilver pulled her behind a thick bush, and willed her garments to be as dark as his. Pulling off his doublet, he threw it over both their fair heads. He willed his thoughts to whispers, and veiled Ariel's.

The steps approached, treading the path where, moments before, Quicksilver and Ariel had kissed.

So, it was true. Sylvanus had guessed, or spied, or somehow learned of Quicksilver's intentions, and now Quicksilver himself would be cast away from the hill, with no power, to become prey to unnamed creatures who hunted his kind. He would be sent throughout the world—neither mortal nor elf—an elf without power, a creature of little more than wisps and wishes, and those very wisps wishing themselves away to nothing, day by day as they dwindled. Quicksilver would become, what? Perhaps prey for legendary creatures, like the Hunter, creatures so old that their origin had been lost in the minds of both elves and humans. Himself, Quicksilver had always suspected the Hunter of being a god of his own kind, and possessing only the kind of reality that elves gave him, by their worship and belief. But the oldest legends spoke of his feeding on elves, of his hunting them as his quarry.

The steps came closer. Ariel squirmed and breathed deeply, as though she might say something. Quicksilver shook his head No and, once more, put his hand over her lips.

The steps halted, just on the other side of the bush, behind which Quicksilver hid.

"Here we should be safe to talk," a voice said. Pyrite's

voice. "Well enough away from the court and that foolish nursemaid."

The foolish nursemaid? Could this be the same Pyrite who had heaped compliments on the woman's common looks? Did Pyrite then, have plans of his own? What plans?

"You said Lord Sylvanus had a task for us," another voice prompted, a voice kept too low for Quicksilver to identify.

A task? Quicksilver's heart beat fast. A task? Had Sylvanus, then, decided to dispose of Quicksilver, the heir to the throne? Elves could be killed by other elves, if enough power were brought about, and Sylvanus had enough power.

But would Pyrite lend himself to this? Pyrite who'd just professed his friendship for Quicksilver?

So, it would be thus, Quicksilver thought. Not even exile, but death. Death and nothingness beyond. To sleep. Perchance to dream. Quicksilver almost longed for it. But in that sleep beyond the grave, what dreams might come? His hand clenched the ornamental dagger at his side, and he waited and listened. If he listened to his would-be assassins, chances were he could deter them and forestall the evil hour yet. His other hand he held tightly over Ariel's mouth, feeling her lips pressed against the palm, her regular breath over it.

"A task indeed, an easy one, that will win us the gratitude of our king." Pyrite's voice resounded with easy self-satisfaction, with the enthusiasm of a man who sees recognition and riches within reach of his outstretched hand, his for the plucking. "That man who has wed the nursemaid, that butcher's apprentice, or farmer, or whatever he is, stands in the way of our king's ardor. But for him, the fair one would have our king. As it is, though, she sees herself bound by the vows taken before her god.

Were her husband out of the way and she a widow, she wouldn't long resist the blandishments of her better."

"Who is he, then, this mortal?" the whispering one asked. "And how can we ambush him?"

"Our king has gotten from the woman that her husband's name is William Shakespeare. He is young yet, and dark-haired, and twice daily he must walk from Stratford to Wincot and cross the forest, to fulfill his lowly calling, whatever that is. According to our king's spies, even now he'll be walking back. It should be easy to ambush him by the great oak, at the turning to Stratford. There we shall kill him. The mortals will never guess. They will take it as a murder committed by bandits, a killing for his purse. And the woman, Nan, will be free to make free with our sovereign."

Quicksilver's heart beat at his throat, his hand clamped tightly, tightly, on Ariel's mouth.

So, it wasn't his life his brother sought, but his brother's plan could, nonetheless, spell the death of Quicksilver's plot. He thought of young Will, foolish and trusting, and comely and sweet. Quicksilver must stop this assassination.

However, if he stopped Sylvanus's plan, wouldn't Sylvanus find out? And what punishment might he not mete out to the young brother who stopped him attaining his heart's desire? A brother that, already, found no favor in Sylvanus's heart?

Quicksilver took deep breaths and thought, and thought, while the conspirators spoke near him, and Ariel stood beside him, still, still except for her breath that tickled the back of his hand, and her lips pressed, warm and soft, against his palm.

He would have to kill all four of the conspirators. All of them. But Pyrite was Ariel's brother and his own oldest friend, not to mention a duke of the Realm, a favorite of

Sylvanus, through the King well connected in the hill power, and strong enough to oppose his elven power to Quicksilver's own. The other ones, from their deferential tones to Pyrite, their softly whispered comments, though still elves, and therefore still Lords of the Hill, would be pages, lowly knaves, second sons and bastard ones, and their ilk. Quicksilver doubted too that any of them stood as high in Sylvanus's favor as Pyrite. Them, Quicksilver could dispatch quickly.

The thought of killing his own kind made his blood rankle. The thought of killing Pyrite made him tremble. To kill his own friend would make him a fiend, like monsters in human stories.

But for the villain, Sylvanus, to die, those who guarded him and followed his orders must be defeated.

Yet, perhaps there was hope. Pyrite must believe Quicksilver. Together they had played at fair Titania's feet, together hunted the green forest. And Pyrite had professed his affection for Quicksilver just this morning. Perhaps Pyrite would agree to lie about the results of his ambush. Perhaps he would agree to lie for Quicksilver.

Oh, Pyrite wanted to advance in the kingdom, but surely, once Quicksilver acquainted him with Sylvanus's treachery, he would see that his best advantage lay by Quicksilver's side.

Quicksilver swallowed. One way or another he must stop them, he must stop Pyrite. It must be done. And weren't they, anyway, contemplating murder themselves? Oh, surely murder of a mortal was not nearly as bad as killing elvenkind, as mortals died quickly and their lives were worth little more than the lives of fireflies in a summer night. But killing them remained murder, the extinguishing of a thinking mind. To do it, as Sylvanus would, to gratify gross lust and base emotion, must be a crime.

The boy had been warm and alive, and real in Quicksilver's arms. And they would kill him, to clear the path of Sylvanus's lust. Sylvanus must die, as must his servants. Without Will, Quicksilver could not even dream of killing Sylvanus.

Quicksilver heard the conspirators retreat, their steps distancing themselves, light and almost inaudible on the forest floor.

That young man they were so intent on killing was as alive as they were, for the brief while his life lasted. Quicksilver remembered his solid form that he'd clasped in his arms, remembered Will's voice replying to him, the youth's confusion at the interference of the fairy world in his life.

He remembered Will's lips, his mouth that tasted of wine and life, his arms that had embraced Quicksilver's body with so much eager intent, such powerful urgency.

The conspirators were gone; Quicksilver was alone with Lady Ariel.

Her mouth freed, she said, "Milord, it was my brother, who ... I didn't tell him of your brother's deed. I couldn't, since Pyrite is his closest liegeman, but ..."

"Your brother is safe, milady," Quicksilver said. "Your brother is safe. I'd never give him away. I'll try to speak to him and dissuade him from his fatal purpose, but no more. I prize your brother above mortals." He smiled, a facile smile that made his facial muscles smart. He must get her mind from this, he must make her forget what she'd heard. Ariel had been orphaned as a baby, and Pyrite, ten years older, was all the family she had.

Pyrite must be spared, for fair Ariel's sake.

Quicksilver must distract her and quickly and then he must hasten to the great oak in the forest. He marveled at how careless his voice sounded as he said, "There was something we were pursuing, what was it? Oh, yes." Voraciously, he lowered his mouth to Ariel's, while his hands worked, unnoticed, at her bodice.

Her eyes on his were hungry, helpless, all thought vanished from them. She didn't attempt to ask any more questions. Her mouth sought his with blind eagerness. Never had a traveler in the heat of the sun longed for water as much as she did for his good turn.

And as he laid her down on the forest floor, Ariel might have forgotten Will, but Quicksilver did not.

Scene 6

❧

A tavern such as frequented by working-class men. By the blazing fireplace three bawds sit, scantily attired, though their clothing has seen better days. Three long tables, with benches of the same length take up all of the smoky space. At the tables sits a motley of men, most in russet suits of ill cut, covered in obvious mending. On the walls there's a suspicion of frescoes covered beneath years of grime and grease. A fat woman moves amid the tables, refilling the thick white clay cups the drinkers hold.

"That's my Marian, Marian Hacket, she is. Thighs like butter and breasts like cream, could envelope a man till kingdom come." The man sitting next to Will on the tavern's long bench reached a hand for the arm of the alewife, and held onto it while he spoke in the high, querulous voice of one who's had far too much to drink. "Here, Marian," he went on. "Tell my friend Will that all will be well. His wife left the poor lad, you see. He has nothing to go home to."

The smell of sour sweat from the man, and the cleaner sweat of the alewife mingled with the sweet scent of fine

ale as the woman poured a good head of golden brew into
Will's white ceramic cup, and then into that of the man
next to him.

"Not *left*," Will said, surprised at saying it, surprised at
hearing his own voice rise high and as whining as that of
the old drunkard's next to him. "Not left, she didn't. They
took her by force, they did, with their fine manners and
their velvet suits. And she danced . . . she danced with him
nightlong." His words shocked him as if a stranger had
pronounced them. What fool was he to go telling all to a
stranger at a poor alehouse in Wincot? Foolish Will, foolish, so foolish that within six months of marriage, he had
lost wife and daughter and all. He felt a desperate sadness,
a terrible pity for poor, overworked Will Shakespeare,
who had nothing but an empty house to go home to. He
felt sorry for the foolish lad as though he were someone
quite different from himself.

"Pssssshhhhhh!" the man next to him said. "It's getting
so a poor workman can't even keep his wife no more. If
it's not one thing it's another, and now gentlemen in velvet and all. Would you credit it? I tell you, friend Will,
there are stranger things under the sun than any philosophy professor could dream up. Stranger. Just the other
day, crossing Arden Forest, I saw a troop of the little
people, roaming across, dressed all in green. Would you
credit it?"

Will wanted very much to credit it, but his tongue had
become like thick cork and he held about as much control
over it as though it *were* cork.

"I know, friend, you think me crazy, but I'm not crazy.
Not I, Christopher Sly, by birth a peddler, by education a
cardmaker, by transmutation a bearherd, and now by present profession a tinker. Ask Marian Hacket, the fat alewife
of Wincot, if she know me not: if she say I am not fourteen pence on the score for sheer ale, score me up for the

lyingest knave in Christendom. And Christopher Sly tells you the world has gone mad and nothing has been right no more. Why, these last ten years or more, someone has put a blight on all the colors, so they all run together, and my meat has lost its taste."

"Perhaps because you taste your ale too well." The ale-wife had returned. She set her large white pitcher of foaming ale on the table next to Will and said, "Son, should you be here? You look scarcely old enough to be out of doors at sunset, and you're not from these parts, are you?"

Will focused his eyes with an effort.

The woman placed a fat white hand on his shoulder and squeezed. "You're the petty-schoolmaster, are you not? The one as comes from Stratford?"

Will nodded. "The sun . . . setting?" he managed, despite his thickened, unwieldy tongue.

"More than half set, already. You shouldn't be here this late," Marian Hacket said.

Will would have liked to explain that it had seemed a good idea to stop in and get some supper, since there would be none waiting him at home. But, because there would be no one at home, Will had, by a declension of his self-pity, ended up eating nothing and drinking far too much.

Marian Hacket struggled to get him up, pulling him by the strength of both arms. Her warmth enveloped him, her large breasts pressed against his side. Her fat doughy hands pressed into his arms as she held him. She succeeded in getting him to stand on his own, shaky legs.

The room spun around Will—tables, and long benches, dispirited drinkers and smoky atmosphere—but he stood, gritting his teeth and cursing his dizzy head. What had come over him, to drink himself into brutish stupor?

"There you go, son. You're too young to sit near the

likes of old Sly. You get yourself home, and who knows? Mayhap your wife will have come back."

Will wanted to hope, but he couldn't. He remembered Nan's dancing, and the palace he couldn't enter.

Marian escorted Will to the door, her breasts pressing against his shoulder, her body holding him upright.

As they reached the open front door, a draft of fresh air from outside, cold and untainted by either smoke or fumes of spirits, revived Will.

He found his feet and stood on them, leaning no more than a few degrees off the vertical.

"There you go," Marian said, feeling the shift. "You'll be all right now, won't you?"

Will nodded, not sure of telling the truth.

Outside, two horses were tied beside a spacious, clean-looking horse trough.

Will bent down and dipped his head in the cold water. The cold braced him, like a hard slap will brace a crying woman or a sniveling boy. Standing again, some of the cobwebs clearing from his brain, he shook water from his dripping curls. Water trickled down his back, soaking his doublet and, insinuated itself beneath his collar, running down the middle of his back.

The cold discomfort helped him wake up.

He looked about him, regaining his wits. Marian had told the truth, and it was later than the time he would wish to cross Arden Forest alone. The sun had all but set and only a few, desultory rays lit up the narrow Wincot street.

Workers hurried home, and women called their children inside.

Will had better hurry home, also, to Henley Street, where at least he had a bed and a safe place to stay. And maybe, just maybe, there would be news of Nan. If the mad dream he'd walked in was true, and Nan, his Nan, had indeed been taken away by the people under the hill, then maybe the dark lady would really come to him and show him how to recover his lost wife, his infant daughter.

The thought of the dark lady made Will's blood run faster and braced him with yet another kind of feeling, another form of surging energy.

If he believed every other part of his dream, he still found it hard to credit how beautiful the dark lady had looked.

"Friend Will, have you a weapon?" a voice asked from the tavern's doorway.

It was old Sly, who'd somehow made his way from the smoky interior and now stood, or rather leaned, against the age-stained doorway. "Because if you don't, I'll be glad to help you. I was a peddler, and I—"

"I have a dagger," Will said, and lifting it from its sheath at his waist, he showed it to Sly. An old dagger it was, very old, covered all over with cabalistic signs and odd incrustations. Will had found it in his father's shop, when he'd gone in search of a weapon—thinking even a rounded glover's knife might do—to keep him safe on the way through Arden Forest.

Footpads were few and far between there, and the last ones caught had been hanged when Will was a little boy; nevertheless he wanted to feel safe. And this knife he'd found, fallen behind his father's workbench, looked functional enough despite its odd handle and odder triangular blade. Most likely it was either an inheritance from his grandfather, or something his father had taken in surety for payment and then forgotten.

"A good toad sticker," old Sly said. "Yet, if you want a sword . . . there are strange things in Arden, made all the stranger at night. If you ever tangle with the people under the hill, remember, the one thing they can't stand is cold iron, forged and honestly worked for humankind. Use chains or knives, or closures and they'll all work, so long as they're iron. . . ."

But Will shook his head and, his hand on the handle of the strange old knife, which he didn't expect to need, he walked out of Wincot and onto the path across Arden Forest.

Scene 7

ලග

A path through Arden Forest—a poor kind of path, of the sort beaten over centuries by peasants making their way between neighboring towns. Shrubs and great trees grow hard on either side, leaving but meager passage open to travelers. Where the path winds about a large oak tree, a group of fairy lords—dressed as though for a party— block the narrow trail. Will stops in front of them, gazing in disbelief. From behind Will, running sure-footed amid shrubs and the roots of trees, Quicksilver comes, his sword out and ready.

He shouldn't have stopped to dally with Ariel, Quicksilver thought, as he ran, his breath caught in his throat, coming in short bursts of remorse and fear.

The sight of the four fairy lords, Pyrite and his three friends, facing the hapless mortal turned Quicksilver's blood to ice.

So now the traitor would thus prostitute his vassals, and make them ambush mortals and interfere in a kingdom of which they had no ken. Bad enough that Sylvanus had the nursemaid kidnapped, and left no stock behind, or none that could deceive her husband, a Sunday child. Bad enough. But this was lunacy, a trespass into the realm of mortals which the rules of the universe would never tolerate.

Sylvanus would bring disaster to realms both human and fairy and, conjoined, plunge them into the abyss.

Quicksilver ran, his legs pumping hard. Ariel had been sweet, her love freely bestowed and more eager than any he'd ever experienced. Her caresses had almost succeeded in making him forget Will's kiss, and they had, certainly, succeeded in making him forget the passing time.

He saw the elves advance toward Will.

Pyrite walked amid them, beautifully dressed, as always, this time all in checks—doublet and breeches both fashioned of priceless silk, in colors so bright they dazzled the mind and stung the heart.

Oh, what a poor assassin, what a shoddy highwayman Pyrite made, that even in treason he must remain bright, even in dishonor shine like a new polished kettle.

Pyrite's sword, like Quicksilver's, had been fashioned in one day by an elven smith, of the purest crystal, solid as a diamond, bright as ice, sharp as the scythe of death. It glittered as Pyrite drew it out of its sheath. Pyrite's fair features contorted in a smile half-gloating and half-embarrassed as he advanced on Will.

Just then, Quicksilver ran around the elven lords, in a burst of speed, reached Will, and stopped by his side.

Pyrite's eyes widened in shock and disbelief.

"To me, to me, milords," Quicksilver yelled as he grabbed Will by the rough wool of his doublet. "Or can you only duel with nurselings, mere miserly mortals, creatures that start dying in their cradle, and before they ever learn the ways of life, go back to the dust whence they're fashioned?" Quicksilver pushed Will behind him, shielding the mortal's slim body with his own. "To me, Pyrite." Quicksilver bared his teeth to his lifelong friend and tried to shock him into renouncing his treason. "Pyrite, whom I've called my friend and with whom I played in my cradle, like that Greek god it was who played with serpents."

Pyrite blinked. He had enormous eyes, blue like the periwinkle and innocent as an infant's. For a moment, he was confused, Quicksilver's words meeting their mark and making him think about the wisdom of his actions. Then he shrugged, and bared his teeth to Quicksilver, in return. "Serpents, milord? Was that not Hermes, god of thieves and traitors? And was he your milk-brother, nursed from the same tit of treason?"

"Treason, I? Treason? I do not seek to murder mortals and set the realms at war."

Pyrite raised his eyebrows at that. He opened his mouth, closed it, only to open it again. "How come you here?" he asked. His sword, which he had raised for the mortal, never flagged, but was held halfway up while his expression rearranged itself into confused worry.

"I'm here to protect the mortal from the designs of the traitor. Where else should I be?"

Pyrite spared a look behind Quicksilver, at Will, and leered, an unhallowed grin. Pyrite, more than the rest of the court, was privy to Quicksilver's tastes, Quicksilver's follies, Quicksilver's false steps. "Oh, the mortal, is it? Is this one yours? Have you claimed him? Very fond of mortals, are you not, my friend?"

"It must be a family affliction," Quicksilver answered. "As my lord brother, the traitor, the usurper himself, likes mortal flesh well enough. At least I do not command others to taint their honor and kill the rivals who stand in my way." He looked aside, in a calculated expression of disgust, and spat on the forest floor.

From above came a rumble of thunder, and the light of the more than half gone sun disappeared faster and faster, veiled, like a candle covered by a snuffer.

"You call him traitor, you?" Pyrite asked. His voice acquired a tone of justified outrage. His bright eyes opened in startled wonder, and his sword rose, now almost fully up. He braced his legs apart, balancing solidly on the uneven ground, in the position of a swordsman ready to parry.

Quicksilver raised his own sword, prepared to meet the thrust should it come. He had been so resolute, so ready to face dishonor and kill for the sake of his vengeance, if kill he must. But now his desire for vengeance flagged. True, he still needed the mortal alive to avenge his parents. But Pyrite did not back down, as Quicksilver had hoped. Must Will's life be purchased at the cost of Pyrite's death?

The sudden glare of a thunderbolt revealed Pyrite's amazed face and, behind him, the three lords, his accomplices, standing in amazement, frozen like some tableau painted long ago and enshrined in the solidity of wood.

A passing glance over his shoulder showed Will to Quicksilver. Will, who stood behind Quicksilver, appeared frozen or transmuted into some inanimate object.

None of them looked capable of movement.

None but Pyrite, whose eyes burned, whose cheeks flared in offended color. "You can't speak thus of Lord Sylvanus. He is our king, the king of our kind. You'd betray him for a mortal? O monstrous traitor! I arrest you, of capital treason against the king and crown. Obey, audacious traitor; kneel for grace." Pyrite's eyes filled with madness, with the eager fire of the devoted courtier who sees a chance to score points in his lord's estimation.

Would this fire be quenched? Could Pyrite be brought back to his senses? He must be mad, driven mad by being fed the power of the hill directly through Sylvanus. Sylvanus, the fool, the base traitor, would be giving too much of that power to Pyrite, who wouldn't know how to control it. And the power would make Pyrite mad. Drunk.

"I'm not doing this for a mortal," Quicksilver said. If only he could convince Pyrite, and win him to his cause. If only Pyrite knew his reasons, if only there were time to explain them. Oh, why hadn't Ariel confided in her own brother?

Ariel and Pyrite, had there ever been two such, hatched from the same womb? She, timorous and meek, asking for love; he hot and brave, and foolhardy daring.

"And who am I betraying?" Quicksilver said. "I should have been king, and in attacking me, it is you, false friend, who are the traitor."

As the words passed his lips, and he could no longer call them back, Quicksilver knew he had erred. These words, rather than damping the fire of Pyrite's anger, like oil poured onto a raging fire made it blaze anew.

Where friendship and offense had warred in Pyrite's eyes, now offense won the match, overcoming much-weakened friendship, which hadn't fed in years uncounted, and bringing him to earth with a quick stab. Just as quickly did Pyrite's sword lift and Pyrite surge forward, dancing on light cat's feet. By the glint of lightning, his teeth flashed, very white and clamped together, as though to prevent the eruption of some fatal word. And yet, despite the clenching of his teeth, words emerged: "Aye, Quicksilver, aye, I'll be a traitor then, when you are king."

Not even thinking, not daring to speak, Quicksilver lifted his sword and parried a blow aimed with all of Pyrite's considerable force.

And Pyrite thrust and Quicksilver parried.

Quicksilver found his voice. "Desist, Pyrite, desist. I would fain not hurt you." Quicksilver felt the blows vibrate through his sword to shake his whole being. He must, somehow, quell Pyrite's madness, and speak to him, again, as a friend, and tell him of Ariel's vision and Quicksilver's own just cause.

"You feign as you are and can't help feigning," Pyrite answered. His sword sought out a place to strike, like the serpent, well-nursed and taken to a warm bosom, will find the weak spot in which to lay its venom.

A twig snapped with a loud crack under Quicksilver's foot.

Quicksilver parried, but barely, the tip of his sword withstanding the crashing clash of Pyrite's charge.

Chill, chill sweat ran down Quicksilver's forehead to sting his eyes. Lifting his arms felt like Herculean labor and lifting his sword to stop Pyrite's blows was infinite hardship, terrible pain.

Pyrite had to be drawing on the power of the hill to sustain his fury, while Quicksilver dared not, could not, dip from that bright current. He could feel it run on past him, like a shimmering brook flowing just outside a parched traveler's reach.

But if Quicksilver reached for that abundant power, that tempting flood, then his brother would know of his endeavor and all would be lost. Nor would Quicksilver survive.

Pyrite pressed close, each blow stronger, his dancing feet moving nearer and nearer, until the two of them were fighting, face to face, their bodies almost too close to maneuver against each other.

"Desist," Quicksilver said again, desperate. "Desist. I am your friend."

Pyrite said nothing, only pressed closer and closer, till Quicksilver could feel Pyrite's hot breath on his face.

Quicksilver stepped back, step by step.

Above, thunder sounded like the hooves of horses in battle, and the bright sword of a forgotten god cleaved dark, roiling clouds in twain to illuminate the Earth in an unreal, glaring white, unforgiving light. Like the light of reason shining upon long-cherished delusions.

Fool that I am, fool, Quicksilver thought, and stepped back step by step, back along the root-mined path, knowing that a stumble, a false step would bring him to his doom.

Will was forgotten, as were the other three elven lords, though in some corner of his mind, Quicksilver guessed them to still be there, still where he had seen them last.

Only Pyrite mattered, and this duel fought close, close, as their emotions had always been close and tenderly nursed, closer than in a love affair. From childhood, they'd known each other's weaknesses and strengths, each other's joys and sorrows.

And never, till now, had a sword come between them.

Pyrite's pale face, lit up by the white light from the heavens, looked even whiter, with nostrils flared, like those of a purebred horse about to rear.

Could Quicksilver unsay what he had said, and somehow uncall the name of traitor that he had called his friend? No, that would not do. It would not stop Pyrite now, nor detain his charge. If, besides a traitor, he thought Quicksilver a coward, it would only serve to speed home the fatal blow.

Quicksilver's only hope was to survive, and tire Pyrite until, his body spent, Pyrite's mind engaged in thinking once more.

Quicksilver's foot, stepping back, settled atop a rounded root, and his ankle turned, to find balance. The sharp pain shot up his leg to his hip. He faltered, but kept moving, kept standing, kept parrying. No time to be hurt. No time to stop. No time to fear.

The sweat that rolled into Quicksilver's eyes stung and burned, blurring his vision. Breath panted out of his dry mouth. Harsh, broken breath like storm winds, blowing uneven destruction upon the landscape.

The temptation to reach for the power of the hill, the

temptation to get strength and healing and new force from
that accustomed source almost overpowered Quicksilver,
but like a mortal saint faced with temptation, he withstood
it and parried and backed up. He wished for words to
explain to Pyrite that Sylvanus had murdered both king
and queen, and that Quicksilver had it from good source,
from Pyrite's own sister. But his mouth was dry with an-
guish and tiredness, and he could not find words. He swallowed and summoned what saliva he could to his mouth,
and swallowed again, tasting dust and mustiness, a fore-
taste of the grave itself. "Pyrite, stay. I must tell you about
Ariel, what Ariel has—"

"My sister? You will hide behind her name, now? You,
who always spurned her?" The words that should have
calmed Pyrite, instead seemed to act upon him like spurs
on a runaway mount, driving him to greater madness. He
lifted his sword up over his head, and the lightning flashed
on it, as Quicksilver tried to lift his own sword to parry
the coming blow.

But Quicksilver's sword weighed too much and his
arms felt bruised and half-torn from their sockets and he
could not, he could not . . .

Lightning flashed and, from the darkness, the dark-clad
Will shot out, holding something in his hand. The something flashed, and Will shouted, "To me, milord. To me,
who was your first intended victim. I am ready for you."

Pyrite turned, struck, surprised, and then an unholy
smile shone on his perfect features, and his sword rose
even more eagerly.

The human dove beneath the lifted sword, and his
weapon which, at close quarters, Quicksilver saw to be a
short dark dagger,—buried itself into Pyrite's shoulder.

Pyrite drew startled breath, and made a sound not quite
a scream. His hands opened, dropping his sword, that fell

straight down to the hard soil of the path, its blade penetrating the dirt, its hilt vibrating in midair.

Will withdrew his dagger and stared at it. It glowed bright red, and shone with its own light, as its good forged iron tasted the blood of fairykind.

And Quicksilver, torn between the mortal who had saved him and his own elven friend, who had betrayed him or whom he had betrayed—he couldn't tell which— yelled, "What have you done?" to Will, and whispered, "Are you hurt?" to Pyrite.

Pyrite, pale-faced, shimmering with a strange milky light, his lips gleaming even whiter than his face, clutched his shoulder and backed up, eyes wide open, glaring, but still looking dark, dark like the absence of all light. "Hurt. Aye, I am hurt. I am done for. Oh, it burns. May the Hunter devour you, Quicksilver, you and Sylvanus both. A plague on both your houses."

"Come, come, it can't be much," Quicksilver said, trying to smile, while Pyrite's white, chalky face gave his words the lie. "It can't be much. A mortal dagger and in the shoulder, only. It is the shock of cold iron that you feel, but it will soon be gone and you'll feel better. It's only a scratch to one like us. Nothing. It can't even be very deep."

Pyrite smiled, a ghastly smile. Glowing drops of blood dripped from his shoulder, staining his bright garment, mingling with the rain on the forest floor. "No, it is not so deep as a well, nor so wide as the palace door." His voice had a blank, brittle quality—odd, like a glass that breaks, far off, in another room, and can only be guessed at. He looked in mute horror down at his shoulder, where his wound showed as a darkness with blurred edges. Across those blurred edges bright magical blood flowed and dripped. "Not at all that deep. But it is enough. It will serve. Ask for me tomorrow and you shall find me a grave man." He smiled again, and his smile, his whole being, flickered, like something only half glimpsed out of the corner of the eye, before becoming solid again. His hands clutched his shoulder convulsively and he drew in a breath as if in pain. "A plague on both your houses. All your houses. Yours and Sylvanus's and this creature's . . . This mortal creature. Harmless, you said he is. Defenseless. Fine defense, this. To scratch a man to death."

His eyes, shining with a strange white light, turned to Will, who stood, transfixed, in that glare. "A braggart, a rogue, a villain. Why the devil did you come between us? A plague on both your houses." Again he flickered. "You have made worm's meat of me. Of me, who am an elven lord and to whom death should be a far-off mockery, a scare for mortals, a harmless bogeyman."

He flickered again and changed form, somehow, as though a strong wind blew out of the trees, speeding him to darkness. "A plague," he said again, his voice sounding as if it came from a long distance off, like a ghost heard in dreams and ill-remembered. "A plague on both your houses. Your houses, remember. You are both cursed." Wind that Quicksilver couldn't feel blew Pyrite away, as though he were no more than a pile of rustlings forgotten from the late harvest, a worthless pile of oak leaves, fallen and dried. It drove him—a mere shimmer of colors, a glimpse of his bright suit and his staring eyes, in a whirl-wind, across the tops of the centenary trees, dispersing him, till he was no more.

Yet his voice resounded still, more like a remembered echo than a real voice: "Cursed by Pyrite. You, Quicksil-ver. And you, wretch. Both you, my prince, and the mor-tal, for whom I'm killed."

As the last echoes of the last word faded, rain fell, hard and driving, blinding, scouring Quicksilver's face, his panting chest, like a whip. He looked at Pyrite's sword, on the ground, and at Will, who stood beside him, soaked all through by the sudden downpour, and shivering as water dripped from his hair and ran down his face.

"I don't know who you are, but you, you tried to defend me, and I don't know who you are." Will looked terrified.

Quicksilver nodded. Will didn't know who Quicksilver was? Oh, yes, he'd never seen him in this aspect, had he? From somewhere, Quicksilver found assurance, a voice that showed a calm that he didn't feel. "You did well." His heart mourned for Pyrite, but his vengeance clamored even harder for satisfaction. "Do not worry. It will be well. It will all be well." He knew he lied. A glance at where the three eleven courtiers had stood discovered them gone, and Quicksilver felt his knees go weak under him, like ties that become loosened with wear.

Sylvanus would hear. Sylvanus was hearing, even now, of his brother's treason, of Pyrite's death. Pyrite's unholy death. Quicksilver stifled a sob.

And yet, Quicksilver must go to the hill, the hill to which he belonged and whence his power came. He must go back, try to justify himself.

Quicksilver had a vision of Sylvanus on the throne, hearing from Pyrite's rogues. And Ariel standing nearby? Meek, harmless Ariel—what would she feel about this? Would Quicksilver lose his last friend?

Quicksilver shook with fatigue, and nausea clutched his middle.

From that other, colorless, in-between world, he could feel his parents' shades reach toward him for vengeance.

He hoped Ariel would know this was the only way to avenge the dead king and queen, the only way to restore order to the universe.

He'd promised Ariel to keep her brother safe, and her brother had been killed for Quicksilver's sake. For the sake of Quicksilver's vengeance.

a boy. "You are of them—of the hill people."

The fair-haired man—creature—nodded. His hair, bright as moonlight, seemed to shine with its own light in the dark and the storm.

Rain poured down—cold, hard rain. Will lifted his hand to his forehead to brush aside the wet hair that had got pasted there, and wiped water from his face in a futile gesture, as more water came rushing down, drenching him like a strange baptism, an unhallowed blessing. Will had killed. With this hand he had stifled a thinking brain, with his dagger put an end to a speaking voice.

The creature wept, water from his eyes mingling with the water pouring down on him. He looked up at Will, eyes all red, rimmed with grief and shrouded with pain. "Yes, I am of them, and he was my friend whom you have . . . killed."

"But if he's of you . . . Was he not immortal?"

The creature laughed, a hard, bitter laugh, like broken ice, its shards pointing all outward, to impale and cut. "No. Not immortal. We live long, but we are not immortal, and cold metal poisons us, if kept in us long. However, it shouldn't have killed him that easily." The blond courtier stood up and brushed with the tip of his gloved fingers at the smear of reddish mud on his knees. His eyes shimmered like lakes where a good spring rain has collected. "May I see your dagger, goodman, may I see it?" He asked it politely, too composedly for one so emotional.

Will's hand went to the handle of the dagger he had sheathed, but it stopped there. "If you are of them . . ." he began. Should he give a dagger to the person—creature—who'd just fought, as he put it, his oldest friend? Would he not kill Will, this elf whose friend Will had killed?

But he'd come into the fray to defend Will.

The creature laughed again, one of those frightening laughs with no joy in it. "Come, boy, come. I came into this to protect you, to keep your head on your shoulders, not to strike it off." He held his hand out for the dagger.

His voice sounded familiar, but in a way that Will could not quite understand. He'd always had a good memory for sounds, and he knew not this timbre, nor this tone, yet the voice sounded, nevertheless, like one he'd heard before.

It also sounded commanding, full of power, used to demanding and not begging.

Will handed him the dagger, wooden handle out, and the creature held it, by the wood. First, he looked down at the thing in horror, as if Will had just handed him a snake. Then, he probed, with the tip of a tentative finger for the dagger end. A blue flash, a sound of sizzling, and a smell of scorch, and the creature took the tip of his gloved finger to his mouth and handed the dagger back to Will. "An evil thing," he said. "More enchantments and curses on it, boy, than I could dream of heaping on anything." He paused, blinked, and went a shade paler, his eyes full of sudden understanding. "Unless I were making the knife and sharpening it to slay the power of the hill and the rulers thereof. Keep it, boy, keep it. It will serve you well." His face set itself in a hard grimace, looking as though years unnumbered had carved runnels down his perfect skin.

Amazed, Will accepted the dagger, and slid it into its sheath, thinking how strange it all was, how odd. Who was this creature, and why had he come to Will's aid, when Will most needed it? Why had he set himself against his own kin and friends for Will's sake, and why did he speak now of giving back to Will a weapon he thought so dangerous?

If this were a guardian angel, it was a mad one.

"Why would you defend me, milord? And why would they attack me? Even if they are people from the hill, why set themselves against me? They already have my wife

and daughter, both." He heard his own voice echo piti-
fully, as the voice of the poor man claiming the loss of
his single ewe lamb, and the full misery of it struck him,
till he had trouble not crying. Yet he kept his eyes dry.
Let the stranger, this unnamed creature, cry if he wished,
but Will was a man and a married one. He would not lend
himself to such displays.

He could not see the creature's expression, but his commanding voice came out with a sneer, a force, a desperate
strength of hatred and disdain. "They attacked you because the king of elves, the King of Fairyland, has decreed
that you must die, so that he can have your wife for his
own."

Will turned startled eyes to the creature and found,
etched on the creature's face, such an expression of hatred
that his hand went to the sheathed dagger.

But the creature looked away and spat on the ground
in great disgust. "The coward, the traitorous usurper who
sits on the throne of elvenkind," he said. "Don't you remember?" He looked back at Will, his eyes softer, though
a little impatient, like the eyes of an adult contemplating
a slow child. "I told you yesterday that you must kill him,
if you want to have any hope of winning back your wife."

"You told me?" Will asked amazed. "You? I've never
seen you."

The stranger's cheeks tinged a light pink, and his small,
pulpy lips squeezed themselves into an impatient line.
"Oh, I didn't tell you myself, but my . . . sister . . . my sister Silver told you. Do you not remember?"

"Your sister?" Gulping air as he remembered that lady
of the night before, her rounded breasts pressed against
his arm, her slim-waisted form walking next to him, the
touch of her soft hand on his arm, Will foundered. "Your
sister?"

The creature smiled, an ironic smile, and bowed a little,

and made as if to take off a hat he wasn't wearing, "I am Quicksilver, Prince of Elvenland, at your service, Will, son of John Shakespeare. My sister sent me to protect you, that I might keep you alive and you might get your wife back, yet. My sister has a most tender regard for your safety." The smile might be mocking, or it might be appeasing.

Will couldn't tell which. He felt blood rush to his cheeks, thinking of the lady Silver, and he tried to speak in a way that would not aggrieve the lady's brother. Did elves have honor, and mind if it got stained? He remembered how furious the other elf—the one Will had unwittingly killed—had become at the mention of his sister's name, and he shuddered. "I . . . I too have a most tender and respectful regard for the lady your sister."

Quicksilver drew in breath like a man drowning, but exploded in laughter all the same. A brittle laughter, shaky and afraid of itself, looking all around for dark corners where fear hid that might slay it. He turned to face Will, with something like a devilish light playing in his dark green eyes even while tears still shone there. "Ah, Will. A tender regard, then? Not a firm one? Silver will be disappointed."

Will felt the blood rush all the faster to his cheeks, and looked at the ground of the path, the hard ground, turned to mud by the incessant rain and trampled by men's feet in a mortal fight. The stains of supernatural blood on the ground stood out as vivid as ever, shining in soft, puddled patches.

"Come, come, boy," Quicksilver said. "I will walk you to the edge of your town, where we might meet your own kind, and keep you safe from mine. Three of them ran off, and who knows what deviltry they might not be stirring?" His face turned grave, all amusement gone from it.

He started up, a little ahead of Will, and Will, obediently, walked behind him.

They walked a long while in silence. The elf's footsteps made no more sound than a leaf fluttering gently to the ground. Will's own footsteps were lost in the constant patter of rain, the growl of thunder. Rain lashed them and soaked them, and stole their warmth like a greedy thief.

Halfway through the path to Stratford, when the air became tinted with the smell of burning wood, Quicksilver looked back over his shoulder and asked, "That dagger, where did you get it?"

"From my father's workshop." The hard, driven rain filled Will's mouth, forcing him to spit it out. "A year ago, when I found I must walk all this way from Wincot, I borrowed the dagger from my father's shop . . . in case I should meet footpads, or highwaymen abroad."

The elf chuckled, a cold chuckle that sounded like ice breaking. "Some footpads you meet, Will." When he looked over his shoulder, again, he didn't appear amused. "And where did your father get it?"

Will shrugged. "I don't know. I found it in his shop, behind some pelts, and I thought I might as well use it. Why?"

"Oh, nothing much and no reason." The elf's voice betrayed much reason, indeed. "Is this your father who hides in his house and lets his business dwindle?"

Will felt a prickle of annoyance. Had he told Silver that much? He remembered her beauty and her lilac smell making him drunk. He might have. He might have, at that. But must she run and tell it to her brother? "Aye," he said. "My father who claims creditors will come and collect from him if he shows himself." And then, with a spur of filial pride, he added, "Though he owes no man anything."

The elf didn't answer that for a while, and Will thought the conversation had been forgotten. They walked in the dark forest, under the pelting rain. All around, creatures ran and scurried in the underbrush, their sounds announcing their flight from this unseasonable rain.

What creatures, and of what kind? Animal, or supernatural? And how would Will pull himself from this tangle, where his wife was gone and his life half-forfeit, entailed to a realm he didn't even understand?

Worried, immersed in his own problems, he barely heard and even less remarked when Quicksilver said, under his breath. "Aye, *no man*. Your father owes *no man* anything."

Scene 9

❧

The entrance to the fairy palace, wet marble steps glim-mering under the rain. From inside the open, arched doorway, spill light and music. Enter Quicksilver, rush-ing up the steps.

Climbing the broad stairway of the fairy palace, Quick-silver looked up, wondering if his brother, the trea-sonous king, had already been told of Pyrite's death. What reception had Sylvanus prepared for Quicksilver? Did his death wait within?

Though he could see the throne room from the outside through the open door, he saw no person within, as if courtiers had deserted the room or else gathered near the walls, out of Quicksilver's line of sight. Light and warmth came from the doorway, as did a feeling of normalcy. Music played, the same music that graced the beginning of every royal reception—soft music that didn't intrude on conversations or flirting.

If Quicksilver but closed his eyes, he could imagine Pyrite alive and well within the white palace, prattling in his vacuous, pretty way to everyone and about everything. But Pyrite wasn't within. Pyrite would never be there again. He'd been slain by a strange, cursed dagger.

Quicksilver shook his head at his own thoughts. No, no and no. The dagger should not occupy his mind now, and the dagger was not the most relevant matter now. At this moment, with danger hemming him in on all sides, Quicksilver must consider that his brother would have heard how Pyrite had died. Pyrite had died, not in a duel, but in a fight that Quicksilver had precipitated. He'd been killed before discharging the mission Sylvanus had given him. Duels happened and elf killed elf, and normally it entailed no more than a loss of dignities, a diminution of the power that the guilty elf could withdraw from the hill for a time.

But this was different. Though Quicksilver had committed no murder, he had, indubitably, caused Pyrite's death.

What manner of wrath would Quicksilver have incurred? Would Sylvanus see his brother's deed as treason? And, if not, would he still pretend it to be such, so as to use it as an excuse for getting rid of his brother, who should have been king in his stead?

At the top of the stairs, Quicksilver rocked back and forth on the balls of his feet. His fine leather slippers had got scuffed and dusty in the fray. In fact, all of him felt sticky with sweat and grimy with dust and he must look frightfully disheveled. He'd used magic to keep himself from getting wet, but for cleaning himself, making himself presentable, he'd have preferred a warm bath in his own apartments. Malachite would gladly get Quicksilver's bath ready, or if not gladly, at least efficiently, as he had done thousands of times before. So, why should Quicksilver not go first to his own room? Why not bathe and rest, and then confront Sylvanus?

Pulling his doublet down and brushing mindlessly at the caking of mud and blood on the black velvet, Quicksilver started to turn away from the front door, ready to go down the stairs and enter through the side door into his own apartments. But just that one movement, that peek down the stairs and around the corner, revealed to him a bulky figure, in black diamond armor, leaning outside the door Quicksilver would use.

A guard. A guard in full war armor. That door was never guarded, in the normal way of things. The realm was at peace and didn't fear invasion, and lower beings could not, would not, dare the magic of the hill and enter through the door to where their betters gathered. So, why the guard?

Quicksilver could think of only one reason, and the reason he thought of ran like an icy finger down his back, the chill of it making his bright, pale hair stand at the back of his neck.

So he would be arrested if he went in that way, would he? Then he would, doubtless, also be arrested the moment he stepped into the throne room.

Squaring his shoulders, pulling down his disreputable doublet, adjusting his tangled, knotted hair and combing it through with his fingers, Quicksilver turned to enter the throne room.

If he was going to be taken, then he would be taken in front of everyone, where Sylvanus would at least be put to the trouble of holding a mock trial. Quicksilver would not be caught in a dark purlieu where he could be finished by odd magic, like what had killed his parents. Like what had killed Pyrite.

Taking a deep breath, attempting not to shake, though he felt as though ice flowed from his mind to encase his body, Quicksilver made for the open door of the palace and walked in.

No sooner had he stepped through the broad entrance, than two dark shapes, twice as bulky as Quicksilver himself and almost twice as tall, detached themselves from either side of the inner doorway. Guards, giants in full battle armor, arrayed as though to meet a foreign enemy.

Quicksilver ground his teeth and forced a smile onto his lips, and gave the guards the same careless nod he'd given them every day of his adult life, when entering or leaving through that door. If he was going to be taken, he would be taken as if he didn't expect it. Not like a guilty coward, cringing from punishment to come.

The guards ignored his nod and closed in fast, one on either side of him. Their steps clanged hard against the marble floor, the echoes of them resounding in the broad salon.

Quicksilver sped forward, trying to appear to walk casually, as if unaware of armored doom striding on either side of him.

It was useless, of course. Their steps, twice the span of his, left him no space to run. At the last second, Quicksilver felt like doing just that: running, galloping, throwing himself forward, losing himself in the throng of courtiers that he knew must be in there, somewhere. He'd run. He'd hide. He'd vanish. He'd defy his brother's justice to come and find him.

Only he couldn't see the courtiers, at least not as individuals or groups. Tears, sweat and fatigue blurred Quicksilver's vision, allowing him nothing but the impression of an amorphous, moving mass ahead. And the distance between him and that chattering mass seemed as endless, as unlikely to be crossed on mere tired legs and sore feet as the depth of the ocean, the span of the Earth.

The diamond-clad hands grasped Quicksilver's arms. The diamond that covered each finger was a thin sheet, cunningly hinged and worked by the brownies of the underworld, faithful servants of the king of elves, all.

The king of elves.

Unable to run, the pressure of the guards' hands on his arms tight enough to cut off his circulation, Quicksilver looked up and blinked, and blinked again, wishing he could wipe the sweat from his eyes.

On the throne sat his brother, powerful, mighty Sylvanus, looking down with an expression that tried to reflect pity and horror and showed, all too clearly, triumph.

Quicksilver had expected trouble, but not this much trouble. Not to be arrested as soon as he stepped on the broad marble staircase of his brother's palace—the palace that *should* have been his.

"How now?" he asked, with a show of bluff, shrugging his shoulders and attempting to shrug his arms away from the iron grip of the guards who, still holding Quicksilver tightly, divested him of both swords and his dagger. "How now, you hold me so? How dare you? I am your prince, sweet Titania's son, great Oberon's heir." As he spoke, he tried to reach into the power of the hill for strength to break away from the clutches of Sylvanus's guards.

But he found his pathway to the hill power blocked, as though the heavy stone lid of a tomb had dropped over it, an impenetrable barrier against his entrance, like a heavy oaken door braced with iron.

The power of the hill, turned away from Quicksilver, flowed to the guards, Sylvanus's mastiffs, and his slaves. Quicksilver turned his head to look first at one guard, then at the other. Both of them remained anonymous, their faces hidden behind black crystal shields that left age, identity, even gender to be guessed at. Sylvanus had outfitted his subordinates as though for combat against a full horde, obviously not trusting them even to resist the only weapons Quicksilver had left: his power of seduction, his slippery speech, and his honeyed tongue.

Nothing for it, Quicksilver thought, nothing for it but to face the traitor and to face him in front of the full court.

At least now Quicksilver had nothing to lose. He would be able to talk to Sylvanus and fling in his face the name of traitor. All the dark deeds Sylvanus had committed in secret, in the dark of night, would now be shouted from the rooftops.

A great weight that Quicksilver hadn't been aware of was lifted from his shoulders. Despite the grip on his arms, the heavy tread of his captors on either side of him, despite his being half-dragged in a most undignified way and his blood-smeared, dirt-caked clothes, Quicksilver felt freer than he had in years.

Conscious of a small smile tugging the corners of his lips upward, he regained his feet and, by almost running, walked by himself, between his guards, more dragging them than being escorted, up the broad red carpet to the throne.

Sylvanus sat on the throne, his features set in as thunderous an expression as the storm outside. Behind him, at one side of the throne stood the three cowards who had fled from the forest when Pyrite had died. To his other side—all pretense obviously being abandoned—stood the nursemaid, looking uncomfortable, overdressed and scared, in a gown spun of the finest red silk and embroidered in glaring white. Her very pale face had settled in an expression that might be either terror or stubbornness, and whose true nature Quicksilver could not guess without knowing the wench.

On either side of the throne, a throng of courtiers jostled and pushed each other so that, despite being calmer now, Quicksilver still couldn't discern faces or remember the names that went with them.

In front of the throne, the guards stopped, and, with a push of their hands on his shoulders, tried to bring Quicksilver to his knees. But Quicksilver had braced himself and withstood the push and smiled wide and innocently at his brother. "Why, my brother's majesty, what a pleasure this is, that your affection makes you so anxious to see me that you call me to your presence, hastened by your very own guards."

Sylvanus's already thunderous countenance grew stormier, and darker clouds collected upon his brow as he narrowed his eyes and hid his gaze. His lips pressed together very straight, disapproving. "Silence, traitor." He leaned forward, to glare down at Quicksilver. "Traitor, murderer, slave, who with your very hand killed the best of my vassals, the best of this kingdom."

"Not by my hand, and not killed him." Quicksilver grinned at Sylvanus, wanting but daring not to turn his head and check the massed crowd of courtiers for Ariel's slim figure. Did Ariel know? "Not by my hand, but the hand of the one he sought to kill." Was Ariel here, and did she know that her dear brother, her last defense in this harsh world, was gone? If here, what did she think, what did she feel toward Quicksilver, who'd been his reported murderer? "The mortal you'd have had him kill has slain him, in self-defense and to preserve his own life."

"A mortal?" Sylvanus thundered, disbelief in his scornful roar. "Would you have us believe, then, jesting brother, that a mortal slew Pyrite, Duke of the Air Kingdoms, Commander of the Army of the North?"

A small scream sounded, at Pyrite's name and, from the corner of his eye, Quicksilver could see a white-clad figure and a commotion of elven ladies all around it. Ariel? Or one of Pyrite's many lovers?

How many times had Quicksilver mocked Ariel's affection and run from her embraces? Yet now, flanked by guards and disgraced, hated and despised by all, he wished, he wished with all his might, he could run to her and embrace her and comfort her in her loss. They'd both lost Pyrite, both of them, friend to one and brother to the

other. Of the few allies Quicksilver had in this court, one
was dead and the other one alienated, perhaps forever.

What dark star had Quicksilver been born under? Under
what crosslight had he been whelped, that his destiny must
always run thus, contrariwise to his intent?

He thought of Pyrite's parting words, his dying curse,
and felt a shudder travel up his spine, piling dread upon
his angry words. Cold sweat formed and ran down Quicksilver's back, and he shivered with a dark premonition.
"A mortal, aye, a mortal, my brother, and well armed,
armed even with a dagger spelled to slay the sovereign of
Fairyland." The idea of saying this had come out of nowhere, or rather, had formed of the powers of that odd
dagger and its being so near—within reach of Sylvanus's
plotting. Only, the mortal who had first used it, used it to
kill Titania and Oberon, in truth couldn't be Will's father.
Had he been the murderer, then Will would be an orphan.
No. The old man wouldn't have struck the blow. But he
had, perhaps, procured the weapon, or perhaps found it in
some field after the murderer had been annihilated. That,
if nothing else, would explain the man's fear, his odd con-
fabulations. If Will's father had seen a mortal put to death
by an elf, and knew not why that had happened, surely he
was afraid of suffering the like fate. Yes, that would be
it. But the executioner of that other mortal must have been
Sylvanus alone, and it must have been quickly done, before the hill felt it and sensed the need to punish the crime
by murdering the human.

Oh, it was possible, possible, though passing rare, for
an elf to be killed by a human, and for the human to
escape ill fate. But no human could murder the sovereigns
of elvenkind and remain unscathed.

Quicksilver woke to reality, called by the silence that
greeted his words. In truth, it was not so much silence as
an odd sound, a sound of withheld breath all around. The

skittering, flying fairies cast a paler light as they heard what, no doubt, all of them regarded as a threat.

"The mortal you sent to have slain, and who has killed Pyrite, has gone free, since it wasn't royal blood that he spilled. But what of that other murderer, brother, the one who did your dark deed for you? What has become of him?" Quicksilver went on. The momentary distraction of the guard on his right allowed him to use that hand to brush at his doublet and compose the diamond at his throat. Immediately the guard regained a firm hold on his wrist. Quicksilver turned his seemingly innocent and curious eyes toward his brother as he asked, "And, bye the bye, does that fair lady by your side know that you ordered her husband to be killed?"

From the sound of harsh breathing, the gasp of the mortal, her face gone slack, her half-open mouth, Quicksilver guessed she hadn't known, and breath came more easily to his chest.

Sylvanus opened his mouth and then closed it, and shot a half-timid look over his shoulder at the nursemaid, who stared at Quicksilver, her eyes very bright, whether with tears or anger, Quicksilver could not tell.

What a clod Sylvanus was, what a fool. Had he not anticipated this would happen if he interrogated Quicksilver in public? Had he thought, then, that Quicksilver's mouth was stopped for good? And what had he thought would hold it shut? The fear of what, when Quicksilver already stood accused of treason?

"I had my reasons," Sylvanus said, to Nan, and then turned back to Quicksilver. "My reasons you well know, knave, serpent, slave, and know them for good ones. None I can explain to this assembly, but good enough."

"Aye, good enough. Good enough, I warrant, for you, my brother. You'd kill the mortal because your bed is too large and too cold," Quicksilver said.

A repressed collective titter from the ladies' side of the room, the sound of coughing that hid male chuckling, rewarded Quicksilver.

He felt almost like himself, charming and facile, but he knew that feeling for a false hope. No matter how much he embarrassed Sylvanus, he would not walk from this assembly free, nor even alive.

Sylvanus's voice shook with fury, as he next spoke. "A wit you have, my brother, and a murderous wit. I did not without reason swat at the mortal fly that buzzes on the edge of my kingdom, but even if I had, what of it? What does it signify? How does it compare to the murder of your friend, your best friend whom you did slay or at least connive at slaying, for no mortal can acquire such power to do harm to fairy without help."

"Aye, and whose help—" Quicksilver began. He could go no farther.

This time, Sylvanus had been prepared. He stretched his hand, the power of the hill coming with it, striking Quicksilver on the mouth like a punch.

Quicksilver's head rocked on his shoulders, rattling his brain. He bit his tongue and tasted blood. Swallowing, he tried to speak, tried to find words, but could not. Not in time.

"You're banished, serpent, from the hill. I'll nurture you no more, nor shall you be known as prince of this Kingdom," Sylvanus said.

And like that, even the small power that Quicksilver had been using, couldn't help using, to connect himself to hill and kin, was pulled.

The pain blinded him. Had Sylvanus pulled Quicksilver's beating heart out of his chest and held it, trembling before his living eyes, it could not have hurt more.

The voice Quicksilver hadn't been able to find now scratched out of his throat, in a loud, formless scream of pain that inflicted yet more pain as it broke through.

For a moment there was no other feeling, but that torturous pain that worked its way to each and every one of Quicksilver's pores, that stopped his heart and blurred his sight and brought his very brain to a screaming halt.

Little by little, sensations intruded through the crimson tide of pain. Quicksilver realized he'd fouled himself, but had little thought to spare even for such humiliation. The pain remained with him, more subdued but still there.

The scorching iron of torment had been withdrawn but in its place remained a constant and omnipresent sting, the protest of his body not used to subsisting without the power of the hill and scarcely knowing how to draw breath without it.

Like a puppet, whose strings are cut, he felt his arms and legs, his very flesh, go slack, and he sagged within the grip of Sylvanus's guards, and found voice for no more than a mewl, when it should have been a roar. "You can't banish me," he said, his words small and timid, losing themselves in the expanse of the great salon and maybe not reaching any ears at all, not even those of the nearest row of courtiers. And even that voice cost him so much effort, so much insane strength that he sweated just with pronouncing the words. "You can't banish me. By elven law and our parents' will, by the power of all that's sacred and that prevents a murderer from profiting from his vile act, you cannot inherit, and I am the king. The king of elves."

He might as well have proclaimed himself the king of humans, the lord of the world, or the ruler of fools. It was all the same. Sylvanus had ceased paying heed to him and looked over his shoulder, talking urgently to the nursemaid, who glowered at him and whose voice, sharp and inquisitive, could be heard in an asking tone, though her words could not be discerned, or not by Quicksilver.

Quicksilver, attempting to collect to him the meager power that was his and his alone, tried to stand on his own feet, but couldn't touch the ground with firmness, because he was being dragged, very fast, along the red carpet, by the two crystal-masked guards. His slack and powerless legs could not support his hurting body.

In this way the guards carried him to the outer stairway of the palace, and there pushed him down the steps.

He fell, as he couldn't help falling, unable to regain his footing. He hit the marble edges hard, on the way down, catching now leg, now arm, now head, now back, until, sore as though beaten by a thousand foes, he found himself in a kneeling heap at the foot of the steps and realized, with cringing shame, that he'd torn his suit in the precipitous descent.

He heard a scuffle behind him, the sound of rushing footsteps, and then the voice of the nursemaid, rolled *r*'s and broad vowels and all, raised in shrewish defiance: "I thank you, milord," she said. "I thank you for saving my husband's life. My blessings go with you, no matter who else curses you."

Pain torturing his bones, mincing his flesh, Quicksilver gathered himself. He couldn't stand but, kneeling, he half turned, bruised and quaking, to look at the stairway.

The woman, Nan, stood at the door, pushing through, as though to come out. Two guards held her back, pulling at her arms. A massed crowd behind her, too, as if more courtiers gathered there, seeking to pull her back, or perhaps to get a last gloating look at Quicksilver's piteous disgrace.

Admiring the force that gave this woman the will to stand against the very power of the hill and the disapproval of the court, Quicksilver bowed low in acknowledgment of her words.

Then she did allow herself to be dragged back in, disappearing from view. The guards resumed their accustomed position.

With enormous, incomprehensible pain and small, aching torment, Quicksilver drew himself to his feet. The rain that fell ceaselessly as it had this whole afternoon, soaked him to the skin. What little magical power he had ached, rendered too shredded and raw by its separation from the whole of the hill for him to be able to use it, even for such a small task as keeping himself dry. But the rain revived and refreshed him. Its clean coldness washed away dirt and soothed the knot of pain his body had become.

Unsteady on his feet, swaying, he looked at the palace and tried to comprehend the enormity of what had just happened. If Sylvanus had killed him, it would have been more merciful. Instead, he had sent Quicksilver away, cut off from the hill, neither elf nor mortal.

Quicksilver shivered, contemplating his new state, his horrible fall. His little power would wear down as surely as a mound of dirt wore down under the storm, and the time would come when his power was exhausted and the craving for magic would consume him. In such a state, would not his now fallible flesh lead him to enormity? What crimes would he not be willing to commit for just a touch of the hill's power? Would he not become one of those dark demons that humans feared?

Worse, the ancient legends spoke of even darker things, of a god-demon of untold antiquity, the Hunter who rode through the sky with spectral dogs, and chased down the supernatural prey of Fairyland. An elf without the protection of his hill would be all too prone to becoming such quarry.

Quicksilver blinked, shook his head at the thought. He'd never believed in the Hunter as such, nor had anyone provably seen the Hunter, for centuries untold. Elves like humans could make up stories to scare themselves. The Hunter was a myth, a word to curse with, and as such possessed only of the power that belief gave him. Quicksilver refused to believe. He refused to fear more than slow, slow, inevitable dwindling, and the temptation it would bring, the need to feed on human emotion, on human pain, and through it acquire a touch of power.

Quicksilver looked at the white palace that had been his parents', and shook his head. Not him. Never. Rather beg Will to use that dagger of his on Quicksilver's own unlucky heart.

And yet, he couldn't do that. Not yet. Not while his parents stood unavenged in the land of shadows. For if Quicksilver had brought tragedy on his own head, by his pride, his rash interference, his lack of confidence in Pyrite, his parents had done nothing to deserve their deaths, and they must be restored to the wheel of life.

Quicksilver nodded. He might never see the inside of this realm again. But his brother would not reign in it long, nor happily.

Knowing what would happen, but willing to test it, to confirm the loss of all he had been, Quicksilver raised his foot to the first step of the stairway that had felt so solid as it bruised his body and macerated his muscles. His foot went through it, as though it were fog.

He had been severed from the hill, as unable to enter it as Will. It had become as impenetrable to him as to mortals.

Scene 10

The same back alley where the story started. Will reaches down to open the same wooden gate, then stops.

Stooping in his accustomed way to open the familiar gate, Will stopped.

This time, no fear disturbed his thoughts, no strange premonition. His fears were all rational, all well-founded. The elf's—Quicksilver's—strange words at parting tortured Will's reason, not his heart. Half-heard then, they now loomed upon Will's mind obscuring all other thought.

What did John Shakespeare owe, and to whom? Why would the elf say that John owed *no man* anything? He'd said it after asking Will about the dagger.

Standing in the dark and the pouring rain outside his gate, Will pulled the knife out of its soggy sheath and tried to examine it. He remembered the blue spark that had flashed when the elf touched it, the eerie glow that contact with elf blood had brought to the ancient blade.

Now it looked like nothing much. A dirty old blade that Will had found moldering behind forgotten pelts in his father's shop. Surely the cabalistic signs on it were just decoration, misdirection, trying to make it look older than it really was, and more important.

But Will could not be easy in his mind. He remembered the flash of fire, the fantastical, magical elf dissolving into a pile of wind-blown rubbish. Fingering the dagger's blade uneasily, Will tried to remember the moment he had decided to intervene in the fight between the elves.

He remembered standing amazed, scared, while the two of them roared insults and attacked each other with their odd swords. Thinking about it, he recalled how his hand had strayed to the dagger handle and how, all unmeaning, he'd found his hand clasped upon it, holding onto it with intent and force.

Then, the urge to intervene had taken him, as though the dagger itself had whispered *yes, yes*, and sent a surge of confidence and an urge to do murder up his unwilling arm, to cloud his amazed brain.

Shivering, partly because of the freezing rain, partly because of the thoughts in his mind, Will returned the dagger to its sheath.

All these events were mad, he decided, and he a madman, led screeching and laughing with no reason, down a public street for the entertainment of passersby. What he should do is put the whole matter out of his mind, and open the rickety gate to his parents' yard and go inside, to his lonely, deserted home, and have the rest of the fast-souring ale that Nan had left brewed, and eat the rest of the hard, stale bread she'd baked two days ago, and retire to his cold, lonely bed and not think, not think at all.

But Will had trouble not thinking. All his life he'd been like a curious fox, nosing here and there, and routing all about, not so much for the possible prize, or meal, or prey, but for the joy of knowing what hid behind every rock and peeked from behind every tree and the secret meanings to be uncovered in the proper and prim poems taught by moralizing school teachers.

He couldn't lie down in an empty house and not know what made it empty and by what agency his Nan had been taken away. Nor could Will look at this dagger at his waist and not wonder at whose hand he had almost lost his life, or by whose power this dagger had been given the singular virtue of killing supernatural beings.

Taking a deep breath, he reasoned that since this weapon had come from his father's shop, it must have been set there by his father's hand. The elf had said that John Shakespeare owed no *man* anything. Did John, then, owe something to a creature not human?

A shiver ran down Will's back. Had the supernatural world of the hill affected his life long before Nan had been seduced into it? Had John's failing business been part of a hill curse?

Will's gaze wandered to his parents' back door, shut against the rainy evening outside. Even through the closed door, he could hear Joan's shrilling and Edmund's wailing.

It was possible that his father sat there, in the hub and wheel of family life, listening to his children squabble and to his wife complain. But, more likely, John hid upstairs, in his room, where he usually sought refuge from both ghostly creditors and his wife and his querulous offspring.

If Will went in through the back door, he'd run headlong into his mother, who, like a Cerberus guarding the infernal regions, would bar Will's way and prevent his going upstairs and asking his father what this dagger meant and what contact his father might have had with the hill people. However resentful and unloving Mary Shakespeare might be to everyone else, she never vented her discontent with life on John. Though he was the architect and cause of their misfortune, by a perverse turn of strained affection, Mary would protect him from the consequences of his own folly.

With sudden decision, Will turned his back on the alley and the garden behind his family's house, and, with renewed courage, walked in the pouring rain, along the muddy alley, away from the Shakespeare backyard, and toward Henley Street proper.

Despite the rain and the lateness of the hour, Henley Street still bustled with activity. Whateley's draper shop remained open, lit by a meager oil lamp and crowded with customers, as was the glover shop of Gilbert Bradley— all the more prosperous since his friend and neighbor, John Shakespeare, had stopped tending his competing business. In front of Hornby's smithy, under the awning, the tailor, William Wedgwood, stood leaning forward with every appearance of eager conversation.

As soon as Will walked onto Henley's cobbled ground, his boots still muddy from the alley, curious gazes turned to him. In a town like Stratford, where he had lived his whole life, every deviation from routine was noted, every neighbor's new affliction became a juicy topic of debate and comforting moralizing maxims.

With a suppressed sigh, Will realized he must be the object of much curiosity indeed. Surely by now Nan's absence had been noted, as much because no one would have seen her in the daily round of a Stratford housewife, as thanks to Will's mother's good offices and sharp tongue.

All would know that Nan had left, but few would credit that she had gone with any gentlemen, as Mary Shakespeare maintained. Instead, Will thought, they would laugh at Mother Shakespeare behind their hands and tell each other that, in her twenty-six years of life, Nan had only managed to hook that young Will, almost a babe and as innocent. How could she now, married and a thin and haggard new mother, have attracted rich gentlemen?

No, Will thought, as he nodded at Mistress Whateley, who stood in the doorway of her house, gazing with wild expectation into the street. No. It would be thought that Nan had gone back to Shottery, at least until some wit uncovered news of her not being at Hewlands.

Will would be pitied. To the widespread opinion that he'd made a rash and unfortunate marriage, would be joined the idea that Nan couldn't abide Mary and for that reason had left him.

Was it pity that Will saw in Mistress Whateley's dark eyes? Will gazed at the woman until she turned away.

Perhaps not. Mistress Whateley looked scared, as did her husband, who attended to his customers in the still-open shop. Will remembered that the man had two brothers who had been papist priests, and who were said to still hide somewhere about.

So, the Whateleys minded their own cares, and might not even know of Will's.

But Gilbert Bradley surely did. Looking out from amid his hanging pelts and the tables that displayed his collection of fine gloves, he gave Will a grave greeting, his eyes intent and sympathizing.

As for Wedgwood, the tailor—a suspicious character said to still have a wife in Warwick, whence he'd come, despite having got another in Stratford—no doubt the news he gave Hornby, the smith, related to the Shakespeare household. As Will passed the smithy, where Hornby stood with his hammer resting whilst his iron cooled on the anvil, both men stopped talking and regarded him with an amazed expression, which couldn't have been more searching had Will been a marvelous being, a dragon or a unicorn, or another fantasy dredged up from faraway lands and the imaginations of ancient scribes.

Wedgwood, Will noted, held the sheers and measures of the tailor's trade in his hand and, in his hurry to bring whatever gossip he'd brought to the smith, had thrust his feet into the wrong slippers—the left one in the right foot and the right one in the left foot.

Nodding his head and keeping his gaze averted, Will made it to the front door of his parents' home. It was unlocked, as it would remain until the family went to bed.

Pushing it open, Will slid into the front hall. This room had seen better days, and Will remembered those days, when polished trunks of good wood, and fine benches graced it, and his father cobbled together great deals within, trading wool and barley like children trade pretty pebbles at their games. It still didn't look shabby, or not as shabby as the Shakespeare lifestyle had become. There was one fine walnut trunk, ornamented with a fine pewter vase that Mother Shakespeare had held onto as the last vestige and proof of her own almost gentle birth. On the walls, too, there remained three of the painted cloths left to Mary by her prosperous yeoman father, Robert Arden, descended from the great Arden family who had once owned all this great region of fields and forests.

Slowly, carefully Will closed the door and stepped gently into the front room, careful to avoid making the floorboards creak. He needn't have worried. Any noise he might have made lost itself in the shrieking of his siblings and other noise from the kitchen. His mother's voice was raised in upbraiding—from the sound of it—Gilbert, Will's eighteen-year-old brother: "And if you think you'll be a Latin scholar—"

Will shuddered and tiptoed across the room.

One of the painted cloths represented Judith driving the tent stake into Holofernes's brain. The other one detailed, in vivid realism, the dance-flushed Salome holding up the gory head of John the Baptist.

By the stairs, on the way up, a painted cloth, lovingly lifelike, showed the massacre of innocents, with red-handed soldiers striking off the heads of wailing infants.

These cloths and their painted mayhem had riveted Will's eye and imagination as a child. When he was very young, he'd feared walking down the steep stairs in the night, lest the painted Judith or the realistic Salome should step down from her cloth and kill him.

Now he gave them but a cursory look, and their images spoke to him only of pointless death and violence, and of turmoil much like that which submerged his life.

He started up the stairs. Though the top of the stairs was the same as in the house where Will now lived—a mere square cut out of the top floor's boards—when walking into the upper floor, Will found himself in quite a different place. The space into which he emerged was barely large enough to hold a standing adult and on each side from there, a door opened, and a wooden wall extended, dividing the space into three chambers: Will's parents', his sister's room, and the boys' room.

The air smelled heavy with human waste. Will wrinkled his nose. His mother had neglected to empty the chamber pots, again, and, from the heavy, sour smell, for more than a day. The last few years that Will had lived in the house, he'd often done it himself, in the evening, carrying the waste to the outhouse so he didn't have to smell it all night long.

The door to the left led to his parents' room and Will opened the door and stepped into a roughly square bedroom. Its walls met at the slightly crooked angles that betrayed the work of an inexpert carpenter. The chamber's exiguous space barely compassed a bed and a shabby pine trunk. Shutters closed the one small window to all but the scant light and little air that filtered between their imperfectly joined boards.

On the bed sat John Shakespeare, fully dressed, in a russet suit, shabbier even, and more outmoded, than his son's. He turned toward the door as it opened and stared at Will, amazed, as if he'd never seen such a creature as his oldest son, and didn't know what to make of this wondrous apparition.

"Blessing, Father," Will said, and bowed his head.

"Will!" his father said, in great wonder, as if Will had been traveling, and long gone, and had now come back to regale his family with the tales of his unbelievable adventures. "Will. How are you, boy? How do you fare?"

"Well, and well enough, Father," Will answered. His father looked much like Will himself and, as such, stood before Will as a warning of what the ravaging years would do to his smooth pale skin, his proud, jet-black curls. His father's hair had deserted the front of his head, leaving his forehead high and unprotected, a vast, domed expanse that met with a receding line of curly hair gone more grey than black and more white than either. He'd lost weight since Will had last seen him, and his gaunt, pale face, covered in lines, looked like much creased and erased vellum that will neither look even, nor lie flat. His mouth, once firm and proud, had softened and drooped and even now, as he looked at Will, John's lips sagged and seemed to tremble, as though in constant terror.

"Does your mother not tell me that your wife has left you, boy?" his father asked. And, in a sudden animation of gaze, an almost smile of his slack mouth, he added, "Are you coming back home, to live with us? I told you, you should learn my business—the shop needs tending and I cannot . . ." His voice dwindled away to inaudibility.

Will shook his head, not answering either question. "Father, your creditors, they are not human, are they?"

His father's eyes turned up to meet Will's. Darker than Will's, a chocolate-brown, John Shakespeare's eyes resembled the eyes of a loyal mastiff, a good hunting dog, faithful to his master and ever ready to fetch whatever quarry the master had uncovered. Right then, staring at Will, John's eyes looked like those of a dog whose master has kicked him for no reason. "Creditors?" he asked.

Will huffed, an impatient sound. In his last years in grammar school, when his father's fortunes had already started declining, and his presence in the shop was a some-time thing, but while the old man still retained his pride and standing, Will and John had often argued—long, barbed, hopeless arguments. The young rooster trying to oust the old, his mother had called it, responding to their discord with an indulgent laugh and a shrug.

Will, in the surety of his grammar education, had found his near-illiterate father, who but knew his letters and not that well, an encumbrance and a shame. Again and again, despairingly, he had argued with his father about his archaic beliefs, his hopelessly limited vocabulary, his narrow view of the world, and his deference to those he called his betters.

Over the last two years Will had repented of those arguments. Feeling the weight of having to earn a living crush his young shoulders, he had, for the first time, understood why his father lacked the interest or the energy to learn Latin or study philosophy.

But now, looking at John's slack mouth, his empty, injured eyes, Will felt his impatience return, and impatience animated his voice as he said, "Father, someone just told me you owed no man anything, but he said it as though he meant you owed something to someone who was not a man."

"A man?" John's gaze traveled, helpless and hopeless, the length of Will's gesturing arm, then returned to Will's face, and looked at it in measuring wonder.

Will walked closer to his father, put his hands on the

old man's shoulders but refrained from shaking him. "The people of the hill, Father, what did you do for them? Do you know anything of a magic dagger and what it was used for?" Thinking it might help, tired of his father's dull, unwitting look, as vague and as blank as a babe's, Will brought his dagger out and displayed it in front of his father's eyes.

John's slack mouth opened and let out a long scream, like the wail of a man pierced through the heart. He clambered fully up on the bed and away from Will and the dagger.

"He promised that he would protect me," Will's father said. "He swore he would keep me safe and nothing would happen, but night after night their ghosts come, and in my dreams they walk and demand vengeance." The words came out in a gibbering torrent, and John covered his face with his hands and rocked back and forth on his worn mattress. "The Queen Titania and King Oberon, or so he said their names were, and not mortal, for sure not mortal, nor would I have slain mortal blood, mindful I am of my immortal soul, but these creatures are not mortal nor do they have a soul, so he said, but they haunt me, and soulless though they might be, their shades walk, mourning and pitiful, and demand that I avenge them or free them, and he said he can do nothing for it, nothing, though he arranged for the dagger, and had it bespelled, with the words and the mystic symbols of his people, upon primeval iron, but he said that he couldn't keep me safe, should I show myself and he—"

"Who, Father, who?" And Will leaned forward, dagger still in hand, trying to get sense from his father's gibbering mouth, his scared, searching eyes.

"Unnatural son." His mother's voice sounded behind Will, from the door into the room, and, before Will could turn around to face her, he felt her hand on his shoulder and, off balance, found himself spun around and pushed against a wall.

"Unnatural son," his mother wailed. Her hair, which had been very pale blonde and was now white, had been for some time confined in a braid at her back, but now escaped in a halo of straggles and wisps that surrounded her face like a hedge of thorns. And, despite privations, she had remained round and soft, like fermented dough, her spherical face looking like a fine doughy pudding with plums for eyes. "Unnatural son, would you kill your father?"

Off balance when he was grabbed and pushed, Will slammed into the wall with full force, and struggled to catch his breath. Kill his father? Remembering the dagger in his hand, he brought it up and looked at it, before mastering a pale smile. "No, Mother. I would just know where this dagger comes from."

But his mother had started speaking at the same time: "If it's for your inheritance, I must tell you there is none to be had, for we have used the last of our money to bring you up and make you such a fine lord that now you disdain—"

"Mother," Will said, annoyed by her misunderstanding him, by her insisting on speaking as though he, of all people, didn't know very well that there was no inheritance to be hoped for here.

"Do not you interrupt me. Our money has made you a fine learned gentleman, hasn't it? And fool enough to marry the Shottery wench." Her doughy cheeks trembled. "And fool enough, now to attempt—"

"Mother, I never attempted against my father's life. I only wanted to know where he got this dagger." He lifted the weapon for his mother's inspection.

This produced a wondrous effect. Never before had Will seen his mother speechless.

She stared at the dagger and at Will, and her hand went up in reflexive habit and traced the sign of the cross again and again on her forehead. "You found that, then," she said, her voice strangled. "You found it, then. We should have buried it, but I was afraid it would call the attention of the good neighbors to us."

"The good neighbors?" Will asked. All their neighbors were good. Well, excepting maybe Wedgwood, and perhaps the Whateleys, although his mother certainly wouldn't object to the Whateleys's priestly connections. "The good neighbors, Mother?"

She crossed herself again and her bow-shaped mouth quivered. "The people under the hill."

Will's father whimpered from the shadows on the other side of the bed.

"They came to your father and offered him good luck forever if he should only kill their tyrannical rulers. And your father . . ." Mary cast a pitying look at her husband. "Your father, fool that he was, took the offer, thinking that he wouldn't be slaying a Christian thing and no harm could come to him." She crossed herself once more. "I told him not to involve himself in such dealings, with such creatures, but there, he did it, and now they haunt him and he fears their revenge night and day." She turned to Will and her expression changed from fear to anger. "And now you, unlucky child, unchancy whelp, have to come and show your father that dagger, and attract the eyes of the creatures to our home."

"Nan was taken by them," Will said, hearing his voice but not believing he said this, even as the words resounded clear if flat in his own ears. "By them she was taken and by them held captive." He slid the dagger back in its sheath as he spoke.

His mother stared for a moment, her dark eyes uncomprehending. Then she cackled in gloating laughter. "So, that's who took her. I've been wondering. Well, they're welcome to her and good riddance. That whelp of hers, you'll find, was theirs and none of ours. A witch she is and a slut, and has had commerce with them before, you'll find." As she spoke, in a half-whispered, malicious current, Mary grabbed Will's arm, guided him to the door of the room, and half shoved him toward the stairs while she closed the door behind them. "Leave her be there, and do not get yourself enmeshed with those creatures. You come back and live with us, Will, and be the man of the house, and look after your brothers and sisters. Your father cannot do it. Your poor father . . ."

Will started down the steps, ahead of Mary, moving faster than he would normally have, seeking to evade her sermon, her pleas, seeking to be alone so he could think.

But she followed him close and fast and, at the bottom of the stairs, before he could head out through the front door, she had clutched his wrist. "Your poor father lives in fear of the creatures' vengeance. But he has said he will teach you the glover's art. Surely you remember enough from when you helped him, as a boy. You'll need only those refinements requisite to becoming a master in it."

He shook his head, and tried to escape toward the door, but his mother pulled him toward the hallway. "Well, and you were always a stubborn one, but you know you'll come to it, you know. You'll come back home and stay with us, and live with us again. Yes, you will and you know it." She pulled him down the hallway. "And meanwhile, you'll need food. I'll wager you haven't even eaten yet, have you? Come, child, come and eat. How can you survive without a woman to keep house for you?"

To tell his mother that she couldn't keep house for herself would be unkind and unfilial, but even so, Will had to bite his tongue to prevent himself saying it.

She pulled him all the way into the kitchen with its odors of soot and old cooking.

Will's brother Gilbert, a sullen eighteen-year-old, sat at the table, with his well-worn book of Latin grammar spread open in front of him, working steadily by the meager light of the guttering mutton-grease taper set in a candleholder in the middle of the stained and scarred oak table. Beside him, Richard, barely nine, worked steadily on a pair of wax tables, drawing numbers and letters on the flat sheets of wax with a wooden stylus. Joan sat by the smoking fireplace, mending some dark wool garment. Edmund ran hither and thither, glad of his own two legs and the freedom that walking on them gave him. He ran toward Will, and grabbed hold of his legs, and looked up at his brother with a radiant smile.

On the wall hung another one of Mary Shakespeare's precious painted cloths. This one, blackened by soot and disfigured from hanging in the damp kitchen, showed the prodigal son coming home to the arms of his old, long suffering father. In his childhood, this had been Will's favorite painted cloth, but now he was glad of the smoke and dirt that obscured the images on it.

He was not a prodigal, he told himself. Nor was he coming home. This was not home, but a dark hideout, into which had vanished his parents' good fortunes and what had been once a happy family life.

"All wet," Edmund told Will, still looking up at him, still smiling.

"You're right, I'm all wet," Will said, conscious of his soaked wool suit for the first time since entering the house. He smiled down at Edmund and ruffled the boy's curls.

Edmund watched him with a gap-toothed smile.

Would Susannah one day smile at her father like that? Would he recover Susannah before she was this age? And if not, what would Susannah think, what would she say, of her father? Would Susannah be raised in that not-quite-real world of fairyland and grow up calling father to that creature on the throne?

Will's mother had said to stay away from the hill people. And had not his father, before him, fallen into the trap of agreeing to kill a sovereign of elves, to his own undoing? Had it been Lady Silver who'd gulled Will's father into such precipitous ruin? That would explain how both she and her brother knew of John Shakespeare's downfall.

And yet, Will would swear that the young gentleman, Quicksilver, had been shocked at the knife, and at its being in Will's hand, and at its effect on the blond assailant.

Will remembered Quicksilver's grief. He'd cried true tears over his friend-turned-enemy. Could it all be a lie? Had such a cunning play been enacted for his father too? Or was this different and would Will be righting what his father had set wrong?

Will wished he could see the future, scry the entrails of events to be, tell what would happen tomorrow and the day after, and know his doom or his fortune beforehand so that, knowing them, he could lay his plans accordingly.

His mother bustled to the keeping cupboard and then to the fireplace, poured some greasy broth into a clay cup for Will, and set it, with a piece of bread, on the table, next to Gilbert.

A glance at his brother's work showed Will a laboriously written essay, full of corrections and erasures. Gilbert lacked the quick mind that had allowed Will to sail through grammar school with little effort and time enough for pranks and carousing. In contrast, Gilbert, who looked much like Will in stature and feature, earned each one of his achievements, through painstaking study, much repeating, and effortful memorizing of every required thing.

Strange thing, at least as far as Will believed, was that

all the masters seemed to prefer Gilbert to his brother. Perhaps because Gil was slower to laugh at their mistakes and would never, ever, dream of making a joke at their expense.

Richard, too, like Gilbert, was slow but conscientious, working laboriously and doggedly, at schoolwork.

Only Edmund, Will thought, promised to be like his eldest brother, a free spirit, laughing and full of joy. Although, Will thought ruefully, perhaps Edmund should learn by example to look where his joy took him so that he didn't find himself early married and ill-paid.

Edmund, seeing his brother gazing at him, clambered up on his lap and leaned his face against Will's soaked jacket.

"Put the babe down," Will's mother said. "Or he'll be catching his death from your wet clothes."

Will and Edmund ignored her. Will gave his mug of broth a dubious look, thinking death might very well lurk in that also.

But he'd eaten nothing at the alehouse, though he'd drunk more than his rightful fill, and, tortured by alcohol and hunger and the tension of the last few hours, his stomach turned on itself, in acid rage.

He took his bread and dipped it into the broth, fishing out a tangled forest of fine-cut cabbage and a couple of fat pieces of mutton. Normally, he would have turned his nose up at it, but not now. He was too starved from the long walk home. He hadn't eaten since the night before, having neglected both to have breakfast and to take anything with him to eat while at Wincot.

Even so, with his taste sharpened by hunger, the broth did not taste good. But it was edible. Will ate the solids, fished out by the bread, then drank down the liquid in a quick swallow.

"How do you expect not to catch a fever yourself, sitting there soaked?" Will's mother said. She stood in front of him, hands on her hips, on either side of her broad, black skirt. The apron in the middle of that skirt was not so much white as different tones of yellow and green, where different spills had tinged it over the week.

Nan always kept her apron white, and changed it when it got dirty. She had three or four of them, always ready, fresh-washed each Thursday.

Will sighed. "Hard to catch a fever," he said. "In this warm weather."

His meal—to grace it with such an undeserved name— was done. Leaning against him, Edmund breathed regularly, slowly. Had he fallen asleep, then, despite the wetness of Will's clothes?

"Oh, I suppose you'd know it all," Will's mother said. Her hard, dark blue eyes glared at him. They'd been soft, he remembered, when he was very young. Soft and yielding like a spring sky, always ready to grow moist with tears of joy or sadness and shower those blessings upon all comers. They'd grown hard like the waters of the Avon veiled by ice. "You'd know it all, and guess it all, and go about your life as if you learned better than your elders and those who have established the way of life we lead."

"Mother," Will warned, guessing where it would end, from past harangues.

"No. No. But listen to me in this, if nothing else, child, listen to me. Do not become entangled with them, under the hill." Once more she crossed herself, on the words. "Give them a wide berth and trust them not. For lies are their very essence and substance, their being engendered by the father of all lies."

Will started to rise, slowly, slowly easing Edmund onto the bench, and attempting to lean him against Gilbert, who recoiled from the babe's touch. He needed to think, but he couldn't do it in his mother's presence and under the heavy shower of his mother's philosophy.

Abandoning his efforts to balance the sleeping, limp Edmund against the skittish Gilbert, Will stood up and carried the babe to Joan, by the fireplace.

Joan looked up with a scowl. "Can't you see I'm mending?" she said, lifting a wool stocking with a puckered seam along its length. The seam looked to Will like a mouth pursed in displeasure.

"Aye," Will said, and smiled at Joan, ignoring his mother's continued ranting. "You're mending very ill. But take the babe, take him to his bed. I must be gone."

"Be gone where?" his mother asked, picking up on the conversation, as if the comment had been addressed to her. "Be gone why? The strumpet has left and taken her child with her. You can have your old room back and live in it, with Gilbert and Richard and Edmund. Why don't you go up and change your clothes? There's an old suit of your father's—"

"No, Mother." Will raised his eyebrows, expressing long-suffering lack of patience to Joan.

Joan giggled, put down her sewing, and opened her arms to receive the sleeping Edmund.

"There's a girl," Will said. "There's a good girl. Thank you, Joan."

"And where will you be gone? To the empty house?" his mother asked, from behind him.

"Yes, to the empty house." Will turned around and faced his mother, squaring his shoulders. He was taller than Mary by a full head. When had that happened and why hadn't he noticed until now? "To the empty house, Mother, to think."

His mother started crying. "Only promise me you'll leave the hill people alone," she said.

Will shrugged and made toward the door, but Mary interposed her own body.

She wiped at her tears with her stained apron. "When I bore you, how happy I was, and how I thanked God for sending me a son to replace the two daughters who had died. And now, how I wish it had been you and not Margaret who lay in a coffin in the churchyard. For a strumpet's sake, you'd get yourself killed and leave your family unprotected." She cried with abandon. "Is this the gratitude you owe your sire, who gave you life and who supported you above your deserts when you were little? Is this it?" Again, she took her apron to her cheeks and wiped her tears, leaving behind more green and yellow smears. "Promise me, Will. Promise me you won't meddle in such matters."

But Will walked around her and out into the rainy night, his thoughts in turmoil. He scarcely paid mind to his mother's crying, her loud wailing, the tears that rolled down her cheeks, and the increasing smears left by her apron on her wet face. His father had trod this same road before? He wasn't in this nightmare alone? His father had tangled with *them* before?

He thought of Lady Silver hanging on his arm, telling him that if he killed the usurper of the elves' throne, he would have his Nan and little Susannah restored to him, and set the world aright. He thought of her perfume, her warmth, her cloying nearness, and felt a tightening in his groin, and wondered if the thing that had thus affected him existed at all. Or was she an illusion, nothing more?

He would go to his house and there he would wait for Silver's appearance, and her explanation. And then he'd decide. But he feared no ghost and no apparition, like the ones who tortured his father, if by braving them he could get his Nan back.

As he opened the back door to his empty, dark kitchen, he thought that a haunted life with Nan would be preferable to a quiet one without her.

Scene 11

☙❧

In a clearing in the forest of Arden, Quicksilver sits against an old tree, in his male aspect, one hand at his sword, another on his belt.

Quicksilver sagged against the trunk of a large oak tree, and tried to gather the strength to walk farther. He'd had enough stamina, barely enough, to drag himself away from the palace, out of sight of those who would rejoice in his weakness and his torment.

But here, a scant hundred yards from the palace, he collapsed against the tree, and slid down till he sat on the spongy moss of the forest floor. He let tears of fatigue and pain run down his bruised cheeks, mingling with the cold rain that soaked through his fine clothing and turned it into a sodden mess.

Beneath his right eye, his cheek throbbed, where he suspected a purple bruise would form later.

His power suffered like a creature eviscerated, raw and bleeding where its innards had been torn out of its living body. It screamed pain along his physical nerves, pounded his brain with the thought of its torment. His body, his physical body itself, felt not so far from evisceration. He'd examined himself for broken bones and found none, but his bruised and abraded flesh throbbed with rhythmic pain from his fall down the stairs.

Tears flowed down Quicksilver's face, while the night turned darker, the rain heavier, and lightning zigzagged across the sky, far away.

Through the fog of tiredness in his mind, Quicksilver knew that he was late, that he should have been somewhere, that he had an appointment. Like an image from someone else's dream, he remembered himself and Will walking and talking along the forest path. He'd promised Will that Lady Silver would come to him tonight, hadn't he?

But how to manage it? The transformation itself would take no power. In fact it took power—a small but continuous drain—to prevent himself from changing between male and female aspects at random. But he would need to change his clothes before meeting Will, and that would require willful use of his magic skill and his dwindling, painfully raw power.

Oh, there was still magic in Quicksilver, to be sure. There would be. Not in vain had he been engendered by the sovereigns of the elf race. But the magic in him was only his, a small trickle when compared to the great river of the hill—a small spider web, nothing more, while the hill's magic was a net tied together with diamond threads.

Quicksilver felt tired, old, worn out by this hour's severance from the hill more than by the fifty years before it.

He must gather himself together, call to himself what power he had. He must avenge himself on the traitor. He must recover his position and his place in the hill . . . which was to say that he had to become king, since Sylvanus would never allow Quicksilver back in the hill while Sylvanus ruled.

Quicksilver recalled Pyrite's death and wished to the

human gods and the terrors of elvenkind, that he didn't
have to drag his own, worthless carcass through his futile
life. If only it had been him and not Pyrite who'd vanished
in a flickering of color, a scattering of nothing, echoes of
power eaten up by the forest and carried somewhere by a
supernatural wind. If only it had been him, bleeding his
supernatural life onto the forest ground.

If only his too, too solid flesh could melt, taking with
it his pains, his bruises, his cowardice, his all too fallible
character. Oh, if only he'd never been born and Sylvanus,
happy and powerful, were the rightful king of Elfland.

But thinking of Sylvanus reminded Quicksilver of his
parents, of Pyrite. All of them were gone; all of them now
resided in a world of dwindling shadows, and would remain there till they ceased to exist or until Quicksilver,
their son, their friend, won their release.

Quicksilver cackled. He could no more release those
loved shades than he could run, or fly, or rule elvenkind.

The thought was like a chill wind, and leaves and plants
around him fluttered with it, as if it had been, indeed,
physical wind. Quicksilver wrapped his arms around himself. How could he exact vengeance from his oppressor?
How could he regain his position in Elvenland? He had
no power, and he was alone. For the first time in his life,
he had neither friends nor admirers, not even one syco-
phantic hypocrite wishing him well.

Hatred gathered within the huddled mass of his misery,
like thunder that erupts from dark clouds. Hatred for Sylvanus, for the hill, for the broad halls, the marble floors,
the delicate, impossible columns, the trappings and set-
tings of Quicksilver's own former happiness.

Standing alone in the forest, he sent his hatred outward
from him. Hatred for the tyrant who had despoiled him
and, not content with that, had torn him from the hill and
as good as killed him. No, worse than killed him. Quick-

silver smarted at the pain, the injustice of it, and thought of Sylvanus in a hot gust of detestation. Oh, that hatred could be all that Quicksilver was, and Quicksilver become his hatred and his hatred Quicksilver, so that no more would the prince be fallible or scared, or hurting, but would be instead the towering rage, the diamantine edge of hatred. Oh, that his hatred could grow hair and teeth and claws and fangs, and crawl through the forest like a beast, and steal upon Sylvanus's satisfied majesty, and satiate its raw craving in the steaming heat of Sylvanus's entrails. He wished for no more.

A noise like horses, the echo of a hunting bugle sounded, over the roiling discontent of thunder, echoing Quicksilver's own cravings, his painful thoughts.

For a moment he thought that the sound came from within, that it was the echo of his own call to the hunt—the hunt for his vengeance and the satisfaction of his hatred. Then the bugle sounded again and with it mixed the joyous barks of dogs who have uncovered prey. Quicksilver realized that the sound came from outside, from the forest drowned in unseasonable rain.

Who would be hunting in this weather? Certainly no human. The puzzle awakened Quicksilver's rational mind, and he worried at it as a dog at his bone. Sylvanus? But no. Sylvanus would be busy appeasing the nursemaid and any—did Quicksilver dare believe it?—voice that might be raised to protest Quicksilver's expulsion. As for the other lords and ladies of the court, Quicksilver couldn't imagine their braving the ruin of their silken clothes on such a pursuit as hunting during a storm.

No, none of them would. They were too satisfied with their condition, too contented with their honors and powers. Too satisfied, even, to protest the expulsion of the crown prince, the rightful heir to the throne, the one who should have been king. Quicksilver ground his teeth and, while the barking of dogs sounded ever closer and the hunting bugle made itself heard again, he wished he could walk into the court and strip the lords and ladies of their finery and of their power, beat them, and throw them out of the palace and make them all go bruised and naked into the storm outside, so they would know, for once, what had been inflicted on Quicksilver, their unmourned prince.

You can. Out of nowhere, a voice came, a booming voice filled with the sonorous echoes of rolling thunder, with the thunderclap's majestic uncaring. *You can.*

The words were not pronounced and the voice echoed not so much in Quicksilver's mind as in his sinews, in the very fibers and nerves that wove his body into being. His heart started up, of its own accord. The Hunter? Oh, nonsense, the Hunter didn't exist. It would be another of the pantheon of beings that elves or humans or both had created and given life to by their belief. A jumped-up supernatural phantom who thought to scare the more ancient and true race of elves.

Smarting at the insult, Quicksilver managed to stand up by clawing his way up the trunk of the oak tree, then leaned against it for support. He'd not let some godling see him as weak and damaged and easy prey for its tricks and goading. His macerated body hurt with every movement, but he stood, and with his magic vision alert peered around tree trunks, and behind and beyond them, for a hint of this being's nature and appearance. He saw nothing.

Some of these once-divinities had become so debased as to be little more than insects. Yet the voice had sounded booming, as if it brought great power behind it.

Supernatural laughter sounded.

Great. It would be a prankster god, or a minor faun, one of those who had clung to the elven race and, on the peripheries of it, gone on existing. With their goat feet tapping to the beat, they'd often join dances in the woodland glens. But they were minor nuisances, with little status, no more important than the serving fairies. How would one of them dare address a prince of Elvenland, even a fallen prince? Quicksilver clenched his hands tight, in painful, angry fists.

The bugle echoed again, and a great wind shook the trees and swayed the bushes. Like frozen breath, it gusted over Quicksilver, making him shiver and causing his teeth to chatter.

Up, the voice said. A hunting horn sounded.

And up Quicksilver looked, past the sparse canopy of the trees, to the lowering skies that hung over the ancient trees of Arden.

Against the leaden grey skies, a darker shape loomed, the shape of a gigantic man astride a horse, holding a horn. Around that shape, other shapes, immense feral-looking dogs, clustered and growled, and nosed forward with impatience, as though smelling Quicksilver's weak magic, his dwindling strength.

Fear clutched at Quicksilver like nausea, coiling around his bruised body like a chain of good forged iron that sucks away what strength and power it finds in elven flesh. The sound of his own heartbeat deafened him. He wanted to run, but he could do no more than take a step back and shake his head, and say, "You don't exist."

The figure on the horse threw its head back and laughed, a full-throated laugh. Its mirth made Quicksilver shiver and he clamped his teeth together, to avoid their chattering noise announcing his cowardice to the forest. Through clenched teeth, he spoke, his voice indistinct and flat. "And if you exist . . . if you exist . . . then you prey on us." His voice lost itself without echoes into the roaring storm. "On my kind. And I'm your quarry." He wished that his kind had prayers, aversion rituals, of the sort with which humans used to attempt to exorcise elves. Ineffective those rituals might be, but they gave the one who used them a momentary feeling of protection. Quicksilver hadn't even that delusion to hold as a shield between himself and his approaching end. He thought of Pyrite cursing him to be devoured by the Hunter, and his mouth worked, worked, searching to create the words of an nonexistent prayer, a protective spell.

The Hunter shook his head. *Some of you are my prey, but not you, little one. What you have, the power you hold, is not worth my harvesting. I prey on those still connected to the hill, so through them I can suck the hill's living power. Not on you, little one. Not on you.*

His words dripped with derision, revealing Quicksilver as a small, scurrying thing, a hare with fur and tough, gristly meat, a prize no hunter would claim. He was just that now, no more. A creature that might be trampled beneath the hooves of the Hunter's supernatural horse, but one that had nothing to fear from the Hunter's weapons, his well-aimed lance.

In a voice that barely sounded above his booming, beating heart, Quicksilver asked, "But then why . . . why come for me?"

Because you have vengeance in your heart and hatred in your soul and both call to me, as to a like mind, the Hunter said. He climbed down from his horse, each motion so human, so natural, that it made his dark shape, the power that bristled from it, seem even more obscenely impossible. Striding like a man or an elf, the Hunter stepped down onto clouds and descended majestically, as though walking down an invisible staircase toward Quicksilver. His horse and dogs stayed behind, and the horse neighed softly, extending its neck as if to look down at its master. *For you, and others like you, I have an offer. Take the power from me, and I'll give you enough for your vengeance. Enough for all you wish.* He stood quite close to Quicksilver, and close by he looked even more impossible and more human, both. His face was chiseled with beauty that made elves seem half-haphazard things, lumps of clay thrown together by a blind potter. His black curls looked like they'd each been sculpted and woven and made the most perfect expression of his nature. But his thundercloud-grey eyes seethed with coldness, with dark that was the absence of light. And, though he wore a normal enough velvet suit of dark red, the color of old blood, over his perfect humanlike shape, where the chest should be that housed a living being's heart, was nothing: a void, a roiling darkness, boiling like a cauldron and swirling like a dark, sucking whirlpool.

You have great things in mind, that you'd do if you had power, the Hunter said. *I'll give you power.* Slowly, the Hunter extended his hand to Quicksilver. It looked like a human hand, strong and square, covered in dark red gloves. From that hand, all around it, a river of power flowed, such as made the hill's power small and miserly. *Take it,* the dark, booming voice said, sounding like velvet sliding across the night sky. *Take it, take it, little one, be done with it. Why hunger when you can have it all, the strength and power of the beings that existed before humanity? Take this old power, from when the stronger ancestors of your kind reigned alone and romped through the sacred glades, feasting and flirting and fighting and, in their wars, their feuds, their assassinations, offering sacrifice and homage to me.*

Quicksilver stepped back still farther, though everything in him called him to that supernatural, extended hand, to the power that flowed from it like manna from the human heaven. Hungry, cold, filled with fear, Quicksilver longed for that power, for that strength. Strength enough to crush Sylvanus like a gnat. Strength enough to live and love and be loved. Strength and power enough to make Quicksilver the greatest sovereign of elvenkind.

Yet some ancient instinct spoke in Quicksilver, whispering amid the thundering of his desire for power. Some instinct that made him step back and back and back, feeling roots under his feet and sliding around the trunks of trees. That power came from sacrifices, from unhallowed sacrifices of elven blood and elven might. The Hunter had said it. The power would be tainted and, like the creature's clothes, stained with old blood, with magical perversion. This was no benevolent sprite of the woods, but an ancient, dark predator, full of hunger and evil. Why would such a one offer Quicksilver strength and power?

"The price?" Quicksilver asked, his voice just above a rasp. "The price?" He remembered Titania telling him, in the happy days of his long-ago childhood, that a magical being must always tell you the price of his magic.

The booming laughter sounded again. *Cunning, are you?* the Hunter said. *Oh, we'll be great allies, little one. Yes, there is a price, but a small one. After an eternity of enjoying my power, or when you have nowhere else to go, you will be called.* The Hunter lifted his other hand, which held a dark bugle. *And then must you come and be with me, throughout eternity.* Around him, dark furry shapes clustered, as though called by his words. *But you'll never die, and you'll never fear again, and you'll be stronger than all men, stronger than all elves.*

The dogs nuzzled at the Hunter's legs in a confusion of grey fur and glittering red eyes. They gave off a smell, not the normal smell of canine fur and well-fed flesh, but a smell as of an open grave. Quicksilver gagged and stepped back.

They looked more like wolves than dogs, but even for wolves they sported too heavy a jaw, too massive a skull. They must be primeval wolves who first had clustered around men's fires, and fed on men's scraps. Or maybe on the scraps from primeval elven fires. The Hunter was that old. Quicksilver could feel that in the ancient, sparkling power that ran from the Hunter's hand, and clustered around the creature's shape, and stretched blue-white tendrils toward Quicksilver, calling to him with its promises of vengeance and power.

The dogs neared Quicksilver, sniffing at the reaching tendrils of power, whining. They looked at the power and then at Quicksilver, with baleful glowing red eyes.

Come, boy, come, the Hunter said. *Will you take my power or not? I'll not wait forever.*

Quicksilver's head reeled, and he trembled. This was how it must feel to Will to face Quicksilver himself. To him, Quicksilver must be as the Hunter to Quicksilver, a strange, unfathomable power. Only Quicksilver was using Will for his own purposes. How did this creature mean to use Quicksilver? "I don't know," Quicksilver said. "I don't know if you mean me no harm. I don't know what your question is, nor what I'm answering."

To be or not to be? the Hunter asked, a suggestion of laughter behind his words. *To be alive and well and powerful, or to dwindle away until you're nothing, less than nothing, not even a memory in your people's mind?*

To be or not to be, Quicksilver thought, and repeated the words to himself like a prayer, a magic talisman. His knees shook and his body ached. He longed for the power in that proffered hand; longed, like men long for immortality. He could feel it, sparkling and cold, and strong. His for the asking. He could mend the bruises and tears on his body. He could avenge himself on Sylvanus and his treasonous court, and crush to nothing his enemies beneath the heels of his dancing slippers. Only touch that open hand, only accept that power, and Quicksilver could have it all. Power and life everlasting. The price was no price.

No price at all. To be one like the Hunter, to live with him. Quicksilver smiled. Why, to live forever was a reward, not a price.

Almost on its own, Quicksilver's hand started forward, to meet the proffered source of such blessings.

The clustering shapes around the Hunter growled and stared, and whined for the taste of Quicksilver's flesh. But if Quicksilver lived with the Hunter, he'd be protected from his dogs, would he not?

Quicksilver's hand stopped. He looked at the dogs. To be with the Hunter for eternity. What could that mean? The Hunter held no court. He had no companions save his dogs.

His dogs. Quicksilver stared at the whining pack, their glowing eyes. Their rotting-corpse miasma surrounded him.

As if with his mind's eye, Quicksilver saw this was the answer to the riddle. If he took the Hunter's power, then the price would be to serve as the Hunter's dog for eternity, nosing out prey for this ancient evil.

"No," he yelled.

Think, the Hunter said. *Think. I've not lied to you. You'll still have your vengeance. And living in another form has to be better than dwindling away to nothing.*

Of a sudden *nothing* seemed like blessed, sacred rest. An unending sleep.

Quicksilver backed away from the outstretched hand, from the stench of the dogs, from the Hunter's dubious offers.

Still he must force his legs away, step by step, drag his body away from the current of power, like an unwilling horse being pulled back from an overflowing trough. Evil it might be. It was evil. But yet it was power. Power to live again as a prince, not a beggared outcast.

Power for an elf's long lifetime.

And slavery forever.

Taking a deep breath, Quicksilver shook his head, and shaking his head, he backed away amid the trees, afraid that his craving would betray him, afraid that, on its own, his thirst would reach for the river of cold, ancient power.

Instead, he stared at the dogs, who ceased snarling and growling, and sat down on their haunches, and began howling, like mortal dogs announcing death. The hairs on Quicksilver's neck stood on end. Now he would be rent by these creatures. Having refused to become one of them, he would be given to them by the Hunter as their fodder. And yet, he thought he would rather have that. He marveled at this realization. He'd rather die than serve this creature through eternity.

Die, then, the Hunter said, and, like that, he vanished, leaving nothing behind but the roll of thunder and slate-grey clouds ahead.

Trembling, shaking, cringing, Quicksilver had trouble believing he lived still. He listened to his heartbeat, and felt his soaked velvet suit hug his body in an icy embrace. Rain dripped on him, steady and cold. The freezing wind that had announced the Hunter died down.

Quicksilver took a deep breath. He must go somewhere. He must leave this forest and find something to do, someone who would help him.

In the darkness, dainty footsteps sounded, and Ariel's voice called out, "Milord."

In pain and fear, Quicksilver turned, willingly, too, at the call of this familiar, friendly voice, and smiled at Ariel in what he hoped would be a soothing manner. By superhuman effort he extended both hands to her, or not to her, but to the reflection of hill power that she represented.

How strangely clean, how magnificently warm that power seemed after the Hunter's icy, tainted offerings.

In Quicksilver's cold world Ariel shone like a blazing

fire to a traveler lost in a snowstorm. Paler than ever, she looked, and grave, like a statue carved in unforgiving marble, and her eyes shone like little points lost within wide bruised rings. Yet the power of the hill glowed all about her, and the current and glory of it flowed and pulsed through her. She had never looked so beautiful.

But she stopped and shied from his extended hands, and from his touch recoiled, as if it were a proffered sword or a coiled serpent ready to strike. Instead, she stretched out her hand till it almost touched his face, but not quite. She spoke, looking at him, her eyes large and wondering, as though not sure what she said or to whom. So might a blind woman speak and peer into the darkness that engulfs her sight for hints of that which she addresses. "Oh, serpent heart, hid with a flowering face," she said. "Did ever dragon keep so fair a cave? A damned saint, an honorable villain. Was ever book containing such vile matter so fairly bound? Oh, that deceit should dwell in such a gorgeous palace. How could you slay my brother, Lord Treason?"

Quicksilver's words caught in his throat, like so many briars in a thorny mass through which he must yet speak. "I did not kill your brother, fair Ariel, nor would I. He was killed by Sylvanus's machinations, by his foul deeds, his setting against one another the races of men and elves."

"But men and elves may war enough, milord, without you leading my brother to death."

"I led him not to death, nor did I—"

"Hush, hush, did you cross swords with him?"

Quicksilver swallowed the denial he wished to speak, and spoke instead the strangled truth. "Yes, but—"

"No, no *buts*, then. Was it while you crossed swords with him that death came, stealthy like a thief in the night?" Ariel looked as never before, white as a marble

statue and just as noble, dignified in all parts, drawn up
into herself: a woman-statue of merciless judgment. And
in judgment she looked upon Quicksilver. "Did death
come to him while thus distracted, while crossing swords
with the one he called his best friend?"

"While we dueled did his death come. The wretched
mortal . . ." Quicksilver's voice dipped and drowned itself,
like a man overwhelmed by waves. Even in this extremity
it hurt him to call Will wretched. The boy had only been
defending his defender and for the love of this protector
that he knew not, had he slain the friend of that protector.
The friend who'd been trying to kill Quicksilver and who,
had Will not slain him, would have tinged his hands as
deep with Quicksilver's life as Quicksilver had been splat-
tered with Pyrite's own. This tangled web spun itself in
Quicksilver's mind, leaving him as sick and sore in mind
as he was in body and power. "But the boy was trying to
defend me, milady. Your lord brother, he sought my life
with hot breath and eager sword."

"Did he raise his sword to you first?" Ariel asked, still
cold and remote and remorseless, a judge on the bench,
admitting no heat of human passion, no warmth of grief,
not even a passing look of love like those lovesick looks
she had bestowed upon Quicksilver, unrequited, so many
years long.

"No. I raised my sword, I did, to protect the mortal on
whom my vengeance depends." The mortal he had kissed.
The memory of Will's lips on his still made his blood
burn. Oh, forget the circumstances and the sure death that
Will was fated to meet. Forget the pain of Quicksilver's
banishment from the hill and his humbling encounter with
the Hunter and that Quicksilver existed, now, as nothing
more than a dwindling force, an elf cut off, mortal but not
of mortal stock, capable of feeling the feebleness of nature
without being, in himself, natural, yet if all this hadn't

happened, would Quicksilver not be singing at the memory of Will's touch, the raw force in the half-grown body, the strength of the boy made man? Would he not be sighing over the boy who would walk with a man's steps in the unsure world, parting all curtains and opening all doors?

"Oh, even now. Even now, milord, vengeance is the only tune your heart knows, and the mortal means no more to you than my brother did, than anyone did . . . than I did."

Quicksilver frowned in puzzled wonder. Did Ariel want him to say he loved the mortal? No, it couldn't be. "My parents," he said. "You told me they must be avenged, and for their sake I must get someone to kill—"

"Speak not of your parents or their sake," Ariel said. "Yes, for their sake you should avenge them. You, yourself, not the poor boy and not my brother, and none other. You, milord, you. But you, Lord Egotism, will walk abroad thinking only of yourself and for your own sake send others to their doom. You want vengeance because Sylvanus humiliated you. Even before you knew of your parents' true death, wasn't your heart full of bitterness? Did you not dress in mourning and parade your vengeful judgment in front of your brother's court? Did you not seek to go to Tyr-Nan-Og, that from there you could harass and torment your brother?"

"Faith, I did not, I only wanted—"

"Oh, do not lie to me." Ariel, this strange Ariel, all righteousness and judgment, drew herself up, stern and harsh. "Do not lie to me, Lord Hypocrisy. I've long since seen through your lies and your embraces, and I should have . . ." Her voice trailed off, and she shook her head. For just a moment, tears sparkled in her eyes as she swallowed and the old, soft-hearted Ariel showed through.

But before Quicksilver could get a pleading word into

the narrow opening of her heart, Ariel's expression closed again.

In her ice-cold eyes, Quicksilver saw himself reflected, small and greedy and cold. He saw himself parading his offense, his righteous injury before the court, even after the court, by its own vote, had accepted Sylvanus for its king. In that clear mirror of memory he saw the tired expressions, the annoyance on the courtiers' faces. He'd made himself a buffoon as certainly as if he'd dressed in pied-piper colors and gone about telling jests and making puns. No wonder no one had raised a voice in outrage when he'd been so unjustly expelled from the hill. No wonder. Had he not acted in such a sour, self-proud way, there should have been indignation, protests, at a prince of the blood being thus cast out, dismissed, with so little cause.

But now, in the sparkling clarity of his mind, Quicksilver saw the faces of the courtiers at his brother's final audience with him. Those faces that had been veiled to him during the argument now appeared clear, each individual and detailed, and perfect, and each one reflecting the same scornful judgment as Ariel's beautiful countenance.

Quicksilver moaned and hugged himself against the cold, the freezing rain seeming ever more frigid to him, as if it leeched at his vital warmth and threatened to embalm him forever in ice.

He'd been on this path, the path to be cut off from the hill, ever since his parents had died. Perhaps even before that. He remembered his wild childhood, his haughty, prideful demeanor, the way he'd always assumed he was the center of everything, and must be obeyed.

Had he not, perhaps, by his own ways, driven Sylvanus to feel he must do murder so that he could inherit, rather than let carousing, unfeeling Quicksilver control the destinies of a whole people? Would not Sylvanus feel righteous and justified?

But, even while his heart stood amazed, Quicksilver's mind rebounded in recovery, and he heard his own facile voice, trying to explain away things. "You accuse me of all crimes because I'd use a human for my revenge? What would you expect of me, then, milady? That I would love the boy? I, love a human, milady? A human? They're but vile creatures and short-lived and . . . you said yourself, loving us brings them madness, drives them to mad twirling in a dance for which they know not the tune. If I loved that boy I would not love him, and not loving him I love him that he might hate my enemy and strike for me. That is all, milady, milady, nothing more." He gazed intently into Ariel's reddened eyes and wished her to believe him, wished her to be appeased.

Oh, let it all be jealousy on her part, and let her ire abate on realizing that she now had no rival to his heart. Let her embrace him, and call him sweet milord. Let her share with him the warmth and the power of the hill, even if at a remove. He wished it so hard, he almost believed it, but he saw her face marble-white and granite unmoved, and knew not what else to do. Oh, so many years he'd been indifferent to her, and now this.

"Even if it were so, milord, even were that human something unimportant, and not a thinking creature with his own love, his own wife, and his own dreams, if you don't love the boy, why did you allow my brother to be killed? Oh, that I should live to see this and that, having lived, I see yet. I could have forgiven your transgression, milord, came it from love. Love is such a many folded folly that within it even the most sane of men might be a lunatic, even a sage might commit imprudence. But you did it out of your cold heart, milord, out of your conceited mind. You are ice, milord, and will never warm up. All

my love was vain. Milord, I want you to know, from the
hill you are barred, from the hill gone, and from me—I
loved you well."

Quicksilver felt tears come to his eyes at the confession
of that love, once bestowed upon him, if not ever received
as willingly as it was given. For that love, now, that uncomplicated craving, he would have wished away his right
arm, his right leg, his useless heart. "So I believed it," he
said.

"You should not have believed it, for it was false. I
loved you not."

This on the tail of the other, made Quicksilver stand
and rear, a bear surprised by a low-charging dog, a wild
animal at bay in the world of hunters. Must he, then, to
his sins add casting the fair lady into madness? "More the
fool I," he said. "More the fool I, who was deceived."

"Oh, yes, you were deceived, milord, thinking I loved
you and I, too, a deceived fool believing that I loved you.
I looked upon you and saw all qualities and joys of our
race, the glass of fashion, the mold of form, the expectancy and rose of fair state, and I thought I loved you well
and that one day, one day you would love me. And I had
the long life of elvenkind to wait out your good graces. I
sat, thus, like patience on a monument, smiling at grief.
Was that not love?"

Quicksilver opened his mouth, but dared not speak for
fear of inciting her to greater madness. Her reddened eyes,
dry and burning like coals in an ill-extinguished fire,
seemed to him to light up something in his cold elven
soul, something he'd never known was there. Had he
loved her, thus, unbeknownst to himself? Or just loved
her love, the knowledge of it, the comfort and joy of
knowing himself dear to her?

She shook her head, to his lack of answer. "I tell you,
lord, I tell you, it was love, but love for a vain object, a

delusion, something like what a human maiden might glimpse in her fantasies when she wishes to see the future and prophesy her marriage night. You are not who I thought and I have not loved. Now you are parted from the hill and I from you. To think that for this I denounced you to your brother, betrayed your plans to him. To keep you near."

"My plans?" Quicksilver asked, confused, lost in her words and her imagery, wondering what she could mean. Had she told Sylvanus of his intended vengeance, then?

"Your plans of going to Tyr-Nan-Og, of marrying there," she said. Her voice rang all hollow, like an unsound bell cast in a poor foundry.

"You?" Quicksilver did not wish to believe it, and yet believing it, he couldn't mind it.

Just a day ago and this would have been the consuming interest of his life, and his rage would have been boundless. But now, cut off and forsaken, he felt as though nothing mattered. All these words were no more than stones falling over his grave, and the dead neither cared nor felt. He had died in leaving the hill and, thus, this was nothing more than the corpse of the Quicksilver who had been that walked and talked, and dragged its sorry self across the forest, looking in vain for what it could not recover. And Ariel was his judgment, as real and terrible as the one that humans believed awaited them after death.

There was no judgment so terrible as seeing himself without deception.

Ariel's dry, grieving eyes, fixed and intent, empty of all but purpose, turned toward his face. "Yes, I, I, I. I told the king, and I got the servant fairies to capture by their magic the images of your courting the foreign Queen. I. Ariel. Fool Ariel, wanting to keep you near, even at the pain of your pain. I did it. So you would stay and learn to love me. I did it. And thus, I, fool Ariel, caused my brother's death." She laughed hollowly.

Quicksilver stared at her, in horror. So, treason had come from such a quarter? And was it treason when, in fact, all the intention of it had been for love? Well . . . was Pyrite dead, though Quicksilver had never intended such? Treason it must be, though in Ariel's fair face and dressed in Ariel's soft intentions.

A thought of another possible treason crept into his mind, and his hair stood up in thinking it. And this one mattered, it mattered much. "Milady, tell me you did not invent your dream of my parents. Was it also a tale, what you spun to me, your idea of my parents' murder, their vile death, their wretched condition in a world of shadows?" As he spoke, he grasped both her arms in his hands, and held her unkindly tight. "Tell me."

But she shook her head slowly, and tears at last crept into her blue eyes. "No. No, that was true. That, and the vileness of it."

Quicksilver took a deep breath, not sure he believed her, and yet her words breathed power and strength into him. He'd gone about this all wrong, and yet now he could only go on with it. If she spoke true, he couldn't be dead, yet. Nor could death offer him the rest he craved. Even the ghosts of dead humans would return to the world when they had a mission. Quicksilver had a mission. If Ariel spoke true, then he still had his vengeance to do. And if he did his vengeance, even if he didn't win kingship by it, yet his parents would be released from their nowhere existence, and Pyrite would not have died in vain. But what if Ariel had spun the tale to get his attention and now denied spinning it to avoid the consequences of his wrath?

Yet his wrath was a poor thing, now that he had been cut off from the hill. Why would Ariel fear it?

And Will had that dagger, that magic dagger that no mortal should have and that could only have come to him through the agency of a treasonous elf.

And yet, what if that dagger was more ancient yet, the mute testimony of some forgotten crime? It was said that the Rollrich stones—a circle of magic stones to the east, that had been there since time immemorial—were all that remained from elven royalty so old that their names and histories were gone and forgotten. Maybe that dagger had been used in killing that royalty, turning their magic flesh to stone.

But no. No. The dagger's own iron would have disintegrated in that long a time, and its spells gone back, absorbed by the magical force of the world itself.

So, the dagger was recent, and Will's father's ailment all too plain. Sylvanus was a traitor and Quicksilver must avenge his parents.

Looking upon Ariel through eyes full of tears, which distorted his vision of her and made her look, herself, like a ghost, a trembling vanishing vision, Quicksilver nodded. "Farewell, milady. Forever and forever farewell. Goodbye. My vengeance waits and it is the only thing I have to live for."

Ariel stared at him a moment longer, her eyes huge and glazed with shock. A sob tore through her lips. She backed away from him, slowly, until, three steps away, she turned and ran, tripping over roots and branches, catching her dress on brambles, leaving bits of lace and straggles of silk hanging in her wake like the abandoned flags of a retreating army.

Her footsteps lost themselves in the distance; her figure disappeared among the trees, first a glimmer of white amid the trunks, then a glimpse of brightness—now seen, now covered by the dark trunks.

Quicksilver stood alone in the dark dank forest. He took a deep breath of moist air into his lungs.

To be or not to be? the Hunter had asked Quicksilver . . . and Quicksilver knew not which he'd chosen. And yet, he must make a decision. Enough indecision and moping about with an air of aggrieved majesty. The new, exiled Quicksilver could not afford such posturing.

To stand around Arden Forest would win him nothing, except the Hunter's attention. He thought he heard, far away, the echoes of the hunting bugle.

Will awaited the lady Silver.

Quicksilver sighed. He knew it was more out of fear than calculation, more out of wishing to be with a creature weaker than himself, than out of true thirst for revenge that he allowed his shape to change into that of the dark lady. By a supreme shivering effort of what remained of his intent and power, he changed his clothes to suit.

The dark lady thus limped through the forest, as shaken and humble, as truly helpless, as Ariel had ever been.

Scene 12

∽❧

The kitchen of the house on Henley Street. The fire burns in the fireplace, and Will sits on the long bench at the table, looking into the flames. A fat black-and-white cat sits on his lap, licking its paws contentedly. The ancient dagger lies on the table.

The lady was late.

Will sat by the fire, striving to keep awake and force his eyes to remain open, though they wished to close. The flames in the broad fireplace leaped and roared orange and gold, forming weird figures and strange shapes that glared back at Will, like the shades of a nightmare.

A black-and-white cat sat on Will's lap, the same cat that had been Nan's and that she'd brought with her from Hewlands. Every time Will nodded off, his sagging body leaned forward and threatened to crush the cat, and the cat dug its sharp claws into Will's legs, bringing him awake.

Will thought, his thoughts merging into dreams, the same way that the golden flames melted into blue shadow and then into spitting orange fire, over again.

That Nan's cat—as skittish of others and possessive of

his mistress as any familiar of his witch—had agreed to let Will hold him was a wonder that struck Will's mind, over and over, each time bringing new astonishment.

The poor thing had to miss Nan as much as Will did. Will nodded off and woke, looking at the fire, the image of the dark lady in his mind. Where was she? Why so late? He had an odd feeling about her, as if death had struck her on the way here.

But elves were immortal, or at least so long-lived that they must seem that way to mortal ken, were they not? And was Lady Silver not an elf? And was she not young? He saw in his mind's eye the elf he'd struck with that knife that now lay on the table looking so common and so inoffensive. Again he saw sparks of color flying away on a wind that Will could not feel, a wind that rustled no leaf, moved no blade of grass. If elves were almost immortal, how had Will killed one?

His mouth tasted bitter, the ale from the alehouse mingling with the taste of his mother's unpleasant soup. Will thought of his father, hiding in his room, crying with horror at the sight of the dagger.

John had talked of someone who'd made him kill the sovereign of the elves and fairies. As the dark lady wished for Will to kill the king of elves. And if he did, would the dead elf haunt him forever, as those others haunted his father in his dark dreams, like righteous nemeses pursuing the guilty murderer and leading him, howling, into madness?

For just a moment, he thought he felt the elf from the forest path standing behind him, a sad shade in a multicolored outfit.

A plague on both your houses.

The elf's voice sounded, loud, in Will's ears, and he woke, shaking, the sting of the cat's claws on his thighs. It was an evil dream. Nothing but an evil dream. Will was not a murderer. He'd set out to murder no one. If he'd killed, he'd only done it to defend himself.

But how to defend yourself? the voice that wasn't there, that wasn't anywhere but in Will's own mind, asked, unabashed. *How to defend yourself, when you already had an elven protector, crossing swords with your would-be killer? Why did you not turn and run, run to the safe haven of your home and away from the strange quarrels of supernatural beings?*

Because he was not a coward. Not a child.

Will flinched from the words his own mind formed, and started as if a stranger's hand had slapped him, while his—much too clear—thoughts told him that he'd killed the elf to prove himself a man. That was the same foolish reason he'd lain with Nan before his marriage. For the same reason he'd found the job in Wincot and worked there, so far away from home, instead of taking over his father's business here, close to home, where he could have prevented Nan from being kidnapped.

All of this, all his mad, rushed actions since finishing grammar school, a year and a half ago, had served only the pride of Will Shakespeare and his need to prove himself a grown man and better than his father. Nothing and no one else.

Will groaned, and the black-and-white cat dug its claws into Will's leg in protest.

Petting the cat reflexively, in an appeasing, unthinking gesture, Will felt shame, such as he'd never felt before. He'd always been fairly sure of himself, nay, proud of his own achievements. From the time when he'd been little Will Shakespeare, the alderman's son, the pride and joy of his mother and the wonder of the petty-school schoolmaster, Will had always had much too good an opinion of himself and his own prowess. And to keep that good opinion in the face of his father's failing fortunes, Will had rushed headlong into a hasty marriage, a poor job, and fatherhood, for all of which he was scantily prepared.

He wished there was a hole deep enough, somewhere on Earth, to hide himself. But no. In marrying Nan, even if he'd courted her to prove himself a man, he'd found a wife willing and ready to make him her husband. If only he recovered Nan, he'd make her a good husband. No more going to Wincot, no more insanity, trying to prove himself a different man from his father. He'd learn what he didn't know about the glover business from the old man and, in John's stead, make the Shakespeare glover shop prosperous once more. And he'd be the best husband that Nan could wish, the best father that Susannah, or any other child, could want.

He nodded off on this vision of domestic happiness, with his heart full to overflowing of true repentance, and woke up to a knock on the door—less a knock than a desperate, cavalcade of fist upon wood.

Will jumped. For just a heartbeat, he thought it would be his Nan out there, under the pouring rain. His Nan, come back to him, now that he'd repented and would be a good husband.

He lifted the fat cat from his lap, eased him to the flag-stoned floor.

The knock sounded again, impatient.

Will opened the door, his heart beating up near his throat. Let it be Nan and Susannah. Only please, let it be Nan, and Will, her faithless husband, would learn to live for her, for her alone. But the door, once open, revealed not Nan but the lady Silver.

Wet and looking cold, she leaned against the doorway as though strength failed her. She'd wrapped a cloak around herself, but so haphazardly that her soaked black hair showed around the hood, while most of her dress remained uncovered. Water dripped from the dispirited straggles of her tresses to soak through her white dress, delineating her generous curved bosom and emphasizing her narrow waist. And yet she looked somehow smaller, thinner, somehow diminished in her beauty and seductiveness. Her pale face appeared almost ghostly, like the visitation of one long dead, and her silver eyes looked out at the world with the gaze of one who mourns.

The face that her black hair framed, showed dark bruises and a broad, purple discoloration beneath her left eye. Her white gown fit her ill and as she moved great tears in the fabric displayed the tender, bruised flesh beneath.

The dark cloak, half-falling from her head and shoulders, dripped rain-soaked and limp, with great stains on it like old blood, and no more grand than the scarf of a peasant woman.

"Milady," Will said, bowing, as he would have, had she come in full state to his door. "Milady Silver. Come in." He stepped out of her way. She had come to tell him how to get his Nan back.

She smiled, just a little, as though gratified by his attention, even as her eyes filled with tears, and she looked guilty of unconfessed crimes. She entered the kitchen, and looked toward the fire and smiled again, a pale smile, a shadow of her former joy.

Removing her dripping cloak, she dropped it, with the carelessness of someone raised with servants, in a soggy heap by the fireplace. Thus revealed, she looked yet more frail. She shivered along the length of her slim body and stretched her hands greedily to the heat of the fire.

Her hands looked blue and bruised, and each finger was bent slightly, as though cramped, like the fingers of a much older woman.

Suddenly she marked the dagger on the table, and a more pronounced shudder coursed down her body. She breathed fast, in short gasps, as she half turned to look at Will with arched brows. Her silver-colored eyes were dull, swallowing up the light but reflecting none.

Will felt pity for her, and a tenderness, a protective care he'd never have felt for the grand lady he'd first glimpsed in the forest. This new feeling gathered around the core of lust that she'd first inspired, and coiled there, making Will ache with longing and tremble with need and almost believe himself in love with this woman . . . this creature he scarcely knew. No, his mind protested, No. It was Nan he wanted, and Nan he craved.

Yet he knew not where Nan was, nor what she did, and this elf lady stood in front of him, bruised and battered and in need of protection and love.

He stretched his hand to her shoulder, where the rent fabric showed creamy pale skin, but withdrew it again without touching her. He remembered too well his longing for Nan, the feeling that he needed Nan more than anything—food or drink, or the very air he breathed. He remembered how guilty he'd felt that he'd used Nan, shamelessly used her, to convince himself that he was a man. No more. He would use people no more.

Yet this lady needed him. And yet, she was not real. Nan was reality. This woman, real though she looked, was of a piece with the nightmare his life had become. She belonged to the forest and its whispered secrets, to the shaded pathways where supernatural villains ambushed him. He didn't want her, or any part of her. He wanted Nan and Susannah and his tidy, rational world the way it had been two days ago. And he'd be a good father to Susannah, a good husband to Nan, and a good son to his much-abused parents.

The dark lady looked at the dagger, then back at Will, her gaze a questing look, alarm at his silence making it tense, like the strings of a drawn bow.

Will thought of his father's fears, thought of what his mother had said. Was his mother insane, as she seemed, or was it the world that had gone insane around his family? "I have heard . . . stories, milady. Stories about . . . my father? My father and this dagger?"

The lady's eyes widened, in mute wonder, and her lips shaped bewilderment as she whispered back, "Your father?" She spoke as though the very words were unknown, as if the idea of Will having been sired were strange and alien. She attempted a small, timid smile. "Your father, Will?"

She was not going to make it easy, he thought. And yet he must know. He had to ask her. "My father said someone told him to kill the King and Queen of Fairyland. He said this person told him they were oppressors and not the rightful rulers. . . ." He shrugged. He couldn't quite tell this supernatural creature that his father had thought it would be no crime, since the elves were not natural. "A folly, but he did it, and since then, night or day, he sees their ghosts and he believes they will come and take vengeance on him."

The lady stared at him, her wide silver eyes unbelieving, or rather unthinking. They were like silver buttons on some great gentleman's jacket, unseeing, unreflecting, showing nothing of what the wearer thought or felt. "Your father?" she repeated, as if the words were unknown, a fragment of some great lost language spoken by the people before the deluge. "And your father lives?"

Will frowned. "He lives but a poor sort of life. He lives in fear of vengeance, of retribution."

The lady's pale lips formed a word, but didn't pronounce it, then opened on expelled breath and said, "No. And he lives?"

She shook her head, as if to an answer he hadn't given. "But he should have died. When releasing the power of the hill—when killing the king and queen—fair Titania, powerful Oberon—he should have been dead, there and then, the vengeance of the hill upon him. How can he be alive?"

"But I killed an elf myself. And I live still."

She shook her head impatiently. "The elf you killed was not a sovereign. Although all elves are tied into the power of the hill, it is the king or queen who controls it, who, in him or her, holds every other power. Killing them brings instant loss to the whole hill, and immediate, un-avoidable retribution."

Will was tired. He'd waited long, and he'd worked hard during the day, ruling over his little tribe of shiny-faced savages, and he'd drunk too much ale and he'd been at-tacked and he'd killed. For the first time, he'd killed, if not a man, then a creature so much like a man that there was scant difference.

What the dark lady had said added up slowly in his addled brain. Slowly but surely it formed a pattern and made sense, if sense of a sort he didn't like. "But," he said. "But you said I should kill the elf king. You said . . ." He stared at the lady and on her face read, in rapid suc-cession, guilt, dismay, and guilt again. "You said that I would get my Nan back then. You said that. And now you say that if my father killed the king and queen, then he should be dead."

The lady shook her head and smiled, the quiet smile of an adult watching a child's harmless tantrum.

Her smiling assurance made Will's voice small. "If I kill the king . . . will I die?"

The lady Silver's eyes regained some of their spark, as if she lit it by an effort of will. "Ah, Will," she said. "Ah, Will. But, you see, Titania and Oberon were rightful and just monarchs, full of might and power, while Sylvanus . . ." Her voice trailed off. "And you'll have my protection, Will. My own protection."

Smiling like that, she looked very pretty but still helpless and frail.

Will felt her charm, but not strongly enough to cloud his mind. He thought that his father must have had someone's protection, too, the protection of the person who'd ordered the murder. Yet, that protection didn't prevent his being haunted. But still, Will's father was alive.

Will walked over to the dagger and picked it up.

Silver turned to face him, her features a mask of shock. She took a step back, then another. "I mean you no harm, kind master Shakespeare. Indeed . . ."

But Will shook his head. "It is I who means no harm. No harm at all." And with outstretched arm he made as if to throw the dagger in the fire. The metal would no doubt survive the flames, but maybe its evil power would be purged. Did not fire purge and cleanse?

"Stay." The dark lady stretched out her arm hastily, to prevent his flinging the dagger in the fire and, in her hurried movement, touched the dagger's blade. Blue fire sparked and the lady screamed, and took her naked hand to her mouth, and sucked on it. "Keep it," she said, around her fingers. "Keep it. It will serve you well."

Will brought his arm in slowly, and looked at the dagger. "Serve me well?" he asked. The dagger glowed with an inner light, as though having tasted the blood of one elf and sensing the presence of another, it longed for another meal. He set the dagger down on the table and looked up at her. "You said it would serve me well. Serve me well how, lady? I want my wife and daughter back, not anyone's life." Will sat down slowly, on the bench next to the table. "And what has this elf king done to deserve death? Already, I've killed . . ." He thought of the ghost he'd dreamed up and shivered. Maybe Will's father had a reason for his fears.

The lady hesitated, then sat down across the table from Will and leaned forward eagerly, till her face was within a hand span of his.

Nan's cat, who'd been sitting at the table, watching it all with a cat's skepticism, hissed and spat and sought refuge above the keeping cupboard.

The lady Silver's eyes looked into Will's with intense, aching need. "The king must die to expiate his treason. His treason in having his parents killed and stealing the throne from me." Like that, sudden tears sprang to her eyes and rolled, fat and sparkling, down her pale face. "His crime has set both worlds wrong. Only his death, the vengeance for his awful crime, can make the world right and give your Nan to you again."

Will's heart contracted, and he squeezed Silver's hand in his.

He'd never been able to resist a crying woman.

Thus had Nan cried, on that far off day when she'd told Will that no one would ever want her, that everyone called her a shrew, that she'd dance barefoot at her sisters' weddings and for their sakes lead apes in hell. Nine months later, Susannah had been born.

Will leaned across the table and squeezed the elf's small hand. It felt and looked cold and frail in his, all too human, with delicate bones and a faint blue tracery of veins beneath the smooth, pale skin. Will squeezed it, seeking to give the lady some of his own warmth, some of his own strength.

Her parents? The throne? The realization that he faced royalty sank into Will's sluggish mind, causing his jaw to go slack, like the jaw of a fool walking through a great town.

"Milady," he said, and attempted to stand, and would

have done it, but for her small hand that still held his hand fast. "I did not know you were a princess. And I do not know . . . Milady, I do not . . ." He wished to tell her he was rough, a farm boy, a village boy and ignorant of all courtly stuff, human or supernatural. He wanted to explain that he didn't know how to deal with princesses, mortal or not, and that he was bound to hurt her with his crude words, his crude gestures, his uncouth touch.

He couldn't express himself better, though, than by holding her hand tight. He remembered that she had kissed him. She, the princess of an ethereal world. He'd always wanted to be better than he was, but he'd never thought he'd climb so fast. A smile, only half mocking, shaped itself on his face. An enchanted princess had approached him. An enchanted princess wanted his help. "You say we have to kill this traitor, then," he said. "And that this"— he touched the dagger with one finger—"will do it? But who will pay for it, milady, and how?"

She looked at him with heartbreaking sorrow. She gave him her other hand, too, grasping at his hands like a drowning man clawing for the riverbank. "My parents were killed," she said, "these five years ago, at the behest of my older brother." Her face pinched in sorrow. "That dagger will do the trick and dispatch the traitor. I know from the grief it caused poor Pyrite." Her eyes brimmed again and, while she looked up and met his gaze, something came and went behind her stare, like a veil quickly lifted and then dropped again. "My brother told me what it did . . . how the poor elf dissolved into another world. . . ."

"But your brother . . . Your brother, Quicksilver?" Will asked, puzzled. Her words circled round and round inside his head, beautiful and senseless like the ditties sung by schoolchildren at their merry games. And like his pupils singing, it made his head spin. "I thought—" He didn't

know how to explain what he thought. He'd believed that
her brother, the king, was her foe. Were they, after all,
friends? Was she, then, on the side of those that had sent
the men to kill Will? No, it couldn't be, Quicksilver himself had said that the king wanted Will dead. "How many
brothers have you?"

The lady looked at him, her silver eyes wide open and
her expression intent. Again there was that feeling, of a
curtain opening for just a second and then closing before
Will could get an idea of what it hid. "Two brothers," she
said. "Two brothers. Quicksilver and I—we were one
birth. My older brother, he has stolen the throne. From
us."

"But if he's older, perforce . . . Is he not the heir?"

Silver smiled, flashing bright, tiny teeth, the teeth of a
mouse in a human mouth, the sharp teeth of a woodland
creature showing between the pulpy softness of a woman's
lips. "No. Among our race, it is the younger that inherits,
or the girl. It is assumed the older one will go throughout
the world, seeking adventure. It is the younger child who
follows in the parents' footsteps." She clasped Will's
hands, hard, her strength better suited to a swordsman than
to a woman's frail muscles. "It is our law, and under our
law, I've been dispossessed."

An odd arrangement, but who was Will to complain?
If she said she should have been the heir, then she should
have been the heir. And yet, his doubt remained. "But who
will pay for this killing, milady? Is there not a price for
murder, even if merited murder, even if just vengeance?
Who will pay for it?"

The lady sighed. She stood up and walked around the
table to stop in front of Will, and sighed again. Great tears
fell down her prominent cheekbones, rolled down to drip
from her pointy chin.

Will pulled his handkerchief from his sleeve, and offered it to her. She took it, wiping her face without seeming to effect much drying. The fresh source of her grief provided a continuous spring to her tears and made them fall again and again down her face like a river ever renewed.

"I've never killed anyone," Will said. "Nor much of anything. A . . . a few hares, but never . . . Lady, could we not make him redress your wrong another way?"

She laughed. "What, infirm of purpose already?" Her silver eyes gazed into his with all-consuming intensity. "What about Nan—do you not wish to rescue her?"

Will's mouth worked in vain, conjuring no sound. A perfume of lilacs, thick and cloying, flowed from the dark lady and made his blood pound along his veins like an army deployed for assault.

He loved Nan, he thought, but he wanted this lady. He wanted to lay his head on her bosom, he wanted to compass her svelte waist within his hands. He wanted . . .

"Don't you love me?" the dark lady asked.

His hand reached out to the lady Silver's shoulder and clasped the wet, frayed gown. "How come you here, like this?" he asked, his voice small, his thoughts all at odds with his labored, slow words. "How come you with clothes in tatters and why do you look hurt?"

The lady glared, hot temper burning like twin hearth fires in her eyes, lips trembling and nostrils flared.

"He expelled me," she said. "He. Expelled. Me. From hill and dale and the haunts of our kind and our tribe. From the dancing glens and the power circles. He. Expelled. Me. Me, who should have been king and ruled over elvenkind, my every wish obeyed, my every whim feared."

Will wanted to point out that she was a woman and that, at most, she might have been queen, but not king. He dared not. She looked like Nan used to look when describing the men her father had thought suitable for her, and the marriages he'd tried to force her into by intimidation and guilt.

Silver's eyes flashed, like droplets of molten silver, and her white face became whiter, while her lips retracted to show her sharp white teeth beneath, clamped tight and menacing.

Will wouldn't point out anything at all. He stood up and backed away, awed at this fury, this unleashed storm.

The lady's gaze fell on him and seemed to remark his furtive shying. Her expression softened, her face relaxed. Her lips let go their raging tautness and went soft, shapelessly soft and yielding. "Oh, Will," she said. "Oh, Will, not you. I'm not angry at you."

Like a high-tempered stallion that takes its own way regardless of the wishes of its rider—like a storm that rages despite human prayers—like any other natural force, the lady changed her mind and her course. She stood and approached him. Her hands reached for Will's shoulders and pulled him close, and her soft, trembling lips pressed upon his.

The world contracted to that kiss. All of Will's wishes, all of Will's senses, all of Will's thoughts became no more than that mouth that opened onto his, that tongue that probed his, those white teeth playing against his own.

Running his tongue over the lady's sharp, pointy teeth, brought Will an odd pleasure on the edge of pain.

Never had a woman kissed him like that. Not like that, till he felt his whole body and mind consumed and that his soul itself was in danger of igniting at this touch. The only woman he'd ever kissed was Nan, and Nan . . .

Nan mattered not. Her image crumbled within Will like a dried flower, long kept in an unopened book. All thought of his guilt and atonement left with her. Nan was like the memory of a childhood toy, enjoyed while childhood lasted and then forgotten. She was a pale tatter in the wardrobe of memory, compared to Lady Silver's purple splendor.

Will encircled Silver's waist with his hands, and she fought not. He kissed her hard and deep, and she shied not away. His hands roamed everywhere, learning the depth and breadth of her flesh, and she protested not.

Their breathing accelerated in unison until, breath by breath, they raced each other to a pinnacle of dizzying, gasping ardor.

The lady untied her dress and let it fall, then dropped her chemise after. They swept down like curtains that open, and revealed her tall, limber body. Will had to lift the hands he'd placed on either side of her waist to allow the fabric to drop to the floor. The shimmering cloth puddled around the lady's ankles. Amid it she stood, like Venus born of water and from it engendered, clean and guiltless.

The light of the fire shone on her white body, her perfect skin. No hint of blemish marred her. No childhood illness had left its mark there, no scarring had formed from early falls. The virgin silk of her skin looked as if it had but just left the weaver's loom. The slight broadening of her hips looked large only because her waist was so narrow that Will could encircle it with his two hands.

Encircle it he did and, pressing close, he made bold to steal again a kiss she would willingly give.

He'd never been thus tempted, he'd never craved this much. His hands on that fair skin felt like pilgrims that, having crossed the parched desert with no sustenance, had reached the shrine where they longed to worship, and there worshipped again and again, unsatiated.

She pressed close to him, her firm, round breasts heavy and hot against his doublet. Her hands unfastened his doublet and shirt, breeches and hose, as though she knew those clothes as well as she knew her own. Those small white hands worked fast and silently, seemingly self-willed, even while her mouth remained joined to his and her tongue disported amid his teeth like a hunter in accustomed glades.

When Will was naked, shivering in his drafty kitchen, she knelt and showed him the other secrets her tongue knew and other hidden, shadowed valleys of pleasure that Will had never visited.

The flames in the fireplace leaped in newly minted golden splendor and cast a molten heat over their conjoined forms.

Nan's cat spat and hissed atop the keeping cupboard.

Later they went upstairs, to the oaken bed, and there, while the rain tapped on the roof and the wind whistled a mournful tune through the cracks in the shuttered windows, they strained the rope supports of the mattress and wore out each other's sportive invention.

Scene 13

❧

Will's bedroom. It is yet dark, but greyish daylight filters in through irregular cracks on the shutters. In the light, dust motes dance. On the bed, half-uncovered, Will sleeps with a smile on his face. Standing beside the bed is Quicksilver, naked, returned to his male aspect.

Quicksilver could not believe what he had done. He stood by the bed and shook with righteous indignation at his own folly.

It must have been the cutting off from the hill, the withdrawal of his ancestral power. It must have been meeting the Hunter, feeling so small, and the loneliness, and the rain and that damned knife, which the boy bandied about so cavalierly. It must have been seeing his best friend cut down, and losing the regard of the only elf lady who'd ever regarded Quicksilver.

He glanced at the bed. Well . . . All that and Will. The boy was sweet and gentle and oh, so preoccupied with the lady Silver's distress. He'd offered sympathy, and sympathy was something that Quicksilver had been offered but rarely.

Kind, brave Will had come to protect Quicksilver in the

forest, even though he had to have known that Quicksilver was an elf and, as an elf, commanded powers and strength that Will could not even guess at.

Quicksilver thought of all his friends, everyone who, during his maybe too contented childhood had never offered smiles, or attention, or reproof, to Quicksilver, the crown prince, the great one, who needed nothing from anyone.

Here was someone who thought Quicksilver needed help and gave it unstintingly. Help and love, and sweetness besides. Much too good, much, to waste on vengeance and bitterness.

Quicksilver let his gaze frame the boy's black curls, the soft curve of his youthful cheek. Damn, but Will looked good, and loved better. Almost as well as Kit, maybe more eagerly.

Yet, was that reason for Quicksilver to allow his wits to be overwhelmed? Was it reason enough for him, like a fool, to get himself naked, and vulnerable, in the mortal's own house? Damn it all, Quicksilver knew very well that whenever he woke up, he found himself back to his male aspect and how would young Will Shakespeare react to a naked male in his bedroom?

Even now Quicksilver trusted not the lady Silver's desires. Should he allow himself to change into her, she might well remain here, contented, the rest of her mischanced life. And doom the boy to madness.

Quicksilver started walking away from the bed. An ill-laid foot made a floorboard squeak, and the bed covers rustled as Will stirred. Quicksilver looked toward the bed and sighed and, almost without thinking, lifted his hand and held Will's sleep over the boy's dark head, keeping him submerged in dormancy, quiet and dreaming, until Quicksilver should leave the house.

For this Quicksilver still had enough power. Meek and

soft power, like the light of a guttering candle, but strong enough to subdue mortals.

Quicksilver hugged himself against the chilly air. He longed for his own room in the hill, for the satin sheets, the broad, soft bed, in which he'd slept most of his life. He longed for his bath, where he could rid himself of dried sweat and grime. But the hill was barred and nothing for it, now, but the narrow beds of humankind and humankind's rare and inconvenient baths. Unless . . .

Again, Quicksilver looked toward Will and frowned, and sighed, all in one. A beautiful mortal, Will was, but what good would he be, once the insanity that started with the love of elevenkind commenced coursing through his veins, turning his blood mad?

Quicksilver shuddered thinking of Kit, the timid divinity student whom he had loved for a scant summer and who had become a vociferous heretic, a promiscuous lover of bawdy houses, a spy and counterspy in the deadly realm of mortal politics, running hither and thither, from France to Scotland and everywhere between and offering his services to the Crown and the Catholics and everyone who promised him money and thrills.

Quicksilver had used Kit, he now saw, just as the Hunter had proposed to use Quicksilver. A like mind calling to like mind, and nothing more, but Quicksilver had not paid for it. Kit had.

No. Quicksilver did not wish that for Will.

A voice still within Quicksilver, the voice of the Quicksilver who'd ever got his way and done what he wanted, told him that he must go on with his plan, that Will might as well die killing Sylvanus as go insane by craving the supernatural love he could not have, the warmth that elevenkind could not bestow.

But the other part of Quicksilver, the part that had resisted the Hunter's evil, and listened to Ariel's speech and been heartily shamed by it, cringed from such thought.

No, no, it had been a night, a night and nothing more. Will would live, Will would survive this. He would grow to be a prosperous fat burgess, happy in his wealth, who would buy himself arms and land and, eventually, a nice tomb upon Stratford church. His little daughter that the fairy land now held would marry some wealthy Puritan, a doctor or a lawyer or some sort of learned man, and Will would brag of them both and their connections. One of his descendants would attain nobility.

As for Quicksilver's vengeance, Quicksilver would forget it. Forget it and leave Will, and go, like the cursed thing he was, and dwell in some vile part of the forest, and there dwindle away peacefully.

Will's forehead had beaded with the fine sweat of contented sleep. His rosy lips parted. He snored softly. He smelled warm and young and healthy.

Quicksilver looked on him, transfixed.

No, Quicksilver would never again cause another's death. Pyrite had been enough of a sacrifice to Quicksilver's vanity, his cursed pride.

Let Sylvanus rule Elvenland. He would be good enough with it, now that Quicksilver, that thorn in his side, was gone.

As for Titania's and Oberon's shades . . . Quicksilver felt tears sting his eyes. He had failed them. Another guilt he'd have to learn to bear.

The thought of his parents put a chill in Quicksilver's body. The wind outside picked up, blowing through the cracks in the shutters with renewed force. Rain rattled against the shutters, too, a rat-a-tat-tat of ominous portent.

Where had Quicksilver left his clothes?

Hugging himself, trying to collect his scant wits about him, and think where, in the wild lovemaking, his clothes had been taken off, he started down the stairs, step by step, then step by step retraced his steps back up, for one more look at Will sleeping on the bed.

Pleasure and sleep, mingled, had painted Will's cheeks a light pink and touched a deeper tint to his lips, like nature upon ripening an apple will make it blush a more intense red. One of his arms lay flung above his head, curved somewhat, like the arm of a conjurer about to unveil some grand trick. His other arm was crossed over his still hairless chest, which lay uncovered. Below that, the covers gathered in a tumble, hiding the middle of Will's body. From beneath the tangle, Will's legs emerged, long and almost hairless, shapely and muscular, the legs of a man who walked much.

Quicksilver leaned over the bed and touched his lips to Will's sleeping lips.

In his sleep, Will smiled and sighed.

Quicksilver turned his back on him, resolutely this time, and forced his feet, step by step, down the stairs. No, and no, and no, and no. He would not make a fool of himself, nor could he afford to. He would not ruin Will's life more than he already had. Enough, enough already. Now Quicksilver would go, in shame and penance, and expiate his reckless joys in the darker recesses of the forest. There he would die, like some hermit of old, if not saintly nor blameless, at least having worn the edge off his sins, blunted them, made them homelier.

With such worthy thoughts, Quicksilver made it downstairs.

Crossing the dark, shuttered workshop, Quicksilver wrinkled his nose at the smell of rotten eggs and aged pelts that were part of the glover's trade. That such a base creature as Will's father, one who dealt in the skins of dead animals and cut and fashioned them into gloves, that such a creature had sired Will . . . Worse, that such a creature should have the power to kill elvenkind . . . And where had that dagger come from? And wouldn't it be better if Quicksilver took it with him?

Quicksilver ran down the hallway and into the kitchen.

His clothes lay where he remembered them, all of a pile by the now cold fire. Will hadn't banked those fires the night before, busy as he'd been feeding other fires. And neither he nor Quicksilver had cleared the remains of the banquet with which they'd fortified their flagging appetites halfway through their sport. Quicksilver had conjured bird and fowl and fine venison from the lands hereabouts and, by his power, had them arrive roasted and prepared to the Shakespeare kitchen. There, Will and he had eaten until they had satiated that appetite. Now, the remains of their meal cluttered the uncleared board, looking faintly repulsive. The same fat black-and-white tomcat who had, the night before, observed their lovemaking with curious eyes, now rooted amid the food, and cast a suspicious look and a warning growl at Quicksilver.

Quicksilver sighed, thinking how much power he'd used to bring the food here. But the little power he retained would have to do. He had enough for his diminished purpose.

Quicksilver wished his clothes back to their male aspect and restored them to their prime by an effort of wishing, that left him panting and drained. He put on shirt and doublet and breeches and boots. Then he found the knife on the table, and rolling it in a scrap torn from his shirt, he slid its threatening solidity into his sleeve.

Fully attired, he bid a mental farewell to Will. What had happened this night past would never happen again. Quicksilver had woken sure of this knowledge. He would not, ever again, lie with Will in that bed, not in either aspect.

Thus resolved, he slipped out the door and into the rainy garden outside.

The thought of saintly death warred in his mind with his wish to live and enjoy himself. He should seek out another hill that would admit him. Now, Quicksilver could go to Tyr-Nan-Og. But would the queen there take a pro-script? Well, if not, he could always have his well-merited death. But first, he must leave Will alone and restore him to the life he'd had before the hill had meddled in it. For the fine future he'd forecast for Will, Will must have his wife back. And how could Will accomplish that?

The sacred Summer Solstice Dance, when mortals could intrude and seize a changeling, and thus recover him, was held at a different glen every year, at the whim of the king. Which clearing would Sylvanus have chosen? Quicksilver could send Will looking and spend all of Will's mortal life in that endeavor.

But as cold rain hit Quicksilver's head, he thought that Ariel would know. Ariel had shown friendship for the woman Nan. Surely she'd want to restore Nan to her true lord.

Still, going near the hill, seemed too much pain for too little gain. What did Quicksilver win by such an effort? On the heels of that thought, he reared, startled. Was he then so like the Hunter, never giving aught that he didn't mean to be paid for in triplicate? Was that why his mind had called to the Hunter's?

No. He would go to the hill, and humiliate himself be-fore Ariel, to restore Will's wife to Will. He would do it despite his aching heart, his muted jealousy. He would do it though he gained nothing from it. He would do it to prove himself different from the Hunter. He never wanted to attract attention from such a one again.

He'd go near the hill and there wait, and wait, until he saw Lady Ariel or someone who would agree to call her to him. Perhaps he could even reach as far as to have his magic touch her privately, and call her to him, and beg, and cringe and cry if needed, till she told him what he needed to know.

A great peace fell over his heart. All would be well, for others if not for him.

Walking out, under the pouring rain, Quicksilver noticed the child at the door of the house next to Will's, a pixie-like thin girl who looked somewhat like Will. He gave her no more thought, as he walked out of the garden and into the woods.

The best time, the only time, for Quicksilver to find Ariel would be now, now before his power depleted itself to nothing, before his craving became too great, before he became a thing of air and shade and little more. His vanity didn't wish for Ariel to see him that way.

Walking through the woods in the rain, he smiled to himself. He must get it out of fair Ariel. A doubtful prospect, considering her wrath at him. And yet, she'd always been kind. And this was not something he wanted for himself, but for another.

He must woo the lady and represent to her the sure necessity of their alliance.

If nothing else, he thought, as his smile faded from his lips, it might help keep his mind off Will. Will, whom he was starting to like much too well.

Scene 14

೪

Will's bedroom, the shutters closed against the rain, and scant light filtering through the warped boards.

Will woke with the creaking of a floorboard across the room. He struggled to open his eyes, but found it hard going.

Another board creaked, at the foot of the bed, closer to him. He felt that someone was there, close, close by.

Will's head hurt and his brain roared like ill-tuned virginals. That was Will's first thought, and the second, fast on that, was that his mouth tasted like a midden.

He opened his eyes, which hurt on opening, and stung with the light, as though he'd been monumentally drunk the night before and were just now wakening from that drunk. What he saw was like a refraction of light on a spider web, as though his world had been fractured and his brain struggled in vain to reconstruct it.

As he blinked, he heard a voice say, "Will, are you awake?"

The voice was Joan's, but Will couldn't imagine what his sister was doing in his room, nor could he think of any plausible reason for her presence. His thoughts moved through his mind, slow and quiet, on hesitant feet, like ghosts fleeting through the land of the living. He brought himself to sitting, surprised that his bones didn't creak and that he didn't fall apart with the movement. His stomach clutched and hurt, and nausea climbed the slope of his throat. He swallowed back the bitter bile. His sight cleared enough that he could see Joan standing by the bed, staring at him as if the night past had transmuted him into some monster. He reached for the blanket, to make sure his privates were covered, and wished his head would stop pounding.

"Will?" Joan asked.

He closed his eyes, waiting for it all to quiet and for his body, again, to become a good servant to his mind.

Behind his closed eyes, his headache pounded, and, to the rhythm of it, his recollections danced like gaily garbed clowns.

There had been a lady—a fairy lady—dark as the night and fair as the day. A lady, Will thought, and marveled at it.

She was a princess, a fair, enchanted creature such as Will had read about but never expected to meet in real life.

Into his kitchen she'd come to ask him to do justice on her behalf. Justice. He, Will, had been asked to do justice by a lady of high birth, an ethereal lady from the land of fairy tales.

She'd come to him in the kitchen and they'd talked of knives and . . . one knife in particular. He flinched, thinking of what his father had done with that knife. What crimes had been committed and how dark a revenge awaited? And should Will kill again, kill the new king of the elves, and should . . .

He couldn't think straight. His brain wouldn't follow from word to word, from sentence to sentence. Instead, it gave him the image of the dark lady and made his blood course faster through his veins, while he remembered what she'd felt like in his arms, and how she'd kissed him, and she'd . . . He blushed, remembering the remainder of the night.

But, oh, what pleasures two bodies could wring out of one night. That, too, was like a dream, a tale he'd never been told and had never imagined. He'd suspected naught beyond the sweet but plain twinings he'd known with Nan.

On opening his eyelids again, he knew what pained him and what illness this was that made his brain so sluggish— he suffered from hangover, as if he'd drunk two casks of good French wine. But he'd drunk nothing, save the ale those hours ago, and a little more ale the lady said she'd conjured from the tavern. And he'd drunk ale too long to be drunk by that little.

He must be drunk on love, and the roar marching through his veins must echo the pain of parting. Love, when taken in excess could be as debilitating as ale, as maddening as good wine. A wondrous thing.

This thought made Will spry; the memories of the night past made him smile; his own joy made him laugh.

"Will?"

Oh, yes, Joan. Will brought his gaze to his sister, who stood by the foot of the bed, her face flushed pink, her expression like that of one with a private joke.

"Yes?" Will asked, the word reverberating through his pained head. His voice rasped and droned like rusty bellows.

Joan smiled. Her wide-open eyes were dark and cunning, filled with knowledge that shouldn't come to one so young.

Will had a moment of panic. What had Joan seen? And what thought?

"So it is you now," Joan said, still smiling, her small, bow-shaped lips curled in an amused smile. "It is you now who consort with velvet-clad gentlemen." She put her hand on the oak footboard, and caressed it with a slow touch. "I wonder what our mother would think."

Will's mind felt so strange, so wrapped up in super-natural fogs and miasmas and vapors of otherworldly things, that he couldn't, for a moment, make out what Joan might mean.

Then he caught the cunning look in the girl's eye, a sharp, expectant look that he associated with tavern shills and cheaters fleecing the unwary in games of chance. She had seen something, and for that something, to keep that something secret from their parents, she wanted . . . What? Money? Gifts? Or simply the attention of her older brother, whose attention she'd lost almost a year ago, when all his thoughts and all his actions had started re-volving around Nan?

But why did the girl babble about gentlemen? What gentlemen? Was there something wrong with her eyes? Will could have understood her talking of the dark lady, and promising to keep that secret for a prize. And though right now Will felt like shouting it all from the rooftops, the glory and ecstasy of that uncalled-for love, that sur-prising joy, he knew that tomorrow, and the day after, and yet another day, he might rethink it all and not want the company that graced his bed to be bandied about on dark corners, smiled at over the smith's cold forge, seamed over by the tailor, handed over the draper's counter like so many tawdry goods.

That was not what he wanted for his dark lady. What he wanted . . . A series of disconnected images crossed Will's mind: the lady Silver in his bed, and in his kitchen, in his garden and walking about Stratford streets, like Nan had. Children graced with the lady's fantastical beauty, with her quick, parrying mind. He never put such images in words, not even to himself. He knew, in his bones and in his sinews and in that knowledge that permeates every man and, comes down the generations, weaves itself into every pore, every fragment of him, that this thing he dreamed would never become reality.

The lady was supernatural, a creature of fire and air, of enchantment and thunder, immaterial and weightless as those fantasies that men weave late at night and can't recall in the morning.

The lady was made of the same cloth as the ancient goddesses who would condescend to lie with a mortal but could never compass their power, their strength, to a mortal form, nor abide beside that mortal as the mortal aged.

Something in Will rustled, whispered, that those whom the gods loved went insane, and perhaps he was insane already, to even allow such images to cross his mind.

Annoyed with himself, more than with Joan, who still stared, her eyes wide and cunning and full of secret, insalubrious knowledge, Will got up, holding the blanket in front of him, and rasped out in anger: "What, child, what? Speak or be gone." With the blanket held in front of him, looking much like a gypsy woman dancing in a fair and appearing to be nude while taking good care to keep the essentials concealed, he pranced here and there, around the room, looking for his clothes with no success. "What you say makes no sense. What gentlemen, child?"

"If it's your clothes you want, they're in the kitchen," Joan said, slow, amused, her voice that of a grown woman. "Where, no doubt, the good neighbor pulled them off you last night, when your magical party was progressing and all that food was consumed. . . ." She tittered, her tongue touching her lip.

What did this girl know, and where had she learned such mannerisms and dissolute insinuations?

Will backed down the stairs, not an easy feat considering that he must hold the blanket in front of him, for the sake of Joan who followed him and looked on, still amused. With quick, awkward movements, Will draped the blanket around himself like a toga worn by the Romans. It made him think of Plutarch and imagine himself a persuasive Marc Antony standing before Caesar's coffin in an ancient forum.

But his position was much less dignified. He had— nothing less—to justify his pleasures and his choices to his little sister, aged fourteen and full of more mischief than a fourteen-year-old should be. The girl should have been supervised. She needed more than her lax, crazy old mother. She needed someone who cared what she did and where she went. She went walking about after dark. Had she seen the dark lady? "If you talk of the lady," Will said, reaching the bottom of the stairs, and backing through his father's workshop, avoiding by instinct the broad work-scarred tables. "The lady who came here last night came to me on business. Grave business. Involving . . . death and business. Business and business . . . and . . . well, business . . . such as you . . . you couldn't understand, if you tried."

Joan tittered again. "Which part of this business was removing your clothes in the kitchen? And what part of it was played by the gentleman who crossed our yard, early morning, right after sunup, and disappeared into the forest? And why did he look like the fat cat who has swallowed the plump bird?"

"Gentleman? What are you talking about, child?" Having backed all the way to the kitchen, Will found his clothes scattered on the floor, and the remains of his wild, riotous banquet littering the humble, scrubbed pine table. With one hand holding his would-be toga, and the other grabbing his more common and comfortable breeches, he attempted to slip the breeches on without dropping the toga. Not an easy task, made all the more difficult and perilous, by Joan's curious, watching eyes.

"I know what you don't. . . ." Joan said, in singsong mischief.

She sounded, Will thought, like his pupils when they had played a prank on him and waited impatiently for the trap to be sprung so they could laugh and mock at his haplessness. He managed to pull his breeches up, and let the blanket fall while he finished fastening them.

"When Mother is in one of her moods, late at night, I've taken to wandering in the garden, playing, you know . . ."

Will didn't know. The idea of a girl's life, a woman's life, had always seemed boring to him. What could there be to an existence in which letters weren't learned and there were no ancient works to peruse, no maxims of wisdom to memorize? What could enliven a life that was entirely circumscribed by home and church, children and mending, shopping and husband?

Will couldn't think of it, except to thank God that he had been born male and capable of learning. But he knew Nan had whiled away her time in Arden Forest and there learned freedom in a way her home did not allow.

Had Joan, too, learned forbidden language from the brooks? Had she tasted freedom amid the trees? Or was hers a small freedom, the freedom of the garden and the enclosure, the silent moment away from a prattling mother?

Will put his shirt on, and then his doublet, and fastened them both. He opened his door to look out. Through the pouring rain, he couldn't tell the time of day, but he felt as though he'd slept much too long, slept later than he should have. He should have been halfway to Wincot by now.

There was too much light, even if only the diffuse, grey light of a rainy day. And there were too many sounds, the waking sounds of Stratford—doors opening and the clip-clop of horses along the thoroughfares. Somewhere nearby a rooster crowed.

"I saw the gentlemen that came to spy on Nan," Joan said.

Will started to reply that there had been no gentlemen, then realized there probably had been—the advance guard of the hill, scouting out a prospect for kidnapping—and shut his mouth with a snapping sound.

"Oh, I don't say as Nan consorted with them," Joan said and smiled, a small dimple forming on the side of her cheek. "I never found *her* clothes strewn about the kitchen."

"Oh, leave off, already," Will said. He grabbed the wooden bucket from near the door, to get water from the well. Nan used to get it at night for him, and leave it set out in the basin for his morning washing. But Nan wasn't here.

Swinging the bucket peevishly, Will pushed the door open and strode outside into the pouring rain, with Joan following.

Why he bothered, he couldn't tell. After all, all it took was five minutes in this rain and he was washed enough, clean enough. Surely he didn't need any more washing. Yet he would get water and scrub his face, and do a proper washing, although by the time he reached Wincot, even if he wore a cloak against the rain, he would be wet and dripping all through.

"But I saw gentlemen in velvet skulking and hiding around the wall, and among the plants, and also the strange fairy lights, the small ones, that came and looked in windows and rattled the shutters." Joan walked behind Will, her steps a small echo to his. "And I followed them, back to the forest. Edmund and I followed them, to see where they lived."

Will reached the well, a raised cylinder shaped in stones, with a square hole on top and a rope coiled beside it. The rope could be tied to the bucket, so that one could lower the bucket into the well and get the water. "Where they lived?" he asked. He started tying the rope to the bucket's wooden handle.

"In the forest," Joan said impatiently. "And I saw their dances and their walks, their affairs . . . It's quite like a court, like the court of our queen must be—all great gentlemen and ladies." Joan chuckled. "I know your gentleman, Will, I know him well."

"I do not have a gentleman." The rope tied to the bucket, Will started lowering it into the well.

"Oh, but you do, though you might not know it. Was it the lady you saw, Will? The ill-colored lady, with dark hair and white clothes?"

What did the girl know of the lady Silver? Curse Joan's unsupervised childhood. Curse his mother's detachment. Curse him, himself, as busy as he'd been with work and Nan and Susannah, that he hadn't noticed how far astray the girl was going. And she'd taken Edmund near the people of the hill? Had she never heard of changelings? No, perhaps not. So many things had changed since Will was a child and the war between papists and the proper religion had tarnished everything and turned even legends and ancient knowledge into crimes.

"So, you do not know that this same lady is no lady, but just a disguise for the gentleman with blond hair and a midnight-dark velvet suit?"

"Oh, what nonsense, child." Will felt the bucket hit water, and started hauling it up, the weight of the water on his arms, his straining shoulders. "Nonsense. The dark lady . . . a woman in all parts, I assure you." He bit his tongue, having said more than he intended to, and pulled at the rope and turned to look at Joan.

She shook her head. "Oh, no. The gentleman is the true form, though he changes to the lady and back again. Many times I've watched and seen it." She smiled.

Things were coming together in Will's head. Silver and Quicksilver knew things that they said the other had told, but who would give such intricate descriptions, every detail observed?

And hadn't Silver been banished, she said, for defending Will? But it had been Quicksilver who'd come to Will's defense. . . .

And there was something else, the thing that had bothered Will all along. From his great memory for voices and sounds, he unearthed the voices of the two, Quicksilver and Silver, and realized what had sounded so familiar about Quicksilver's voice.

Silver's voice. Quicksilver's voice. It was only one voice. The same voice translated, now to a higher register, now to a lower one.

His hands let go of the rope, and the bucket fell into the well.

Scene 15

✢

*Nan's room in the fairy palace. She has just finished
nursing one of the babies and now sets the child, with
infinite care, back in the cradle. Nan wears a dress of
golden silk, and looks rested and self-possessed. Beside
her, sitting at the end of the bed, a wan Ariel embroiders
in pastel colors upon pale silk.*

Nan set the fairy princess down in the cradle. Such a
beautiful baby and so good that Nan had become
quite attached to her, almost as much as to her own daughter. Off and on she wondered if, when she managed to
leave here—and she *would* manage to leave here—she
should take the fairy princess together with her own bun-
dle.

She was sure Will would welcome the baby, and both
could be raised, side by side, as their own. But she worried
about the fairy princess' nature. Could she live away from
the hill?

Nan shuddered, as she remembered the expulsion of
Quicksilver. How he had looked—that bright, supernatural creature. Of a sudden, all light had gone from him, all

strength, and he'd collapsed like the discarded peel of a withered apple.

Pulling the blanket over the princess, adjusting Susannah's sleeping form, Nan cast a sidelong glance at Ariel. How wrong she had been there. How foolishly wrong. Watching Ariel, at Quicksilver's expulsion, and now remembering how Ariel had gone after him, only to return wild and crying, like a woman scorned, Nan knew it was Prince Quicksilver whom Ariel pined for, and he whom she worshiped in the cathedral of her heart. Not the king at all.

And now, without Quicksilver, the little elf maiden had gone even more colorless, more dispirited. Not that she complained, or even talked about him. To Nan's overtures, she'd replied by turning her face away and concentrating ever more on her broidery.

A knock on the door called Nan's attention. Nan lifted her head and tied, with nimble fingers, the crisscross laces on her bodice, which hid her milk-heavy breasts.

She needn't have bothered. When Ariel opened the door and looked out, she found no person, only a flock of the tiny fairies, who twinkled in lights all around her.

Grave, serious Ariel turned around, her pale, peaked little face set in anxious urgency, "Milady, they say the king has summoned you, and bid you come to the small audience chamber. They will show you where."

The small audience chamber sounded like much too intimate a place. Nan shook her head. "No, you bid the fairies stay and watch the babies and summon us if aught goes amiss. And you show me where."

Ariel inclined her head in assent and gestured at the little fairies. Then, gathering up her ample skirts so as to walk unencumbered, she turned and led Nan out of the chamber and down a maze of corridors.

The corridors in this place were such—ending in round

halls from which myriad doors opened, and leading to staircases that climbed and descended seemingly at random—that Nan was sure she would never learn her way about, even if she should live out her life here.

A shiver ran down her spine.

No, she would *not* live out her life here. She would not. She could not. Oh, the food was good, and life was easier than in Stratford and, unlike Will's parents, everyone in the hill was ready to make her welcome, to amuse her and entertain her in every possible way.

The temptation was great and, walking along the marble corridors, her elegantly cut skirt sweeping the floor, Nan admitted to herself that she could learn to live like this, with servants and maids to do her bidding; with daily perfumed baths; with soft, heavenly beds.

But she couldn't live without her Will. And he would be mourning her, lamenting her, since she'd disappeared. He would be suffering for her and wondering where she was and what had become of her. That, or he thought her dead, and, either way, he'd be a suffering Will, a weeping Will, a subdued and mourning and quiet Will. A mockery and joke upon himself.

She couldn't bear the thought of him like that. She couldn't bear the thought of him, lost and helpless, within the manipulating schemes of his conniving mother. She could not.

Ariel stopped in front of a golden door, and knocked.

The door opened and Sylvanus himself, powerful Sylvanus, of the square shoulders, the broad, straight back, the narrow waist, the strong voice, stood looking at them.

Since the night before, when Nan had screamed at him and called him all manner of insults, from spineless worm to murderer, things had been cold between them. He had not asked her to join in the dance by his side, and she wouldn't have done so had he asked. Leastwise, not if she could have imposed her own desires over the strength of his glamoury. Now she greeted him, remaining coldly distant, and looking as strong as she knew herself to be.

Behind him, she saw the whole of a small room, furnished with a chair and nothing else. The walls shimmered as though built of jade, and though no candle was visible, the room glowed with diffused light. Firefly fairies danced up near the ceiling, flashing their fire in a way that Nan had learned to recognize as excitement or anxiety.

It had been long in coming, this summons. Last night, after she'd learned of his attempt on Will, Nan had remonstrated with the king and told him what she thought of powerful men who seek to kill weaker ones. Knowing he couldn't know of it, yet she preached at him, the story of the poor man and his one ewe lamb.

She'd been at her best, shrewish Nan, the one who'd scared suitors and lovers well away from her door for more than ten years running, and now, she thought, now the king would want to tell her that she was no longer welcome in his hill, and that he was desisting from his pursuit of her.

The king gestured for her to come in, closed the door behind her and Ariel, and sat on the broad chair at one end of the room.

Neither she nor Ariel were offered chairs, so it seemed as though he sat on a throne and they, his courtiers, stood respectfully before him. "Ah, my dear," he said, and looked toward Nan. "My dear, my dear, my dear. Would that I could spare you the pain . . . but there . . . I have to tell you . . ."

So, now it would come, Nan thought, and almost smiled. He was going to ban her from the hill. And good riddance. She'd go back to her room and get Susannah, and leave this cursed place with a song in her heart. She turned to Ariel and smiled, but Ariel looked grave, frowning, as though sensing a trap.

"And Lady Ariel," the king said, "you're welcome too, even if I did not send for you, since what I have to say concerns your interests also."

The lady Ariel turned even paler, and Nan thought maybe the maiden had reason. Maybe the king meant to marry her and make her a mother to the little princess. And maybe it was a worse fate for Ariel, but maybe not.

She would be a queen and have power such as the banished prince could never give her. And, from what Nan had understood, Ariel's affair with the prince had never been a happy one.

So, let the foolish girl pale and ponder. It was none of Nan's business, anyway. Soon Nan would be away from it all.

The king of elves looked at Nan, puzzled, as though he couldn't quite understand the joy that bubbled up from her eyes and erupted through her expression, like a spring that pierces through hard rock, to rise to the surface of the thirsting soil.

"I have ill news to acquaint you with," Sylvanus said, and stretched out his hand, palm up, as if expecting a peace offering.

Nan's heart clenched upon itself, like a fist closing. Ill news? Had the miserable creature managed to undo Will? But no, it couldn't be. Even beaten and expelled, Prince Quicksilver would defend Will, Nan was sure of it. There was a man—well, an elf, but man in all essentials—who would stand for justice. She had known it from the first time she saw him, alone and grave, dressed in black and somber, amid the gaudy, chattering crowd.

One of the flying fairies swooped down, carrying something in its tiny, perfect hands. It deposited the something in Sylvanus's extended palm, and flew away, flashing white and yellow light that, for some reason, gave Nan the impression of a secretive giggle.

Beside Nan, Ariel gasped, a small, timid sound, betraying fright and little else.

The king of elves lifted his hand, and gazed intently at the object it held—which looked like no more than a droplet of water—spherical, transparent, minuscule.

Within the compass of his gaze, it grew, till it seemed to occupy his whole hand, like a monstrous, glowing pearl.

Within it figures moved, figures that made human sounds.

At first, Nan—surprised by the novelty of seeing images in an enlarged drop of water—couldn't understand what she was seeing, nor could she make head nor tails of the figures that moved within the light. Then, little by little, she started to see it. Two people, a man and a woman, moved in that small globe, against a familiar backdrop.

The kitchen, the cat atop the keeping cupboard, all of it made Nan's heart ache with recognition. Her home. But who . . . ? Then she recognized Will, and her eyes widened at how he held the dark-haired strumpet who melted in Will's arms.

Her reason paralyzed, her brain stopped so that she couldn't even feel justifiable ire, Nan stared at the two people making love within that droplet of water. She marked all that happened in the kitchen and followed with wide, horrified eyes, the couple's ascension of the rickety stairs to the upper chamber and Nan's own oaken marriage bed, the bed that Will's aunt had given them at their wedding. The best bed Nan had ever seen. The best bed they would ever own.

Her breath caught in her throat. She had never seen Will so enraptured. Her clumsy, tentative caresses had never wrung from his lips such joy, never brought such shine to his eyes.

This woman, who was she? Nan didn't know her from Stratford, and she would have known such a one, even in that small a rendition. This woman's face, once glimpsed, could never be forgotten.

This is what Will had deserved all along—a woman of ethereal beauty, a fit target for his poems, a fit anchor for his dreams.

Beside the woman, Nan saw her own self, juxtaposed in her mind's eye—graceless Nan, with no beauty, no joy, nothing. Her form was plain and her face as haphazard as a barley cake thrown together for Whitsunday. There was nothing to Nan but that plainness, that earthiness of field and forest. How could she compete with this creature of fire and ice, of sculpted joy and dancing music?

Before her eyes, the scenes of Will's encounter with the dark lady unrolled, and Nan clasped her skirt within her hands and tightened them so much that it felt as though her nails would go through the heavy satin. But they didn't. And Nan neither cried out nor screamed. In truth, there was no reason to. She felt nothing, except maybe a small relief that Will was not mourning, not in pain.

Another, stronger gratitude formed, that Will had found someone more worthy of him. Someone like him, young and full of that fire that always eluded Nan except in anger.

She now saw how their bed must have been boring for him, Nan knowing nothing and guessing little of the art of love—her imagination narrow and restricted in such things. Now she understood that their love had all been on her part. She had loved and he'd let himself be loved.

Nan, foolish Nan, tired of being an old maid, tired of her father's house, had taken this beautiful youth and led him by the hand to fornication and fatherhood and marriage.

Mary Shakespeare had known it all along. Nan had been a harlot, a slut, disquieting Will's dreams with her all too solid body.

Now Will had finally found a woman who would be perfect and inspire him to the heights of his abilities. Nan had always managed to bring him down.

Clasping her skirt hard, pressing the fabric into bunched wrinkles, Nan felt as though she'd died and been buried.

In those few minutes, standing there, watching Will and his new love, Nan had forgotten her purpose, her intention, the animating strength that had kept her going from disaster to disaster and from grief to grief all her life, unbowed. The wish to make her father love her no longer drove her. Her father was dead now and, long since, Nan had become accustomed to the idea that she'd never measure up to the strong sons he'd sired before her and of whom he was proud as of true olive branches, fit to grace his patriarchal table. And she no longer needed to be married.

She *had* been married, to the astonishment of her sisters and the head-shaking of her bewildered brothers. Married not in the grand wedding she had wished for, but in a small, confined ceremony under the falling snow, in Temple Grafton.

Oh, that she could undo that ceremony, and give Will the freedom he deserved, so he could pursue his joy with his new love. Oh, that she'd seen that falling snow, that lead-colored sky, for the omens they were. Oh, that she'd paid attention to Mother Shakespeare's justified glares and muttering.

One by one, Nan reviewed all the half-whispered comments she'd heard from the woman since the unchancy day when Nan had intruded on the Shakespeare family.

Mary had said that Nan didn't deserve Will. Faith, that was the truth. And she'd said that Nan had taken Will and made him hers, like a thief that robs from an innocent man. And faith, that too was the truth. And she'd proclaimed that Will was so much better than Nan, and could have found a better wife anywhere, around any corner, if only Nan had let him. And faith, that rang true also, and Will had found his better match as soon as Nan had absented herself from his life.

Nan held her teeth together so tightly that she could not have spoken had she wished to.

The lovers on the oaken bed shown in the drop of water had fallen asleep, still sweetly entwined in each other's arms. The light went out within the drop of water, which returned to that which it was—a drop of water, nothing more.

"I'm sorry you had to learn it this way, my dear," Sylvanus said. "But now you see why I must kill your husband."

Kill him? Kill Will at the height of his joy, when he'd finally found sweet love? Nan started at the thought. "Oh, milord, no. You must not kill him. Let him enjoy his new love in peace and faith—let him be happy. I am, to him, as good as dead, being already in another world. The bond between us is severed and there's nothing, nothing at all holding us together. Let him be luckier in his second match than ever he was in the first." Her voice sounded distant and strange to her ears, as though her words were uttered by a stranger. She noticed Ariel, beside her, cast an amazed gaze in her direction.

Nan should be amazed too. From the corner of her eye, she marked that Ariel had regained color, and breathed rapidly. Did the show, then, interest the fair maid and perhaps awaken in her marble countenance an interest in the marriage bed? For the first time since Nan had seen her, Ariel's eyes shone with animated purpose, intensity and joy.

The king looked as though he'd add something to his words, but then didn't. He lifted his hand, and one of the flying fairies took the drop of water. He looked at Nan with a concerned frown, then at Ariel with an inquisitive glance, and then shrugged as though to signify that all women, human or elven, were insane and he, a mere male, not able to understand them. "Will you then, milady, consent to marrying me?" he asked Nan.

The words reached Nan's ears, but didn't penetrate to her brain. No association formed between the sounds, which, isolated, remained just sounds, with no meaning. Amazed, she looked toward Ariel, as if to ask what strange language Sylvanus could be speaking and what it might mean.

Ariel smiled, and, turning to Sylvanus, spoke in a gentle voice more persuasive than anything Nan had yet heard, "The lady needs time to think, milord. Surely you understand. Such a question after such news . . . It is too much and she can't answer yet. But give her time in her room, alone, time to compose herself, time to think, and she will have an answer for you, I am sure."

Nan couldn't understand what Ariel said, either. Unlike the words of the king, Ariel's words she heard—each well-pronounced syllable—but she could no more make sense of them than she could of the king's. What did the girl speak of? Nan, compose herself? Had she ever been more composed? For the first time in her life, Nan saw herself for what she was: the compounded ugliness of her heart, the drab darkness of her soul. All her life she'd wanted that which was not hers, and, coveting the affection or the joy that belonged to others, she'd pushed herself into other people's lives, and bent them, and twisted them, and made them that which they weren't supposed to be.

Oh, that she'd never been born.

In the harsh light of this sudden understanding, she allowed herself to be led, like a child with no mind or purpose, down the endless corridors. Lady Ariel led her, Ariel's cold little hand clasping Nan's.

Grand courtiers, and fawning, well-dressed ladies curtseyed to Nan as she passed and Nan thought how foolish they looked and how sad it was that creatures so perfect should bend their knee to her, who was unimportant and pasty, and ugly—some warty thing grown from the ground, with no more charm and no more beauty than a fungus that springs after a rain from the side of a mighty oak tree.

Their curtseys and fawning attention so diverted her, that by the time Ariel threw open the door to Nan's room, Nan was laughing, giggling at the top of her voice, a girlish giggle such as she'd never heard from herself.

Ariel gestured, anxiously waving her hands, demanding silence, pointing at the cradle where the babies slept.

Laughing, Nan collapsed on her bed, and still laughed, till tears ran down her face. When she could laugh no more, when strength failed her, when her tears stopped, she found herself staring at Ariel.

And Ariel, looking concerned and worried, looked concerned and worried for Nan only. Not for herself. For the first time in the days Nan had known Ariel, the elf displayed no great grief, no overwhelming worry.

Nan blinked at her, in surprise. It was as though the scene they had witnessed, captured as it had been in the droplet of water, had given Ariel some great, secret joy.

Nan frowned at the elf maiden. Had the images somehow been contrived? Did Ariel know something about this? "I see what the king showed us gives you great joy," she said.

The elf blinked. "Oh, no, milady. Or at least . . ." Her small pink lips shaped a secretive smile, and she shook her head, and still smiled. "Or at least not in the way you think. I'm sure your husband is a good man and that he loves you. You must understand, though, that the glamoury of elvenkind can cloud any judgment. You've felt it yourself and only withstood it because you are a rare, strong woman."

"A shrew, you mean?" Nan asked, but even as she asked it, her mind pursued another line of thought, like a dog that abandons his appointed prey to roust a bird from a distant bush. "Glamoury of elvenkind? Was that lady, then, of elvenkind?"

Ariel looked at her, and blushed, and gasped, and blushed again, and took in a deep breath. "Someone will tell you, anyway, milady. I thought they might already have, and I am surprised they . . . No, but there, I'll tell you. That was an elf, yes, but not a woman. It was the prince Quicksilver, himself, in his other form."

Sure she was being made sport of, Nan lifted her brows, creasing her broad forehead. Her eyes flashed in annoyance at being thus played with, like a child led into a foolish game. "What nonsense. That was a woman, not a man. And do you think my Will so thick and childish that he wouldn't know the difference, when it came to it?"

Ariel giggled. "Oh, he would know the difference but there would be no difference. Quicksilver, you see, is a dual creature, male and female both and both in truth when he so chooses. Your Will would not know the difference."

The room swam, as if water had been poured in and moved each object to unfelt currents. To the distance Nan had felt before, now was added an even odder discomfort.

The perfect lady of Will's love was a perfect youth but, even as a youth, Nan thought, the prince Quicksilver far exceeded Nan in beauty and charms. Oh, let Ariel talk of the glamoury of the elven people. Was it not glamoury that Nan herself had cast over Will? Surely she'd never allowed his brain to perceive what he was doing, marrying an illiterate, aged spinster.

And then again, how it looked, now that Quicksilver had interposed his body to save Will. No wonder. No wonder. And Nan had thanked him. Feeling uncomfortably hot and embarrassed, Nan turned on Ariel with shrewish spite: "You seem very happy, milady, that the prince you love dotes on my husband."

Ariel took in a sharp breath, then smiled, a small smile. "Oh, I'm happy, milady, very happy. You see, I thought him ice, but he loves. And he loves a human—a rare love, rarely felt by our kind. I know his dissembling look and that's none of it, and I know what he does for calculation, but this could bring him no advantage. So he truly loves and there's hope that his icy heart will melt to me yet. I have almost eternity to wait."

Nan sighed. Eternity. She could have eternity, too, or close enough as made no difference. She could live for centuries, here in the fairy hill by Sylvanus's side. And she need no more interpose her shadow between Will and his true love.

How they must have laughed, both of them, when Quicksilver told Will that she had thanked him for saving Will's life.

Nan felt as though her heart were a balloon, pricked, all the blood escaping from it and leaving her gasping in vain for life. "You will go," she told Ariel. "You will go and tell the king that I will marry him. Tomorrow night, at the great solstice ball, I will eat the elven food and become his wife."

Scene 16

❧

*A small Elizabethan schoolroom with a single, narrow
window high up on the northern wall. Long benches are
ranged all around the walls, and on the benches sit
twelve shiny-faced small boys holding the horn-protected
sheets of writing known as the hornbooks. One small
blond boy reads from his hornbook, while Will, standing,
listens to him.*

Will nodded, while his pupil read.

"... who aren't in heaven," the little blond boy
read, laboriously appearing to decode the mysteries of the
Paternoster written on the paper that the transparent sheet
of horn protected. "Hollow be thy name."

Normally, Will would have stopped this unrighteous re-
citing of the Lord's Prayer. As it was, the other students,
smaller boys and bigger ones, all laughed at the pupil's
declamation. The boy's name was Robert Haite and he'd
memorized the Lord's Prayer and somehow memorized it
wrong. Will couldn't seem to make him understand that
the words he said might have anything to do with the
mysterious signs engraved on the paper in front of him.
And if Will called his attention to the correspondence be-

tween symbols and pronounced words, as he often had, Robert would no more than turn round, innocent eyes toward Will and listen with rapt, breathless attention to all Will said. To forget it the next minute.

But this time, despite the titters of his fellow students, and the boy's very poor rendition of the prayer, the petty master nodded as though Robert had said everything perfectly.

Will noticed the mistakes, as well as a vague expectancy around him, a hush that said that, faith, the petty master had been distracted the livelong day.

But he had other worries. No blasphemy uttered with sweet schoolboy innocence could pierce Will's preoccupation.

Tension started to show in the boy's face, in a nervous twitch at the corner of his mouth, and the way he kept looking all around, when the expected rebuke did not come.

In Will's mind thoughts and feelings warred about the fair youth who was the dark lady. He'd lied to Will in that. Well, he'd lied to him in a lot besides. Eyes wide open, thinking over the conversation with the dark lady the night before, Will realized that she'd refused to tell him what would happen to him once he killed the fairy king.

She took him for a rube, a knave with no more mind than a hare hurrying ahead of the dogs to certain doom. The fair youth, the dark lady, that person who was both had no more regard for Will than a man for an old suit he wore, that served a need and was discarded afterwards.

But Will would find a way to defeat the elves, and get them off his back, and turn them from his family, like a curse averted.

While his pupil desecrated the Lord's Prayer, Will thought and thought of Nan, who had been taken from him. His guilt had returned to haunt him, his certainty that had he been a better man, a better husband, Nan would never have been taken.

And now, to his manifold sins, Will had added adultery, the staining of their marriage bed with someone who wasn't human, someone who, almost certainly, wasn't even female.

The memory of the dark lady's charms was pushed out of the way, and Will longed for Nan, his sweet, uncomplicated Nan who'd never lie to him and never, never make him feel like the fool he was, led around blindfolded by other people.

His students' titters grew so loud that Will pulled himself from his thoughts. He looked sharply at Robert's glowing face, his wide, innocent eyes, and, for the first time, realized the boy had been shamming all these long months. He could read well enough or, if not, at least he knew that the words he said were wrong.

Fool that Will had been, fool, that even a petty-school pupil could fool him. He'd half a mind to whip the boy, but why whip Robert when the whole world had been laughing at Will? And, looking at the boy's innocent expression, Will saw a reflection of himself and the jokes he'd once played on his masters.

The light coming slantwise through the leaded glass of the high window above the row of benches looked scant enough, and the sounds that came through were the sounds of workmen hurrying home for supper, and mothers calling their sons back in. This day, this awful day of guilt and doubt, had passed and night neared.

"Go," Will told the solemn assembly of dark-clad little boys, who all stared at him, having understood, through some mysterious alchemy, that their prank had been caught out, and now awaited punishment for their mischievousness. "Go home, all of you, and pray that the

Lord make you as smart as you think you are."

Chastised by his very restraint, the boys left and it was not until a good while down the muddy road in front of the school that the first one let out a whoop of joy and another one called out a challenge to a race.

Will listened to their merry noise, receding down the street, as he locked the schoolhouse door.

Ah, for their freedom, their certainty, the carefree days of his own childhood.

Will must find out how to counteract the dark lady's charm. Even knowing her for what she was and knowing himself duped, could he resist her blandishments if she were to appear?

Who could he ask for help on dealing with unruly elves? *Not* his father. Will shuddered at the thought. And not his mother. He'd taken Joan to her this morning, with admonitions to keep the young girl inside and out of danger. His mother had, predictably, made it out to be Will's fault and turned it all on him. But maybe she'd listened enough to keep Joan safe. Maybe not.

So, other than his family, to whom could he go? Too long he'd listened to Quicksilver-Silver, too far believed in him-her. Now Will needed a mortal advisor and knew not where to turn.

Starting down the street, trading nods with his casual acquaintances in Wincot, Will saw movement in front of the door to the alehouse ahead, and thought of Christopher Sly. A drunkard the old man might be, and insane he might have sounded. And yet, Will remembered his words about the knife, and about the dangers Will might incur in the forest.

Was Sly, then, more than he seemed to be?

Will stopped at the door to the alehouse and looked in.

The place still looked as Will had left it—was it only yesterday?

Had he not known better, he would have thought nothing had changed and that the same people had sat here, through the day and to this evening.

When he'd come in yesterday, he'd been so hungry, so miserable, that he hadn't noticed the smell of the place, a moist, heated mingling of body odor and both sour and sweet ale—sour where it had spilled on the floor, sweet in the jars.

"Now, now, is your thirst such?" Marian Hacket stopped amid the tables, with the white ale jug resting on her rounded hip, and looked up at Will. "Will you be coming here every day now, lad? You're too young for this."

Will came a step into the house, and blinked at the darker, smokier light inside the place, which rivaled the dark, overcast day outside. He shook his head at Marian, but did not say anything. He hadn't come for the ale, but what he had come for he didn't want to say aloud, where all could hear him.

Sly was nowhere to be seen, though the space he'd occupied on the bench remained empty, as though other drinkers feared to take his place. "I was wondering about Christopher Sly," Will said. "Have you not seen him? I thought he might have something to tell me."

Marian's soft face creased, and she pursed her lips. Taking a deep breath, she set the jug of ale on the stained table. "Now, that's strange, for he has left something for you." She walked over to the hearth, where the dispirited bawds sat, their half-hearted smiles displaying near-toothless mouths. From a corner near the fireplace, she retrieved something dark, that clinked metallically as she lifted it, and made her frown in carrying it on her arms, as if it weighed much.

"There," she said and deposited what, up close, Will could see was an iron chain, in his arms. "There. He left that for you, and said it should be the answer to all your problems."

Will remembered the old man telling him that the creatures were afraid of cold iron. Was Will supposed, then, to bind the dark lady with this metal, and with this bond cause her to tell him the truth? It had to be. Nothing else could be true. But how did Sly know of Will's real troubles? And how did he know what Will needed? "Who is Christopher Sly?" Will asked. "He said he was a peddler and that—"

Marian was shaking her head. "A peddler he is not, unless what he peddles be some goods we can't fathom, boy. I saw him talking to you and wondered . . ." She lowered her voice to a whisper and looked frantically around, though none of the drunkards or bawds seemed to take any interest in their conversation. "I've known him since I was a little girl, helping my gram with the serving, and he always has looked the same. At the height of summer and the height of winter, and the days just before, he'll come and drink, and talk like a local, though no one hereabouts knows him except from being here, on those days. My grandmother used to say he was a great lord who played the pauper for his own amusement. My grandfather said he was one of the ancient gods, Lug, god of merchants and liars . . . And so he might be . . ." Her voice trailed off and her hand, as if on its own, made the sign of the cross over her round face, then wiped itself to her apron with nervous haste. "And so he might be, but I didn't say it, and you didn't hear it from me. Only I've never seen him take such an interest in someone, and I wonder what trouble you can have got yourself into, lad."

Will, too, wondered very much what trouble he'd got himself into.

He nodded gravely, to Marian Hacket's words, and nodded again when she said, "My prayers go with you, boy. May the good Lord protect you."

"I thank you," he said. "I thank you." And, shouldering the heavy iron chain, he set out for Stratford.

highest tower where the green flag of Elvenland flew, a
golden mesh of power encased the hill and protected it,
as if invasion were eminent. Could all this be defense
against a single, near-powerless elf?

The power of the protections drew Quicksilver in, sure
as food will draw a famished hound, but his mind told
him to keep away. Now that he was not of the hill, that
net was no beneficial protection to his unprotected head.
Rather, like the net that surrounds a fish and pulls it to his
doom, this net would spell the end of Quicksilver and the
death of all his meager hopes—his hope of love, his desire
for atonement.

Yet he longed for the palace, for its comforts, with a
physical longing such as he'd never felt. Somewhere,
within those walls, Quicksilver's valet worked, perhaps
tending the room from which his lord was now barred.
Somewhere within those walls, Quicksilver's bed was
made, waiting his rest. Somewhere within, his marble and
jade bathroom waited his good pleasure.

Outside, rain poured down the back of Quicksilver's
neck. Even his small comforts, his keeping himself dry in
a rainstorm, his conjuring of food to feed himself, would
demand too much magic. The power he had in him now
was all he'd ever have and the hill would not be there to
draw upon as a never-ending reservoir. Even the magic
he'd used on Will, to draw food to the table, to send the
boy back to sleep in the morning, even that had been hard
spent and Quicksilver might well come to regret it.

The thought of Will brought such confusion of feelings
to Quicksilver, such a tangled mess of mobbing emotions,
that he forgot hunger, boredom, and the cold rain.
Thoughts of Will covered Quicksilver in the warmth of
their remembered love; the fear for the boy, who might
go insane from that love; the shame that he'd allowed
himself to fall so low as to care for this human; the dread

of his own death that must now come, now that all hope of toppling Sylvanus was gone. And over all, over all, the certainty that sweet Titania and gentle Oberon were fading into nothingness, even as their unworthy offspring failed.

Quicksilver rubbed his face with his soaking velvet sleeve, wished he could dry himself, and cursed the weather. If it weren't raining, Ariel might come out on some errand, or perhaps to wander the forest, to ease her heavy heart. If it weren't raining, ladies-in-waiting or valets might walk about, speaking of the great dance tomorrow, and where it would be held . . . and he could take that intelligence back to Will, if nothing else.

Instead, the rain fell unrelenting, leaving the palace grounds deserted and giving Quicksilver little choice but to hover there, within sight of the white palace and its tempting golden power net, and to hope against hope that something, something would happen to give him a hint, a clue.

He couldn't address his parents' shades, and once more ask them for guidance. He felt too tainted, too low, too weak. And he'd given up on the vengeance they'd demanded. So, how could he ask for their help, now?

The chilly rain seemed to drain Quicksilver of even the little power he had, and he sat down, his back against a rough tree trunk, and closed his eyes.

"How now, milord? How now? Asleep?" Ariel's soft voice intruded upon Quicksilver's sleep, and for a while he didn't know whether he dreamed or wakened.

Half opening his eyes, he saw the lady bending over him, and yet didn't know if this vision was a product of his deranged brain or a real being, walking in the world of touchable things and knowable truths.

"Oh, alive," Ariel said. "You're alive, milord. For a moment, seeing you there, so piteously forlorn . . ." Her small oval face registered a startled awareness that he might not wish to be called "piteously forlorn," and she smiled apologetically. "But there, you're soaked, milord. Soaked through and through," she said as her hands sought to grip his arms and slid on soaked velvet. "Wet and cold," she said, as her hands moved from his arms to his face and, resting against the chilled flesh there, felt to Quicksilver like small beacons of warmth and comfort.

She did something he couldn't so much see as feel, like the draping of a warm blanket over his cool flesh and, of a sudden, the rain no longer wet him, and his body regained a measure of warmth. He looked at Ariel with gratitude, as he opened his eyes fully and sat up.

Funny how, from his new view, outside the hill, Ariel looked like a goddess, a creature full of power and glory. And on the heels of that, he wondered whether that was how he, himself, had appeared to Will, whether Will had been dazzled not by Quicksilver's female aspect but by this fatal glamoury of Quicksilver's kind. Confused, worried about his obsession with Will, and what the boy might think or feel, Quicksilver blinked at Ariel, "You are speaking to me," he said. "Have you . . . forgiven me, then?"

The lady didn't answer. She inclined her head, in a half affirmative, but turned her face from Quicksilver and sighed. "You love the boy," she said. "You love the mortal, Will."

Blood rushed to Quicksilver's chilled cheeks, making them glow with the heat of shame. He turned his head away, himself, to hide his red cheeks from her, but he couldn't hide the awareness of them from himself.

Ariel smiled at him, an odd smile, as though he were a slow child, stuttering through his first words. "Love forgives a lot," she said. "And I love you, milord. If I don't comfort you, who will? Who will soothe your misery if not me?"

That smile puzzled him as did the words that followed.

Love. Ostensibly, she referred to her own love for him, but was that all? Something in her smile unnerved him, something in her idea of him made him uncomfortable. She behaved as if she knew something he couldn't even guess at. As though she knew what he was feeling better than he himself knew.

Still, in the warmth of her affection, he found himself comforted, and her charms, which he'd disdained before, seemed now overwhelming. Her smile was a radiating sun, her body, clad in her white gown, a thing of marvelous shape, her features—small and neat as they were—appeared beautiful, a beauty on the verge of the supernatural. Her spun-light hair framed her face in a blaze of glory. And she gazed on him with kindness.

By the light of her kindness, he raised himself slowly. Slowly, he stood up. "You've forgiven me, then," he said.

She shrugged with hypnotic grace. "Forgiven you, milord? What was there to forgive? My brother's death . . ." Her voice caught, and a sob choked her. "My brother's death and my brother's decision to attack the mortal were both wrong. My brother did a vile thing and in committing it, died, as though the gods would not allow him to taint himself with such disgrace. Being killed with the same dagger as your parents"—she took in a deep, shuddering breath—"Killed by the same weapon, he went to join your parents, and with them he waits till the right order of things should be restored, and you can ascend the throne. Then shall he be released, to rejoin the wheel of creation, to be born again, to elvenkind." She spoke with certainty and her eyes had that faraway-looking blankness of when she spoke out of her dreams and prophecies.

Quicksilver thought of Pyrite, Pyrite released anew, to be born a babe, innocent, in the world of elvenkind. And perhaps, Quicksilver thought, long as the lives of his kind were, perhaps Quicksilver would yet regain his friend in another form.

If he carried on his vengeance. But . . .

Something like a twinge of pain seized his heart. "I cannot do it," he said. "Will . . ." How to tell her that Will was inexpressibly dear to his heart, that he could no more send the boy to his death than he could, unflinchingly, open his own veins and spill his magical blood upon the cold ground? "I can't hurt Will. I thought . . . We must give him his wife back, send him his way unfettered."

Ariel looked grave. "Aye, his wife, milord, his wife . . ."

Something in her tone made Quicksilver's mind misgive itself. Could something have happened to Nan? Let her not be dead. Quicksilver felt his former chill renew itself, all the chill that Ariel had dispelled. Not dead. Let the wench that Will prized not be dead. Let him have her back, and regain his mortal happiness.

Quicksilver realized that, having given up on happiness of his own, Will's happiness had become all that he put stock in and hoped for, as mortals hoped for salvation. "What happened? What happened to Will's Nan?"

Ariel shook her head. "Why nothing yet," she said. "Nothing yet, but she has agreed that tomorrow, on the stroke of midnight, she'll eat the nectar, and become one of us, and marry Sylvanus."

Quicksilver shook his head. "Not Sylvanus. Not . . ." It couldn't be. She couldn't desert Will. Didn't she love Will? Besotted with the youth, Quicksilver couldn't imagine anyone seeing Will and not falling into worship like a struck devotee before a god. "How so? How?"

Ariel blushed, and her blush made her so radiantly beautiful, so overwhelmingly enchanting, that Quicksilver's knees buckled and trembled and he had to struggle to keep his mind steady.

"It was your night with him," Ariel said. "The fairies captured it on charmed dew—none of my doing, this time—and brought it to Sylvanus, who displayed it before Nan and me and thus . . ." Her voice trailed off.

"The night just past?" Quicksilver asked. He let his hands fall from her shoulders. "How you must despise me."

"Oh, I do not. Indeed, I do not." She put her hand on his shoulder. "Were it not for that, I might never have known. Your lips might lie, but your heart does not. It was love I saw, love. Love on your part, I don't know if on his. The glamoury . . ."

"Oh, yes, the glamoury," Quicksilver said, and said it bitterly, for he knew it true. "It was my glamoury he worshiped and not me. And even had it been me . . . it is not all of me and I could not . . ." He put his hands on her shoulders again. "Listen, milady, you must tell me where the midsummer dance will be held, and there I will have Will meet his wife, and there claim her back, by the ancient rites, before she commits the fatal folly of joining herself to Sylvanus."

"Of course," she said. "If you'll bide and listen. But the boy must come early and forewarned, because all is in readiness for this wedding. Even now I should be tending to Nan's gown and the presents arriving from every elven kingdom. The party, the wedding, and the rites of summer are all to the take place down the rushy glen, down where the water pools by the riverside and reeds grow. The humans fear the site, because of the sucking mud, and there we can disport in peace. Or so Sylvanus has judged, and he means to disport long and well, since it's to be his wedding night."

Quicksilver nodded. "I'll hie to him, then," Quicksilver said. "And I'll tell him. And you, milady, try to keep his lady from doing something too rash too soon."

Ariel nodded, but her big, questing eyes still stared at him. "What about Sylvanus? What about the traitor, and the vengeance you owe your parents and my brother?"

Quicksilver sighed. "I can't do it, milady. I'm not strong enough, never was, to face Sylvanus and the power of the hill. Not even when I had the power of the hill in me, much less now. Much less now. I am, myself, a dwindling power, a fast-vanishing strength. Forget me, my lady. Be happy without me. I am nothing and no one and the world will be better without me."

Ariel stood sternly, like a judge, a queen, a stern, terrible power. "Fie, milord. You are as extreme in your modesty as in your pride, and both modesty and pride in such immoderate quantities are crimes still. Fie. You have strength and you have power, mightier and greater than hill power. It is the power of right that moves through you and makes you stronger than yourself."

Quicksilver arched his eyebrows. Beautiful words, and he wished he could believe them, but he couldn't. Having tasted his own fallibility, and the evil that tainted him, he now feared to work more mischief by any attempts at righting wrongs. Before, he'd caused Pyrite to die, and now what? By threatening Sylvanus, who might he kill? Sweet Will? Or Ariel herself?

He smiled, a sad smile and, reaching over, touched his lips to Ariel's warm lips. "Farewell, milady, farewell. If we had time, I might have loved you yet as well as you could hope. But I must go to Will and tell him how to recover his good wife."

Ariel looked at him, and appeared sad and wondering and desperate, all in one. In a hot breath of urgency, she said, "Think what I said, think. Justice has its own sword, and right its own strength. Now, go. Go to your love, but forget not that my love shall always be waiting for you."

Her voice was so assured that for a moment, for just a

moment, he almost believed her, almost believed that he could take revenge on Sylvanus himself, and survive it and claim her love.

But as she stepped back, he felt her power go with her, leaving him. He felt the rain start to wet his just-dried velvet.

She paused, an angel arrested on the verge of flight, and turned her concerned, pale face to look at him. For a moment she hesitated as though not sure that he was worthy of her mercy, that he was worthy of her confidence. "Remember, milord, on the glen by the riverside," she said. "Where the rushes grow thick and the bullfrog calls nightlong. There shall we dance tomorrow night. There, Will may find his wife and you may reclaim your crown."

Like that, she turned and ran, back to the white palace. She ran with unreal grace, skipping over the roots of ancient trees and avoiding obstacles, while seeming to dance across the forest floor.

Quicksilver stayed, looking at her run. The rain fell hard, driven, seeping through soggy velvet and thin silk, and chilling his weak body through.

Ariel—a supernatural creature with fantastic powers—disappeared into the world he'd lost, and he was left alone with his cowardice.

He loved, he loved he didn't know whom, but, just at that moment, he loved Will and Ariel both, and though he knew it impossible, he wanted for Will to have his wife back and to be happy that his happiness would feed Quicksilver's joy, and for Quicksilver to win back his kingdom, that he might lay it at fair Ariel's feet.

Quicksilver's heart swung like a pendulum between Will and Ariel, suspended, helpless, from Quicksilver's own dual nature. And no matter how the pendulum swung or how hard, if he carried on his vengeance, he would lose the only two people who mattered in his life.

And if he didn't carry on his vengeance, he would lose them still and he would die, a poor, powerless thing, by the wayside. And the world would melt in the wake of his death, the elven sphere and the mortal sphere, and perhaps even the divine sphere thrown out of temperance, destroyed by this wrenching rearranging of the order of things.

Quicksilver took a deep breath of cold, wet air. When nothing can be done, something must yet be done. He must make a choice and live to rue it, bitter as any choice must be.

Walking through the forest, hungry, cold, scared, he half dreamed himself a young peasant woman and Will's wife. Had dreams been possible, he would have been just that, and happy ever after, for the brief span of mortal life.

But in reality he remained something other, a tangle of physical body and magic—the raw power that had formed when the hearth had first been created from the burning heart of the sun. He remained such a creature of power and magic, of fire and air and fallible, aching flesh. And he must somehow find it in him to fulfill his destiny and be a king.

Scene 18

ᔕᕟᕍ

Will's kitchen. The cat atop the cupboard watches with skeptical gaze, while Will waits by the door, holding the heavy iron chain in his hands.

Will prayed that the dark lady would not come. Standing there, in his kitchen, holding the iron chain, he couldn't help but remember their love, in this very place. He felt like the worst of traitors.

What if she meant him no harm? What if her love had been as real and warm as it felt? What if she came, all kindness, to bestow love on him yet again and he surprised her thus, with this chain?

Behind Will, the fire hissed and spat, and the everlasting rain that had fallen over the last three days lashed against the door and window, and rattled and sang on the pavement outside, its noise sometimes so intense that it could almost be mistaken for a weary walker's feet, dragging toward the door.

The lady had seemed so tired, yesterday. Tired and belabored and bruised. Thinking of her as she had looked, so helpless and frail and needing comfort, Will almost dropped his iron chain. But not quite. At the next breath a thought of Nan, a longing for her as he had known her—strong and sweet and unbearably dear, a woman of his sphere, proper who belonged to him alone—made him clutch the iron with renewed vigor.

The chain felt heavy in his hands. Colder to the touch than any other metal Will had ever held, it abraded his hands as he held it, its links rough like the branch of a tree with the bark still on it.

Where had this chain come from and through whose hands? Like most young men with a grammar-school education, Will knew enough about Roman gods, but precious little about the gods of his own ancestors, who'd been driven into the twilight of nonbelief by those same Roman divinities who would later be sent, howling and shivering, into everlasting nothingness by the light of the Christian faith.

Lug. God of liars and thieves. Will tried to picture in his mind what such a god would look like and superimpose it on the remembered countenance of Christopher Sly, by birth a peddler, by education a cardmaker, by transmutation a bearherd, and now by present profession a tinker. He'd said he was a tinker. Not a peddler, though he'd said that later, and not a smithy, but a tinker. An important distinction. What did Christopher Sly tinker with?

Will had a feeling that Christopher Sly neared and spoke in his ear, in an inebriated whisper ripe with the smell of ale, "I mend more than plates, young Will, and set more than pots fit to boil again."

But who could trust a god of liars, the local brother of that ancient Mercury?

The cat changed positions atop the keeping cupboard and, backlit by the fire, cast its enormous shadow on the wall in front of Will. Will recoiled from that projection as though it were a demon come from the depths to swallow him. Looking over his shoulder, startled, he saw the cause of it and smiled, and returned to his vigil.

Listening carefully, he thought he heard light steps approaching along the alley.

The lady came.

Or maybe some child had been forgotten late out of doors and now slunk under the rain to the bed in which he should, long since, have reposed.

Almost suspending his own breath, holding it in, Will tried to hear, all the while attempting to calm the turmoil in his soul.

Silver had lied, he told himself, her aspect of frailty was a mere ruse with which such as her snagged men from their better purposes, lovers from their better intent. And, to the mellow protests of his heart, he replied with stern warning that she wasn't even a lady, nor a man, but a thing caught between, a thing that could only belong to that realm of nightmare whence the whole hill came. And maybe they were fallen angels, for how else could such evil dwell in a single being?

Will was not so foolish, nor so blind, that he could blame the whole of his transgression—his taking of another to his marriage bed—on the lady's persuasiveness or her perfidious nature. Well he knew how eager he had been.

Such fantasies had long haunted Will and, juxtaposed with his meager experience, his all-too tame upbringing, they might have driven him to commit adultery, someday, some other day, when far from home.

But that would have been later, and no one need have known, and he would have been more settled, more sure of his ways. And he would never, never, have mistaken such bawdy love for the real thing.

He'd loved the elf creature. He'd loved her and considered replacing Nan's sweet truthful love with the lady's false one.

And the lady had, she had, tried to convince Will to kill the king of elves—her brother or no, who could tell—which would have killed Will, or, if not killed him, led him to the same sort of madness that held his father in its thrall.

The steps came all the way to the door, and a meek knock sounded.

Will froze, the chain in his hand. What if he opened the door and it was Joan, or a neighbor on the other side, come to borrow a cup of flour, a jar of ale? What if he encircled with chains a good wife of Stratford?

The knock sounded again, a tempting music, and on the heels of it a faint, sweet voice, called, "Open up Will. Open up. I must talk to you. I must tell you how to recover your Nan and—"

Reaching over, Will unlocked the door, and, with his foot, shoved it open, even while he knit himself with the wall so that he and his chain, both, would be invisible to the lady outside.

"Will?" The lady stepped within. As she had the night before, she wore a cloak wrapped around her head, only this time the wrapping had been better done, and Lady Silver walked with a more assured step. "Will?" She turned her head to the side where he hid, but too late.

He jumped from his hiding place and wound the chain all about her, like a python holding the lady in a lethal embrace.

Blue light flashed the first time the chain touched her and blue light went on flashing. Blue light bathed the kitchen in weird reflections.

She screamed.

From atop the keeping cupboard, Nan's cat spat, hissed, and howled, in a symphony of strange distress.

The lady collapsed to the floor, as if the weight of the chain had crushed her. On the floor, she writhed and screamed, adding a cacophony of sounds to the blue-white brilliance of unhallowed splendor that emanated from her and the chain.

Amazed, scared, breathless, Will stepped back and closed the door. All he needed now, all he needed, would be for Joan to see this spectacle and report it widely enough to have Will arrested for witchcraft.

His eyes dazed by blue-white fire, his ears pierced by the lady's screams and the cat's strange lamentations, Will shivered and tried to look at his handiwork.

He'd expected a sulfurous odor, but there was none, only a strange stench of scorch, but without any taint of infernal fires.

And he'd expected—he didn't know what—that within the chain the lady would turn into some strange creature, some giant aphid, some monstrous toad, something fantastic and inhuman and not to be pitied.

Instead, the blue dazzle subsided, as though its fire had consumed whatever magical strength remained in this being. When Will could see again, what he saw was strange and wondrous indeed, but all too human, almost pathetically so.

The blond man, Quicksilver, whose hand had defended Will from the brigands in the forest, lay in the tangle of iron chain, his eyes closed. He looked dead and his whole noble countenance had been cast into that dignity that sculptors try to give noblemen's statues that rest upon grand marble tombs. Even Quicksilver's hair, moonlight-bright and wild, spread like a fan beneath his head and half-pulled over his face, could not detract from his dignity.

Below the neck, he looked like something quite other. His body had changed but his clothes hadn't. The fine white dress that had so fetchingly encased the lady Silver's cleavage, now lay, split and rent, across Quicksilver's broad chest. And from the ample folds of the white skirt, an unmistakably male leg protruded.

The whole looked both noble and pathetic at once and, struck by it, by Quicksilver's apparent death, Will took two steps back, then another two.

He hadn't meant to kill. He hadn't meant to injure her—him—seriously. He hadn't meant ill, not at all. He must go. He must run from this supernatural murder, from the vengeance that would come as its aftermath.

Will might be able, yet, to endure the ghost of Pyrite whom he had scarcely known and hardly betrayed. But Will knew better than to imagine he could live with Quicksilver's noble ghost, Silver's enchanting one.

And yet, how does one run from a ghost? If the times of papacy remained . . . Will looked at the creature on his floor and more imagined than hoped to detect a very faint movement of the chest, like breathing. Was color returning to the high, waxen cheekbones?

No, no. It was naught but a reflection of the fire.

Will had murdered the elf. He must leave. In some other land, where monasteries still kept their timeless rules, Will would openly affirm and expiate his sins with self-applied scourge and unfailing fast. He'd become, mayhap, adept at herbs and their secrets and use such to help star-crossed lovers. He would . . .

"Will?"

Did he imagine it, or had the creature spoken? Or was it already his ghost, that haunted Will?

"Will?" Quicksilver's long blond lashes quivered upon his cheeks and with immense, visible effort, he managed to open his eyes. "Will?"

The dark green eyes turned toward Will, where he stood in the shadows.

"Will, oh, curse it, Will." Quicksilver's voice, faint, little more than a whisper, sounded like Silver's own, lamenting lost love. "Why did you do this? Why? I loved you well."

Will had backed up until he was flat against the wall. He wanted to go and remove the chain from this creature and then open the door and watch him run out into the darkness outside, never to be seen again.

But, much as he wished it, Will could not do it. For some reason, having Quicksilver address him in Lady Silver's voice, and hearing Quicksilver speak of love, scared Will more than anything yet. He pressed his palms flat against the rough plaster of the wall, and breathed fast, in scant breaths, like one wounded.

"I only came to tell you . . ." The creature on the floor took a deep breath that sounded as though it broke the stays of his chest with filling it. "I came to tell you that the sacred solstice dance will be held in the rushy glen, by the riverside and that, if you go there, you will see Nan." He took another deep, painful-sounding breath.

Once, Will had kept vigil at the bedside of a dying neighbor and these breaths sounded much like the last breaths a moribund might take.

"If you hold her, though she change aspect and transform into all manner of monstrous things, if you hold her still and hold her fast till she stops changing and the sacred dance is done, then will she be yours, Will, yours forever."

At this speech from the creature, who was patently not dead, obviously still able to discourse, Will felt as if he recovered strength and anger. What was this? What was this, but another confabulation, yet another lie from that pretty-lipped liar? Wildly, Will looked to the table where, he thought, he'd left his magical dagger. He'd kill this creature, kill him, cut his lying tongue out of his mouth.

"I can't lie, Will," the creature answered. "Not while wrapped in cold iron."

Will stopped. "How would I know if you lie not? Is that not the tragedy of the liar, that even when he speaks the truth he will be doubted? You have lied to me too well, milord, milady, whichever you might be."

The creature's lips—the lips that, even in this manifestation, looked so much like the lady Silver's—parted.

Will felt that had it more power, the creature would have laughed at the thought of what Will had said. And yet, the eyes that looked on Will reflected such sadness, such never-ending sorrow as if the sins and follies of a million years had come to repose there, like the tatters and ruins of long forgotten kingdoms might be submerged beneath a cold and ancient river.

"Will, if I hadn't been forced into my primary aspect, would I have taken it?" With slow, slow effort, the creature raised its head to fix Will with the full glare of those doleful green eyes. "Or would I judge, and knowingly at that, that you would be more moved by a woman in this plight? Come, Will, I lie not." Breath hissed in and out of its parted, pale lips. "This once, I lie not."

"So it is true?" Will asked, all of a rush, feeling the rightness of the creature's arguments and knowing that unless it was more deeply cunning than Will could ever combat, it would indeed have remained female the better to control him. "So it is true that I might have my Nan? If I hold her fast?"

"If you hold her fast," Quicksilver rasped. "But it must be done tomorrow night. For tomorrow night, lest you rescue her, she'll marry the elven king."

"Marry?" A chain, much like the dreaded iron chain, seemed to drop on Will's heart, causing it to writhe and twist in agony. "My Nan, marry another? But she married me and she . . ."

Quicksilver shook his head. "Glamoury. By the—Damn it, Will, you should know it."

Will knew it, of course. Hadn't he, himself, danced a jig to the elf's tune? So Nan was like that, also—beguiled, driven, by some strange creature, into realms the human mind couldn't dream.

She'd been offered a throne and a king's hand. Should Will even try to recover her? Should Will interrupt her bliss, disturb her pampered state? Would she, who must now have silks and gold and fancy jewels—he remembered her dancing amid the courtiers in the translucent palace—would she wish to return to this poor kitchen, the daily round of back-breaking work, the humble love of her humble husband?

Will looked at Quicksilver and shook his head.

The elves were beautiful, but all deceit. He couldn't let Nan be lost in this land of illusion. Didn't some of the legends say that the palaces that appeared so grand were, in reality, dank caves and poor huts, and that all of the elves' gold and silver added to no more than a handful of slimy leaves, picked, rotting and festering, from the forest floor?

"Will . . ." The creature's voice had gone weaker, weaker than the wind mourning outside, weaker than the softest of whispers. So weak, in fact, that Will wasn't sure it had spoken. "Will, please let me go. Remove this cursed iron that sucks my life and power and strength from me. If you do not, I shall vanish and become a dark creature of the night, of the sort that drowns little children and smothers maidens who forget their prayers."

The voice still sounded gallant, and still had the ironic, humorous tones of Quicksilver's speech. In such a tone, he'd told Will that John Shakespeare owed no man anything. And yet, and yet, Will guessed beyond the words a truth he'd never heard from this source. And the voice whispered upon the kind of ears the human body doesn't have. Mystical ears that understand the speech of angels. The lips that seemingly pronounced those words didn't move.

Quicksilver had laid his head back down, and closed his eyes, and his face reverted to its marble-statue dignity, its distant deathlike coldness.

"If you do not release me," the whisper-sigh went on. "If you do not release me for the memory of our love, then release me out of self-interest. Only take these chains from me and I shall be to you a good slave, a faithful bonded servant. I'll carry the wood for the goodwife and supervise the little ones at their play, and never, never cross you in anything. In anything, Will. You have my word, as an elf under the awful curse and burn of this cold iron. Only let me breathe without this chain."

The thought of the dark lady—or for that matter, the fair youth—as his bonded slave, made Will's blood tremble and his heart fibrillate. The temptation to accept such bondage glimmered before Will's eyes like fairy gold. Who, in Stratford could boast such a grand equipage? A prince from under the hill, bound and harnessed by Will, little Will Shakespeare, the grammar school graduate, the petty-schoolmaster of Wincot.

At the idea of it, Will's mouth watered like a miser's at the sight of a mountain of gold.

And yet, he knew better, had learned better. For trying to prove himself a man, Will had already caused Pyrite's death, and Nan's kidnapping, and Joan's exposure to unsavory kingdoms, and the wrack and ruin of all Will held dear.

And this creature—Quicksilver, or Silver, it mattered not which—this creature of air and fire and eternity, could it be bound, would it accept as its lot the bondage to Will's meager household? And if it would, how would slavery lame and twist its magical beauty?

No, no. Better let it go and see it no more. Even in its aspect as Quicksilver its glamoury shone too strong and Will found himself admiring Quicksilver's straight nose and stern chin, and he feared for his reason and for impulses and instincts that had never, in truth, given him a doubt before.

"Will?"

Will sprang forward, awakened by this word that was almost no word at all. Was it imagination or did the body of the fair youth flicker and go transparent, within the confines of the chains, like the body of the elf in the forest, before his death?

Will found himself tearing his knuckles and hurting himself in his haste as he lifted Quicksilver's uncomfortably hefty bulk, and untangled the iron chain from the wealth of fabric, the mess of skirts, and untangled and untangled, throwing the free end away from Quicksilver, so it would not touch him, and no more leach his magic.

The chain now felt warm to the touch, like metal that has lain too long before the fire.

The last link of chain came away from Quicksilver, and Will cast it violently from him, to land in a pile on the floor beyond the table.

Quicksilver lay cold and unmoving, a faint bluish tint marking the advancing flag of death upon his cheek.

"Milord?" Will asked. Had it been too late, then? Had Quicksilver died already? Was he dead of Will's slow mind, of Will's clumsy fingers? Dead?

Gently, Will laid his hand on the elf's face and, unthinkingly traced Quicksilver's perfect jaw line. "Milord, I do not want you for a slave. You owe me nothing. To keep you for a slave would be as wrong as to enslave the stag that romps through the forest and force him to pull a

cart beside a mule. To enslave you would be to cut the
wings of the falcon and confine him to a tiny cage, that
the doves might mock him.

"Only wake, milord, and you are free, the forest yours
to roam, the Air Kingdom and province of your kind open
to you. Go, milord. Go." Will found his voice clogged
with tears and tears in his eyes. Did he love this creature,
still? Did he love him, even in his male aspect? Was it
glamoury that made Will's heart tender, like a freshly
skinned knee, at the sight of Lord Quicksilver, like this,
poor and powerless and near dead?

Quicksilver's eyelids moved. His blond eyelashes fluttered against his cheek, then lifted, canopying his green
eyes, and he looked at Will, uncomprehending, as if the
mortal spoke a long-lost language.

Will removed the hand that had rested on Quicksilver's
face, and, carefully, too carefully, stood up, stepped back.

Quicksilver sat up slowly, looking about, bewildered.
Then he looked at Will, and drew his eyebrows up in
puzzled wonder.

For a breath, Will feared that Quicksilver had forgotten
who Will was or what Quicksilver was, or what he might
be doing here, in this mortal abode. Will feared that he
had accepted Quicksilver's bondage by freeing him and
now both would be chained to such roles, master and slave
forever.

"You do not want me for a slave?" Quicksilver asked.
His mouth opened a little, at the wonder of it. "You could
have power over a prince of the Air Kingdoms and you
turn it away?" With obvious, aching slowness, Quicksilver
leaned on the bench by the table, near which he'd fallen,
and brought himself up slowly, until he sat on the bench,
an incongruous figure of a fine gentleman, in a lady's
court dress.

"You are too fine for my commanding," Will said.

"Yours is the nature that will go on living centuries after I'm in the tomb and shut in the darkness of forgetting. No one will remember my name on Earth and yet, you will still live and still look as spry and strong as you do now, and possessed of all your faculties and . . . and your fatal charm."

A little color crept into Quicksilver's cheeks, and a spark returned to his eyes, making him look alive again. His faintly colored lips lifted in a smile. "Ah, Will, I owe you more . . ." Quicksilver looked down at himself and saw the tattered dress, and frowned at it as if not believing he'd allowed himself to go around thus attired. "I owe you more than you'll ever owe me. Mortal though you are, you have given me the gift that my kind dreams about and speaks of as men speak of the fantastical treasures of Croesus." Still looking at the dress, Quicksilver made an intent expression, and the dress flickered and palpitated, and changed, and, in the next moment, Quicksilver was attired in gentleman's clothing.

Only this time it wasn't the dark velvet he had so long worn, but a glistening confection of gold and pearls that flickered in splendor and dazzled in shining glory.

Will stared, uncomprehending. Last night, the lady had worn tatters, and this night when Quicksilver had changed, his clothes had remained the same female clothes the lady had worn. And yet now he had changed his clothes with a look.

"It's the power you've given me, Will." Quicksilver smiled at the youth, an indulgent smile. "You see, most elves draw power from the hill, and a little of the power of the hill is attached to each of us at birth. This power, this strength, is no more than the captured fires of creation, that shine through us still. Without the hill, our power does not replenish itself from that primeval force, and eventually dies. But there is other power that can be got, most of it dark. Any strong emotion produces power and harnesses a little of creation's fire. And any strong emotion can feed an elf. But most of us live our entire lives on the surface of emotions. We feel desire but not love, joy but not abiding happiness. Even the love we feel for other elves is a light thing, a bauble, requiring no overwhelming trust, demanding that we withstand no hardship, forcing us to know no pain. Most elves find it easier to feed on emotions of humankind, particularly the strong and raw power of human ire and fear and suffering. Thus do you hear of demons who hunt dark lanes and forgotten forests. But there is another power." Quicksilver stood up, all in one fluid motion, his ease of movement regained. "There is another power that comes from emotion, if an elf manages to attain a higher emotion, most of all, love for a human, that most unequal of passions, that most trying of affections.

"If a human loves us . . . if a human loves us, he can give us wings. And thus you hear of all the fairy princesses awakened with a kiss."

Will opened his mouth to protest that he didn't know that he loved Quicksilver. Oh, he found the lord as unbearably beautiful as the lady, but from that to love was a long step, and Will didn't think he loved anyone but his Nan.

Quicksilver closed the space between them with three easy steps and rested his cold finger on Will's lips, commanding silence.

"Hush, hush. I know well you don't love me. That's not what I mean. We are, Will, cold creatures, with neither joy nor great capacity to love among ourselves, much less beneath ourselves or beyond ourselves." He smiled, and his eyes shone with merriment. "And yet, in rare instances we can be made to love, truly love, even a human, and if we are . . . if we are . . . Then we capture the fire of creation in our own heart. With the hill or alone, Will, I shall never want for power, and that's the gift you gave me, Will, for I love you well."

Will opened his mouth again to protest that such love was too much for him, as overwhelming and embarrassing as unrequited hate.

But Quicksilver shook his head. "Promise me you'll go to the rushy glen by the river. It's a good five hundred steps, straight toward the river from the oak where Pyrite ambushed you. There you shall see—blessed that you were born on a Sunday—you shall see all the fine ladies and gentlemen of Fairyland, assembling for a grand ball. While you're yet unobserved, mark what your Nan is wearing, for Sylvanus, the king of elves, my treasonous brother, will try to confuse you and change the aspect of everyone's faces. But it is unlikely he'll have that much power at his command as to change apparel. And when they start dancing, you seize your Nan and hold on tight to her, no matter what seems to happen. They can do no more than spell you with illusions. If you hold on to Nan, she will remain with you and still be yours when the dance is ended. Do you understand, Will?"

A fine glove of silvery fabric now covered the hand that Quicksilver laid on Will's shoulder, while he looked to Will for assent.

"I understand," Will managed, overwhelmed by all the strange events that his eyes had witnessed, events that his mortal eyes denied and his mortal reason protested against. "And Susannah?"

"Susannah will be given to you with her mother. She was only taken with her mother, and is not a changeling of her own nature."

"And you? Will you be there?"

Quicksilver looked surprised, then laughed. "I might be, Will. I might well be."

Before Will could anticipate it, or forestall it, the elf lord bent and touched his lips to Will's, in a brief, velvety touch, and then he was gone.

The door never opened and Quicksilver didn't step toward it. He simply vanished.

For a moment Will wondered if he had died, like the elf in the forest, but he heard Quicksilver's laughing voice in his mind, answering, *No, Will. But I now have enough power to move as I should, on fire's own wings, and not as your kind moves, on painful feet. Goodbye, Will. Goodbye. Remember me.*

Of a sudden, Will was alone in his mundane kitchen, with nothing to show for his adventure but a rusty pile of iron chain in one corner.

The cat jumped down from the keeping cupboard to the table, and bumped Will's arm with its head, as if to ask if he intended to fetch its mistress.

"Of course," Will said. And yet he wondered about the tests and trials he would have to endure to get his Nan back. And would Nan want to come, now that she'd been offered the kingdom of Fairyland?

Scene 19

❧

The rushy glen by the riverside. Amid the rushes, a wedding table is set, and on it cakes and confections of such miraculous nature that they look as though they might at any minute take flight.

Nan thought that the place should have smelled brackish—of stagnant water and rotted vegetation, but it didn't. Her wedding banquet table—a golden piece of furniture, with spindly legs—sat by the riverside in a spot where shallower ground invited the river in. There, the river had taken a bite out of the forest, forming a murky pool, where green rushes grew and lilies floated on the stagnant water.

But the wedding table, for her second alliance, was set right atop the rushes and the murky water and there stayed, as though on a carpet, balanced and even. And the air all around smelled of flowers, as if they feasted amid a perfect spring meadow.

And though rain fell everywhere, and Nan could see it, it wet neither her nor any of the elves, nor did the servants, carrying fantastic confections to the lace-covered table get

wet, nor the cakes—spiraling, soaring spun-nectar white-
ness—run, nor the tablecloth sag.

Sylvanus had led Nan to the thrones set up at the end
of the clearing—tall thrones as gilded and perfect as the
one in the throne room in the palace. He'd seated her in
one of the thrones, but he, himself, had declined to sit on
the other.

Like a market peddler, adept at gaining the friendship
of his customers, the High King of Elvenland in Avalon,
moved, instead, amid the multitudes of well-dressed courtiers, their numbers swollen far beyond those that attended
the evenings at the palace, and spoke to each of them in
a concerned away, and pressed their hands in earnest of
his honesty.

Through the sweet music that a large orchestra of elves
played at a corner of the clearing, Nan could hear the song
of frogs by the riverside, and coming across it all, again
and again, Sylvanus's powerful voice. "Quicksilver" he
said and then again, "Quicksilver" and "Quicksilver," yet
again, the name laden with deep sorrow, infinite sympathy. It seemed to Nan, on hearing it, that all these noble
lords objected to the expulsion of Prince Quicksilver and
that the king had to mention it, again and again, to explain
away the cutting off of a prince from the hill, and justify
his stern measure.

All the same, Nan wished he wouldn't mention the
prince, wished his name were not pronounced near her.
Hearing it, brought to mind Will and the dark lady cavorting on Nan's own bed.

The thought still sent a shock like molten lead flowing
through Nan's heart. How could Will? How could he?

And yet, looking around the clearing, she thought that
she was about to contract marriage with an elf, to become
an elf, like him, part and parcel of his world and never
again able to return to her own world, or to Will. Wasn't

her treason greater than Will's? So Will had spent a night with someone else. Was he, then, the first husband to thus stray? And did many a man not, after such a false step, find his feet again and keep to the path of his marriage and the bed of his wife the rest of his days?

She felt something like a bitter laugh push its way through her lips, but she stopped it in time. If it were only one night . . . If Will had repented . . . But, for all she knew, Will continued cavorting with his dark lady who was really a fair gentleman. Even now, Nan supposed, they'd be beneath the covers in the house in Henley Street, finding new ways to cloy their jaded appetite.

Like that, Nan gazed across the clearing, past the milling crowd of courtiers all in cloth of gold and fripperies of velvet and silk, and saw . . . Will! He stood at the edge of the river, but in the mortal world, so that his feet sank in the mud to the ankle. The rain that fell soaked his poor wool suit, and made him look like a wet cat, when all its fur—the ornament and grace of its state—clings to its poor frail frame and leaves the cat nothing more than a bag of bones, pitiful and pitiable.

Nan felt a stab of annoyance. Will would be ruining his suit, the idiot. And worse, he'd be destroying his boots, the fool man. As though it were easy, on their meager income, to have his boots resoled when they wore thin, much less this, to have to replace sole and uppers and all.

Such was her reflexive indignation, before she thought that it would be none of her business. Will's clothes, his shoes, should no longer worry her. She would be Queen, Queen of Fairyland, alive and hale and happy, long after Will lay asleep and gone forever beneath the dust in Stratford Cemetery.

The thought should have brought her joy and exhilaration and a sense of freedom. Instead, it brought a disconsolate, deep mourning, like the crying over a dead child. Reflexively, Nan looked to the side of the throne, where the double cradle had been set and where grand ladies and great gentlemen of Fairyland sighed and cooed over the babies' perfect, chubby features.

One of those ladies detached herself from the group. Grand, dressed all in spun silver, her head ornamented with gaily colored feathers, the lady looked like a stranger, and it wasn't until she got close that Nan recognized Ariel's small features.

"He loves you, you know," Ariel whispered. "He's come to fetch you away."

"Loves me?" Nan started, then looked at Will again, at the edge of the clearing, his gaze fastened on her like iron called by a magnet. Ah, so he loved her, did he? And how was it that Ariel knew of his presence? Looking at Will, at the way the elves walked around him and through him, Nan was sure no other elf saw him.

"I cast a veil over him," Ariel whispered. "Oh, they'll know he's there when he interferes in the dance, but, until then, I'll keep him safe from the ravages and defenses of our kind."

Safe. "Foolish girl, why do you bother? What do you think you'll accomplish with this? Are you keeping him safe for me, or have you become a procurer for your lord Quicksilver and will, for him, find what his lewd love requires?" Speaking thus, in harsh words, Nan wished to shock Ariel and half expected the elf girl to yell back her response, like a housewife at the Stratford market.

But instead, Ariel smiled. Her pale blue eyes glowed with a light they'd never shown before. "Love is never lewd and my lord Quicksilver has forsaken his claim for your sake. He loves that much."

"Love." Disappointed at Ariel's meek answer, Nan realized that she'd been trying to start a fight because she wished to cause a spectacle and force this whole court to turn toward her. No more would they press Sylvanus's hand. No more would they mutter sad things about the transgressor, Quicksilver, no more would they walk past the throne, where Nan sat, with just a nod and an arching of eyebrows. If Ariel had started a fight, they'd have been forced to see Nan and react to her. "Love—you believe in that, do you? You believe in a man's words? Ah, girl, girl. Men were deceivers always."

But Ariel laughed. "Deceivers, maybe, but you see, Quicksilver is not a man and his dual nature deceives him more than anyone else. For many years, tumbled by it, he's not known which of his end is feet and which head, and he's gone through the world like an oyster, shut in on itself veiling the pearl of love it is capable of. But the oyster is now open, the pearl displayed, and this treasure . . ." Ariel shook her head and tears shone in her eyes. "It was your Will who pried the shell open. And it is for your Will's love that Quicksilver wishes you and your husband reunited. And for Will's sake, Quicksilver has asked me to help. And for his sake, I will."

Nan stood up. Even standing up, despite her shiny, rainbow-colored gown, she attracted no attention. Not one of the courtiers turned to look at her, not even Sylvanus, busy as he was, in conversation with several imposing high lords.

No glance but Will's followed her, but Will's gaze was so steady, so intently fastened on her every moment that she felt as though it were a hot, smothering blanket that made her sweat with the strength of his regard.

To deny him, to tweak him, to keep him doubting and guessing, Nan walked down the three steps of the throne, to stand beside Sylvanus, as he spoke to the high lords.

"Quicksilver was ever an improper elf," Sylvanus was saying. "Not, I'm sure, my brother true, not the son of my father. And that improperness has stained the hill. That's what is causing this unseasonable rain, this distemper of colliding spheres. You know, certainly, that when a hill's power becomes tainted, it affects the movement of the other spheres, and thus—" He stopped. Nan had come up to stand beside him, and put her arm through his.

She could feel, across the clearing, Will's startled recoil, as if she'd slapped him. As she should have. She smiled, happily.

Her happiness lasted a scant moment. The three lords who'd been talking with Sylvanus, now turned toward her with frowns of such portentous disapproval that Nan's smile wilted on her face, replaced with a tenseness of shock, a confusion of embarrassment.

"Milord," she said, wanting to prove her power over the king. "Are you not going to introduce me to these high lords, and let them know the woman you expect to be your helpmeet?"

Sylvanus looked down at her and tried to remove his arm from her grasp. "Milady, you forget yourself."

"Forget myself, how? Am I not going to be their queen?" She fixed the lords with her best shrewish glare. She wanted them to look on her with respect, to curtsey and bow and scrape and make Will more than ever mad with jealousy at her new state. "Should they not know me and bow to me?"

But the lords only glared harder, and Sylvanus's voice had a deep chill in it, which raised a snow-covered fastness of disapproval as he said, "Milady, your sphere is the nursery and the kitchen, the supervising of the babes and the meals and the upkeep of the palace. Not the sphere of politics and the business of men, for which your gentle nature, your inferior brain, ill qualifies you."

Nan took her hand from Sylvanus's arm, and gladly too. Gentle nature? Inferior brain? Who did the fool think he was talking to? Some maid, with milk still upon her breath, dawdling her time upon the village green until her father, in his superior wisdom, gives her away like a new shirt or a well-tamed horse to a man he deems worth it?

What a fool, what a disgraceful idiot. How could he claim to love her, if he knew her not?

She opened her mouth, ready to remove all illusion from Sylvanus's foolish mind, to make the misapprehension fall from his eyes like scales.

She would surely have done just that, had the music not changed at that moment.

The sounds that had been a fair accompaniment to gentle conversation now became an insistent drumming, a thrumming of disquieting chords, echoed and repeated by all hearts, picked up by all feet. Without a word, the courtiers started pairing, noble lords picking noble ladies, taking them in their arms, and, with them, spinning, round and round, as if music itself moved them.

Ariel, dragged away by a gentleman all in gold, stopped long enough to whisper in Nan's ear, "Your true husband will take you in this sacred dance, and do what he might, do what anyone might, don't let him let you go, or you shall be forfeit."

And then she was gone, her step light as she joined the many couples dancing round and round in mad joy. The gentleman who seized her and led her, Nan thought, looked much like the banned prince, Quicksilver himself. Except that Nan had heard that since his parents' death he'd never worn anything but black, and this gentleman was dressed in gaudy gold and laughed with ease as he led the smiling Ariel.

Tearing her gaze away from them, Nan realized that she, herself, was being tugged into the dance by Sylvanus's thundering majesty.

She followed, half-spirited, not feeling the beat and pull of the music as the elves no doubt did.

But her heart did drum a mad song as she neared the place where Will hid. And she flinched and startled to see that he looked not at her but at the whole company, eyes amazed, going from face to face, as though not sure where she was.

The fool boy. Could he not see her? Would he let her go now, and miss his chance at having her back?

Oh, gladly would she go back to him now, heart and soul. He'd never told her that her brain was inferior or her nature gentle. Her Will knew her, and loved her despite knowing her.

But if he didn't seize her now, what good would that be? She'd be lost to him, forever a captive of Fairyland.

Scene 20

❧

The same enchanted glade, where fairy couples dance, round and round in mad, joyous cavalcade. Will stands amazed, at the edge of it, worried and fearful, as couples dance by. All the ladies, in every couple, wear Nan's face.

So many couples, so richly attired, pirouetted past Will that it made him dizzy. And the music of the fairy orchestra resounded and moved in his blood, making him nauseous, as witless as a babe who knows not his name and smiles at all who approach his cradle, rewarding friend and enemy alike.

And all the ladies, in every couple, had Nan's face and smiled on their gentlemen with Nan's besotted smile. Was Nan besotted with the fairy king? She had seen Will, Will was sure of it, but she had ignored him. Did she no longer love him?

He'd marked Nan's dress, an odd white glimmering fabric that shone all over, under the light, with the reflected brilliance of the rainbow. But now every woman, every single one, seemed to wear Nan's dress and, with her face, dance besottedly round and round and round.

And all the gentlemen's faces looked softly blurred.

Twice—as by looking at the gentlemen Will could track it—twice the whole enchanted company went dancing past him, round, round, and round, a mysterious fairy circle he could not penetrate.

Will's heart sank within him and, under the rain, standing in mud, he felt like the most miserable, the last, of beings.

Quicksilver had told him that Nan would be forfeit. If she didn't get rescued now, she'd be forfeit, lost forever to Fairyland. And Will, poor Will, would trudge alone to his cold home, to be an object of pity to his neighbors— the chattering Wedgwood and the smith Hornby—who would relate over the day's work how poor Will fared, and how his case was not expected to improve, and how it was said, far and wide, that he drank and that his life was in a shambles since his wife and daughter had left.

Other rumors would start, too, when time went by and no one saw Nan and no word came of her having settled somewhere else. Rumors that Will, or maybe Mary, had killed both wife and babe and buried them in the backyard of the house on Henley Street, amid the flax patches and the fat, round roses.

Time would go by and people would stop talking to Will. No good, then, reviving his father's shop, for no one would come in when Will was there. And babes, on the street, would shy away from him, and far and wide the dreadful ballad of the schoolmaster who'd killed and buried his wife and his infant daughter would be sung at fairs and sold in cheap booklets, to quaking passersby.

All this Will saw, as the inevitable course of his life, while the magical dancers passed him in their joyous cavalcade.

That man in the golden suit—was he not Quicksilver? He'd thought Quicksilver banned from the hill. But this elf had Quicksilver's same manner of moving, his graceful step. Had Will been lied to, yet again? The lady with whom Quicksilver danced had Nan's face, but she looked even more besotted than the other Nans, her face very close to Quicksilver's, and his, blurred like those of the other gentlemen, close to hers, as if they had eyes only for each other, intent and close on their own conversation.

Those looked like marriage negotiations, if Will had ever seen a marriage negotiated, and he felt a pang of something he was willing to admit might be jealousy as he saw the dancing couple do the whole circuit of the clearing and return, dancing toward him, intent still on their close negotiations.

Suddenly their arms reached out. Quicksilver and the woman who wasn't Nan, though she looked like her, each reached out an arm and pulled Will into the dance.

Of a sudden, though there was still mud beneath his feet, Will didn't sink in it, and, instead, danced on a hard, polished floor. His eyes couldn't see it, but his feet could feel it, as, on their own, they moved to the rhythm of the fairy music.

"Fool boy," Quicksilver said, in his odd, amused yet soft voice, that denoted more affection than Will had ever wished to inspire. "Did I not tell you to mark what she's wearing?"

And the lady with Nan's face and Nan's body, who nonetheless talked in a softer voice, said, "She knew you would grab her, but you didn't. Why not? Have you changed your mind?"

They dragged him on and on in their joyous dance, even as they spoke, and Will shook his head, and swallowed air to feed his movement, as he kept up with the elves' fast, graceful movements, and tried to explain, "No . . . my mind . . . remains . . . the   same . . . But   Nan . . . every-one . . . even . . . this lady . . . looks like Nan . . . with the same . . . clothing." He gasped for air and watched anger twist Quicksilver's noble features into a knot.

"The villain," Quicksilver said. "I was right. He doesn't have power to alter everyone's clothing, nor could he do it without protest from the ladies. But he changed your vision. Oh, damn, Will. We'll take you to her."

Dancing round and round, and round and round, faster and faster, they started passing couples, weaving around them, improvising a mad dance of their own that took them, around and around faster than Will's feet could move.

Both lady and lord held Will, his feet off the ground, dragging him on in their merry dance, too fast, Will thought, too fast for any of the other couples to have time to discern that here danced three and not two.

They collided with another couple. Lord and lady extended their arms, pulled a woman into their group, shoved her into Will's arms, and, letting them go, danced on, just two.

The man left dancing alone, his feet following the music but his face stricken and shocked, was the same ponderous majesty that Will had seen, once, sitting on the Elvenland throne.

He tried to catch up to Will and the lady in his arms, the lady who had to be Nan.

Quicksilver and his lady danced close by, now clearly visible, and Quicksilver fixed the king with a basilisk stare, and under that stare, the king spun slower, as though dancing while immersed in molasses. All the other couples passed him by, and he spun in place, under Quicksilver's forceful glare.

Nan felt warm and soft in Will's arms, much the same as she'd felt when, together, they'd danced in the churchyard at Temple Grafton, last year.

"My faithless husband," she said. And it was Nan's

voice, shrewish-sharp and yet tinged with abiding sadness.

Had he hurt her that much, then? "Your faithful husband, milady. From now on, no other will do for me, no one else shall fill my arms."

"Oh, I pray you, how many have you told that to, milord, and how many times?"

"None, Nan, none other, for you I married, and you I took to my bed." The dancing made his breath short and cut the fine declaration of love he wanted to make to his Nan.

"You took another to your bed, too." Nan's voice was sharp as a well-honed blade, but her eyes were soft and full of tears. "To our own bed, our best bed, given us by your Arden aunt and by me cherished . . ."

"Fool that I was, fool," Will said. "And foolish with longing for you I took another. Forgive me, Nan, forgive me. Love you me not well?"

Nan shook her head. Her eyes were soft but her face all hard, disciplined to hardness and joyless judgment. "Ah, no. No more than reason."

"Oh, sweet Nan, do not be so. Wouldn't you come home with me? Though you never came to any man's call."

She looked, for a moment shocked, surprised. "I never came? I came to your deceiving call, fast enough."

"Then come to it, again. Do you not remember our home, our hearth, and the joy of being together?" Will was not so foolish that he dared mention their bed. He cast about for another enticement and said, "Your cat misses you so well that, in his suffering, he will even consent to come to my calling."

"Foolish cat, then. Foolish. Fooled like Nan by sweet-talking Will," Nan said. A faint twitch made her seem to almost smile. "And yet it is true that, hard though it is to conceive, there are men worse than you. You've never bid me come and go, at your whim, as other women's lords might have done. And you never told me I had a weak brain."

"A weak brain? Forbid it. I am not that foolish, my Nan. I promise I'll never more bid you come, never impinge on you when you do not wish. Even now, I beg you to come, I do not order it. Come home, dear wife, and be my own. Hie home with me, with our Susannah."

Nan smiled now, openly. "Yea, I'll come when you bid me. But remember, I'm not doing your bidding henceforth. I won't depart when you bid me to."

"Stay till then. For I'll never bid you go, and if you but abide till then, you'll abide forever. For *then* will never come."

"Then is spoken," Nan said, and, despite her words, she smiled. "Fare you well now."

"Foolish Nan. Thereupon will I kiss you."

"But no. For if a fool kiss you, your lips shall be tainted with his foolishness, and I will not be a fool."

"But you borrowed foolishness from my lips," Will said. Dancing like that, round and round, he'd forgotten the seriousness of their situation and the very serious striving he must do for his Nan's hand, her renewed regard, their baby's freedom.

He held Nan in his arms, he smelled her, her soft perfume of roses beneath the other perfumes of Fairyland, and he thought himself safe, safe and home at last, in his Nan's arms. How could he ever have thought that he longed for anything more? Who could long for anything more? "Let me borrow my foolishness yet awhile, and kiss those lips, where my foolishness does ill sport itself." He pushed his lips close to Nan's half-parted red lips, full of temptation and hinting at sweetness like a well-ripened grape, enticing and intoxicating.

But Nan turned her face, so his lips touched but the soft

niche of her cheek and she laughed, "Neither a lender nor a borrower be, Will, neither a borrower nor a lender."

But even then, in their striving, Will knew he had won her back.

Happy in his happiness and lulled by their joint dancing and Nan's sweet body next to his, Will didn't remember the king, nor did he look to see whether Quicksilver still kept him immobilized.

"Will, look out!" Quicksilver's scream, from seemingly very far off, startled Will, and yet he remembered what he'd come to do, and tightened his arms around Nan, hard.

Just in time. The ground beneath their feet seemed to open up, and suck Will down, like a whirlpool of water will suck at the unwary swimmer and threaten to devour him.

Will felt his feet pulled at and then his ankles, both of them disappearing beneath the murky water and the mud. Nan, on the other hand, remained on the invisible hard floor on which they'd danced, and was being pulled, insensibly, out of his arms.

Will held on. He held onto her waist with all his might, linking his hands together behind her and whispering softly, "If I hurt you, pardon me, love, pardon me."

On those words, and while Will's arms ached and strained with holding onto Nan, but Nan wouldn't sink and he wouldn't go down beyond his ankles, the scene shifted.

Nan screamed, "Will!" and let go of him, and flailed at him with her not inconsiderable force, her large, work-capable hands belaboring his head and shoulders, her arms pushing away from him.

So startled was he by her attack, that it took him a moment to realize he had become engulfed in flames, that flames shot out of his doublet, outlining his arms, bursting from his every pore, his every breath. Once he noticed them, he felt the pain, the agony of burning spreading along every nerve.

Nan, too, must have felt the burning, for her body contorted and she fought, trying to get away from Will's burning arms.

In horror, Will watched his arms, which encircled Nan's waist, melt in the flames. The smell of his own burning flesh made him cough. Yet he lived, like the immortal salamander, within the flames.

"Hold on, hold on," Quicksilver's voice said. "It is but an illusion."

The king stood, separating Will and Nan from Quicksilver. On Quicksilver's words, he extended one hand, and Quicksilver reeled as though punched. The king extended his other hand and kept Will and Nan engulfed in flames.

Quicksilver knelt, on the ground, immobile. Blood ran from his mouth. His eyes glazed. He looked transparent, greyish, like a pale thing on the edge of dissolving.

Will watched his own flesh burn, helpless, and knew not how to keep Nan in his immaterial arms.

Nan pushed at him with the force of panic, wishing to save herself from the flames, and his arms, which he couldn't see, hurt even more than the rest of him.

Odd, how burning into nothing hurt less than the tiredness of holding on by force to a strong wench.

Will breathed fire, and it burned his lungs with every breath. He existed only as an exhalation of pain. Through it, without breath, without strength, without voice, he found the power to yell, "Quicksilver. Help."

He'd thought, always, that asking for help would make him sound like a little boy in the world of men. But now, he asked for help and, though the object of his request seemed as helpless as himself, Will felt new strength grow inside him. He held Nan steadier and she, surprised at his scream, stopped struggling for a moment.

"It's an illusion, Nan. You will not burn," Will whispered with his new strength.

Far away, at the other end of the clearing, Quicksilver stirred, but, through eyes blurred with tears and smoke, Will had trouble seeing what the elf prince did.

Scene 21

❧

The same clearing. Quicksilver kneels, overcome by the power of the hill embodied in Sylvanus. Near him, Ariel speaks, trying to push him forth into battle, but he kneels. His mouth bleeds, where Sylvanus hit him with the power of the hill, as if with a fist.

What a fool Quicksilver had been, what an idiot. The salty taste of his own blood made him realize how stupid he'd been.

So, his craving for the boy had given him desperate strength, desperate enough to allow him to dress himself in glittering gold and brave coming to the Summer Solstice Dance and join in the merriment. And he, fool that he was, had believed himself in love, in real love, and had thought that such love gave him magic.

He'd even led the boy to his Nan, though Quicksilver's heart split with the pain of letting Will finally go, of giving him up forever to his farm wife. Yet, while Quicksilver's jealousy watched, and his envy spied out of his eyes at the man and wife as they talked and danced together, Sylvanus had overcome the feeble hold that Quicksilver had on him, and made Quicksilver the defeated prisoner where Quicksilver would have reigned victorious.

And here Quicksilver knelt, while foolish little Ariel wished him to get up and fight, as though he could.

Sylvanus's power encased Quicksilver and held him in place like an iron fist closed over a gnat. Now would Sylvanus crush him, with good reason and in front of the whole court. Here ended ill-fated Quicksilver. Scared and shamed, tasting blood and smelling his own sweat of fear, Quicksilver knew his whole life had been in vain. He closed his eyes and waited for the final blow.

Instead, he heard Will's voice, raised in panic, "Help, Quicksilver, help."

Will's scream woke Quicksilver from the tolling of his many pains and inevitable doom. Quicksilver looked up, though looking up should have been impossible, held as he was by his brother. Just in that moment, Will overcame the illusory fire. Flames went out on his arms and along his body, showing Will's body perfect as it had been, and his eyes amazed and scared.

Will had defeated the flames. In a fluttering of hope, Quicksilver rose upon one foot to stand. But reason crushed hope before it took wing, as Sylvanus rounded on the elf prince and Quicksilver realized that Sylvanus had only let Will go so he could give his full attention to his rebellious brother, who had moved when he should have been immobilized.

On Quicksilver, Sylvanus turned the entire might and fury of the hill. "Disobey me, will you? And flaunt your disobedience in front of the whole hill?"

Quicksilver looked at Will and thought that if he could move for Will, at Will's voice, then he could move at any time. The power of his love for Will was true. It must be true, and ever renewed when he looked on Will's dark curls, his pale skin, the raw gracefulness of his half-grown body, every time he remembered that Will had let him go free when he had offered himself as a slave. That power filled Quicksilver, infusing him with white-hot strength. In the grasp of that strength, that power, Quicksilver stood up.

"Challenge you, yes, challenge you, Sylvanus, who stole the kingdom from me, and who holds it against all laws of nature. I heard you speak, brother, before the dance, of the laws of nature and everything being out of kilter, the spheres clashing one against the other with the wrongness of it. You are wrong, my brother. You're the wrongness."

"I?" Even as he spoke, Sylvanus sent the power of the hill, as an invisible, burning force, to hit Quicksilver on the chest.

The impact, scorching and crushing, pushed Quicksilver away and sent him sprawling backwards, past the illusory floor of Elfland and onto the mud of the glen. The mud cushioned Quicksilver's fall, but still his chest hurt where the power had hit him, and the heat of it seemed to have scorched his heart and lungs and throat, making them feel raw.

"Why would I be wrong?" Sylvanus strode on the invisible floor suspended above the mud, and stood over Quicksilver. "Just because you were born the younger? What does that signify? What does it matter, that accident of birth? For two thousand years I was Titania's and Oberon's only heir, their only hope of succession. And then you came along, you imperfect spawn. Why should I yield my place to you and be content to see you smirk and take it?"

Mud squelched as Quicksilver struggled to raise his head. He had to gasp and swallow air to be able to speak through a throat that felt burned by the discharge of power. His voice came out croaking. "Unfair, perhaps, but is nature not unfair? Does not the mother hare sometimes, on birthing, eat half of her litter that she might survive? Who knows if the ones that were eaten were not the best part of the whelp and the others, that survive and enjoy the freedom of the fields, the much inferior product?" He summoned the power of his love and, mud-spattered, managed to levitate back up to the illusory floor of Fairyland through which Sylvanus had willfully pushed him, and to slowly, painfully, bring himself to his feet upon it.

"Imperfect, I am, perhaps, and yet I stand, and I am your rightful sovereign. Kneel to me, Sylvanus." As he spoke, Quicksilver threw the force of his new-found power, his love for Will and all its strength, toward Sylvanus, to make him kneel.

The knees of the king buckled for just a second, but then he stood again, and smiled. "Kneel to you? Sooner would I kneel to the Hunter himself."

Quicksilver held fast, but Sylvanus laughed and strode about, mocking Quicksilver's new-found power. What power could Quicksilver have that was greater than Sylvanus's?

With all the force he could summon from his aching body, his fearful spirit, his loving heart, Quicksilver pushed at Sylvanus. His power was the only thing keeping Sylvanus from throwing another power charge at him, and he meant to keep Sylvanus thus incapacitated until he knelt. Sylvanus would kneel or Quicksilver would die. And if Quicksilver died, what would become of Will?

Quicksilver pressed fast, fast, and held Sylvanus in an unmerciful grip, and sweated with the effort of it, while Sylvanus laughed.

"Dark spawn of a mistaken night, return to the shadowy place where you were conceived and plague us no more," Sylvanus said.

Quicksilver could see the faces of the dancing court, who had not yet judged this important enough to interrupt the sacred dance for the sake of it. Lords and ladies smiled at the innuendo about Quicksilver's origins.

"Why do you not rule together?" a courtier asked, dancing by, and smiling, only half-mocking. His name was Basalt and he, a great southern lord, passing fair, was ever ready to broker a peace or offer a solution for any striving. "It is plain you are both great lords."

"I cannot rule with a murderer," Quicksilver said. He wished to clean the mud from his golden suit, but he could not, not while he had to use all his strength against Sylvanus, just to keep Sylvanus from attacking. And all his strength was insufficient. Sylvanus appeared not to feel it, countering Quicksilver's strength with another power, stronger than the hill power and deeper than hill power had ever run. Sylvanus's power pushed back Quicksilver's, as a stronger opponent will overpower the other in a wrestling match. Soon, he'd be wholly free. Soon, he would attack Quicksilver with renewed fury. "And my brother has stained his hands deep in regicide. *He* killed our parents."

At such a statement even the sacred music, that must go on the whole half-hour before and half-hour after midnight, stopped. The dancing couples trembled in their dance, then came to a standstill, amazed.

"I never killed our parents," Sylvanus said. He looked shocked, his honest face strained with the surprise of such a base accusation. The accusation had, indeed, surprised him so much that Quicksilver managed, for a moment, to get a firmer grasp on him. But as he recovered, his strange power, once again, gnawed at the edges of Quicksilver's hold on him. "How could I, and the stain not be visible to the whole court?"

"You did, villain, you did." Quicksilver was aware of

sounding insane. Even Will, standing across the clearing, stared at Quicksilver with disbelief. "You killed them by another's hand." Quicksilver reached into his doublet and pulled out the cloth-wrapped knife he'd concealed there almost two days before. He held it up by the handle, and the cloth fell away from the blade and, in that assembly of magical beings, the cursed iron blade shone with an evil blue-white light. "You had this blade fashioned, perhaps fashioned it yourself in the darkness of the night, in those days when you were supposed to be courting your now late wife, and you gave it to a mortal named John Shakespeare, and had him use it to sever the life thread of Titania and Oberon. You. Murderer."

Quicksilver let the knife drop, blade down, so it stuck and vibrated in the muddy ground, giving off an eerie glow.

Sylvanus looked at the knife and then at Quicksilver, with the sheerest incomprehension. "John Shakespeare? I know the burgess. Does he not keep a glover's shop and is he not alive? How could he be alive, brother, if he had slain royal elvenkind?"

Here Quicksilver was caught short. He knew not how John was alive, nor how Sylvanus had managed to preserve him from deserved death. Sylvanus's power started reaching behind the binds, bursting through Quicksilver's hold, here and there, like a sleeper thrusting an arm through moth-eaten cloth.

A murmur grew around the clearing, and the small fairies flew here and there, blinking their concern, their doubt of Quicksilver's accusations.

"You lie," Sylvanus said. "And facts give you the lie. You see, my fair lords, my kind ladies, this base creature lies and sullies my name that he can rule alone." As he spoke, he opened his hand, and, as if without meaning to, let a concentration of power fly at Quicksilver's mouth.

Quicksilver saw the gesture and put up all his power as a shield, from which the power charge rebounded with a fizzling sound. But to put up his power, he had to let go of Sylvanus, who seemed to grow and visibly gain power in that instant.

"I don't need to lie," Quicksilver said. His voice had an hysterical edge, and he tried to think, to think what he could do to prove Sylvanus the liar and the murderer he was. "I alone am the rightful heir, and though I cannot prove your greater crime, I can prove others. You have interfered with the spheres of man. Against our ancient law, you have got a nursemaid for your daughter and have no intention of returning her to her husband when her term of service is over. And more, you didn't leave convincing stocks in their beds, either the woman's or the babe's, so that they both are known to have disappeared. If you hadn't committed that even grosser, darker transgression of parricide, this would be enough to set the worlds of men and elves at war, and that would make you unfit to rule alone or by my side. Give up, Sylvanus. Kneel to me. I am your king."

Sylvanus stared at him, his expression diamantine, his eyes unfearing. "Liar," he said. "Liar. May the Hunter consume your treasonous soul. You killed your own best friend for no reason, and his shade walks the world and will consume you. How dare you aspire to the throne of Elfland, and accuse others of the heinous crimes that taint your perverse soul?"

Quicksilver flinched. In his mind, he again saw Pyrite, bleeding in a dark clearing, saw him dissolve, felt the dread of his death anew. He looked at Will and faltered. Will and he, himself, and their love, had killed Pyrite— driven the enchanted dagger into the body that should have been almost immortal. Pyrite's bright, handsome face flickered, in a countenance of death before Quicksilver.

Will and he, both, were tainted by Pyrite's death. Pyrite had cursed them. How could Quicksilver's love for Will, then, give him power?

As Quicksilver's resolve faltered, Sylvanus bared his teeth in a smile. "Be gone from the hill, liar, traitor. Be gone. Dare not approach this hill again."

The order was given with power that turned it into magic. Quicksilver, defenseless, felt the compulsion to obey, and had to grit his teeth to remain in place. Only Ariel's hand on his arm, Ariel's fingers grabbing firmly enough to make him feel pain, steadied him and prevented his feet dragging the rest of him away.

Sylvanus had turned from him as if he'd ceased existing. "And you, good man." The king looked at Will. "You will forget the wife, of whom you were never worthy, and you will also go—"

"I recognize Quicksilver as my true lord." Ariel's voice rang, high and desperate. "And give him all my power."

Like that, her power joined Quicksilver's, bracing and shoring up his failing strength, and clearing away all but the bare remnants of Sylvanus's compulsion.

Renewed, Quicksilver realized that the king was trying to make Will forget and leave Nan. And that, Quicksilver could not allow. Will could not be made to leave Nan. Quicksilver swallowed, and, still feeling the vapors of the compulsion that Sylvanus had imposed on him—a shuffle of his feet, a fading desire to be out of the clearing—he realized that the only way to corner Sylvanus was to put him under compulsion to tell the truth. Such simple magic, worked in full view of the court, would be understood by all. They would all know that an innocent man would tell the truth. But a guilty one would not speak, would fight the compulsion with all his might. And Sylvanus was guilty.

With new power and renewed outrage, Quicksilver

flung compulsion at Sylvanus in clear-spoken words. "Tell us what you know of our parents' death," he said, and pushed the compulsion, like a sharp prod, onto Sylvanus with the words. "Tell no untruth, but tell us all the truth."

Sylvanus opened his mouth and then closed it, and bit his small, pulpy lower lip so hard that it bled. A tendril of blood ran down his chin, as he glared at Quicksilver and swallowed audibly.

"My power is yours, Lord Quicksilver," Basalt said. "If he'd committed no crime, he would have spoken."

Basalt was duke of an immense domain, leader of a faction almost half the size of the main hill. His considerable power allowed Quicksilver to throw his compulsion forth with even more force, trying to drag truth from Sylvanus's reluctant lips.

Sylvanus stood and swayed, and looked as though he'd like to swallow his tongue before it betrayed him.

"If he lied not, he would tell," someone else said.

"Lord Quicksilver, you are my king."

"My one king."

Through his fatigue and his concentration on the compulsion he wove, Quicksilver heard them. He felt their fresh power join his, healing pain he hadn't realized he still felt, the pain of severance from the hill, the raw, bleeding edges of lone power. His aches, magical and physical disappeared, as one by one, more lords pledged to him.

From the feel of it, he thought, Sylvanus and he received the hill's loyalties equally, Quicksilver having fewer lords, but among them, those with the greater power.

The court argued and worried, and both sides tried to convince others to join them.

"If he is innocent, why will he not talk?" someone said.

"Yes, but do you want Quicksilver for a sovereign?"

Yet the ones who mistrusted Sylvanus slowly increased and a slow, steady trickle of power drifted into Quicksilver's growing reserve, increasing his strength like reviving water and a good night's sleep, and fresh baked bread, and all that was wholesome and good and nourishing.

Quicksilver held the compulsion over Sylvanus, and Sylvanus, unable to overcome it, unwilling to talk, clamped both hands over his mouth and, concentrating hard on not speaking, fell to the invisible floor of the glen and writhed about on it, like a wounded thing.

A voice Quicksilver recognized as his servant, Malachite's, said, "Milord Quicksilver spoke truth. Faith, in the past I've been disloyal to him, but now he is my king and has my power."

More power, smaller power, the lower lords and bastard sons of Fairyland trickled into Quicksilver's mounting arsenal. Connected to the hill again and this time from the top, he felt and knew his fellow elves as he never had and, at the back of his mind, gently tried to send to each of them mind-messages that would soothe their fears and promise that his would not be a wild rule. He let them see his heart, with its determination to serve the hill above all things, and they responded, opening their powers more fully to his use.

Sylvanus held less than the fealty of one in ten lords. Sylvanus was defeated.

Connected to the hill again, Quicksilver felt powerful and strong, and sane as never before. "You leave, Sylvanus," he said. "You leave, traitor." He pushed compulsion upon his dethroned brother. The other lords of the hill who had not yet sworn to him would, in time, when they saw his wise rule. No one could expect Sylvanus to rule now, with such a small following. "You are a murderer and a traitor, but I'll not taint my hands with your blood. Go and never again come near this hill."

Just then, at Quicksilver's moment of gloating, relieved triumph, a hunting horn sounded in the distance, a call that made Quicksilver's breath stop, mid-drawing.

The Hunter? It couldn't be the Hunter. Yet, who else would be hunting this late at night and in the pouring rain?

Quicksilver felt chill sweat run down the middle of his back.

Had the Hunter come for Quicksilver? Did the relish Quicksilver had taken in his vengeance incite the Hunter's dogs to his pursuit? Now he would indeed be worthy prey, connected as he was to the hill.

He looked at Sylvanus, who still writhed on the floor of the ballroom. Sylvanus's hands covered his mouth and, on his side, he patently tried not to obey the compulsion to leave the hill. The result of it was that he crawled, like an abject animal, around and around in the center of the floor, inching ever so slowly toward the edge of the clearing, surrounded by a ring of astonished courtiers.

From above, came the noise of a horse at full gallop and the baying and whining of hunting dogs.

Quicksilver shook. It was the Hunter. Come for him. By an effort, he softened his voice and his heart and tried to absent any sign of gloating from his speech as he stood over Sylvanus and said, "Go for now. Should you prove worthy, perhaps we will have you back, sometime. Perhaps even your crimes can be redeemed."

But Sylvanus shook his head, even as the bugle sounded again.

On the storm-dark sky, a shadow formed, of a hunter at full gallop, surrounded by dark, ferocious dogs.

Quicksilver gagged on his own panic and looked around, frantically for a place to hide, and then noticed that Sylvanus was transforming, and stopped, staring at the deposed king, in astonishment.

Sylvanus's form changed and became distorted, and

elongated, and on the forest floor, on all fours, baying to the cloudy sky scarred by thunderbolts, stood a male wolf, as tall and as large as Sylvanus had been. A silver-bright wolf, his maw open, his sharp teeth glittering.

Quicksilver had only time to scream and take a step back. "The Hunter," he said. "He's allied with the Hunter. He's sworn fealty to the devourer of our race." Even in saying it, he had trouble believing it, yet Sylvanus's transformation was undeniable and it wasn't Quicksilver's doing, but the inevitable call of the Hunter. Quicksilver remembered the Hunter talking of having nowhere else to go and being called.

Besides, all around the changed Sylvanus, Quicksilver could see a dark grey cloud of blood-red power, power rooted in pain and suffering and on blood and sacrifice. A lot of power but defeated by the power of love and hill conjoined, that Quicksilver commanded.

What lords still held with Sylvanus now deserted him, and their power surged into Quicksilver's hold. Lords screamed and ladies shrilled, and, amid it all, Nan and Will stood, amazed, while Will's falcon eyes took in these sights that no mortal eyes should watch.

Sylvanus's voice came from the darkness, distorted into an animal growl but still, somehow, Sylvanus's voice with his accents and his proud tone. "Foolish brother. You would rule, you, by the power of your foolish love. Pitiful creature. Long ago, in the mountains of the north land, my mind in despair over being displaced by you in birth order and our parents' affections, I found the Hunter. He offered me power and I took it. Since I joined with him, I can drink humans' pain, like a nectar, and feed on their tears and suffering like a sweet wine, and power spent is only power recovered. Thus I engineered the murder of those foolish, pleasure-loving sovereigns, silly Titania, lecherous Oberon, and covered my tracks so well that the despicable human I used as an instrument neither died nor dared talk of my deed, and went unsuspected. And I almost won. I would have won, were it not for your cursed cunning, Quicksilver." The wolf's eyes glittered with a red light as it looked on Quicksilver. Its half-open mouth slobbered iridescent green drool that went on glowing after it had fallen, past the illusory floor, to the mud. "And now I must go, but you will come with me, and be fodder for my pack brothers."

Quicksilver readied his new power for the jump he knew would come. Awkwardly, he fashioned his unaccustomed power into a shield. As the wolf jumped, Quicksilver held all this power in front of himself like a shield, felt the animal's impact, and heard a sound, as if the creature had hit hard crystal. The creature's face twisted sideways, as it hit the invisible barrier, and left a trail of slobber behind that seemed to drip from the clear air, at Quicksilver's eye level.

But the creature landed on its feet and, turning with malevolent ire, dove at Quicksilver's ankles. Quicksilver realized that his clumsy handling of power had left his legs unprotected, but realized it too late as the creature's icy cold yet burning teeth clamped onto his left ankle. Green saliva mingled with the shimmering red blood of elvenkind.

Quicksilver screamed and dropped his shield, and the wolf pulled at Quicksilver with all its might, throwing him off balance, making him go down on one knee, the other leg painfully extended in front of him as the wolf pulled on it.

This was how the teeth of the Hunter's dogs would feel, Quicksilver thought, rending him and tearing him and devouring him. His mind clouded by pain, he felt terror such as he'd never felt before.

Above him, in the storm-dark sky, the Hunter laughed.

Reaching into all his power, all his strength, Quicksilver wished to throw power at the wolf, in one of those punching attacks that he had so often felt from the other end. Not sure how to do it, he wished the power of the hill through his arm. It sparkled down his arm, feeling somewhere between a tingle and pain and, before Quicksilver even realized what he was doing, power flew from his extended fingers. Catching the wolf in the face, it made the animal unclench its jaws.

Quicksilver wished yet more power down his arm, and sent it flying, tingling, to hit the creature and send it sprawling. At the same time, Quicksilver stood, though his ankle felt as though immersed in live coals.

An animal whine escaped Sylvanus's wolf-form, but it scrambled to its feet and, glaring with unflagging hatred, made for Nan.

Quicksilver, still burning with the pain in his ankle, took long enough to realize what was happening, that the creature had fastened its teeth on Nan's gown.

Will put his arms around her. Nan, her mouth open, shrieked in terror.

Quicksilver set his power like a shield in front of the woman and around her and Will both, this time taking care that the shield met the ground of the glen. If he couldn't have Will—and he couldn't—then at least he would ensure that Will was happy, so that his happiness could feed Quicksilver's joy.

The wolf pulled at the hem of Nan's dress with its fangs, but the fabric tore in its teeth and the woman stayed put in Will's arms, within Quicksilver's shielding.

The beast, at bay, turned this way and that, all around the circle.

And Quicksilver, sparing barely a thought and a trickle of his now-immense power to healing his ankle that he might concentrate better without the pain, responded with fast-moving wit, protecting now this, now that lord and high lady from the intended attack of the creature.

The wolf snarled, a low complaint that sounded like a blasphemy. The hunting horn sounded again, and the wolf-like dogs bayed.

Come, the Hunter's voice sounded, commanding.

The wolf-Sylvanus turned yet again, and unexpectedly, cowered, belly to the ground, and ran between the legs of the massed courtiers.

A flash of lightning crossed the sky and laughter sounded.

Quicksilver's ankle still felt a little sore and he moved too slowly. He turned just in time to see the dark wolf-shape plunge into the lace-bedecked double cradle, and snatch one of the swaddled babes, who screamed and cried at being thus maltreated.

Before Quicksilver or anyone else could react, the hunting horn sounded again and the wolf ran up an invisible stairway, with the baby in its jaws, and plunged into the pack of grey dogs who followed the Hunter.

The Hunter laughed again, and spurred his horse, and his shadow form galloped across the sky, followed by his dogs. The sound of hooves retreated into the distance, and the infant's cries with it.

"My daughter!" Nan wailed. "My daughter."

"It was not your daughter that he took," Quicksilver said.

Nan, detaching herself from Will, ran to the cradle and lifted the babe who was not so blond and not so round and not so pink as the fairy princess had been.

"It is not your daughter but his own that he's taken with him in damnation. I felt her power leaving. They're both gone from the hill." Quicksilver felt different, strong, as if the mantle of kingship, having fallen on his shoulders metaphorically if not yet in fact, had given him strength and dignity he'd never hoped to possess. He knew things he'd never before known, secrets and certainties and facts long forgotten by all living elves, but still stored in the collective memory of the hill.

How could Sylvanus have known this much and yet acted so foolishly? Had the evil that consumed him blinded him to the folly of his actions? Or had the pact with the Hunter, once sealed, been unbreakable?

Quicksilver thought how close he'd come to sealing such a pact and shivered.

"Is she dead? Will he give her as fodder to the wolves?" Will asked, his eyes filled with horror. He'd crossed the clearing to stand beside Nan, his arm around her shoulders, while she hugged their baby.

"No." Quicksilver shook his head. "No. I can feel her alive but cut off from the hill. I think he means to keep her alive, with him, in the realm of the Hunter. There she'll remain, imprisoned, and grow up to be one of the Hunter's dogs."

"But she was a good babe," Nan said. Tears filled her eyes and brimmed over. "She doesn't deserve such a fate."

Quicksilver sighed. "She has not sealed a pact with the Hunter, nor can she, till she be full-grown. And maybe some young mortal, or some elf, will undertake to save her before then. But Sylvanus sealed his pact knowingly and Sylvanus will never be free." On saying this, Quicksilver felt his eyes well up, and looked down to hide the sparkle of tears from his courtiers. From now on, all his emotions would be much too public. And yet he, himself, had been so close to being thus lost into darkness and greed and his need for vengeance. "But we have nothing to fear from him. He can't overcome the protections of this hill," Quicksilver said and added, as much to the frightened courtiers as to Will, who looked tired and scared and sad. "He shall plague us no more."

The rain stopped. As though a giant hand passed across the sky sweeping the clouds away with a gesture, the sky showed deep blue and starry, as it should this time of year. And the moon glowed, bright and full, within a halo of reflected light.

"Pardon me, milord." One of the servants bowed to Quicksilver. "But we had everything prepared for a royal wedding, the sacred nectar, the charmed ambrosia. What shall we do with it all?"

Quicksilver smiled. "Why, have a royal wedding, of course. If milady Ariel will have me."

Ariel turned to him, her eyes shining with joy and her mouth half opened in a smile, long before she said, "I will have you, milord. If you can like of me."

"I look to like," Quicksilver said. "And looking moves my liking." He extended his gloved hand toward her. "Here is my hand, lady, before the whole noble company. And as for you . . ." With his other hand, Quicksilver pointed at Will and Nan, who still stood by the cradle, holding their daughter and talking to each other in the urgent tones of lovers long separated. A fat black-and-white cat had come out of nowhere and wove a path between their ankles, purring loudly.

"As for you two, you shall go, and, for your pains, you shall have the good will of elvenkind as long as you both shall live. And your father, Will, your father, is hereby forgiven his crime. Sweet Titania and gentle Oberon are avenged and will return to be born among elvenkind. You may go." As he dismissed them, Quicksilver wished he had a sign of his parents' return, of Pyrite's liberation.

He looked over his shoulder at Ariel, to see if she had any intimation of their fate—and saw them. Pyrite, ghostly and transparent, bent over his sister to kiss her. Titania and Oberon stood one on either side of Ariel and put the elf maiden's hand in Quicksilver's.

Then, all three shades smiled at Quicksilver, a smile of blessing, and disappeared, in a twinkling of lights, leaving behind the feeling that they'd embarked on a journey that must be undertaken. A journey of return.

Tears shone in most courtiers' eyes. Ariel cried, though her lips smiled.

Indifferent to all but their present happiness, Nan and Will had already left.

Quicksilver could see them on the path to Stratford, two dark shapes now revealed, now hidden, by the intervening dark trunks of ancient trees. Attenuated echoes of Will's chuckle reached him.

Taking a handkerchief from his sleeve, Quicksilver wiped the lady Ariel's eyes, then rounded on the orchestra where each musician stood like a statue, horrified and moved by all he'd seen.

"Strike up your instruments, and let there be music," Quicksilver said. "It is your king who orders it. This is his wedding and not his funeral."

Quicksilver squeezed Ariel's hand and smiled. Everything was well. Everything was well. Will had his wife and, having somehow escaped the price of elven love, the youth wanted for no more.

And, as the first tentative notes of a dance tune sounded, Quicksilver took Ariel in his arms and led her a-dance.

Epilogue

๛

SCENE: *the same foggy, otherworldly place we saw at the beginning of this play, but now the gentleman who introduced the play stands bent over a smaller stage where, as though in miniature, the forest of Arden looms and Nan and Will and their cat walk through the forest. Nan and Will hold hands, and Will holds Susannah.*

The narrator leans over the scene and signals the audience to silence, with a finger to his lips. His other hand still covers his bleeding eye. Something very much like a smile curls his lips upward. But it's a sad smile, full of meaning that no one can decipher. "Watch," he says. "Watch, now. Jack shall have Jill. Naught shall go ill. The man shall have his mare again, and all shall be well." His hand gestures at the diminutive stage. "The man and the woman walk through the enchanted forest in safety. The king has his throne and his queen, whose righteous love is rewarded. Will has his Nan and his baby daughter.

"Even as he walks through the forest, he's thinking he'll be a better husband and a better father and even—in the loving kindness of his heart—a better son. He'll learn the glover trade from his father and never again stir from Stratford.

"But as he walks and makes such plans, the tune he just heard, the spectacle and fury of the fairy dance and the horror and power of elven strife seep into his blood, kindle strange fires in his brain. Fantastical tragedies and mad farces hatch within him like eggs, laid by some mystical insect and waiting only the right time to let their wondrous, magical engendering come to life.

"Quicksilver's love had its price, after all. Returned or not, it had a price. Everything does. But who paid that price? And is Will—who will leave wife and daughter and mother and father behind and trade his small domestic happiness for a spotlight in a world made stage—better or worse off than if he had never come across the unexplained marvels of elvenkind?

"Who is to say? Look." Again the narrator points at the stage at his feet. "Look. He puts his arm around his Nan and tells her that from now on she is all his desire, the sum and crown of his days. And she laughs and leans into him and tells him that he's her king, the only one she wants. They don't know that this happiness is already doomed, that their love is already poisoned. They think they have the future before them, the small future of mortal beings. And maybe they do." The narrator looks up at the audience, and smiles and, for the first time, removes his hand from in front of his eye, showing a whole eye, healthy and sparkling grey. That eye, like its twin, is filled with unholy mirth. The blood that stained his collar vanishes. His angelic smile contrasts with the deviltry in his eyes. "Maybe they do. Maybe it is what you think you know of their future and your past, that which is an illusion. Maybe Will settled down in Stratford, and plied his father's trade, and became a master glover and a dealer in wool. And perhaps I, Marlowe, never died in a tavern brawl, with a dagger through the eye, and was, and am, hailed as the magnificent playwright of Great Elizabeth's age. Or maybe, just maybe, both stories—the play you watch and the play you live—are just tales told by an idiot, full of sound and fury, signifying nothing."

On those words, the narrator vanishes, a thing of air, a wisp of dream returning to the land of what never happened.

Author's Note

ಞ

In writing this book I tried to stay as close as possible to historical fact (elves excluded), but I have taken some liberties with what we know of Shakespeare's life, with geography, and with tradition.

On no better evidence than John Aubrey's theory to the effect (in *Brief Lives*), I chose to make Shakespeare "a schoolmaster in the country." Though this theory is "supported" by his apparent familiarity with the profession, exhibited in plays such as *Love's Labor's Lost* and *The Merry Wives Of Windsor*, just as many biographers assert that his often legalistic turn of phrase points to his apprenticeship as a law clerk. However, since these are Shakespeare's "lost years," meaning that we have no evidence at all of what he might have been doing—and since his plays betray a familiarity with too many professions for him to have worked at all of them—he might well have been a butcher's apprentice, a law clerk, his father's helper in the glover shop, or a dozen other things.

I took poetic license with the geography (as Shakespeare himself often did). I enlarged Arden woods to become Arden Forest—as did Shakespeare in *As You Like It*—and placed both Shottery and Wincot (Wilmcote) in places where Will needed to cross the forest and pass by the elf palace to reach either of them.

As for tradition, my most egregious violation is perhaps the matter of William Shakespeare's marriage, as everyone *knows* he was unhappy in his choice of wife. However, the supposed marital discord rests on very scant and ambiguous evidence: the fact that Anne Hathaway married late, William Shakespeare's absence in London for most of their married life, and a bare-bones, coldly worded will, in which Anne is only mentioned to be left the second-best bed.

This matter of the will can be easily dismissed as William Shakespeare employed no words of affection for anyone in his last testament. In fact, if we believe Ian Wilson (*Shakespeare: The Evidence*, St. Martin's Griffin edition, January 1999), the will read like other wills drafted by Francis Collins, William Shakespeare's lawyer, and therefore bore the mark of the lawyer rather than the willmaker.

As for Anne's small legacy, Anne was left—from all we know—to the affectionate care of her eldest daughter, Susannah Hall. Besides, at the time of Shakespeare's death, Anne would have been in her sixties, an advanced age in Elizabethan England. It is quite possible she simply wasn't competent or strong enough to administer the estate. In that case, his leaving her the second-best bed—which might well have been their marriage bed—was no more than a gesture of affection, a reminder of their happy marriage. There is simply not enough evidence to judge the Shakespeares' conjugal happiness or lack thereof from the will.

As for Shakespeare's working in London, while his family remained in Stratford-upon-Avon: London at the time was not considered a healthy place for children. Even today, it is not unusual, in many parts of the world, for men to go some distance away to seek their fortune, while women stay behind to raise the children. Besides, it is quite clear that Shakespeare always intended to return "home" when his career in London was done, and it's possible he visited Stratford often during his career.

Anne Hathaway's late marriage is another matter. Judging from his plays, Master Shakespeare nurtured a fondness for spirited women, though in his day such women were less than universally appreciated. Perhaps Anne *did* scare away all suitors but Will.

Ultimately the best measure of their marriage is that he chose to spend his London-earned money in buying the best place in Stratford-upon-Avon for his family and that it was by his wife's side that he decided to pass his waning years.

Of all the Shakespearean biographers I have studied, the ones I resort to most frequently and in whose work I can always find the answer to any nagging questions are, in no particular order: A. L. Rowse (*William Shakespeare, A Biography*, 1995, Barnes & Noble Books; *What Shakespeare Read—and Thought*, 1981, Coward, McCann & Geoghegan); Peter Levi (*The Life and Times of William Shakespeare*, 1989, Henry Holt); Dennis Kay, (*Shakespeare, His Life, Work and Era*, 1992, William Morrow); Robert Speaight (*Shakespeare, The Man and His Achievement*, 1977, Stein and Day); Stanley Wells (*Shakespeare, A Life in Drama*, 1995, W. W. Norton); Ivor Brown (*Shakespeare*, 1962, Time); S. Schoenbaum (*William Shakespeare, A Compact, Documentary Life*, 1977, Oxford University Press; [and my personal favorite] *Shakespeare's Lives*, 1991, Oxford University Press.

There are many other, excellent biographers but these form the essential core of my research.

Also used as references were *Daily Life in Elizabethan England*, by Jeffrey L. Singman, published by Greenwood

Press; *The Elizabethan World Picture*, by E.M.W. Tillyard, published by Random House's Vintage Books division; *The Vanishing People, Fairy Lore and Legends*, by Katherine Briggs, published by Pantheon Books; *Celtic Fairy Tales*, collected by Joseph Jacobs, published by Dover Publications; and *Life in The English Country Cottage* by Adrian Tinnis Wood, published by the Orion Publishing Group.

For sheer fun, I recommend *The Complete Works of William Shakespeare*, available in several affordable editions and—to deepen one's understanding and enjoyment of them—Harold Bloom's *Shakespeare, The Invention of the Human*.

The credit for accurate historical details in this novel belongs to my references. The errors are all mine.

As my final justification, I will say, like Alexandre Dumas: "It is permissible to rape history on condition that you have a child by her."

Whether this *first heir of my invention* proves malformed or not, I will leave to my readers' judgment.

Sarah A. Hoyt
Colorado, 2001